THE PROJECT

Lyoto-Straf: a doomsday device on the cutting edge of modern technology. The Russians have it. The Americans must stop them. There's just one catch: A Chinese spy has stolen the project's computer files and he's dead beneath the frozen Barents Sea.

THE PLOT

Sent by U.S. Intelligence, Commander T.C. Bogner has the latest weaponry and sub-surface marine armaments at his disposal. But high-tech resources may not be enough to defeat a deadly enemy in the Arctic icescape.

THE PRIZE

World domination for whoever can get to the bottom of the sea first. It's a heart-stopping race against the clock to retrieve the lost disks—a race Bogner must win to preserve worldwide freedom.

RED ICE

THE TECHNO-THRILLER OF THE YEAR BY R. KARL LARGENT BESTSELLING AUTHOR OF *RED TIDE*

"A writer to watch!"   —*Publishers Weekly*

R. KARL LARGENT

RED ICE

LEISURE BOOKS **NEW YORK CITY**

A LEISURE BOOK®

June 1999

Published by
Dorchester Publishing Co., Inc.
276 Fifth Avenue
New York, NY 10001

ISBN 0-8439-4604-0

RED ICE

ONE

ONE

LOG:
ONE: ONE

Sector 8-B, 8-C: Stavka Straits 2141L
25 October

It was the last scheduled run of the *Drachev* before the ice pack made the voyage impossible. Because of the howling gale, Captain Valeriy Zachinsky had already slowed the aging freighter to six knots.

The ship's outdated navigational system had shown the first indication of malfunction at 2032L, and radio contact with the equally ancient Moskova class icebreaker *Urhan*, now estimated to be some 18 nautical miles east and south of the *Drachev*, had been lost at 2104L. The *glonass* navigational system, which Zachinsky had scheduled for installation the previous spring, remained crated on a Velova dock in the Kresnik Ship Yards, and for all practical purposes the *Drachev* was now at the mercy of the storm.

Zachinsky peered through the ice-painted windows of the wheelhouse at a blinding wall of wet, wind-whipped snow, glancing from time to time at the ship's anemometer, which was recording surface winds in excess of 27 knots and gusts to 38. For Zachinsky it was a matter of increasing concern. Floe ice had been surging over the deck for the past hour, and although he had no confirmation from the second officer, he was certain at least two of the minor forward compartments were already inundated.

Despite his demand for an explanation from the same officer, the shipwide power failure remained unexplained, and it occurred to Zachinsky that if he had been sabotaged, he could not have been more helpless.

At the same time he understood that the man at his side, Lieutenant Gusenko, the *Drachev*'s newest officer, was terrified. Zachinsky doubted if the young native from the flatlands near Trebuchovsky, a recent graduate of the Naval Sciences Academy, had ever seen a storm at sea—and if he had, certainly not one of such violence. The young man's face had assumed a grayish pallor and his hands trembled. His eyes mirrored the opaque curtain of white that reflected up from the wash of light provided by a small standby power unit designed to provide emergency illumination for the helmsman.

As each massive wave, jacketed with the heavy slush of the rapidly forming ice floe, slammed into the *Drachev*, the young Ukrainian shuddered.

"Can you get through to the *Uhran?*" Zachinsky asked.

The young officer looked at him. "It is no use, Captain, I have tried repeatedly."

"Try again," Zachinsky ordered.

Gusenko flipped the toggle switch several times, but the small red diode indicator remained dark.

Still, there was no response from the first officer. Zachinsky jerked off the headphone and stumbled toward the door of the wheelhouse atop the *Drachev*'s creaking superstructure. "I'm going back to the radio shack."

"But—but the winds . . ." young Gusenko protested. "It is not safe." But his admonition was useless. Zachinsky was already gone.

*   *   *

In his spartan cabin two levels below the wheelhouse, an unnerved Zhou Hu tried to steady the candle that enabled him to peer into the contents of his battered attaché case. He was holding a small metal film tin that had been hidden in the lining. The flat, hermetically sealed aluminum container had been designed to make it capable of holding a copy of the complete computerized data file of every critical dimension, element, and construction detail of the Lyoto-Straf-96 project.

Zhou caressed the tiny metal case, forgetting for the moment the terror brought on by the creaking steel plates in the storm-tortured *Drachev*'s hull.

Tingri would be proud of him, perhaps even reward him. Zhou Hu was obsessed with the thought that Tingri could be a generous man, both in terms of what he could do for him in the Party, and perhaps even financially.

For the moment, however, Zhou Hu was content to dwell on the cleverness of Tingri's convoluted plan. First there was the illness of Yaobang and Tingri's influence, which had resulted in Zhou's appointment to the Belushya technical contingent. Then there was Zhou's meticulous 24-month-long, day-and-night cataloging of every facet of the Lyoto-Straf-96 project while his colleagues covered for him and married their system with that of the Russians. The reputation of the Belushya security system was underserved, Zhou had decided—even if the site was managed by former GRU personnel.

Admittedly, the work had been tedious—but in retrospect, he would tell Tingri, it had not been all that difficult. And when, finally, he had completed the arduous task of cataloging the project, and when he was absolutely certain that everything was ready, Zhou had ingested the iodine that created the spots on his lungs. The "mild heart attack" had followed. As Tingri had predicted, the limited and inexperienced

Russian medical staff on Belushya would concur with
the diagnosis that Zhou Hu had tuberculosis and had
also suffered a mild coronary—and as predicted, now
he was on his way back to Tibet. Indeed, Tingri would
be pleased. Zhou slipped the canister back into the
lining of his attaché case and decided to take more
dimen-hydrinate tablets.

As Zhou Hu stood up, still clutching the briefcase
and steadying his frail frame against the arched steel
bulkhead support, he heard a sound he could not
identify—a sound followed by a violent explosion.

Everything happened at once.

The bulkhead buckled, the steel plates of the inner
hull collapsed, and cascading tons of freezing water
roared into his cabin. There was a ball of flame,
the shrieking, tearing protest of violated metal, and
a sound not unlike that when he'd heard his father's
tiny *chinpan* capsize in the swollen flood waters of the
Zengho Jang.

The frigid waters swirled up and around him,
engulfing him, sending him reeling into the chaos of
the deluge. He felt his neck snap as he was catapulted
against the thick metal plates that had once separated
him from the sea. The waters washed over him and he
began gasping for breath. Instantly there was both a
numbness and a terrible pain. His chest pounded, and
he involuntarily began swallowing great quantities of
seawater as if the gesture would somehow prolong
his life.

The surging water quickly became coated with oil
and the flames danced around him. There was a second
surge, and he was cast sideways, his world collapsing
and the fire enveloping him. The heavy brown briefcase
was ripped from his helpless hand, and for the first
time in his life he felt a surge of panic. Now Zhou Hu
was even more intimidated by the prospect of Tingri's
terrible reprisal if he lost the container.

Overhead, a huge beam snapped. The ceiling of

his cabin began to collapse. He felt pain, and then something crushing his chest. He tried to breathe—but there was nothing to breathe. His lungs had filled with the acrid, phosphor-heavy smoke of a decaying, dying ship, and now the smoke was being quenched by the icy waters of what was to Zhou an unknown sea. He felt himself being sucked down into the icy blackness. His head lolled to one side and he clutched at his chest. His eyes blurred and the pain became excruciating. For the first time in his life, Zhou Hu was aware of the sound of silence.

Then there was blackness and shrill, terrifying, electronic sounds—and finally, there was nothing.

No more than three or four feet from Zhou Hu was the briefcase, tantalizingly close but buried under shards of steel plating and a twisted section of bulkhead.

As Zhou Hu was dying, there was one final devastating salvo; the *Drachev*'s boilers exploded and the aging ship was ripped in half. The carcass of the once-proud freighter settled into a shallow trench, a mere 83 feet below what would soon be the icebound waters of the Stavka Straits. Even now, in the lacy tentacles of the rapidly forming and deepening floe ice, there was no trace of her.

LOG:
ONE: TWO

Konsoolstva Weather Outpost: Ludivestik 2145L
25 October

Georgi Voloktin, the meteorologist on duty at the Konsoolstva Weather Outpost, finished his pibal run, relayed his final azimuth and vernier readings into the recorder, and started to climb down the ladder from the observation platform. He had terminated his run at the 250-millibar level because of the instability of his theodolite in the gusty winds.

As he swung his legs over the edge of the platform and allowed his feet to search for the top rung on the ladder, he glanced upward. In the crystal stillness of the northeastern quadrant, he saw a faint distant flash. He blinked his eyes against the cold and looked again. Whatever it was, it was gone.

Moments later, on the ground and only a few meters from the door to the RWB station, he heard an equally faint roar, muffled and brief—a departure from the usual deafening silence. He paused, pulled back his parka hood, and listened again—but there was only the sound of wind and the familiar emptiness of Arctic vastness.

Inside the tiny station, Voloktin stomped the snow from his mucklucks, and removed his parka and

14

headset before he looked at Ilya. Unlike his companion, Ilya was a taller man, spare and taciturn, a man who smoked a short pipe with a curved stem.

"Did Belushya make the last scheduled transmission?" Voloktin asked.

"Yes," Ilya replied. He picked up the printout and scanned it. "AK-7 at 2100Z—why?"

"Anything unusual?"

He shook his head. "No." He glanced at the APR recorder, ambled over to the WMO computer-generated surface chart, wiped off his glasses, and studied the area. "It appears that we have a magnetic anomaly of some sort over the Stavka Straits."

Ilya momentarily studied the data printout and the latest satellite photographs before he shook his head again. "Neither the geostationary or orbiting satellites are recording anything of . . ."

"There was a flash of light," Voloktin began, but Ilya began to laugh before he could finish.

"Sporadic aurora phenomena." Ilya smiled. "It often occurs early in the season. You will probably see the appropriate notation when AK-7 reports on the next transmission."

Voloktin laughed, settled into the chair in front of the computer, and pressed the review key waiting for the Stavka Straits chart between sectors 6-1 and 8-1. Unlike Konsoolstva, which was reporting clear skies and winds gusting to 17 knots, both Murmansk and the remote site on Kichkna Island were reporting deteriorating conditions. He shivered.

"I'd hate to be out there on a ship tonight," he observed.

Ilya laughed. "If the *Akershus* had already been deployed, it would be right in the thick of it."

Voloktin smiled. "Only one more reason why I am glad I am not a Norwegian."

LOG:
ONE: THREE

Sector 8-B, 8-C: Stavka Straits 2146L
25 October

Lieutenant Mikolaï Klyuzov leveled his Sukhoi Su-24 "Fencer" off at 24,000 feet, activated his coder-recorder, and began sequencing the time, location, and situation analysis. The infrared target indicator on the VSD had dissipated.

He showed surprisingly little emotion. He jettisoned the empty AS-9 launcher, making certain he was not over the ice floe when he did so. It was a precaution Colonel Ulitsa had advised him to take.

He depressed the *razgavareevat* button on the voice control panel, rotated the selector switch to the digitized sequencer, and pressed the "record" switch. Klyuzov selected his words carefully; always referencing his flight recorder.

"*Drachev* located by MSD at 2137L—target confirmed by H-77-1. Two passes—4,500 MSL. Heavy cloud cover—no visual contact. Surface winds; SSW –25c pg 39–41, heavy precip: snow intensity, moderate to heavy. Wave height: 10–12 (est) BINOVC. Target lock 2138:47—program 1. Sequencing—lock confirmed; lock checked and confirmed. AS-9 pd 1. Firing time 2139:02. Interval .00045. Audio sensors recorded target impact 2139:47L. Sensor elevation—variable to down 03. Infrared indicators recorded at .05 interval. Confirmation −00 at 2351L. Launcher jettisoned at 2353:45. Confirmation—confirmation. Coded."

Klyuzov released the digitizer and watched the pattern of 5 × 5 clustered digits sweep across the screen. It was 2356:02 when he terminated the transmission.

He had exactly seven minutes to rendezvous with his programed coordinates. By maintaining the Belushya ETA of 0222, no one would be the wiser.

Finally, there was time, a time for Mikolai Klyuzov to reflect on his accomplishment.

LOG: ONE: FOUR

Lyoto-Straf-96 Site: Belushya Guba 0042L
26 October

In the COM-CEN of the Lyoto-Straf, Lieutenant General Kirill Gureko turned to his comrades. He was smiling.

"My congratulations, Admiral Dolin. Assuming Lieutenant Klyuzov's assessment is correct, we can assume that his mission was a success."

Dolin, the former chief of the GRU Naval Directorate, and one of the few to escape President Aprihnen's wrath following General Denisov's attempted coup, was a man of imposing stature. His large, thumb-shaped head, void of hair except for heavy black eyebrows, was endowed with a bulbous nose, full fleshy lips, and massive jowls. He gave his comrades the impression of having no neck. His oversized head simply appeared to be one continuous appendage that protruded from the tunic collar. Now was one of the rare occasions when he smiled.

Across from him sat the Lyoto-Straf's logistics officer, Colonel Vadock Ulitsa. Unlike Gureko and Dolin, Ulitsa was unsmiling. His hands were folded in his lap as he listened to the report; he made no pretense at elation.

"And now, Colonel Ulitsa, now that this somewhat annoying matter has been disposed of, we turn our attention to you," Gureko said. "How long have you known?"

Ulitsa wetted his lips. His hands moved to the table. "Major Chinko indicated her suspicions during her last review and inspection, Comrade General."

"That was over three months ago," Dolin reminded him.

"At Major Chinko's recommendation I put Zhou Hu under twenty-four-hour surveillance. But—it was not until he became ill and was subsequently instructed to return to his country that we were able to determine the extent of his activities." Ulitsa paused a moment and when he continued, his voice was less nervous. He looked at Dolin. "Last Monday he accessed the central data file and used both red and red-red codes. He carried the printouts to the viewing screen and appeared to be introducing data into the configuration models. It was only after he repositioned the paper several times that we realized he was taking pictures. Apparently, a miniature camera was housed in the back of his scanner."

Gureko frowned. "May I ask, Colonel, why you did not confront Zhou Hu at that time?"

Ulitsa sniffed. Obviously neither Gurekon nor Dolin understood his quandary. "There was no way of knowing, Comrade General, whether Zhou Hu was working alone or whether he had an accomplice. We knew that if he did have an accomplice and we arrested Zhou, whoever was working with him would simply be driven further undercover. But when Zhou Hu was ordered to return home, I knew that he would have to take the data with him. That is when I informed Admiral Dolin."

Gureko sank back in his chair. His ruddy, pock-marked face was creased in a perpetual frown. He ran his hand over his hair and studied Lieutenant Klyusov's decoded report.

"Tell me, Colonel Ulitsa, do you believe Zhou Hu had an accomplice?"

Ulitsa hesitated. "We have not been able to verify . . ."

"I did not ask, Colonel, what you have and have not been able to verify; I ask you what you think. Do you think Zhou has an accomplice?"

Ulitsa swallowed and looked down at the table. Then he nodded. "Yes, Comrade General, I believe Zhou Hu has an accomplice."

"Do you have any idea . . . ?" Gureko started to say, but he realized Ulitsa was shaking his head even before he finished. "Then how do you intend to find this unknown accomplice?"

The colonel opened the file in front of him and sighed. His voice was measured and edgy again. "Zhou Hu was a physicist and apparently nothing more. There is nothing in his dossier to indicate that he has any expertise in any field other than the one he professes. Our investigation did turn up the fact that he was at one time a member of the Lingyuan Party at Nanjing University. Two other members of the Sino delegation were also Lingyuan Party members, Yuhan Ti and Quindo Fu Shan; which of course indicates that at one time or another they were affiliated with Tingri. But—so far that is the only connection we have been able to uncover."

Dolin leaned forward. "Have you discussed your suspicions with Major Chinko?"

Ulitsa bristled. "Major Chinko has no particular expertise in these matters. If it were not for Kusinien she would be nothing more than another obscure officer."

Gureko continued to frown. He folded his hands on the table in front of him. "Tomorrow I will return to Moscow. I will report this incident to President Aprihnen. I will tell him that we were aware of Zhou's activities. I will also tell him how we engineered the power failure aboard the *Drachev* and inform him that we instructed Lieutenant Klyuzov to see that the *Drachev* did not reach its destination."

Dolin cleared his throat. "It may also be advisable to inform the president that we now have the remaining members of the Sino technical contingent under surveillance. He will want assurances. You can tell him that according to Klyuzov's mission report, the *Drachev* is now resting at the bottom of the Stavka Strait and that in a matter of a few days, the area will be covered with a virtually impenetrable layer of ice. Tell him that when the Sino authorities begin to question the whereabouts of Comrade Zhou Hu, we will appear to cooperate by launching an investigation. Of course the only thing we will be able to report is that the *Drachev* was lost during a sudden and severe Arctic storm and that, apparently, all hands, including Zhou Hu, were lost."

Gureko nodded. When he spoke, his voice was strained. "As for you, Colonel Ulitsa, I would advise you to uncover Zhou's accomplice—and do it quickly. I speak for President Aprihnen when I emphasize that this is a matter of the utmost urgency. Two Russian naval officers, their crew, and the *Drachev* have already been sacrificed to insure that the extent of our efforts in the Lyoto-Straf project does not leak out. You must take the most stringent of measures to see that our integrity is not jeopardized a second time. You are dismissed."

After Ulitsa left the room, Gureko looked at Dolin. The admiral was pouring himself a drink.

"When is Xo expected?"

"The last day of the month. He is arriving from Stockholm."

Gureko raised an eyebrow. "A curious route," he observed. "Did we know Zhou's itinerary?"

"We examined his papers when he left the site. We

know only that he was scheduled to arrive in Lahsa by the end of the week. If Xo checks in with his office prior to his departure from Moscow, he will know that Zhou has not yet reported in."

"Then we can assume he will know," Gureko decided. "If anything, I suspect they planned a meeting in Stockholm. If Zhou Hu does not arrive at the appointed place and time, Xo is is bound to be suspicious." He laughed. "If Zhou Hu and Xo do not meet, you can rest assured we will know about it."

Dolin nodded. He took out a small notebook and scribbled a few lines. Then he looked up. "Then we have come full circle. Do you not agree that we have suffered with Ulitsa long enough? I consider the Zhou Hu matter to be sufficient cause. As far as I am concerned, he has blundered for the last time."

"You can be certain we will be offered Major Chinko as a replacement, Admiral."

"You have discussed her appointment with General Bekrenev?"

"I have," Gureko acknowledged. "It is what the French would call a *fait accompli*. Bekrenev will inform her of her new assignment when she returns from her father's funeral."

LOG:
ONE: FIVE

The Riddarholm Hotel: Stockholm 2157L
27 October

From where he was sitting, Bogner was unable to see Xo's face, but he could see the reflection of the man's back in the cloudy, ornate mirror that extended the length of the hotel bar. Xo, seldom animated, sat quietly, staring out at the lights of the city. Bogner had actually been close enough at the time to hear the high-ranking Chinese diplomat request a table that would afford him a view of the magnificent old Riddarholm Cathedral on the island.

Now Bogner ordered a scotch and water and waited. He had been riding herd on Xo for three days now. He knew the man's sleeping habits, his eating habits, and now he knew his itinerary. Stockholm, as it turned out, was merely the last stop before he caught an early morning Aeroflot flight to Moscow.

This was where Bogner got off. He took a sip of his drink and looked around the room. "We'll make the switch in Stockholm," Packer had assured him. "Under no circumstances do we want Xo catching on."

Now Bogner was more than ready to lateral the man to his counterpart with Reprisal, whoever or whatever that was. He had been following Xo since the clandestine meeting in an upscale Long Island retreat; enough was enough.

"When you make the switch, hustle back here," Packer had instructed him. Well, this was Stockholm, and he was ready for the switch. His only problem was, he had no idea who his replacement was or how to find him. He had given the signal to the flight attendant at the airport. Maybe she was part of Reprisal—or maybe she was responsible for nothing more than getting the message to Reprisal. In either case, all he could do now was wait.

He turned his attention back to Xo. Xo had ordered a drink and, like him, appeared to be waiting for someone as well. Bogner had no idea for whom, or when to expect the contact. To avoid staring at Xo, he turned his attention to a statuesque young woman at the far end of the Riddarholm bar. She was wearing a chic gray-black suit with a high lace collar, and her long blond hair was knotted in what his former wife, Joy, would have described as a "let's-get-it-on bun." To top it off, she had a full sensuous mouth and rhapsodic eyes that in turn were studying him. He nodded politely in her direction and she returned the gesture.

At that point, Bogner had about decided that Xo could do without him long enough for him to introduce himself to the woman. He was ready to make his move when he felt something in his ribs. It was hard and obtrusive. The voice was even more so.

"Turn around slow," the man said, "and act like you're offering me a light. Oh . . . and don't forget your manners." The voice was encased in garlic.

Bogner reached in his pocket and coiled his fingers around the small Bic disposable lighter Mickie had given him when he left her apartment after Packer's call. For a fleeting moment his mind rocketed back. "No guarantees," she had said stubbornly. "The only thing I'll promise is that I'll try." With that she had handed him the half-empty pack of Camels and the small plastic lighter.

Now the thought occurred to him; why hadn't he thrown the lighter and the cigarettes away? He didn't know. Maybe it was the struggle it represented.

While Bogner ignited the flame, he tried to get a glimpse of his unexpected intruder in the same mirror where he had been watching Xo. Whoever he was, he was bulky, Caucasian, and smelled of garlic. Outside of that, he was wearing a hat and an overcoat.

The man exhaled a cloud of heavy blue-gray smoke, coughed, and instructed Bogner to casually get down from the bar stool and walk toward the lobby.

For a moment, Bogner considered his options. Garlic Breath appeared to be a bit too corpulent to be able to move fast . . . and a bit too wheezy to make a chase of it. Already Bogner was figuring he could outmaneuver the man or move fast enough to get away from him. In either case, he did not want to lose sight of Xo until his replacement was in position.

"Suppose I told you to . . ." Bogner started.

Garlic Breath jammed the hard object deeper into Bogner's ribs. "What you feel, my friend, is the muzzle of a Sig 228 nuzzled up against your vitals. Perhaps I should warn you that under most circumstances this little gem makes a hell of a racket when it goes off. But in this case I've got her quieted down with a G77 gas silencer. If I pull the trigger, a few people in the room might hear a muffled 'phutting' sound, but most of them, including you, wouldn't hear shit. All the bystanders would see and feel is an ultra-fine pinkish mist . . . and a few of them might notice a peculiar odor."

"Who the hell are you?" Bogner demanded.

Garlic Breath prodded him toward the door, through the lobby, and into one of the Riddarholm's spacious men's rooms. Along the way, he picked up an assistant. Inside the men's room he picked up another and began barking out commands. "Claes, cover the door. Gunnar, frisk him."

The one called Gunnar descended on Bogner like a homely hooker. He slapped at Bogner's pockets and clothing until he uncovered the whereabouts of the Steyr SPP 9mm semiautomatic. Then he spun Bogner around, slammed him up against the door of one of the privacy stalls, relieved him of both his wallet and pocket secretary, and stepped back. There was a pause and some heavy breathing. He could sense Garlic Breath and the one he called Gunnar appraising the contents.

"Little bit of everything," Garlic Breath assessed, running his hand around the waistband of Bogner's trousers, "a pneu-gun made to look like a pen . . . and a bionic ear. The guy's a walking arsenal."

"Look at this," he finally heard the one called Gunnar say.

There was a prolonged silence.

"Is your name Bogner?" Garlic Breath finally asked.

Bogner managed a partially muted response. "Tobias Carrington Bogner, Commander, United States Navy."

"Internal Security Agency?"

"ISA," Bogner confirmed.

He heard Garlic Breath let out a string of what he assumed were expletives; some were in Swedish, the rest of them he recognized as decidedly American in origin. There was another pause, and finally he heard Garlic Breath grunt, "Okay, better let him go."

Bogner felt Gunnar retreat and Garlic Breath stepped away. When he turned around, both men were wearing half-sick expressions of incongruity.

"Sorry, Commander," Garlic Breath mumbled, "but we had no way of knowing. A couple of hours ago we got a call from the chargé d'affaires at the Chinese Embassy who indicated one of their diplomats was being tailed. They asked us to inter-cede."

Bogner sagged back against the stall door. "And you are?"

Garlic Breath took off his hat. "Deputy Director Bergdorf, SSB." He nodded in the direction of the one called Gunnar and then the other man, introducing them both.

Bogner sighed, straightened himself, and pushed past Bergdorf. He opened the door to the men's room and looked out. Xo's table was empty.

"Damn," Bogner muttered, "he's gone."

"It should not be difficult to trace him," Bergdorf volunteered.

"Forget it . . . we know where he was headed ultimately," Bogner admitted. "What we were trying to discover was . . . who our boy Xo had to contact along the way. We figured there just might be some holes in the old spy network . . . and there are."

LOG: ONE: SIX

Belushya-Guba 2122L
30 October

"I trust your flight was uneventful, comrade." General Gureko smiled. To Xo, the statement sounded insincere.

As usual, Xo responded to the question without actually speaking; instead he bowed slightly, a gesture he realized Gureko could interpret several different ways.

It was only when the general turned away to look at the electronic situation display of the Belushya project that Xo was willing to admit there were any number of things about his host that disturbed him.

First, there was the coarseness of the man's features. Everything about the man was physically exaggerated: the large, unfriendly mouth, the hibernal, faded blue eyes that appeared to be imposing on rather than complementing his face, the splayed ears . . . and the man's hands. Gureko's hands protruded from his greatcoat like gorged leviathans, and he gestured with the grace of a butcher.

Secondly, there was the matter of the general's deportment. He was both clumsy and crude. Xo had long been taught to distrust a man void of grace.

28

Finally, there was the matter of Gureko's ever-present aura of distrust. To Xo, it was obvious in his every comment and gesture. Xo suspected that the general distrusted him as much as he distrusted the general—if that were possible.

"You have made a great deal of progress since my last visit, Comrade General."

Gureko ignored Xo's observation and continued to lead the way along the steel-grid catwalk suspended over the assembly area.

In the area below them, Xo could identify Section DD-7 of the Lyoto-Straf, a 900-foot-long pontoon graving dock where the third phase of the cylindrical hull section was being assembled. It was nearer completion than he had anticipated.

"Tomorrow morning," Gureko informed him, "the air locks will be opened and the third module will be maneuvered into position by transfer cars. It will be rolled forward and we will begin the process of joining it with modules one and two."

Xo nodded approval. "Then the project is on schedule?"

Again Gureko avoided a direct answer. "There have been only minor problems," he replied. Then he pointed to the large radio-controlled crane in the DD-7 section. "The ground transporters move components from the four sub-assembly areas into this section," he explained. "Frames, cylinder shells, installing frames, and welding of cylinder section pairings must be accomplished before the unit is assembled here and equipment is end-loaded. We have had minor problems with the process."

It was obvious now that Gureko intended to say nothing of the computer problems. Xo looked past him. "And that is where the welds are X-rayed?" he asked.

Gureko nodded. "Since your last visit we have made the HY80 steel standard; weld integrity is critical. There are lessons to be learned even from the Americans. We do not need a repeat of the *Thresher* or *Scorpion* incidents."

Xo had the feeling that Gureko would have offered his observations no differently if he had been delivering a lecture at the Mayachino Technical Institute where Aprihnen had plucked him from his professorship to lead the Lyoto-Straf project.

Turning his attention back to the assembly area, Xo studied it and shivered. He was not dressed for the tour of the underground facility. "Perhaps we could finish our conversation where it is a bit warmer, General."

Gureko seemed both oblivious to the cold and enthralled with the massive technical marvel that stretched out several hundred yards under the ice in front of him. Reluctantly he turned and began to climb the stairs to the engineering area on the C-level.

Xo followed, and at the top of the steel stairs the two men presented themselves to a security camera and scanner. When the green light appeared at the top of the monitor, Gureko pressed a button that opened the air lock. A young Russian seaman standing post just inside the doors snapped to attention. He was hiding a cigarette, but Gureko overlooked it. Xo knew, however, that the general was not the kind of man who would ignore such a breach of protocol. The young seaman would pay later.

The two men proceeded through the spacious, well-lighted engineering section containing banks of computers, and crossed over to the elevator that would carry them to the compound's B-level. Xo realized now that Gureko was taking him to the COM-TAL center for the obligatory technical review. It was part of the agreement; obviously the part Gureko disliked most.

There was little doubt in Xo's mind that being accountable to a Chinese bureaucrat rankled the old Bolshevik.

Inside the COM-TAL there was a large office and

conference table with eight chairs. Two of the chairs
were occupied by men Xo had met on previous visits.
The elder was General Vyacheslav Bekrenev, the former chief deputy of the GRU, a man Xo had heard
referred to as one of the two or three most powerful
men in the loose amalgamation of republics President
Aprihnen referred to as the Commonwealth of Russian
States. Bekrenev, unlike Gureko, was polished and
affable. He stood up to greet Xo.

The other officer was Gennadi Kozypitski, Gureko's
chief technical adviser, a moon-faced man with the
outward appearance of a man-child. Like Bekrenev,
he was acceptably cordial.

Before Xo took his seat at the table, he stopped to
study the large detailed model of the Lyoto-Straf-96. It
was the one that had been exhibited at the Chairman's
reception when the accord was signed. Under it was a
small bronze plaque.

LYOTO-STRAF-96

Displacement:	38,750 tons (submerged)
Length:	831 feet
Beam:	72 feet
Draught:	40 feet 6 inches (surface trim)
Machinery:	twin-shaft Suvorov nuclear re-actor 50,000 shaft horsepower (each)
Speed:	20 knots
Complement:	150 combination (estimated)

On the table, in a file folder lying in front of Xo,
was a translation of the Russian report. He knew it
was intended primarily to be a courtesy since his
hosts knew that Xo was equally fluent in Russian
and German as well as English and seven Chinese
dialects.

Kozypitski stood up. Like Gureko, he was a former
academic. Unlike Gureko, he did not wear a uniform.

He dimmed the lights and walked to a lighted wall projection of the report.

"Much of what we have to say will be of little interest to the chairman," Kozypitski began, "but as we speak, there are two concerns, one technical and one logistical. Both concerns have surfaced in recent weeks."

Xo, a small man with delicate features, waited. He had expected the Russians to announce further delays. It was becoming part of the pattern.

"The first," Kozypitski said, "are reports of increasing American surveillance activity of our Belushya site. On at least three different occasions since 7 September we have detected American submarine activity in the Barents Sea. On all three occasions they spent a great deal of time in the waters immediately off Novaya Zemlya."

"This alarms you?" Xo asked.

Bekrenev leaned forward. "Fifteen years ago the Americans seeded the seabed of the Greenland-Iceland-United Kingdom gap with sound-surveillance devices known as SOSUS barriers. With this device, they could use microprocessors to triangulate the position and speed of our submarines traveling from Murmansk to the North Atlantic. As a consequence, they were able to track our every move."

Xo nodded politely. He was aware of the GIUK gap impediment to secret Russian submarine movement.

The general continued. "They proved to be so effective that we planted a similar set of devices in the Barents Sea prior to initiating the Lyoto-Straf project."

"Are you saying this is an increase over previous levels of American activity?" Xo probed.

Bekrenev took out a cigarette. He gave a casual wave of his hand. "No. But perhaps there is reason for alarm, Comrade Xo, and perhaps there isn't. Our security officers assure us that we have no doubt piqued American curiosity with the large amount of freighter activity over the past three summers. As you well know, Novaya Zemlya is not exactly in the mainstream of world commerce. Increased shipping is bound to be noticed."

"Perhaps it was nothing more on the Americans' part than a training mission," Xo volunteered. "Besides, did you not assure my government that there was no way the construction of the Lyoto-Straf would be detected?"

Kozypitski cleared his throat and directed Xo's attention to the scale model of the construction site. "You must remember, Comrade Xo, it was only recently that it was discovered that the island itself was actually two separate land masses, bisected by a narrow body of water that flows between the Barents and Kara seas. The shelf of ice that bridges that separation has long concealed that fact. Thus the early stages of installation took place under an ice shelf which completely concealed all construction activity. Even the sophisticated American satellites cannot see through thousands upon thousands of years of glacial ice."

Xo's voice was measured. "What you say may be true, comrade, but even in Beijing there were rumors that the Milatov weapons system was being relocated to Belushya Guba. My comrades even then were critical of your General Denisov."

"General Denisov has been discredited," Bekrenev blustered. "He engineered the assassination of President Zhelannov. His blunders are a matter of record."

Xo retained his composure. "I was only reminding the general that the rumor did in fact circulate. Is there any reason to doubt that the Americans heard it as well?"

Gureko, like Xo, was calm. He weighed his words. "President Aprihnen has chosen to reconstruct the union at a pace more moderate than his predecessors.

He uses the stage of world affairs to discuss problems of economy and internal restructure. He defuses the specter of a reunified Republic by talk of other matters. He addresses the American concerns only as a cover for what we are doing not only here in Belushya Guba but Estonia and Turkmen and Kazakh—"

"What General Gureko is saying," Bekrenev interrupted, "is that unlike Stalin or Khrushchev or even Chernenko, Aprihnen chooses to play his role on the world stage in what we feel the world will view as a more moderate fashion. While we reassemble the Union of Socialist Soviet Republics, we want it to appear to the rest of the world that we are, as the Americans say, 'playing by the rules.'"

Xo was growing impatient. They were offering him Party rhetoric instead of answers. "Very well, comrades, but I must point out that you have still not indicated how you intend to handle the American submarine intervention."

"The ways of ice are treacherous." Bekrenev smiled. "We have a plan."

Xo leaned back in his chair. "Then I would be correct if I told my superiors that you do not view this as a formidable threat to the project?" He paused and waited. When no one spoke, he said, "But you also indicated there were other concerns."

"The second round of testing of the HORDE units," Gureko replied. "We wish to move up the test date. But the date will be determined by the availability of the . . ."

Xo Cho Ping smiled and bowed slightly. "And now I have good news for you, comrades; my government informs me that we are ready. We have successfully developed a method of encapsulating the cruor-toxins to ensure that they survive the initial blast."

Bekrenev stood up. "That is excellent news, Comrade Xo." His face was encased in a broad smile. He walked over to a small steel cabinet and inserted a key, unlocked it, reached in, and produced a bottle of vodka. Then he went to the door and shouted for the sentry. "Bring us four glasses."

The young man hurried away and Bekrenev turned to face his comrades. "Comrade Xo brings us excellent news indeed," he repeated. When the young man returned, it was only Gureko who failed to join in the celebration. For him there was still the matter of Zhou Hu—and Zhou Hu's unknown accomplice. Both he and Dolin had decided not to inform Bekrenev until the situation was under control. And at this point control was an elusive commodity; in the five days since the night of the sinking of the *Drachev*, Colonel Ulitsa had reported no progress in his investigation.

LOG:
TWO: ONE

Keplin: Ukraine 0817L
31 October

The earth was not frozen; it was merely corrupted, corrupted by the sooty, depressing layer of week-old snow.

Nearby, two men, one quite old for the task, the other much younger, leaned on shovels and waited. When this one was finished they would dig still another grave.

E-Alexa Chinko watched the two men and wondered how long it would be before someone would be assigned to dig *their* graves. It had occurred to her that neither of the men appeared to be in good health.

Perhaps because of her training, perhaps to reaffirm her outrage, she again counted the number of graves in this latest addition to the old cemetery: 17 rows, more than 50 in each row, all recent. Recent, that is, if you counted the days forward from that April 26th over a decade ago when the disaster had occurred.

Tired of counting graves, she glanced over at the modest tombstone that would be put in place after they left.

Boris Illyavich Chinko
Husband Father Friend

36

Born 6 October 1930
Died 28 October 1994

In death her father had gained no particular distinction; he was only the most recent victim to be buried there.

"He was my son, my only son," the old woman standing next to her wailed.

"And I have lost my father," E-Alexa reminded her. But the babushka, E-Alexa's grandmother, was too immersed in her own grief to console her granddaughter. Instead, she leaned on her crooked cane and continued to chant her centuries-old funeral prayer, Ukrainian in origin. And even though E-Alexa had heard it many times as a child, the old woman had a special way of torturing the words; a way that made them all but unrecognizable even to someone like E-Alexa who had graduated from the Kiev Institute of Science with a minor in languages.

The attending administrator, a former Party official who had been away in Kiev when the Chernobyl reactor failed, had insisted on presiding at her father's funeral. He had conducted the graveside rites and now he was finished. He closed the Manual of Interment, reached down, picked up the customary handful of soil, and threw it on the coffin. Then he turned, and without looking at E-Alexa or offering his condolences, began to walk back to his car. He had instructed his driver to leave the motor running in his Zaporozhet. "I will make it brief," she had heard him tell the man when he arrived.

E-Alexa bit her lip, determined to hold back the tears, and the raw October wind sent a chill through her as she surveyed the dreary scene for the final time.

The grave site was situated on the down slope of a small decline, and the overweight Party official slipped several times as he struggled back up the hill. Still 50 meters from his waiting car, he paused to catch his breath, light a cigarette, and look back at the mourners.

"Pig," E-Alexa muttered. "Koslov is an insensitive pig."

"Shhhh," the woman standing on the other side of the open grave cautioned. "He may hear you. In Keplin the Party still enjoys a certain amount of influence. He can make trouble for you."

E-Alexa scoffed.

The woman was E-Alexa's aunt, Achina Budenny, a former instructor at the Kiev Academy, now removed from her position and assigned a token responsibility in the Bureau of Trade. That had happened when Aprihnen assumed the presidency. The new President of the Commonwealth of Russian States was politically adroit. He defused any number of potentially disruptive situations by appointing known members of the opposition to lesser positions in his new government—where, people said with a laugh, he could keep an eye on them.

"When I speak English, the *pig* does not understand me," E-Alexa reminded the woman.

Achina's eyes hardened. "Do not misread me, I hate the man as much as you do," she hissed. Then she turned away to survey the field of cheap, wooden, orthodox crosses. "It is all so unnecessary. If only he had responded to the crises and not spent his time trying to protect his position, perhaps no more than a handful of these people would be here."

E-Alexa did not respond. Instead she occupied herself noting the names of the people who braved both the weather and the possibility of Party sanctions to attend the funeral. These were names to be filed away, along with the names of those who were able to attend but did not.

Sadly, her father's cortege consisted of only a handful of people: Achina; old Valentin, who drove the burial wagon; Tomas Likli and Pytor Zimrin, friends of her father since his youth; her father's mother; and the widow of Grigorevich, her father's older sister. And, of course, there was Yuri; Yuri attended all funerals. The addled young man had nothing better to do, and even though he was addled, he had long ago figured out that there was the traditional funeral food at the home of the departed after each service. E-Alexa suspected that even with his impaired mental abilities, Yuri had learned that he could sustain himself with the food that was always served in great abundance following the services.

She looked around again and shivered. The chilled mourners, swaddled against the icy Ukrainian morning, continued to stand in silence. Only when she stirred, giving an indication that she was ready to leave, did they begin to move about. The younger of the two grave diggers approached, and his hollow eyes asked the question without words.

E-Alexa looked at Achina and then she nodded. "It is all right to begin."

The young man wedged his spade into the mound of dirt beside the grave and shoved the first shovelful into the hole. The sound of frozen clumps of earth and clay thudded against the wooden lid of the coffin, sending a shudder through both of the women.

At that point, Yuri stepped forward, glanced in both directions, and dropped a small package into the hole. Then he scurried up the greasy, trampled path of snow without looking back.

E-Alexa continued to wait while each of the mourners passed by the grave. Then she took her grandmother by the arm and with Achina's help, assisted the old woman up the hill. At the top of the incline, Pytor intercepted them and insisted on helping the woman to his car. He nodded toward the waiting Koslov.

To E-Alexa's consternation, the Party official was still waiting. Even in the raw air of the early winter morning he smelled of cigar smoke and gin. "On behalf of the Party and Mrs. Koslov," he grunted, "our deepest sympathy. I knew your father well. His passing is a personal loss to me as well."

E-Alexa started to say something, thought better of it, reached for Achina's hand, and started for her car.

For Koslov, even in front of such a small group of people, the silence was a rebuff. "I am not finished," he shouted after her. "All of us suffer. Do you think that you are the only one who mourns?"

E-Alexa stopped and Achina stiffened.

"Just because you are part of the military elite," Koslov said with a glare, "it does not make you any better than the rest of us. If you want to blame this on someone, blame it on Gorbachev or Yeltsin or Zhelannov. If it were not for the likes of them, the so-called reformists, this would not have happened."

"But it did happen," E-Alexa snapped. "Look around you, Comrade Koslov, look around you. How many graves does it take to make the Party admit that your blunders cost my father and hundreds of others their lives?"

"The men who are guilty of this atrocity have been tried and sentenced to labor camps," Koslov reminded her.

"Tell *them* that," E-Alexa snapped. Her hand made a whiplike gesture toward the grave-littered hillside. "See if they are willing to forgive you so easily, Comrade Koslov."

The Party official had nothing further to say to E-Alexa. He continued to glare back at the daughter of the man he had just buried, and mumbled an obscenity under his breath. Only Achina overheard his epithet.

Inside the Chaika limousine E-Alexa, alone now, settled into the warmth of the spacious rear seat. For a moment she shivered, waiting for the anger to subside. Meanwhile, her driver, a young militiaman supplied by the Ministry because of Kusinien's influence, waited for instructions.

"Follow the Moskovitch," she ordered, and the driver, wearing an ill-fitting uniform with the insignia of the new Commonwealth, nodded. He slipped the oversized sedan into gear, and waited for the Moskovitch to turn around and head back to the village.

E-Alexa Chinko, still two months away from her fortieth birthday, reached into the military attaché case beside her on the seat and extracted a small leather-bound journal in which she had been recording the events surrounding the number-four reactor failure. She rifled to the page where the last entry reflected the date her mother was buried, exactly one year and 16 days prior to the death of her father. One year prior to that was the date when her brother had been buried—and before that, the date of the death of her younger sister—all victims of the Party's reluctance to tell the truth about Chernobyl.

She turned the page and scribbled the notation:

Boris Illyavich Chinko
died 28 October
Gurorov Cemetery in Keplin
plot 377

Then she penciled in the word "marker" with a small question mark behind it.

Before she closed the book, she added Koslov's name to the list of other Party officials.

Finally she instructed the driver to take her past the power plant before heading to the village at Diva. As he turned at the crossroad the sign said, "Diva 13 kilometers."

Diva, of course, was still surrounded by the eight-foot-high chain-link fence that the government had constructed around the site following the disaster. The driver brought the Chaika to a halt at the preliminary gate and turned to look at her.

"We are allowed to go no further."

E-Alexa nodded. "I want to look around." She did not bother to explain why. Perhaps it was because she believed that he was too young to understand.

He glanced at his watch. "How long will you be?" He sounded impatient.

"Not long," she assured him. "I am not dressed warm enough to stay for more than a few minutes."

The driver nodded, slumped down in the seat, and tilted his hat forward over his eyes. When he did, E-Alexa wondered if the young militiaman realized that she carried the rank of major in the military.

She pulled her scarf up around her throat, stepped from the car, and felt the biting sting of the east wind. She was wearing a fur coat, the one that her mother had given her, but it was insufficient, and she wished she had worn the greatcoat that was a part of her uniform. Yes, the uniform would have been much warmer—particularly the boots.

She stood for several minutes beside the car, listening to the empty, wind-whipped day. It was both as lonely and deafening as Achina had told her it would be. The music was still being broadcast over the loudspeakers—and the unlikely sounds of Smetana's "Moldau" could be heard even above the constant shriek of the icy wind.

Party officials had placed loudspeakers high atop poles at 200-meter intervals, and the music went on incessantly, 24 hours a day, seven days a week, 365 days a year, year after year. In a letter from her father, he had written: "It is a requiem for the violated—for who is there to listen, to hear, to appreciate—a mere handful of lonely and frightened security guards?"

Was it for the guards? she had wondered. Now, as she walked along the chain-link boundary, the question arose again.

How inappropriate it all was, she thought. A beauty created by the living, mocking the deafness of the dead. Why not Borodin or Rachmaninoff—or even an obscure and brooding funeral dirge—something very Russian?

E-Alexa trudged through the snow that had drifted along the fence line, trying to shield her eyes against the venom of the cold. Could this place really be Diva? Diva, the village where she had spent her childhood, now nothing but vacantness; a collage of empty buildings with broken or boarded-up windows, shops that no longer operated, and the now-silent state-operated small tractor plant, with its smokeless stacks paying homage to a dull, slate-gray Ukranian sky.

Party officials had chosen to cordon the community off at the highway on the edge of the village. Without going through the gate, which was against government rules and regulations, there was no longer a way in— or a way out. The village where she grew up, where she played with her cousins, and attended preliminary school, was now nothing more than a sullen monument to man's blunders. Where ten thousand had once lived, now no one lived. It was no longer safe to inhabit because of the residual contamination. The real toll, E-Alexa was aware, would never be known.

She paused again, buttressing herself against the bitter cold.

Now that she had come *home*, it was difficult for E-Alexa to sort through her thoughts. It was not just what had happened at Diva; there was more to it than that. On the way, she had driven past once-fertile Ukrainian farmland where no one seemed to know how long it would be before the soil would be productive again.

She paused again, and from where she stood, she could see storefronts that faced along Spusk Street, and the small sweetshop next to the old church where Olga had taught her how to make her famous *tort peerozhnaye'*. It was there, in Olga's tiny shop, that she had made her decision to leave Diva and work at the Intourist Cultural Center. At the Center she'd believed she would improve her English sufficiently to be accepted for matriculation at the Institute of Science.

Never in her wildest imagination had E-Alexa believed that such a move would result in her becoming an officer in the military.

She indulged herself in reflection after reflection as she surveyed the stark landscape. It was snowing harder now and she narrowed her eyes, squinting, straining, trying to identify the small two-story house on Levitsky Street where her father had brought her mother after he had fallen from favor during the reign of Stalin. Although it was difficult for her to imagine now, she knew that Boris Illyavich Chinko had at one time been quite at ease in the well-oiled affairs of the Soviet diplomatic service. It had not been his shortcomings as an organizer that had been his downfall; it had been the political paranoia, so typical of the Stalin years, that swallowed him up, disgraced him, and ultimately saw him assigned to a menial position at the Diva tractor plant.

For the moment, E-Alexa's emotions vacillated between anger and nostalgia.

Now, in this nostalgic frame of mind, it would have been easy for her to forget the real reason she had insisted on bringing her father home to bury him. She refocused her thoughts and repeated the man's name over and over: Koslov, Koslov, Koslov. Koslov would be next; the plan was already starting to formulate.

The wind whipped eddies of swirling snow around her legs, and she realized that she had all but blocked out the sounds of the mocking music. Was it Mussorgsky or Rimsky-Korsakov? She could no longer be certain. She wondered if the guards, after so long a time, paid any attention to the music either.

In Moscow, where she had spent most of the years since her graduation, if a composer was not Russian, the work was seldom heard. She still remembered the night the Shevchenko Opera and Ballet had presented an all-Beethoven program; several high-ranking Party officials had walked out in the middle of the performance.

She looked back at the village and then the deserted fields that surrounded it. It was simply gone—like youth and innocence. There was nothing left to do now but turn and walk away. The village of her childhood was a ghost, but it was all she had left. Only the bones remained, starched and bleached and naked bones.

E-Alexa straightened her shoulders. Her resolve was renewed. There was no more time for melancholy and pointless reflection. She turned and headed back to the waiting car.

At the house of her father, E-Alexa sought refuge in the *komnata* where the old *zhensheena* who lived next door had arranged for her to rest. A small group of mourners, consisting mostly of babushkas who were assigned the task of conducting the dirge, were in another room. For some reason, many more of them had been spared. Perhaps it was because most of the men were in the plant or in the fields at the time of the accident.

When Achina entered the room, she closed the door behind her. "When will you be going back?" Achina asked.

"I have a flight out of Kiev tomorrow morning. I am flying back to Moscow."

"Where will you be staying?"

"The ministry has arranged for me to stay at the Belgrade until I receive my orders."

"Are you being transferred to the project?"

"At the moment it is only a rumor. I have a meeting scheduled with General Bekrenev later in the week.

I have been instructed to act surprised when I am informed. It is part of the game we play."

"Then I must conclude that the project continues," Achina said with a sigh.

E-Alexa smiled. "I have been there a number of times on inspection trips. You are right, it is one of the few projects that has not been sacrificed to Aprihnen's austerity program."

For Achina Budenny, E-Alexa's admission was merely a confirmation of the observations of her co-workers when they returned from business trips to Murmansk, Mezan, and Cherskiy. "They say that seldom a summer week goes by that more construction equipment and materials are not shipped to Belushya Guba."

E-Alexa looked at her. "Does that surprise you?"

"Like so many," Achina said with a sigh, "I had hoped that those days were behind us." She paused. "Is it true what they say about the project?"

Before E-Alexa could respond, the door opened and Pytor Zimrin entered. He appeared to be taken aback by the fact that there was someone in the room.

"Forgive me," he said with a laugh, "I was merely seeking a respite from all of that wailing going on in the next room. As an old man, I should perhaps appreciate it. As I was telling Tomas, they are simply getting practice for our eventuality."

E-Alexa stood up and embraced the old man.

He took her hand. "I am deeply grieved for you, my flower."

"I am afraid that I do not feel much like a flower, my old friend, but I appreciate the fact that you are here. I know it has been difficult for you as well."

"It will become more difficult in the weeks ahead," Pytor said. He took out his pipe and filled it with tobacco. "Sit down, flower, there is something I want to tell you."

Achina stood up to leave.

"Stay," he said. "Where family is concerned, there are no secrets."

Achina sat down next to E-Alexa.

"Are you aware that I visited your father when they took him to the hospital in Kiev?" he asked.

E-Alexa shook her head.

"There are matters about which he wanted you to know. He said that he had not had the opportunity to talk to you since you were home for your mother's funeral."

E-Alexa stiffened. She did not want to have to acknowledge that she had waited too long to resolve the differences with her father—even though she had suspected that he was dying. "It has been a while." She sighed. "There were differences in philosophy that were hard to reconcile. He was opposed to the project."

The Milatov project was now in its fifth full year. But the foundation had been laid as far back as the days immediately following the death of Stalin. And the most recent delay, two whole years, had come as the result of the bickering that revolved around the approval of the Belushya site following the reactor failure at Chernobyl.

Then there had been other impediments, weather and logistics, the latter more than the former. The military engineers had been grossly underprepared to convert the tiny Arctic island arsenal into a facility where the E-1-A Novgorod weapons system could be perfected. To compound matters, there was the task of concealing it from the rapid succession of Gorbachev, Yeltsin, and Zhelannov. All were known to be against further development of a weapons system that they felt was both too costly and no longer required. And only now, with the ascension of Moshe Aprihnen to the presidency, had awareness of the project begun to resurface again.

"I am sorry," Pytor said and paused. "Your father

wanted you to know that he resigned from the
Party."

"When?"

"Shortly before his death. It was his statement."

"Did Koslov know this?" she asked.

Pytor shook his head. "Do you think he would have
been there today if he had known?"

E-Alexa looked away. She knew that her decision
to remain active in the Party and support Aprihnen's
policies had displeased her father. She was equally
convinced, however, that he had lost sight of the
political expediency in her decision. If she had not
accepted the appointment, she would have been just
another instructor at the institute—and perhaps not
even that. She had learned the subtle art of compro-
mise—something he had never done.

"You realize, flower, that none of this would have
had to happen. If only the officials at the reactor site
had warned us, many lives would have been saved."

E-Alexa realized that the old man was rebuking the
Party, but she was aware that it was a personal rebuke
as well. She noticed that he had taken his hand away—
and the chasm created by political differences made
the gesture even more poignant.

She leaned toward him and recaptured his hand. She
lifted it and brushed the back of it with her lips. "You
were a treasure to my father," she whispered, "and you
are a treasure to me as well."

Pytor Zimrin buried his face in his hands and began
to weep. When he did, E-Alexa put her arm around his
shoulders and tried to console him. There were times
when she wished she could return to Keplin.

LOG: TWO: TWO

ISA Bureau: Washington 1102L
1 November

Sara had decided to stay at the farm in Vermont for another week. Which for Clancy Packer meant that he would postpone the dreaded 1,200-mile round-trip to retrieve his bride of 37 years for another entire week. But with his plans for the two days scuttled and the Redskins out of town to play the Eagles in a one o'clock TV game, he was faced with nothing to do—at least until game time.

The weekend had not gone particularly well. Clancy did not sleep well when Sara wasn't in bed beside him, and as a consequence he went to bed later than usual and was up too early. On this particular Sunday he had risen at seven, devoured the bulky Sunday edition of the *Post* by nine, and gone in search of breakfast by 9:30. At a small diner in Waverly he'd had two cups of coffee and a short stack before deciding that because there was nothing better to do, he would drive to his office at ISA bureau headquarters in the city.

He arrived there at eleven o'clock. He was not surprised when he found Miller there. But he was surprised to find Bogner sitting across the desk from him. It was the first time he had actually seen his longtime friend since the debacle in Stockholm. The two men shook hands and made small talk.

"I thought you would be spending the weekend with Mickie," Packer said.

Bogner shrugged. "She had to fly to LA. Something about business before pleasure. She promised she would be back in time for Sara's party next weekend."

Packer grunted. He had forgotten about the party. Now he was really dreading next weekend. He went into his office, picked up some papers, laid them down again, and looked out at the traffic on Lombard Street. Funny, he thought, how he never really intended to accomplish anything of substance when he went into the office on Sundays.

"If you guys don't have anything better to do, you can help me wade through this stack of fitness reports; I've been putting them off for the past two weeks."

While Bogner sipped his coffee and watched, Packer continued to thumb through papers until he came to a file folder with one of Miller's cryptic notes attached: "Pack, see this."

The bureau chief removed the envelope and unfolded the one-page document.

To: ISA (Packer-Miller)   DC-7565
From: Wilkens P&S t-3   4433
File date: 9/10 current
Subject: Belushya Guba: All AC monitor
Construction activity on BGI accelerated period 7/1–9/14. Heavy shipments from all servicing ports. 4-W-ss recon indicates heavy dock activity. Tonnage reports show increase all phases. Surveillance continues. Advise—advise. JRW P&S t-3 4433 9/20/ priority IIa

Packer read the memo a second time, shoved it across the desk at Bogner, got up, and walked into

Miller's office. The two men had worked together for the last 18 years, and the lines of authority had long been obscured by time and familiarity.

"I just saw Wilkens's report on Belushya Guba. How long have you been following that situation?"

Miller, unshaven, wearing his usual Sunday attire, a National University sweatshirt and Levi's, leaned back in his chair with his hands folded behind his head. "Month or so, maybe longer," he admitted. "I was just telling Bogner that every time I bring it up to Stinson or one of Langley's people over at NI, they give me the impression there's not much happening."

Packer perched himself on the corner of Miller's desk. "So if it's so damned unimportant, why are we wasting Wilkens's time following it?"

"I didn't say it was unimportant, Pack. I said NI 'gives the impression' that there isn't much to be concerned about. But when you talk to the troops over at COM SAT, it's a hot item with them. I had a couple of drinks with Roger Kramer at the Bellview the other night, and he claims Belushya Guba will be our next hot spot. On the other hand, you know Kramer; his ego is bigger than his IQ. Most of what he tells me I chalk off to martini talk."

Packer turned and looked at Bogner. "What do you know about this, Toby?"

Bogner shrugged. "Pieces here and there. Nothing substantial. I haven't seen it mentioned in any of Spitz's briefings."

Clancy Packer had a sixth sense about cocktail talk, and this time it was sending him signals. "Okay . . . I have no intention of being a horse's ass about this . . . but I repeat, why are we having Wilkens monitor the situation?"

Miller's thin face was creased with one of his wry half smiles. "I guess I've been around you and T.C. too long, Pack. Hell, it's gotten so that I'm suspicious of everyone and everything too."

"Be specific," Packer sniffed.

Miller rocked forward in his chair, stood up, poured himself a cup of coffee, and looked out over the bureau's browning but still-manicured lawnscape. It was littered with fallen leaves. In Miller's mind, autumn had already started to deteriorate. From the middle of October on the weather was all downhill. "It'll take more than a couple of minutes," he cautioned.

"The game doesn't start until one o'clock," Packer reminded him. "Let's have it."

"Okay, let's start with some background. Where are the world's largest known uranium deposits?" Miller asked.

"At least half of them are in Tibet," Bogner answered. "That's at least half the reason we're keeping an eye on Xo Cho Ping."

Miller grinned. "Excellent. Now, where did Milatov first start to develop the E-l-A Novgorod weapons system?"

Packer closed his eyes. "Can't remember the name of the village—but it was close to Chernobyl, right?"

"Diva," Miller reminded them. "Remember how Gorbachev kept insisting it was a tractor factory?"

"Gorbachev closed it down, right?"

"Minor technicality, T. C. Gorbachev ordered a guy by the name of General Viktor Denisov to close it down. But while Gorbachev was fighting a rearguard action with the Party and Yeltsin, Denisov was preoccupied with his own agenda."

"Tractor factory," Packer repeated.

"Yeah, they called it Tashkent Robata, and they wanted the world to think they were building small tractors for some of the smaller collective farms in Siberia. According to our G2, in April of '85, Denisov began converting that tractor factory into a facility where the prototypes for the E-l-A Novgorod would be built. On this one point I have to agree with Stinson at

NI. If that reactor of theirs hadn't malfunctioned, we might never have known about all of this."

"So Denisov *had* to relocate?" Packer probed.

"Why Belushya Guba?" Bogner wanted to know.

Miller shrugged. "Who can follow Russian logic?"

"So," Bogner pushed, "how and when did all of this bubble up?"

Miller slumped back in his chair. "Piece by piece, T.C., piece by piece—and I sure as hell don't have all the pieces yet. Five years ago, our State Department started logging some statistics that pointed to something unusual. When we started digging around, we discovered that the Chinese had increased their trade presence in almost every major Russian port in the North Sea. More and more Chinese freighters were going in and out of those ports, and the Chinese stepped up their mining activity in such places as Yusu and Kangding. Then all of a sudden this guy Xo pops up. When he began going back and forth between Moscow and Beijing like he had frequent-flyer coupons to burn, we sat up and took notice."

"You're throwing a lot at us," Packer said. "Are you suggesting that Xo Cho Ping is somehow tied to this Belushya Guba E-l-A Novgorod riddle?"

Miller shrugged. "Why not?"

"On the surface it doesn't sound like a very likely combination," Packer said. Then he looked at Bogner. "What do you think, Toby?"

Bogner frowned. "We never have been able to tie Xo to anything specific. Maybe Miller has come up with something."

"I'd want something a helluva lot more concrete before I'd hang my hat on the Belushya bit," Packer drawled. "It's too damn far out of the mainstream."

"Not for Moshe Aprihnen," Miller countered. "Seems to me that from the perspective of the Russians, remoteness would be the beauty of it. If your primary objective is to build a weapons system in a location that is nearly impenetrable, where would be a better place?"

Packer stood up and walked over to the large wall map in the conference wing. He located Murmansk, and traced his finger across the Kanin Peninsula and the Karskiye Vorota Strait to Novaya Zemlya. At the south end of the island was Belushya Guba.

"Don't I remember reading a GO report some time back that claimed that there are actually two land masses here?" Packer asked.

"Shelf ice bridges the two," Miller clarified. "One of Wilkens's earlier reports claims we now have pictures showing one of their freighters actually disappearing up the fjord under the ice shelf."

Bogner continued to frown. "So where does Aleksandr Milatov fit into all of this? I thought the E-l-A was supposed to be his baby."

Miller shook his head. "That's just one of several unanswered questions, T.C. I checked with GO and NI, even the State Department. According to them, our official position is, we haven't seen him since the night of the Nobel Prize ceremony in Stockholm. Apparently we're saying we buy the story that he just disappeared into the night."

"Which means we know more than we're telling," Packer admitted.

"I don't think so," Miller argued. "If the truth were known, I think somewhere someone decided to let sleeping dogs lie on this one."

Packer studied the map again, thumbed through the file, and looked at Miller. "So—who's on this—other than Wilkens?"

"Officially, no one. Unofficially, just Wilkens and me. Up until now, there hasn't been enough to justify anything more than just an occasional peek at what's going on. Remember, Pack, everything I've linked together so far is just conjecture on my part. So far none of it actually ties together—what we have now is just bits and pieces."

Packer took out his pipe. "So what do you think, Toby? Think there's enough here to bear looking into?"

Bogner nodded. "It makes it all the more intriguing if it somehow ties back to Xo Cho Ping."

Packer stood up and looked at his watch. "Damn thing stopped; what time is it?"

Miller knew what the old man was referring to. "About forty-five minutes until kickoff."

LOG:
TWO: THREE

Keplin: Ukraine 1804L
1 November

Most of the mourners were gone by the time E-Alexa began to think about leaving. In the empty darkness beyond the bedroom window, the snow had turned to a cold, depressing rain, and even though she had a driver, E-Alexa was beginning to dread the long ride back into the city.

She began to undress, carefully folding the heavy black wool dress between layers of white tissue paper before she placed it in her travel case. She knew it would not be the last time she wore the funeral dress. From what she had seen in the faces of the people at her father's services, it was only a matter of time. Then the thought occurred to her that in Russia, it was death that was fashionable, not attire.

Next E-Alexa placed the shoes with their modest one-centimeter heels in a paper sack, and tucked her lingerie and nightgown into a small compartment in the case's lining. The coat—black Russian fox fur, lined with black silk, willed to her by her mother—was hung in a garment bag and laid over the end of the bed.

Before she put on her uniform, she paused long enough to study her reflection in the mirror. She was still trim, admittedly a little too angular and muscular, but at five feet six inches in height, she carried her 135 pounds well. The deterioration she had heard other women her age complain of was still not in evidence.

Finally, she stepped in front of the mirror, gathered her shoulder-length blond hair together, twirled it, and pinned it into a tight bun.

She applauded herself for bringing her winter issue; the heavy wool gray-green skirt, a thick-fibered white cotton shirt, and a tunic made of the same coarse fabric as the skirt would keep her warm. The hose were standard issue, coarse, warm, and as Achina had observed, unflattering. A fact, E-Alexa pointed out, that didn't matter, because they were concealed by the knee-high brown leather storm boots that were also standard issue for women officers.

She looked one last time in the mirror and, satisfied with her appearance, reached for the Makarov semi-automatic. She checked it, the clip, and the box of 9mm cartridges before placing them in her attaché case and closing it. At last she was ready.

When she opened the door, Achina was in the kitchen with Yuri. When he saw her, he stood up and walked toward her.

"I wait," he said in English. He was smiling.

E-Alexa was surprised. She looked at Achina and back at Yuri. "You—you speak English, Yuri?"

"A—a—li—little," he stammered. E-Alexa could see that Achina had stopped what she was doing and was watching them from the kitchen.

"Under the circumstances it did not seem appropriate to tell you our little surprise until now," Achina said, "and it was supposed to be a surprise for you."

"Y—yo—your father—he te—teach me," Yuri managed.

E-Alexa was stunned. She had known the young man since he was a child. He was, if she remembered correctly, at least 20, perhaps older. The children of her village had always called him "the addled one." No one could even remember where Yuri came from or when he had arrived in Keplin. Most had forgotten that it was Comrade Kretchin who had taken him in. Kretchin had hired him as a chicken butcher at the collective farm in Kirilil, and E-Alexa remembered that it had been a common sight to see him walking back to the village at the end of the day, coveralls stained with the blood of the thousands of chickens he had beheaded that day.

The addled one, all four feet eight inches of him, postured like a schoolboy in front of her. "You like?" he asked.

E-Alexa nodded.

"Me help?" Yuri tried.

As they stood there, there was a knock on the door and Achina opened it. It was the driver. He was holding his hat in his hands and his long, black hair was wet. Beyond him, E-Alexa could see the glistening sheen of the freezing rain that covered the street.

"If you still intend to make it into the city tonight, we must be going. The roads are getting treacherous," he complained.

E-Alexa pointed to her luggage and turned to Achina. The two women embraced and stepped back, each with tears in her eyes. She nodded to Yuri and left.

In the privacy of the Chaika limousine, she opened her attaché case and took out the small, stainless-steel flask. The jolt of the tepid vodka was what she needed.

LOG:
TWO: FOUR

Arlington, Virginia 1437L
1 November

Oscar Jaffe reached for the phone. "Jaffe residence," he snarled. The gruff voice was intended to intimidate anyone who had the audacity to call during a Redskins game.

"Oscar, it's Clancy Packer."

"Pack, goddammit, don't you realize the 'Skins are on?"

"Yeah, and it's halftime, so don't lay that routine on me. All I need is thirty seconds."

"Thirty seconds is all you're going to get," Jaffe growled. He was keeping one eye on the television.

"What do you know about a joint Russian-Chinese weapons venture on Belushya Guba?"

There was a longer than usual silence on Jaffe's end of the line, and Packer knew what that meant. It meant that Jaffe knew something. It also meant he had no intention of revealing anything over the telephone. No one played their cards closer to the vest than Oscar Jaffe.

"Have you talked to your man Bogner?" Jaffe finally asked. "He's been shadowing Xo, hasn't he?"

"Only in the States . . . and only when the Maximum Computer requests it."

Jaffe paused again. "There's a connection." Then he fell silent. When he did, Packer knew he had all he was going to get under the circumstances.

"The usual place?" Packer asked.

"The usual place—the usual time," Jaffe confirmed.

"One more thing," Packer added. "If they don't start getting to that Eagles quarterback in the second half, we're going to get our butts kicked."

"Yeah," Jaffe grunted, "I know. Now will you get the hell off the damn phone so I can get back to the game?"

Back in his den, Clancy Packer slumped in front of the television. The 'Skins had mounted a rally, but his thoughts kept straying back to Belushya Guba. Finally, he picked up the phone and dialed Mickie's number.

Bogner answered.

"What do you know about Reprisal?" Packer asked.

"Reprisal," Bogner repeated. "According to Langley, we don't always know who is running their show. One minute they cooperate, the next we get the cold shoulder. Half of the organization wants closer ties with the United States—the other half doesn't. On the other hand, also according to Langley, they're the closest thing we've got to a reliable conduit into what's really going on over there."

Packer was silent. Finally he said, "Toby, my boy, I got a feeling you and I are going to know a helluva lot more than we ever thought possible about these Reprisal people before this thing is over."

When Packer hung up, Bogner knew the ISA chief had lost all interest in the game.

LOG:
THREE: ONE

Arlington Hotel: Washington 0755L
2 November

After 30 minutes of searching for a parking place, Clancy Packer finally found one at the Arlington loading dock in a stall vacated by a local delivery truck. The sign said, "NO PARKING, LOADING ZONE," but it was the best he could do. It would probably cost him a parking ticket, but he was already 25 minutes late. He decided to take the gamble.

A late-model four-door Ford Taurus, brown, Jaffe's favorite color, was parked across the alley from the hotel's rear entrance. A slender young man in a raincoat wearing a crush hat that drooped down on all sides to conceal most of his features was standing beside it. His head was tilted to one side while he talked on a car phone. He was making notes on a small pad lying on the hood of the Ford. Packer made a mental note to tell Jaffe he was getting in a hiring rut; all of Jaffe's men were starting to look the same.

Packer entered the hotel through the delivery door, worked his way through the Arlington's bustling breakfast crew in the kitchen, and headed down a dark hall to a paint-chipped door marked "EMPLOYEES ONLY." He knocked twice and entered. Packer could have predicted what he would find when he opened the door. Oscar Jaffe never changed; the coffee, the coat, and the cigarette would all be the same. He had been the bureau's field agent in the capital for more years than Packer could remember.

The emaciated-looking little man was smoking a cigarette and sipping coffee from a brown mug with the hotel's monogram on the side, and his raincoat was hanging on the back of the door. The ashtray hadn't been emptied in weeks, and the room reeked of stale smoke and kitchen grease. Jaffe was facing the door . . . because Jaffe always faced the door.

There was a kind of ritual about their meetings. Packer had no idea how the ritual had started. He always took off his coat, neatly folded it, and laid it over the back of the chair before he sat down. On the other hand, Jaffe always looked as though he had slept in his clothes.

Now both men were wearing the disgruntled expressions of fans whose team had lost on a last-second field goal.

"Sorry I'm late," Packer muttered. He reached for the coffee.

Jaffe grunted, and groped in the inside pocket of his suit coat. His hand emerged with a sealed envelope and he dropped it on the table. "I had Markham run it off and bring it over this morning. No doubt you saw him waiting in the alley. Read it. It'll answer some of your questions—but sure as hell not all of them."

Packer rolled the envelope over in his hands. "I'll read it later. Classified?"

Jaffe shook his head, took his feet off the table, and leaned forward to refill his cup. "Hell, yes, it's classified." Out of habit, he lowered his voice. "Now let me tell you what's not in that report. What you've got there is nothing more than a bunch of bureaucratic bullshit. Ever hear of something called 'The Ninth Academy'?"

Packer nodded. "It's the code name for China's ICBM

program. Xo is affiliated with it . . . which explains why Bogner is shadowing Xo whenever he's in this country."

"You got it. But are you aware that some folks believe Belushya Guba is nothing more than a branch campus of the Ninth Academy?"

Packer could feel beads of sweat trickle down the side of his face. The room was warm and there was no circulation. He loosened his tie.

"Next question: What do you know about Tibet?" Jaffe said.

"What the hell is this, Oscar, a test?"

"Not exactly. Like I said, what you've got in that envelope, Pack, that's the so-called 'official version.' Now I'm giving you my version which, so far at least, is nothing more than conjecture based on one helluva lot of reading between the lines, and being told to stay out of something that isn't agency business." Jaffe's voice was as rasping as ever. "And as you well know, I don't like being told to stay out of something."

"Exactly what I'm looking for."

"When the Communist Party took over in Tibet thirty years ago, they threw the Dalai Lama out on his ass. The Party not only dumped the Dalai Lama, but they got rid of the number-two man as well, a cat the Tibetans called their *gyaltsab* or regent. That left only their two prime ministers. They called them *silons;* one was a monk and the other was a layman. For obvious reasons they got rid of the monk too. But it turns out that the layman, a guy by the name of Tingri, had some strong business connections with the power brokers back in Beijing. In fact, some fairly reliable sources think this guy Tingri may have actually been the one that greased the way when the Mao forces took over. Bottom line, Tingri ended up being one of the principal heavyweights in the new Tibetan government. The folder is thin. No one seems to know a helluva lot about him. But we hear the guy is the Sino version of Jekyll-Hyde. Some people love him. Some people hate him. It all seems to depend on whether you're likely to put something in his pockets or not."

"Diplomatic clout?" Packer asked.

"The guy's a heavyweight. He was the only Tibetan asked to participate in the drafting of the the Five Principles of Peaceful Coexistence agreement. That's the document that pretty much governs the border policies between China and Russia. Sources tell us the Russians wanted him on that council because he carries a lot of weight—particularly when it comes to influencing Beijing's views on forming mining policy."

"So what's the connection with Belushya?"

"The Chinese love to tell you that everything happens for a reason—and every reason is in turn tied to a purpose. So work this into your equation. Tingri's daughter married a Party heavyweight by the name of, get this, Xo Cho Ping. Xo, as you know by now, is not a university type, even though his background is as a physics professor from Shenzhen Province. It's been rumored, but never confirmed, that Xo is the man Beijing power brokers gave the task of wedding some sort of doomsday warhead to what we all know as the Milatov project."

"Then this is a joint effort and Reprisal was right?"

"Remember, Pack, none of this is official. I prefer to call my version educated conjecture."

"Okay, so what about Tingri?"

"Good question. His official title is now Minister of Resources in Tibet."

Packer let out a muted whistle. "So what do I owe you?"

"You bring us up to speed on this Xo Cho Ping. Other than what I told you, the dossier in our files reads like a blank check."

"Agreed."

Jaffe paused long enough to take out another

cigarette. He tamped it on the table and lit it, and the smoke curled around his pinched face. It was the anticipated pause. Packer had been through these sessions before; Jaffe had volunteered everything he felt comfortable volunteering. Now it was up to Packer to ask the right questions if he wanted more information.

"Sounds like you've got a handle on this then."

Jaffe laughed. "Hell, no, we don't have a handle on it. I can't prove a thing. The only thing our State Department will admit is that they *suspect* that Denisov moved the Milatov project to that damned island after the Russians determined they couldn't reopen the factory in Diva. The State Department's position is that the Russian economy is in a shambles and that the whole project has been put on the back burner. If you believe that, I've got a ten-thousand-dollar canary I'll sell you. Did the project die? Is it still active? Who the hell knows? I sure as hell don't. If it is dead, why is this guy Xo screwing around in Moscow these days? Nope, Clancy, all I've given you is some of our current thinking—hell, it's not even thinking, it's all educated guesses. The bottom, bottom line on this is—no one seems to know what the hell is really going on. NI says it's not our bailiwick and to stay the hell out of it."

Packer scowled. "Who the hell's bailiwick is it?"

"Officially, NI. My guess is, if anyone on our side of the fence does know what's going on up there, it would have to be your buddy Peter Langley over at NI. Hell, I've talked to him about it. He tells me that 'full disclosure' of what was coming down in Belushya was one of the items on Colchin's agenda the night Zhelannov was assassinated in Negril."

"And Aprihnen is leaning the other way, right?"

"Leaning, hell—Moshe Aprihnen is the one with his finger on the button. One of these days those assholes in Congress will figure it out; when Moshe Aprihnen gets what he really wants, he'll drag us back into the pages of history and the Cold War will look like a tropical paradise by comparison. Even worse, the longer Congress jacks around, the more likely the Milatov project will eventually be fully operational. And if what they say about Sino involvement is true, we can all bend over and kiss our collective asses good-bye."

Packer had been around almost as long as Jaffe. He had been told that listening to Jaffe was a whole lot like listening to J. Edgar Hoover. They were from different eras—but they were cut from the same bolt of cloth. The way Jaffe saw it, there was a ghost in every closet. The thing that bothered Packer was, he wasn't convinced that Jaffe was wrong.

Packer grunted, looked at the envelope, and stood up. "I'll get you a copy of Xo's file."

Jaffe's expression didn't change. "You owe me more than that. You got lucky today, you got a twofer: a fistful of educated guesses and a rock-solid political philosophy, all for the price of one."

The two men shook hands. Packer picked up his coat, and left Jaffe still sipping coffee. He headed back through the Arlington kitchen and worked his way toward the lobby. There he picked up the latest edition of the *Post* and looked for the telephones. When he found them, he dialed straight in to Miller's office. When Miller picked up the phone, Packer checked to make certain no one was in earshot. Even then he lowered his voice.

"Right on target, Robert, my boy. Get on the computer and see what we've got on the E-1-A Novgorod weapons system. It should be old hat. Then see what else you can find. We need to get savvy in a hurry. Jaffe is drawing the same conclusions; he's convinced Denisov moved the entire project to Belushya before he died and that Xo is involved."

"So what's our next move?"

"See if you can get in touch with Peter Langley

over at NI. Find out if he'll talk to us. The sooner the better."

"What if he asks if it's urgent?"

"I'd tell you to tell him the same thing Jaffe told me. I wish to hell I knew. But I think we'd better keep digging."

LOG:
THREE: TWO

Belgrade Hotel: Moscow 1851L
2 November

The flight from Kiev to Moscow had taken a little over 90 minutes after a brief weather delay in Kiev. E-Alexa's scheduled meeting with the engineers from the Tashkent plant had gone well and she'd been able to catch an earlier flight than anticipated. She would have her evening in Moscow after all.

Her flight was landing just as darkness was beginning to settle over the city. The weather was clear, but there were signs of the deepening winter in the air. She delayed at the terminal just long enough to purchase a round-trip flight to Kiev for the following morning with a guaranteed return on the final flight of the day. Then she took a taxi directly to the Belgrade. She realized that Nijinsky would be more likely to meet her if she stayed in the city rather then going directly to her seldom-used apartment near the Pskov.

In the lobby of the Belgrade, she presented her card, registered, spent a few minutes talking to a former GRU colleague who had lost his job when the internal security bureau had purged its ranks of Zhelannov suporters, and then headed to her room on the third floor.

E-Alexa dialed the first number from memory.

"Yes," the voice responded.

"Arbat, please."

"One moment."

She tapped her foot impatiently while she waited. Finally she heard him pick up the phone. Before he could speak she cut him off. "Don't talk, just listen. If you do speak, speak in English. Write this down: eleven o'clock, tonight, at the Baku on Gorky Street. Clear?"

If there was no response that meant he understood. It was their prearranged signal. There was silence, and E-Alexa hung up and dialed the second number. This time a woman's voice answered.

"Inspector Konstantin Nijinsky, please."

Again there was a delay.

When she heard Nijinsky pick up the receiver, she altered the tone of her voice. The clipped style used with Arbat was inappropriate for the inspector. "Good evening," she said, her manner now decidedly more feminine.

Nijinsky recognized her voice immediately and his greeting was, on this occasion, more cordial than tired. "Ahhh, Major Chinko, one of your rare visits to Moscow?"

"Official business, I'm afraid. No time to visit the theater." As usual, she had two tickets to the Bolshoi for him, but she would pass those along later—after she had what she wanted. "But I do have time for a drink. Do you?"

Nijinsky knew how to play the game. It was rumored that Major E-Alexa Chinko was a star on the rise. If that was true, it made her unique. Few women had made any real headway in the military. Besides, Nijinsky knew the value of an exchange with a former GRU agent. There was always new information. "Of course," he replied. "Where? When?"

"There is a small cafe near the Prospekt Marksa

Metro Station called Obraztsov's. I have a nine o'clock train to catch. How soon can you meet me?"

"I will leave as soon as I hang up."

"Give me thirty minutes. . . ." Her voice trailed off as she placed the receiver back in its cradle.

From there E-Alexa went into the bathroom and examined her reflection in the mirror. She seldom used makeup, but for Nijinsky she applied a tinge of blush and some lipstick. Then she undid her hair, allowing it to fall loose around her shoulders. A couple of strokes with a brush proved sufficient. We will see, Inspector Nijinsky, she thought to herself, if a little femininity does not inspire your ready cooperation.

LOG: THREE: THREE

Obraztsov's: Moscow 2010L
2 November

Obraztsov's was a small Lithuanian cafe that seated no more than two dozen or so diners at a time. It was a rarity in Moscow: conducive to quiet conversation. There were only five entrees on the menu, each prepared as it was ordered. E-Alexa had been told that only the borscht was prepared in advance.

She found a small table near the rear of the cafe and waited. Nijinsky was always late and while she waited, she rehearsed her lines and reviewed the details of her plan. It was, she believed, simple enough that the inspector would have few if any questions.

When Nijinsky arrived, the thought again occurred to her that his parents were probably Jewish. He had traditional Jewish features, and there was something about him that reminded her of her father's friend Pytor Zimrin, who she realized, now that she thought about it, was probably Jewish too.

Konstantin Nijinsky stood no more than five feet, ten inches; not much taller than E-Alexa. He had heavy black shaggy hair and a pockmarked face. He walked with an almost imperceptible limp, and had an annoying habit of chewing on a toothpick—even when he was speaking. He reminded E-Alexa of a man who had a total disregard for sartorial trappings. For Nijinsky, clothes were merely a necessity.

For several minutes they exchanged small talk about the presentations at the Moscow Conservatoire and the program he had attended at the Stanislavski and Nemirovich Danchenko Music Theater the previous weekend.

"I believe I told you that my daughter attended the Moscow Repertoire Academy," he concluded. "Alas, it is as close as she will ever come to achieving her dream of joining the state theater."

"Was there a problem?" E-Alexa asked.

Nijinsky nodded and his eyes saddened. He did not elaborate. E-Alexa suspected that the girl had probably gotten in with the wrong crowd, but she did not ask. Nijinsky, lost in his thoughts for a moment, shrugged and offered her a cigarette. She declined, and he laid the pack on the table without taking one himself.

"But enough about me," he said. "I seldom see you, comrade. You are busy with bureau affairs, I assume?" He was studying her through thick lenses that distorted his eyes.

"Unfortunately, even interludes such as this must be combined with business." She sighed. "We talk theater—and then we talk business; bureau affairs."

Nijinsky arched his eyebrows and feigned disappointment. "And all along I thought it was my charm and sparkling conversation that inspired your invitation." His fleeting, slightly crooked smile disappeared as quickly as he had summoned it.

When E-Alexa looked up, she realized that the waitress was waiting for their order. "Vodka and lime water for me and . . ." She pointed to Nijinsky, who indicated he would have the same.

The inspector waited until the woman moved on to another table. "You were about to say . . ."

E-Alexa lowered her voice and leaned forward. "We

are looking for a man by the name of Mikhail Arbat."

The expression on Nijinsky's face indicated that he was not familiar with the name. E-Alexa was delighted. It made her feel even more comfortable with her scheme.

"We have it on good authority that Mikhail Arbat is booked on the last Aeroflot flight from Kiev tomorrow night. It arrives at 9:40. It is imperative that he does not elude us this time. It could be most embarrassing if he does."

"His crime?" Nijinsky inquired.

"Numerous crimes." E-Alexa pointed to her attaché case. "His dossier reflects just how decadent our society has become. Black-market activities, theft— the list goes on."

Nijinsky nodded.

The waitress returned with their drinks and E-Alexa proposed a toast. "To old friends."

Nijinsky smiled and took a sip of his drink. "May I be so bold as to inquire why the bureau has not already taken this man into custody?"

This was where E-Alexa knew that her story had to be convincing. Nijinsky was no fool. It was a known fact that Aprihnen himself had once depended on Nijinsky. It was Nijinsky who sprang the trap that had aborted Kerensky's attempt to scuttle the GRU takeover in the final hours of Denisov's attempted coup. She knew his work to be efficient, dependable, and intelligent. It would have been a mistake to underestimate him.

"Lack of solid evidence. Arbat is exceedingly clever. But this time arrangements have been made. When you take him into custody, you will have all the evidence you need."

"Then what?" Nijinsky pushed.

"Take him into custody. Book him—theft of state property. You will be contacted the following morning with instructions."

"By whom?" the man questioned.

"Does it matter?"

Nijinsky shook his head. "I was hoping it would be you." There was another brief smile, and this time E-Alexa returned it. Before he could counter, she glanced at her watch and reached in her purse. She slid the two tickets to the Bolshoi across the table, and Nijinsky thanked her. Without touching her drink, she stood up.

"It was good to see you again, Inspector. Perhaps the next time we will have the opportunity to discuss our real interests without the intervention of more pressing matters."

Nijinsky laughed. "Tell your superiors that I prefer to deal with you. I enjoy our little exchanges. You are much prettier than any of them."

LOG:
THREE: FOUR

Clancy Packer had called for a two o'clock meeting based on the fact that Miller indicated he needed three hours to pull together information from his sources. Now the two of them, along with Bogner, Purvis Richards, and Ted Balinger of the bureau's resources section, were cloistered in a second-floor conference room reviewing Miller's findings.

Miller closed the drapes and the room was dark, except for the illumination created by the light from an overhead projector. For the last several minutes they had been looking at a series of transparencies outlining tonnage reports and cargo manifests from ships leaving a number of Arctic shipping points. "On this last one, the manifest for the *Meeklova*, we can verify she left Murmansk with a manifest that included twenty tons of a high-quality stainless-steel sheet stock and a like amount of a sophisticated alloy aluminum, also sheet stock. The latter was from their mill in Petrova. Supposedly both the steel and the aluminum were destined for Helsinki. But when the *Meeklova* finally docked at Helsinki, there was no sign of the metals, and she was seven days overdue."

Miller looked around the room before he continued.

"This next transparency is a map of the area and shows the location of Belushya Guba. It also indicates the area under surveillance. As you can see, Belushya is situated at the south end of the island of Novaya Zemlya. Up until a few years ago I doubt if anyone in the bureau had even heard of it. To the east is the Kara Sea—that's pretty much of an unknown to us because the area is salted with microsensors. To the west is the Barents Sea. We know more about the Barents Sea simply because we've been tracking Russian submarine activity in and out of Murmansk for the last forty years."

Balinger interrupted. "Up until a few years ago, Belushya Guba was believed to be nothing more than a fishing village, Clancy, and we weren't paying much attention to it. All of a sudden we started seeing some unusually heavy construction activity there, and we began to monitor what was going on. Five years ago, one of our analysts was reviewing some high-resolution infrared recon photos of the activity and noticed some gradations that hadn't been apparent before. We zeroed in on it, and our thinking is now that there is a total separation of land mass between north and south Novaya Zemlya. In other words, it's two islands—with what some arctic specialists believe to be a permanent ice bridge between the two."

Packer looked at Miller. "Looks like you were right on the money."

Miller continued. "After it became apparent that the Russians were shipping more than just supplies to Belushya, the boys over at NI began monitoring the situation a little closer. And this is what they came up with. What you're looking at now is an actual photograph of the *Kanya-Minsk*. The *K-M* is a tanker/heavy load deck cargo carrier, nineteen thousand GRT and thirty-three thousand DWT. Note—

she has two helipads. We know for a fact that the *Kanya-Minsk* has been dedicated to the Belushya project since late August 1990."

Packer lit up his pipe. "Let me ask an embarrassing question, Purvis. Why were we so damn slow to catch on to the fact that something was going on up there?"

Purvis Richards was an agreeable little man from ISA's Statistical Analysis Section. "They caught us with our pants down, Clancy. We were monitoring everything that moved when it left Murmansk—especially if it turned left and headed for the gap. The fact of the matter is we weren't paying a whole lot of attention to Arkhangelsk and Petrozavodsk. The thing that red-flagged us was when they built two new rail lines to accommodate the heavy traffic in and out of Kem."

Bogner spoke up. "In defense of Purvis and his crew, Clancy, that's a damn beehive up there, and because of the nature of the terrain we've always depended pretty much on what NI tells us."

Packer leaned back in his chair and urged Miller to continue.

"The next three transparencies are shots of merchant carrier activity in the area. Note, in every case, they are being led in by icebreakers. This is an obvious indication that the Russians are starting earlier and quitting later in the season—and the obvious question is why. One thing we know for certain is, it's not because Belushya Guba has suddenly become a popular winter resort area." Miller paused and looked around the room. "Any questions so far?"

It was Packer's turn. He leaned forward and looked around the conference table. "Okay, given what you've just heard, and knowing the nature of the Milatov project, let's suppose that Denisov did actually relocate the whole project to Belushya. What do you make of it so far?"

Balinger pursed his lips. He had a habit of pinching the bridge of his nose when he was thinking.

"When Miller came to me this morning and told me this whole Belushya affair was bubbling up, I asked myself what was new about it. After all, the E-1-A Novgorod weapons system is old technology and, given the current state of affairs, our missile defense system and the state of the Russian economy, the Pentagon hasn't been making much noise. In my section that equates to a 'low level of concern, low priority' mind-set. On the other hand, if Miller is right, there is a new factor in the equation: the involvement of the Chinese."

"Make a guess," Packer prodded.

Balinger cleared his throat. "Seems to me like there are several possibilities. Granted the E-1-A Novgorod is effective, dependable, flexible, and has good range. But we believe we can counter it with a number of systems that are already in place. So I put the Russian element aside and focus on what the Chinese could be bringing to the table. First you have to ask yourself where they have been targeting their efforts the past few years. The answer is lasers. But we know they are years behind both us and the Russians in the development program. Bottom line, they probably don't have anything innovative to share with the Russians in that area.

"One report indicated that they were working on ground-based antiaircraft lasers, but that doesn't tie in to the E-1-A. I attended a conference two months ago where Dr. Tsi, head of the Weapons Development Center at MITGO, delivered a paper on the feasibility and cost factors of developing a satellite-based carbon-dioxide laser with outputs in the megawatt range. His conclusion was nothing more than a reaffirmation of what we already knew. Such a program would be cost-ineffective and iffy."

Packer started to speak. "Then you don't think—"

"Look, Pack, discounting starships, space devices,

and a host of other things that conjure up images of twenty-million-megaton explosions, I think the Chinese are probably contributing something they're more familiar with."

"Be specific," Packer grunted.

Balinger thought for a minute before he answered. "This is nothing more than an off-the-wall guess but— biowar maybe? Or chemwar? They're known to be conducting research in both areas."

"Wait," Bogner said. "Weren't the Russians accused of using chemical weapons in Afghanistan, Laos, and Kampuchea? What would they need the Chinese for?"

Balinger nodded. "As far back as the early eighties the Russians experimented with mycotoxins. They called it 'yellow rain.'"

"And?" Packer pushed.

"It has one big drawback," Richards confirmed. "Selectivity. You piss the stuff out of the sky and it gets on your troops as well as the enemy. So far, no one has figured out how to control the vagaries of wind shifts.

"Binary nerve gas weapons have been around for years, Pack. Several formulas exist. Usually they are two relatively harmless chemicals that can become lethal in quantities as small as a microgram when mixed."

"How lethal?" Packer demanded.

"Fifty times more lethal than cyanide."

Packer stood up, began pacing, and looked at Bogner. "What about it, Toby? If you were making an educated guess about what's going on up there, how would you call it?"

Bogner thought for a moment. "Balinger's theory makes more sense to me. If I had to pick one over the other, I'd say the Chinese have probably brought some new development in biowar or chemwar to the table. The laser theory doesn't hold up: too costly and too uncertain. Besides, the Russians are as savvy in laser development as anyone."

Packer turned to Richards. "Your turn, Purvis."

"I'll go along with the theory the Chinese have developed some new biowar or chemwar technology and that they're investigating—hell, at this point they may be planning to put it in the warhead of an E-1-A."

Packer looked down at the table in disgust. "Damn it, all we've really got is a helluva lot of conjecture, and most of it could fade in a good dose of sunlight. What we need is some solid information."

"We need a peek behind the curtains," Miller added. "So—how do we get it?"

Clancy Packer slumped into a chair at the head of the table. "The floor is open, gentlemen."

"We'll know more after you and Bogner have had a chance to talk to Langley tonight," Miller reminded him.

Packer nodded and looked around the room. "I don't think I need to remind you, for the time being at least, our renewed interest in Belushya should be kept under our hats. After what happened in Stockholm, we have to assume we've got a leak in the line somewhere."

LOG: THREE: FIVE

The Baku, 11 Gorky Place: Moscow 2257L
2 November

E-Alexa Chinko returned to her room at the Belgrade and changed clothes for her meeting with Mikhail Arbat. She was well aware that Arbat fancied himself a ladies' man, and she knew that to be seen with an attractive woman in a fine restaurant such as the Baku would please him. She dressed carefully for the occasion, selecting a skirt, a blouse, shoes, and accessories that enhanced her feminity far more than the drab gray-green uniform she had worn for her meeting with Nijinsky.

Arriving early at the Baku, she arranged for a table near the piano bar, another favorite of Arbat's. When he arrived she noticed that he had shaved and smelled of cologne; an American cologne, no doubt, with a provocative name. E-Alexa prided herself on knowing how to orchestrate the notes of her song.

"Hmm . . ." She smiled as he sat down. "You smell good."

Arbat preened, but she knew better than to expect any kind of compliment in return. Mikhail Arbat's preoccupations began and ended with self, money, and women. An occasional foray into the black market and even more infrequent "assignments" for "people in high places" were simply irritating little interruptions that had to be endured in order to pay for his lifestyle.

It had been more than six months since the two had seen each other, and for the first several minutes E-Alexa allowed the conversation to lapse into small talk about where they had been and what they had been doing. As usual, Arbat overemphasized his involvement in several different ventures in an attempt to make himself sound important.

"And you, lovely Major, what about you?" he finally asked. "Where have you been these past few months?"

E-Alexa's answer was intentionally vague. "Much of the time I have been out of the country—nothing very exciting." She was lying, of course. The black market was a marketplace for information as well as stolen items—and she wasn't about to reveal anything that would be of value to him.

"How shall we do this?" he asked with a laugh. "Shall we dine and then talk business—or would you prefer to talk business first, get it out of the way, and then concentrate on enjoying ourselves?"

"Why are you assuming there is business to discuss?" she teased.

"I wish that were not the case, lovely Major, but I know you too well."

"Then let us start with some wine—we should at least toast the evening before we discuss business," she said.

Mikhail Arbat took her cue. He signaled for the wine steward, an aged, slightly hunched man attired in a white serving coat who moved elegantly from table to table despite his infirmity.

"The lady prefers a Spanish wine, slightly darker than *fino*," Arbat announced.

"Perhaps amontillado," the old man suggested. "It has a subtle flavor and is only slightly sweet."

E-Alexa nodded approval, and the old man disappeared in the throng of late-night diners. It was several minutes before he returned with the wine. Arbat examined the cork, sipped the wine, and heralded his approval.

"And now, down to business, right, comrade?"

E-Alexa lowered her voice. She was eager to get on with it. "There is a man," she began. "He has become, how shall I put it, an embarrassment to certain individuals." She had learned to use the term *certain individuals* when she wanted people to think she was referring to higher-ups in the Aprihnen administration.

"And where would one find this *embarrassment?*" Arbat questioned.

"In the village of Diva south and east of Kiev." She was surprised at how easy it was to issue a death warrant.

Arbat simply nodded. He had accepted the assignment. "I will need certain provisions."

"Your *provisions* have been arranged," she assured him. She reached into her purse and produced an envelope. "Your flight to Kiev leaves tomorrow morning at eight-thirty. It is an hour and a half flying time. Outside the Kiev airport, on the north side of the road, you will find a small restaurant called the Peerozhnaye Hoz. There is a man there who answers to the name of Aureio. Tell him you are looking for a way to get to Diva. That will be the signal. He will hand you the keys to a dark blue Zaporozhet. It will be parked behind the building. When you are finished with your 'assignment,' leave the car at the airport parking lot— and leave the keys in the ignition. You must follow these instructions to the letter."

Arbat nodded his understanding and repeated the information.

E-Alexa chose that moment to slip the Makarov to him under the table, and when their hands touched,

Arbat lingered longer than necessary.

"You are booked on the last flight of the day from Kiev to Moscow. Even if you finish early, do not take an earlier flight. Reason: You will be met at the airport. There you will be paid."

"Now, comrade, what is the man's name?"

E-Alexa was savoring the moment. "Koslov." It was all she could to keep from spitting out the pig's name.

"First name?"

"Evgeni—Evgeni Koslov. You will have no trouble finding him." Then she handed him the last part of the puzzle, a copy of the *Davi Gazyeta* with Koslov's picture on the front page. "He is the fat one—in the middle."

Arbat nodded. "And what about the 'arrangements'?"

"As usual, you have your choice, rubles or dollars." Arbat was already aware of the price he would be paid; that had been established in previous dealings.

"Half and half. The usual place?"

"The usual place," she confirmed.

"And this will please *certain individuals?*"

E-Alexa nodded.

Arbat was delighted. He leaned back in his chair and reached for the menu. "Suddenly I have developed a very hearty appetite," he exclaimed.

LOG:
FOUR: ONE

The Navy Club: Washington 2057L
2 November

Bogner had known Peter Langley for years. The captain
was a 1974 graduate of the Naval Academy who had
gained equal fame as the architect of the highly successful Arca-Dino project, and was an acknowledged
pioneer in the development of the Navy's DSSV and
DSRV programs. About Langley it was generally said
that if it hadn't been for a ruptured eardrum, the result
of a malfunctioning pressure valve during dives on
the Hogs Head Shoals explorations, he would still be
combing ocean floors instead of riding a desk in NI.

Now he was assigned to the Washington bureau of
Advance Naval Intelligence, and served as the section's
primary liaison officer with both the CIA and ISA. At
42 years of age he was still trim, a terror on the tennis
court, a man Bogner liked, and one of Clancy Packer's
most respected confidants.

For the past hour and a half he had been listening
while Packer and Bogner unveiled their concerns about
Belushya Guba, the whereabouts of Aleksandr Milatov,
and the current status of the E-l-A Novgorod weapons
system.

"That's everything we've been able to piece together,"

Packer finally concluded. "I doubt if any of this is hitting you cold. What Toby and I are looking for is someone to either defuse or confirm our suspicions. If you can add anything, we'd sure as hell like to hear it."

Langley pushed his chair away from the table, his gray eyes surveying the club's dining room. For all intents and purposes they were alone. The two officers' wives on the far side of the dining room were engrossed in their own world.

"The club's not very busy tonight," Packer observed. Clancy was always uncomfortable with protracted silence.

Langley shrugged. "Monday. Everyone stays home to lick their wounds from the weekend." He thought for a moment, and looked at Packer while the ISA chief loaded his pipe. "You know, Clancy, it's curious you and Toby should bring this up now. Earlier today, one of the men in my section brought me a videotape. He happened to catch an interview with Ambassador Yerrov on television yesterday. One of the questions he was asked related to Belushya Guba. He said Yerrov hemmed and hawed and finally admitted his government had established a research center for Arctic studies on the island. When he was pressed to reveal the nature of the studies he floundered again. We don't think he was prepared for that question."

"What about the rumor that Denisov moved the development of the Milatov project up there?" Packer asked.

"We heard that—and we checked it out. Apparently he did, but those same sources tell us the project has been put on the back burner because of costs. Over at NI we think Aprihnen is a hell of a lot more concerned about bread and butter these days than he is missile systems. The hounds on both sides of the aisles are nipping at his heels. The official line is that he can't afford to be dumping money into a weapons system that he would have a hell of a time convincing anyone they need."

"You'll have to forgive me," Packer said. "I'm a little on the cynical side where Aprihnen is concerned."

"On the other hand, Pack, you and T.C. have brought up a couple of things I want to check into. We knew about Xo's relationship with Tingri, and we know he's in and out of Russia like a yo-yo. We also heard what happened to Toby in Stockholm." He smiled.

Bogner shook his head. "What about Tingri?" he probed.

"Tingri appears to be the consummate dichotomy. He's wealthy and what's more, his Party affiliation hasn't impacted his lifestyle. He lives high—and like I said, he moves in the right circles. But he has a dark side—and we don't know very much about it. Every time we start poking around, he pulls a string and we're told to back off."

"Surely as many questions as he's raising, we can monitor what's going on."

"We know he stays away from Moscow, Pack. We know for a fact that he has been involved in negotiating several cultural and industrial exchanges between the two countries, China and Russia. But when he disappears behind that pseudo-wall of secrecy that surrounds what's going on over there these days, we can't be so certain."

"Do you think he is involved with the Belushya program?"

"That's just it, Pack, we don't know that he is. So far that's just speculation. Belushya isn't your typical situation. It's a damn village on a remote island in the middle of the Arctic Ocean. It's a hell of a lot like Alcatraz—how are we going to get in there to nose around? Sure we've got our eye in the sky—and we can monitor cargo manifests till Hell won't have it. We monitor every ship—in and out. We monitor every transmission—in and out. We've even got a couple of our silent nukes slipping in and out of their waters, but so far there is nothing to indicate that Aprihnen has anything nefarious going on up there. In some ways we're at more of a disadvantage than we were at the height of the Cold War. In those days they expected us to spy on them. Now we're supposed to be buddies, and friends don't spy on each other—at least not overtly."

"How the hell do we get to the bottom of this then?" Packer asked.

Langley lifted his napkin and dabbed at his chin. He hesitated, then laid the napkin down on the table. "Pack, I've known you for years. You seem to have a sixth sense when it comes to smelling out trouble. It's not like you to go off half-cocked. Let me check around."

Packer nodded. "Better safe than sorry, Peter. There are too many rumors, too many things we can't explain—and too many questions we can't answer. It doesn't add up. Maybe it would if we had all the pieces—but when someone throws up roadblocks when we start looking for those pieces, I get suspicious."

Langley's manner was less guarded when the two women left. "Suppose I told you I might have a card up my sleeve."

Packer and Bogner exchanged glances. "For a moment there," Packer said. "I was beginning to think we had run into a blank wall. How good is this card?"

Langley's face darkened. "I don't know, Pack. I haven't played it yet. Let me go back to the office and make a few calls. I'll call you as soon as I've got something you can work with."

LOG:
FOUR: TWO

Kiev 1013L
3 November

The Peerozhnaye Hoz was, as E-Alexa had indicated, a small roadside restaurant that appeared to survive by selling bread, hard rolls, and an occasional meal to travelers going into and out of the city.

Mikhail Arbat had no trouble locating it. He ordered breakfast while he waited for the two men standing at the end of the counter to leave. They had been involved in an animated conversation about the merits of some obscure local ordinance, but their passions had finally played out.

While Arbat waited, he studied the reflection in the grease-splattered mirror that ran the length of the wall behind the grill. He was looking for someone who fit E-Alexa's description of Aureio.

Finally a swarthy-looking man of obvious peasant origins emerged from the kitchen, and Arbat knew that he had found him. Arbat decided the man was probably a Turk. He leaned forward. "Tell me," Arbat said, "what is the best way to get to Diva?"

Aureio was a fat little man with a crop of matted hair that was both thicker and blacker than Arbat's. He studied Arbat for several seconds with empty eyes shrouded by a prominent brow. Without speaking, he turned and went back into the kitchen. When he returned, he surveyed the room, decided it was safe, laid his hand on the counter, and slid it toward Arbat. When he took his hand away, Arbat realized that it had concealed not only the ignition key but a piece of paper as well. Through it all, Aureio had not even tried to speak. Now he simply turned and began to scrape grease off of the blackened grill.

Arbat finished his breakfast, making certain he did nothing to call attention to himself; when he finished, he left three rubles and five silver kopek pieces on the counter. It was more than enough to pay for the meal. The young woman behind the cash register appeared not to be paying attention to him. She was more interested in the radio.

At the rear of the building Arbat found the Zaporozhet. It was dark blue, a two-door sedan, an older model. It was covered with an accumulation of road dirt and snow, and gave Arbat the impression it had not been driven for several days. Well planned, Arbat thought to himself. It was certainly not the type of car that was likely to draw attention even in a small village like Diva.

To Arbat's surprise the engine started on the first try.

Before he put the car in gear, he unfolded and read the small slip of paper.

Koslov can be found at the site of the former Miska collective farm. It is four kilometers north and east of the village. It is likely that his two assistants will be with him.

There was no signature. Arbat smiled to himself. The GRU directorships may have been officially dismantled, but they still ran an efficient operation. He glanced in the rearview mirror and smoothed his hair. Everything was proceeding smoothly. If the rest of the day went as well, his assignment would be easy.

LOG:
FOUR: THREE

ISA Bureau: Washington 1015L
3 November

Packer had arrived at his office shortly after eight A.M. He had been on the phone and pacing his office for two hours when Langley's call came through.

"Sorry it took so long, Pack," he said.

"Never mind. What have you got?"

"Let me give you a name. You may or may not be familiar with it. Reprisal." Langley repeated it, the second time more slowly, and spelled it.

"There's that name again," Packer said. He scribbled out the name on a piece of paper and held it up for Miller. "Our missing Stockholm contact," he said.

Langley continued. "Suddenly Reprisal is difficult to contact. We think something may have happened. We've gone through this conduit on a couple of occasions—but it has been a while."

"Reliable?" Packer asked. "We've got a lot at risk here."

"Has been in the past."

"How do we establish contact?" Packer asked.

"You're living right. There is an international trade show in Montreal. It starts Thursday. If you can make contact you make it there, at trade show headquarters in the Queen Elizabeth. Have your man leave a note in the concierge's office with a woman by the name of Gladys. Leave a phone number, that's all. You'll be contacted."

"This Gladys . . . ?"

"Don't sweat it, Pack; one-hundred percent reliable. I hired her myself five years ago."

"I owe you . . ." Packer started to say, but Langley cut him off.

"It's the other way around. It looks like some of us over here at NI may have some egg on our face—and that doesn't look good on the old fitness report. Keep me advised."

Packer hung up. "Montreal. Who makes the contact?"

Miller furrowed his brow. "Bogner, of course."

Packer's craggy face creased into a smile and then deteriorated into a frown. "Where the hell is Bogner this morning?"

LOG:
FOUR: FOUR

Diva: Ukraine 1422L
3 November

Mikhail Arbat had little difficulty locating the abandoned collective farm as well as a place where he could observe what was going on inside the farm. He found a small patch of scrub wood on a side road some 100 or so meters from the cluster of buildings where two trucks were parked. He parked the Zaporozhet in a shallow ditch close to a storm culvert and waited.

An hour into his vigil, he saw two men emerge from one of the barns and begin loading crates in one of the trucks. He put down the binoculars, checked the clipping E-Alexa had given him, and decided that neither of the men was Koslov. These men, unlike the one in the picture, were slight in stature. Still, because of the distance, he knew he couldn't be certain.

While he waited, Arbat surveyed his surroundings and attempted to determine what obstacles were in his path. Between the trees and the field, there was a stone road. There were small puddles and patches of thin ice covering the puddles, and that meant that the road was not frequently traveled, a factor in his favor.

Beyond the road was the field. It had been a wheat field at one time, but had obviously lain fallow for some time now. The field itself was dotted with splotches of crusted snow amidst a montage of weeds, rocks, and stubble; he decided that the footing would be tricky.

He made mental notes about the layout—just in case there was trouble. There were seven buildings in all, but the activity of the two men he had already spotted appeared to be centered around the largest one, a barn with two attached silos. The entire complex looked forlorn and desperately in need of repairs.

The weather, chilly and sunny when he arrived in Kiev that morning, had turned gray as he drove toward Diva. Now the skies were overcast and the temperature had dropped several degrees. He shivered, scanned the sky, and cursed himself for not being better prepared for the change in weather. He decided he would not be surprised if it began to snow. He pulled his coat collar close around his throat, reviewed his plans, burrowed deeper into the mound of wet leaves, and waited.

Another hour passed before three men emerged from the large barn and began loading boxes again. From his hiding place Arbat could see gestures and hear faint fragments of conversation. He could not determine what they were saying. Occasionally the men laughed. Finally, the two men that Arbat had seen earlier crawled into the truck and started the engine. There was more conversation, and finally the truck pulled away and turned down a lane that led to the road directly in front of him. To his relief, they turned south out of the lane and headed for the village. If Aureio's information was correct—and it was all he had to go on—Koslov was now alone.

He checked the clip in the Makarov, crawled out of his hiding place, crouched low, crossed the stone road, and began working his way across the field. Arbat considered the field to be the most dangerous part of his mission. If Koslov happened to see him, the element of surprise would be lost, and Arbat was counting on the element of surprise.

By the time he sprinted to the central barn, he was winded. While he caught his breath, he surveyed the situation from his new vantage point. Fortunately, one of the silos was between him and the open barn doors. He waited until he could regulate his breathing, then crouched low to the ground and slowly worked his way to the entrance. The Makarov was ready.

Closer to the door he could hear pounding. He stretched out on the ground and used a clump of damp weeds as partial cover. Inside, the man in E-Alexa Chinko's newspaper clipping was removing tractor parts from a large wooden container and repacking them in smaller crates.

Arbat got to his feet. "Comrade Koslov," he called out. He realized his voice sounded chilled and flat.

The man looked up. He was holding a small generator. "Yes?" he growled. "I am Koslov. Who the hell are you and what are you doing here?" he demanded. "This farm is off limits. It is not safe."

Arbat held the Makarov at arm's length in front of him, making certain the fat man had a good look at the semiautomatic as he walked toward him.

"What—what is going on?" Koslov sputtered. "What are you doing here?"

By now Arbat was courting a nervous smile. He was enjoying himself. "Tidy little operation you have here, Comrade Koslov. And rather profitable, I would imagine. Let me guess. You take old tractor parts that were made prior to the plant closing, repackage them, and sell them for new parts?"

Koslov stared back at him. His thick lips creased in a menacing scowl, but his eyes were betraying him. They mirrored arrogance and, at the same time, his nervousness.

Arbat glanced at the smaller crates. Each was marked with a part number and the name of the factory: Keplin Tractor Works. Under the logo on the containers was the stenciled point of origin: Belushya

Guba. Arbat had no idea where Belushya Guba was, nor did he care.

"I order you off this property," Koslov thundered. "If you do not go, I will call the authorities."

Arbat could feel the laughter swelling in his throat. Why, he wondered, did frightened men like Koslov posture so absurdly? Did they think it would scare away their adversaries? He brought the weapon up to chest level with the barrel pointed at Koslov.

"I bring you a message, Comrade Koslov," he said. Arbat's voice did not hide his amusement.

There was uncertainty in Koslov's eyes. "Who sends Koslov a message with a semiautomatic for a spokesman?" he spat.

Arbat was growing more confident. He had rehearsed his lines. He was *onstage* now. "There are those who feel you have become an embarrassment to the Party, Comrade Koslov. They tell me you have been a naughty boy."

Koslov's eyes darted from the Makarov in Arbat's hand to the container and then back again. "Ahhh," he said, "I get it. Sometimes Koslov is a little thick, yes? You and your friends want, what is it the Americans call it, a piece of the action?" There was the slightest hesitation in his voice. "All right, comrade, there is more than enough for everyone. Like you say, my partners and I—we have a tidy little venture here. You want to be a wealthy man, yes?"

Suddenly Koslov stopped. He realized that even his voice was betraying him now, and his eyes narrowed.

Arbat's finger increased the tension on the trigger.

Koslov's mouth was open, but the words had ceased. His eyes narrowed even though they were empty and glazed.

For some reason, Arbat remembered how executions for state crimes had been described to him. A man was locked in a cell and told to await his fate. He would never know when. The marksman was hidden. The condemned might wait one, two, even three days for the inevitable. But then there would be a single shot—through the brain. The anxiety, it was said, was excruciating. Arbat began to laugh. As he laughed, he began to squeeze the trigger.

The silence was shattered by a whiplike crack. A single report. A small explosion. Pigeons roosting in the rafters began flurrying about, then settled again.

The 9mm shell ripped into Koslov's throat, leaving a hole the size of a copper kopek. The force of the bullet sent the Party official stumbling backward against one of his containers. His hands vaulted to his throat in a futile effort to stop the sudden gusher of blood and the rush of air. He staggered, and somehow managed to propel his bulk forward before Arbat fired again.

Arbat squeezed off three more rounds. There was a series of explosions and Koslov's skull fulminated in red and white fragments, his body torquing into a comical parody of the transition between life and death.

Arbat stood motionless, savoring the moment. Mission accomplished. He turned, and had started back toward the doors before he became aware of the presence of another person. Then he froze.

There had been a witness. The vacant-faced spectator was standing directly in his path, wiggling his hips and panting. He was wearing bloodstained coveralls, and strings of saliva escaped from the corner of his mouth. While Arbat watched in astonishment, the onlooker dropped to the floor on his stomach and scratched his ear with a cupped hand. Then he panted.

Arbat raised the Makarov and fired.

The panting stopped.

LOG:
FOUR: FIVE

Shevchenko Metro Precinct: Moscow 1547L
3 November

It was exactly 3:47 P.M. when E-Alexa Chinko walked into the police station on Shevchenko Street to file the stolen gun report with the prefecta. It was a small but important detail in her carefully crafted plan. She checked her watch when she had completed the forms; exactly ten minutes had passed.

The police official, a paunchy little man with a slash of pink scar tissue over his right eye, scanned her report and reached for a rubber stamp.

"I am sorry to have to put you through this boring routine, Major Chinko. Most certainly this is duplicating everything you have already done."

E-Alexa dismissed the apology. "This is embarrassing, comrade. I feel very foolish. It is my fault, of course. I should never leave such things in my room."

"And you say the thief took nothing else?"

E-Alexa nodded. "I have been through all of my luggage. One does not expect this sort of thing at the Belgrade."

"Even the Belgrade has to contend with hooligans," the little officer said.

"Nevertheless . . ." E-Alexa allowed her voice to trail off. She wanted to be certain that she did not overplay the scene.

"And you have reported it to the proper military authorities as well as the security staff at the hotel?"

E-Alexa nodded. "Is there anything else I should do?"

"I'm afraid that you have done all you can do," he said. "It is up to us now. But I should warn you, a Makarov is a highly desirable piece of merchandise on the black market. By now, your Makarov has probably had the serial number altered and is stowed away in some case until the report of its theft disappears from our stolen goods manifest."

"How will they know when that happens?" E-Alexa asked.

The man sighed. "Unfortunately, Major Chinko, that element seems to know everything that goes on here. Do not give up hope—but I should warn you, it is unlikely that your Makarov will be located. It is best perhaps that you inform your provisions officer that you will require a new one."

E-Alexa stood up and thanked the official again. "I am from the Ukraine," she explained. "I have heard how efficient the Moscow police are. Perhaps I will be fortunate."

The officer preened. "I will see that the report is filed immediately. Within an hour or two, every militiaman in Moscow will be aware of your loss."

As she left the Shevchenko precinct, Major E-Alexa Chinko checked her watch again. She was confident that all she had to do now was wait for word that Arbat's flight had arrived from Kiev—and then it was up to Nijinsky. The stage was set. Soon she would be able to cross Koslov's name off her list.

Her driver was waiting.

There was an hour to kill before her meeting with

General Bekrenev. As the driver pulled away from the curb, she opened her attaché case, took out the small notebook, and scanned the list of names. She drew a line through the name Koslov and a circle around the name of Kirill Gureko.

LOG:
FOUR: SIX

Keplin: Ukraine 1829L
3 November

Tomas Likli was already in the waiting room when Pytor Zimrin arrived. "Is it true?" Zimrin asked.

Likli took his old friend aside. His voice was barely audible and there were tears in his eyes. "It is as I foretold. With Aprihnen we are going back to the old ways."

"Then Koslov is dead?" Pytor's voice was shaking.

"Murdered. Shot through the head."

Pytor Zimrin stared at his comrade in disbelief.

"The pig deserved it," Tomas spat out, "but not Yuri."

Pytor was stunned. "Yuri too?"

"I have talked to the police, but only briefly. The tall one is my nephew. He said that whoever committed this crime shot Koslov four times and Yuri once. It appears that the boy was lying on the floor of the barn when he was shot. He was shot in the back of the head. I am told that it is a miracle he is alive."

"Yuri is alive?"

Tomas nodded. His voice was brittle. "We are told that he is alive—but barely. His mother arrived less than an hour ago; she is with him. I fear that it is only a matter of time. He lost too much blood."

Pytor Zimrin slumped into a chair. He covered his eyes with his hands and began to sob. The room was laced with the heavy aroma of ammonia and disinfectant, and Tomas put his hand on Pytor's shoulder to console him. The uncontrollable sobbing was interrupted only by the racking cough that was a portent of the radiation sickness. Tomas realized that for Pytor, the sickness was already in the final stages.

They stayed that way until Tomas's nephew stepped from the clinic's tiny emergency room, and Pytor regained his composure.

He stood up and looked at the young man. "What— what happened?" he stammered.

Kir Gontar, Tomas's nephew, was a tall man who refused to wear the military tunic of the appointed militiaman in Diva. Koslov himself had appointed him, claiming that he was the only man in the village with the appropriate training to handle the position. It was obvious now that a brief stint as an administrator in the air wing had not prepared him for occasions such as this. Gontar was visibly shaken.

He looked at the two elders with an air of hopelessness. "I will need assistance," he admitted. "I have not been trained to handle an investigation of this nature. I have already spoken to the authorities in Kiev. They are sending an investigator."

"Does anyone have any idea who did this?" Pytor questioned.

"Only what Yuri has been able to tell us."

"Yuri is conscious?" Tomas demanded.

"He comes and goes," Gontar confirmed. "I have attempted to interrogate him, but he is not lucid." He shrugged his shoulders with an air of hopelessness. "I'm afraid I do not understand what he is trying to tell me."

Pytor stepped forward. "I know Yuri well. I have spent many hours with him. Perhaps I can help."

Gontar thought for a moment. "I don't see what it can hurt," he said. "But I must warn you that you have very little time—and he may not be able to hear you even now."

The three men stepped into the emergency room, and Pytor Zimrin was not prepared for what he saw. Koslov's body was lying on a stainless-steel table not far from the wounded Yuri. The Diva authorities had not seen fit to cover the body with a shroud. A large portion of the rotund Party leader's head had been blown away. The area above the shoulders was little more than a twisted montage of mutilated tissue. Pytor Zimrin had served on the Polish front during the siege, and been exposed to the horrors of the death march, but even that had not prepared him for what he saw when he looked at Koslov. His mind rebelled and he had to look away.

Yuri's mother, a short, wide woman with a ruddy peasant face, looked up at the men and stepped back. There was a nurse in the room, but she no longer tended to the boy. There was nothing else she could do. Instead she devoted her attention to a bank of electronic monitors. Pytor caught the almost imperceptible shake of the woman's head when she looked at Gontar.

"Can you hear me, Yuri?" Pytor asked. His voice quaked. He grasped the boy's hand and held it close to his heart.

Yuri's eyes fluttered open. They were glazed and hollow. The pupils had contracted into tiny pinpoints of dull black.

"Did you know the man who shot you?" Pytor asked.

Yuri stared back at him. The specter of the inevitable already hovered over him. His breathing was shallow and labored, his lips dry. The tinny sound of erratic pulsing from the bank of monitors was all that detained the youth from his irrevocable journey.

Pytor Zimrin wanted to try again. But his words were choked off in a wash of emotion. The few words that he had been able to utter were incoherent, garbled by tears that etched their way down his weathered face and into the corners of his mouth. He felt the hand on his shoulder again, and knew that it was Tomas. His longtime friend was shaking his head. Yuri's hand no longer clutched his in return, and Pytor began to sob again.

The boy's mother moved back to his bedside and knelt beside it. Gontar took his uncle by the arm and escorted him from the room with Pytor following. As the door closed, they could hear the old woman wail. This time it was not part of the ritual; now she was crying for one of her own.

LOG:
FOUR: SEVEN

Melrose Apartments: Washington 2213L
3 November

Weary, Bogner had turned in early. Now the sound of her voice came through the dense fog of early and heavy sleep—until he could actually feel her body next to his.

He opened his eyes and saw the silhouette of her face against the backdrop of moonlight streaming through the window.

"You're awake, aren't you?"

"Uh-huh," he muttered, only half conscious, half aware.

Mickie Stanton snuggled closer to him and began to massage the area in the small of his back. He moaned, and when he moaned he knew it made her smile.

Finally he was able to summon all of his senses and he rolled over, pulling her body to him. She was still partially clothed. The blouse, the bra, and her skirt lay in a pile beside the bed, but she was still wearing her panties.

"Take 'em off," Bogner said. "You can't sleep with those things on."

She laughed. "Oh, sure. I'm certain your first concern is how well I sleep tonight."

"Hey—I'm happy; you're home early."

"One whole day early to be exact. Can you believe it: I got the interview I wanted with that Mancennoi character—and the pictures. Brice said if I had all of that, I could come home. So I caught the next available out of LAX—and here I am."

Bogner rolled over, turned on the nightlight, glanced at his watch, sat up, wrapped his arms around his knees, and looked at her. She looked great. "I missed you," he said.

The *she* he had been missing went by the name of Mickie Stanton. She was 38 years old, exactly 17 years older than his daughter, divorced, had blond hair and two degrees. The second was a graduate degree in journalism from Columbia. Bogner was aware that everything for Mickie Stanton tended to be for "the moment." She was a correspondent for *Newsweek*—on an assignment that had her looking into and reporting on organized crime.

Now, lying next to him with her head propped on her hand, she reached up to trace small playful lines on his ruddy face. "Tell me about Stockholm," she said.

Bogner thought for a minute. "Well—let's see. To start with, it's a city built on something like fourteen islands and connected by some fifty or so bridges. Want more?"

"That's not what I'm talking about and you know it."

"Who's asking, Mickie the friend—or Mickie the correspondent?" They had had this conversation before. Bogner knew the woman was already aware of the fact that he would not discuss agency matters.

"No details," she pouted. "I was just wondering whether your trip was a success. Did you find out who this guy Xo was trying to contact?"

Bogner stiffened. "How did you learn about Xo?"

She smiled and tenderly pulled Bogner's head down next to hers. "Because you, Commander Bogner, tend to ramble on in your sleep. If Mickie Baby wanted to make a little spare change, all she would have to do is take a few notes when you're tossing and turning."

Bogner winced. "I talk that much, huh?"

Mickie Stanton nodded. "You do indeed," she cooed. "Now—what was it you asked me to do a few minutes ago?"

"It had something to do with panties, didn't it?"

She laughed. "I believe it did. Ask me again."

Bogner turned out the light.

LOG:
FOUR: EIGHT

Konstantin Nijinsky had spent most of his day taking depositions from two prisoners at Lefortovo Prison. At eight o'clock that evening he closed his briefcase, sealed the audio tapes in cartridge cases, and informed the sector warden that he was finished for the day, reminding the prison official that he would return to complete his interrogations the following morning.

By nine P.M. he had threaded his way through traffic to a small restaurant on Beluba Street, not far from the entrance to Sheremetyevo Airport and the domestic terminal. There was a cold rain, and he was grateful he did not have to find a parking place at the international terminal, where parking spaces were at a premium.

He bolted a quick dinner of vinegar whitefish and cabbage, and caught the tram to the terminal. The flight from Kiev was scheduled to arrive at 9:40, Gate 44-BB. For once, Nijinsky was in luck. The gate was situated at the end of the concourse, and other than a workers' lounge, there would be no place for Arbat to go when he approached him. It seemed almost too easy. Had the flight been on time, he would have had a mere ten minutes to wait. But looking at the

109

flight monitor, he realized now that there had been in excess of an hour's delay in the plane's departure from Kiev. He sighed. He had waited before; he would wait again.

For the third time since he left the prison, Nijinsky extracted the hand-copied file card he had made of Arbat's activities:

```
Name:  Arbat, Mikhail
DOB: 2/7/62    POB: Moscow     Status: s/s/c/2
Height: 6"1'    Weight: 187    Party aff: 9/9/80
Record:
Arrested: 1/6/80 . . . illegal trafficking
          7/7/82 . . . illegal trafficking
          4/1/83 . . . possession of stolen goods
                       (convicted—sentenced to 5
                       years)
          4/6/90 . . . weapons violation
```

It had occurred to Nijinsky that it was both unusual and curious that there was no record of Arbat's activities for the last four years. It was equally possible that his activities in the GRU had sheltered him. Nevertheless, Major Chinko had distinctly implied that it was higher-ups in the now-defunct GRU organization who considered Arbat an embarrassment. The thought occurred to him that a man could, and often did, outlive his usefulness. He studied the photocopied picture pasted in the upper right-hand corner of the card. Despite the poor copy quality, he was convinced he would have no trouble recognizing Arbat when he deplaned.

The complete file, bulky and detailed, indicated Arbat had had a long and checkered career, punctuated by numerous blunders that had resulted in clashes with authorities. Typical in cases like his, there was an accelerated pattern of hooliganism as the man had grown older. But, and Nijinsky had noted this before, there was nothing in his recent record to indicate Arbat was likely to be involved in anything of a felonious nature. He wondered what Arbat had done to bring the wrath of the higher-ups down on him.

Nijinsky purchased a pack of cigarettes from a vendor and waited. Waiting was part of the game. He had often wondered how many hours a week he occupied himself with such boring activity. Once he had even tried to calculate it, but decided that he was in error. It had seemed longer than it actually was.

He found a chair that faced the arrival gate, picked up a discarded newspaper, and opened it to the food section. He wasn't sure why, but the combination of vinegar broth and whitefish, on this occasion at least, was not settling well.

The announcement of the arrival of flight 77A from Kiev came exactly one hour later. Nijinsky folded the paper, stuffed it in his coat pocket, meandered over to the Aeroflot attendant at the gate, and inquired how many passengers were aboard. The attendant checked her manifest and informed him the flight carried a total of 17 passengers. "There should have been more," she said defensively, "but because of the weather conditions, several connecting flights were late arriving at Kiev."

Nijinsky thanked the woman and returned to his seat. A crowd of 20 people, perhaps more, were waiting for the flight's arrival. His mind began to wander again, and he found himself wondering who exactly Major Chinko was referring to when she used the term *certain individuals*. Then he shrugged. What did it matter? His mind tumbled from one thought to another. Did the stunning major have a lover, how choice were the Bolshoi tickets she had given him, and Arbat—did the man realize that he had, what was the word, *offended* someone in the hierarchy?

The green light went on, the doors leading up from the ramp opened, and passengers began to debark.

There was a young couple holding hands, two elderly women with their arms full of presents, three men who appeared to be soldiers on leave, laughing and boisterous—and then there was Arbat. Nijinsky studied him for a moment. Arbat was bigger than he had anticipated, and he moved with an uncommon assurance.

Arbat looked neither right or left, and began walking casually up the concourse toward the main terminal.

Nijinsky fell into step beside him. "Comrade Arbat?"

Arbat stopped. "Panhandle somewhere else, comrade," he snarled. "I am in a hurry. I have an appointment."

Nijinsky reached inside his coat pocket, withdrew the leather portfolio, and displayed his shield. "Inspector Nijinsky, *Noginsk Meeleetsisse*," he clarified. "Please come with me."

Arbat did not hesitate. He bolted for the door marked "Workers Only," momentarily catching Nijinsky off guard. By the time the inspector scrambled to the door, Arbat had already succeeded in climbing the flight of concrete stairs to the next level. Nijinsky bolted after him, burst through the doors to the observation platform, and scanned the area in both directions. There was no sign of Arbat.

The weather had deteriorated; needles of sleet stung Nijinsky's face as he removed his revolver from the shoulder holster.

"Arbat," he shouted, but the sound of his voice was drowned out by the persistent roar of idling jet engines as the behemoths of the Aeroflot fleet taxied about the terminal area.

Nijinsky looked down the darkened walkway. To the east, no more than 200 feet from where he was standing, there was a door. That door was the access to the upper level of the terminal and the overhead tunnel to the international terminal. There were four youths standing next to the door, and Nijinsky shouted to them.

"Did a man just run by you?"

They gave a unified shrug, and he realized they were tourists. Either they did not understand Russian or they did not want to get involved in police affairs.

Nijinsky wheeled and appraised the west end of the unlighted walkway. At the far end was the observation tower where tourists could rent a fixed-position telescope that rotated 360 degrees, enabling them to observe most of the Sheremetyevo complex. At the base of the tower was a shelter built of cement blocks. Nijinsky secured his grip on the blunt-barreled Sverdha automatic and thumbed back the safety. Then it occurred to him that where he was standing, Arbat had every advantage.

It did not take long for Arbat to take the initiative. His first shot ricocheted off of the steel pipe railing near Nijinsky's shoulder; the second creased the fabric of his raincoat just above the left elbow.

Nijinsky's survival instincts took over. He dropped to the sleet-covered concrete and remained motionless in the darkness.

Finally, he heard Arbat's voice. "What do you want with me?"

Nijinsky had decided to play out the scene; let Arbat think that one of his shots had struck their mark. He said nothing. Instead, he chewed on his lip to keep from shivering.

"What do you want, dammit?" Arbat snarled. From the sound of his voice, Nijinsky could tell that Arbat was still some distance away.

For the moment, silence was his best weapon. He did not answer. Using the darkness for cover, he slowly inched the Sverdha around in front of him and gripped the handle with both hands. He was gambling that Arbat could not see any better than he could.

Several more minutes passed before he heard the sound he was waiting for: the crunch of sleet pellets under the soles of Arbat's shoes.

It had all come down to this: a deadly game of cat and mouse. There was a second sound, similar to the first—and then a third. The last one was closer. Nijinsky estimated he was no more than 30 feet, 40 at the most, from the cement-block structure when Arbat had fired the first shot. If Arbat was creeping toward him, he was moving no more than a foot, maybe half again that much, with each step. The footing was treacherous. Nijinsky coiled his finger through the trigger housing and closed his eyes, counting: fourth step—fifth step—sixth step. For some reason each step sounded more definitive—and less cautious.

Nijinsky sucked in his breath. His finger tightened on the trigger. Nine. Ten. Arbat was close now—he had to be. Nijinsky opened his eyes and squinted into the darkness.

It was now or, perhaps, never.

The Sverdha responded. The blunt-nosed automatic belched out a steady stream of lead until the magazine was half spent and Nijinsky released the trigger. There were microseconds when laserlike orange streaks pierced the freezing darkness—and then there was silence.

Again he waited.

Finally, he heard it. It was tangled like a shark in a steel net: the sounds of a man, screams and pleas, interwoven with the ear-bending cacophony of airport clamor.

Now Nijinsky heard hurried footsteps. He turned and saw two men running toward him. They were carrying flashlights and shouting.

"What is going on here?" the first demanded. He was indiscriminately stabbing the beam of light through the darkness. Nijinsky started to get to his feet, but as he did, he heard one of the men let out a shout. The man instructed his partner to shine the light toward him. When he did, Nijinsky saw what the two men were looking at. Arbat's body had crumpled less then ten feet from him. His camel-hair coat was splotched with blood. Nijinsky caught his breath, stood up, brushed himself off, and walked over to where Arbat lay. He reached down to check for a pulse. There was none. Out of habit, he removed Arbat's wallet and checked the identification. It contained everything Nijinsky would have expected, including the red-bordered GRU card. He stuffed the card in his pocket, holstered the Sverdha, and breathed a sigh of relief. Now it would be more difficult to find the answers. But of one thing he was certain; for *certain individuals*, Mikhail Arbat would no longer be an embarrassment.

He looked around, and realized that one of the two men was already on the airport's security phone.

By the time department and airport officials had finished their investigation, Nijinsky was thoroughly chilled. He filed his report with airport security and turned the investigation over to the young homicide officer who had been recently assigned from the Aralov precinct.

He made his way back to where he had parked his car, drove directly to 2 Ploshchad-Sverdlova, and parked in an alley behind the theater. The old attendant at the stage door nodded and went back to his newspaper.

Nijinsky stood in the wings for several minutes watching the performance before he decided to make the call. The phone was near the hall leading to the dressing rooms. He heard the click on the other end of the line.

"Arbat is dead," he sighed.

"Were you able to interrogate him?"

"No," Nijinsky replied. "He tried to escape. I had to shoot him."

"Then we know no more than we did."

"Unfortunately," Nijinsky admitted.

"Does she know?"

"No. I will inform her tomorrow."

LOG:
FIVE: ONE

Bogner and Packer had been reviewing tapes in the bureau's multimedia room for over an hour, making notes, only now and then aware of the dulcet tones of the NI narrator's voice-over explanation of the film clip supplied by Langley's staff. Packer was at the console, fast-forwarding the videotape at some junctures, rewinding at others—adding emphasis to certain of the tape's details.

"Notice," he now said, "the similarity between the design of the E-1-A and the SS-N-3-AA, the one that was designated the Shaddock. Langley's people believe the big difference in the two models is range: one hundred seventy miles for the SS-N-3-AA to almost four hundred miles for the E-1-A."

"Appreciable," Bogner admitted, "but somewhere along the line I got the impression the E-1-A had an even longer range—somewhere between six hundred and seven hundred miles."

Packer nodded. "Entirely possible. NI's estimate is nothing more than a 'best guess.' I was telling Miller, comparing those two systems is like comparing the C1W reactor on the *Long Beach* to the A2W on the

Enterprise. They're both reactors, but that's where the similarity ends."

Bogner continued to scowl. "Look, Pack, I still remember all the high-level hand-wringing when we learned that Milatov was working on the E-1-A project. But we're all equally aware that damn near every guided-missile weapons systems that the Soviets unveiled for twenty years fell short of expectations—and projections. The only ones that seemed to live up to any kind of advance billing were the ones Milatov designed.

"On the other hand, I have to agree with Langley. Milatov always has been guilty of falling in love with his designs."

Packer nodded. "Once sketched, twice built."

"The old boy is hard to figure. He went ahead with the SS-N-3-AA retro design even though he was claiming to be a pacifist at the time. I read his book. He truly believed he was designing a system that would be used primarily in missile-defense applications, and I've always contended that the fact that prototypes were installed on Kynda cruisers proves that the whole system was being designed specifically for that purpose. I don't think Milatov ever intended for the SS-N-3-AA to be operational any place other than Soviet waters."

"That was ten years ago," Packer countered. "Suppose I told you that we have computer models that elevate Milatov's E-1-A design to the next set of logical performance parameters. Those models are damn disturbing. Worse yet, NI claims it's a logical design evolution—and sooner or later some Russian missile maker is bound to stumble onto it. Lockheed and Rockwell are both playing around with it. By carrying the concept to the next generation, we get something that looks like it employs a divert-propulsion system operating through the vehicle's center of gravity. If this is the case, it allows the controller to monitor flight and reposition the missile for a certain sure-death impact."

"I still say it doesn't make sense, Pack. In his book, Milatov insisted it was an antimissile defensive system."

"Suppose I paint the scenario this way. We know Milatov developed the concept and God knows it works. But suppose someone took it from there. Rockwell developed a similar concept for the THAAD missile-interceptor system. We're both saying the same thing—but we both damn well know that priorities change. Who knows what Denisov had in mind or how far they've progressed with it? Remember, we haven't seen hide nor hair of Milatov in years. It may be Milatov's system but it's someone else's project."

Bogner leaned forward. "Okay, I'm not saying I buy what you're selling, but for the moment let's assume you and Miller are on target. What then?"

"Miller worked most of the night. He pulled a lot of strings to get this information. Let me show you a couple of interesting shots." Packer turned off the video display and turned on the overhead projector. "This first shot is of a facility about thirty kilometers north of Gongga Airport at Lhasa in Tibet. Look familiar?"

Bogner let out a whistle. "It looks a hell of a lot like the Pantex Nuclear Weapons Final Assembly plant in Amarillo."

"Very good, Commander, indeed it does—but it's not. The one you're looking at is almost twelve thousand feet above sea level—and it belongs to the Chinese."

Packer lingered for a moment, and then forwarded to the next photo. Bogner could see a warehouse floor full of drumlike containers banded on wooden skids. "Know what that is?" Packer asked.

"Uranium green salt?"

"Exactly. This photo was smuggled out of one of Tingri's plants in Kalimpong in Nepal. The rail spur behind the plant that you see in this picture feeds into the line that goes directly to within twenty kilometers of the facility I showed you one frame earlier. And in case I need to paint in the details, that's where their magnesium cooker is."

Bogner leaned forward. "It still doesn't make sense. The Chinese don't need Russian hardware technology to develop a nuclear weapons arsenal."

"Which brings us to Xo." Packer stepped back from the console and put his hands in his pockets. He was searching for his tobacco. "Langley seems to think he's playing a bigger role in this than we first suspected."

"Why?"

Packer loaded his pipe and lit it. Then he plucked a large manila envelope off of the panel behind the console. He opened it, removed three 8 × 10 black and white photographs, and handed them to Bogner. "Courtesy of the IDID eye in the sky. What do you think they are?"

"Look like big holes in the ground to me." Bogner grinned.

"Exactly, but these are not just your average holes, Toby my boy, they are open uranium mines—by our calculations some of the largest in the world, and they belong to guess who?"

"Tingri?"

"Close. These belong to a consortium, one of the few the Chinese government has authorized. It's called Ni'poe'r Zhan, which loosely translated means Nepal Mining—and it's traded on the Hong Kong exchange. The principals in the consortium are none other than Tingri, our friend Xo Cho Ping, and a man by the name of General Kan. Need more?"

Bogner got up and walked to the window. The early November Indian summer sun stretched across the bureau lawn. He was shaking his head. "A lot of speculation, a lot of smoke . . ."

"Where there's smoke, there's—"

"I agree—it's worth checking out. Where do we start?"

Packer put down his pipe, clasped his hands behind

his back, and began to pace. Bogner had seen the routine before. The pacing was part of the ritual.

"Ever thought about a career as a naval procurement officer, Commander?"

Bogner shook his head. "No. Why?"

"Because tomorrow you become one," Packer said. "Miller will see that you have all the necessary credentials. I'll clear this with your superiors over at NGO. There's an international trade show in Montreal. The doors open tomorrow. That's your cover. By tomorrow night you should have an answer to one of your questions."

"Which one?" Bogner was aware that he had been asking a succession of questions, most of which Packer hadn't answered.

"You wanted to know what our next move was. I think by tomorrow night you'll know."

LOG:
FIVE: TWO

The Kremlin: Moscow 1421L
4 November

For Major General Vyacheslav Bekrenev there was a delicious irony to be savored in the fact that his office was now situated in the quarters formerly occupied by Vitali Parlenko. Parlenko had committed a grievous error in judgment, primarily with people. He had cast his fortunes with the ill-fated Party takeover attempt by Viktor Denisov, and he had trusted Nikolai Kerensky; poor judgment indeed.

Now, waiting for the arrival of Major Chinko, he looked out over the rain-slick courtyard, past the Cathedral of the Annuciation, at the hordes of tourists splaying out from their tour buses.

For Bekrenev it was a time of reflection before the even more pleasant business of his meeting with Major Chinko. Gureko and Kusinien were right. They had convinced him; she was the one for the job. Bekrenev returned to his desk and glanced over the file for the third time in the last hour.

Major E-Alexa Chinko
DOB: 7/7/58   Diva Ukraine: Constituent Republic

121

Moscow University: Institute of Science: Graduated 78
   dd/j/kl
   Institute of Languages 79–80   dd/j/kg
   Party affiliation: 08/04/75—Astopovo Academy
   Service: GRU Security (primary & advanced)
            Naval Directorate/assigned Osipov Yusopov Project, 84–87 (commendation)
            Milatov Project, 88–current

There was more, but Bekrenev chose to ignore it. He had assimilated the highlights; for him, that was sufficient. Before he could turn away from his desk, however, there was a knock on the heavy door.

"Come in." He had made a conscious effort to temper his usually gruff manner.

E-Alexa entered the room. Her hair was damp and she carried her weather coat over her arm. "General Bekrenev." She greeted him with a salute.

Bekrenev ignored the salute and gestured toward the red velvet chair in front of his handsome mahogany desk. "Have a seat, Major Chinko. I must confess that my colleagues told me that you were an intelligent woman. They did not, however, tell me that you were so striking."

E-Alexa smiled. "You are very flattering, General."

Bekrenev appraised her as she crossed the room, waited until she was seated, offered her a cigarette which she declined, lit one himself, and sat down behind his desk. He shuffled the papers and rearranged them on the corner of his desk.

"Are you married, Major?"

"Briefly—while I was at the university. He did not, how shall I say it, share my political views." E-Alexa shrugged. "There are those who would say that it was doomed from the beginning." Her face did not betray emotion.

"He did not share your enthusiasm for the Party?" Bekrenev probed.

"An understatement."

"Where is he now?"

"I have lost track of him." Bekrenev was surprised that she offered nothing further on the matter. Being taciturn was an attribute to a logistics officer.

"Do you know why you have been summoned here today, Major Chinko?"

E-Alexa shook her head. She was lying, of course. Gureko had had too much to drink the night of the Aprihnen reception for the new Chinese ambassador and had let her impending appointment slip, that she was being considered for promotion to chief of logistics for the combined Milatov-Belushya project. According to Gureko, several key officials had suggested her. E-Alexa smiled to herself; she knew who the most influential one had been. Still, she thought it best to keep Gureko's remarks to herself. If her plan was to succeed, then she needed access to him. "Any other family?" Bekrenev probed.

"All deceased. My parents lived in Keplin." There was no need to elaborate. The entire world now knew how Party officials had bungled their handling of the Chernobyl disaster.

"Unfortunate," Bekrenev replied. E-Alexa was surprised by the sincerity in his voice. "Of course there are the inevitable questions about liaisons, Major Chinko. It is indelicate of me, but I must ask."

"You want to know if I have a lover, yes?" She smiled as if to prove that she was not as embarrassed by the question as he was. "In response, I have two questions for you, Comrade General. Are you asking the question for your own information, or is this a matter of some importance in regard as to why I am here?"

Bekrenev laughed. "You have a sense of humor, Major. That is a rare commodity in the ranks of the military these days. Nevertheless, I must point out that you cannot evade my question."

"Perhaps an indiscretion or two, Comrade General, but none currently."

Bekrenev rocked back in his chair and the smile faded. "Now to more important matters. You are familiar with the Lyoto-Straf 96?"

E-Alexa nodded. "I have visited the Belushya site on four separate occasions. I have seen the progress to date, but I am told that the project is being downgraded, it is no longer a top priority."

"You have been misinformed. Under President Aprihnen's guidance, Phase Two has just been approved by the assembly. Our president is most anxious to see the efforts of so many brought to fruition."

E-Alexa leaned forward in an air of confidence. "The design is feasible?"

Bekrenev smiled. "I take it you have heard the rumors too?"

E-Alexa nodded. "When does Phase Two begin?"

"That, Major Chinko, is why you are here. It is set to begin almost immediately. Immediately, that is, after certain little annoyances are cleared up."

E-Alexa sighed. Finally, she thought, the old fool is getting around to it. "Please clarify, Comrade General. What do you mean by 'little annoyances'?"

Bekrenev pushed himself away from his desk and stood up. He walked around to where E-Alexa sat and laid a file folder in front of her. "Open it," he instructed. "Do you recognize the names?"

E-Alexa scanned the list. She recognized most of them. "This is a list of the engineers and scientists that have been working on the Milatov project. Three of them are Chinese."

Bekrenev's face was in shadows. He shoved his hands deep into his pockets and walked slowly to the farthest corner of the room. "They are not only Chinese, Major Chinko, they are dispensable."

E-Alexa arched her eyebrows. "Dispensable?"

Bekrenev walked toward her again. "While we speak, President Aprihnen and his advisers are drafting an official document that will inform our Chinese friends that we are planning an immediate termination of our joint agreement."

"But I spent time with one of their engineering delegations just two days ago in Kiev. I am certain they know nothing of any plans to terminate the development program."

"You are privileged to information that is accessible to only those in the highest echelons, Major Chinko. It will be several days before word of this decision filters out."

"Surely General Bekrenev is aware that all streets have two sides," E-Alexa said. "We may well have their contribution in hand, but they know our secrets as well. When they return home they can begin equivalency studies. I am told that their technology is not that far behind ours."

Bekrenev leaned toward her. "That, my dear Major, is where you come in. It would be most unfortunate if the remaining members of the Chinese delegation were allowed to return home."

"But what about Xo Cho Ping?"

"The illustrious Mr. Xo is not your concern."

"I have been told that he knows a great deal about our efforts at Belushya."

Bekrenev shrugged. "Quite frankly, Mr. Xo is first and foremost a politician and a bureaucrat—he is a technocrat only to the extent that he understands the concepts. Besides, we have other plans for Mr. Xo." Bekrenev straightened, lit another cigarette, and exhaled slowly. "Tomorrow morning, at 0800 hours, Colonel Ulitsa will be relieved of his duties. At that time you, Major Chinko, will assume your new post as director of the security post for the Belushya site."

E-Alexa Chinko stared straight ahead. She did not look at the man. Nor did she tell him that his actions had put her one step closer to her objective. Access to Gureko was now assured. The general commuted between Belushya and Moscow. Sooner or later the opportunity would present itself, and when it did . . .

Bekrenev was still waiting for her reaction. "You are pleased?"

A smile invaded E-Alexa's symmetrical face. "More pleased, Comrade General, than you will ever know."

Bekrenev leaned across his desk and picked up another file folder. Again he handed it to her. "These are your orders, Major Chinko. I would advise you to prepare to leave for Belushya on the first available flight tomorrow morning. Admiral Dolin is expecting you. You have met the admiral?"

"I have," E-Alexa said. With that she stood up and offered a handshake rather than a salute. Under the circumstances, it was a breach of protocol that seemed appropriate.

Vyacheslav Bekrenev shook her hand—and laughed.

LOG: FIVE: THREE

Belgrade Hotel: Moscow: 1818L
4 November

E-Alexa Chinko hurried across the Belgrade's opulent lobby to the elevator. She had not noticed the disheveled-looking man with thick glasses in a chair by the newsstand. But when she opened the door, her phone was ringing.

"Major Chinko," the voice on the phone intoned. It took several seconds for her to realize that the voice was Nijinsky's.

She was impatient with him. "If you'll excuse me, Inspector, I have an engagement. Do you have news for me?"

Konstantin Nijinsky had no intention of being put off so easily. "Yes, and it is a matter of some importance. It will only take a few minutes."

"Very well, Inspector," she heard herself saying. "But I must warn you; I have an eight o'clock appointment and I must pack. I am leaving early in the morning."

"So soon," Nijinsky replied. She was certain his intended tone of disappointment was insincere.

"You may come up," she relented.

Before she had an opportunity to remove her tunic, he was knocking on the door. From her bedroom, she instructed him to enter and have a seat.

"I will be out in a moment," she said, softening her tone. She had reminded herself that he was a resource.

When she entered the room, she had changed from her uniform into something decidedly more feminine, a straight black woolen skirt and a white silk blouse. For Nijinsky's benefit, she'd left the blouse open at the throat.

He studied her with a detachment that she found fascinating. Most men leered. She took a seat in front of the window. The lights of the city framed her blond hair.

"You have him in custody?" she asked.

Nijinsky sighed. "Unfortunately, Major Chinko, Comrade Arbat tried to escape."

"And?" E-Alexa demanded.

"He died in the ensuing chase."

E-Alexa stared at him. Her face showed no emotion.

Nijinsky's left hand thoughtfully rubbed the stubble on his chin. "I was wondering, Major, since Comrade Arbat is no longer able to answer our questions, if you might be able to help us. You see, Comrade Arbat was more than just an embarrassment to *certain individuals*. He was, as it turns out, a murderer."

E-Alexa repeated the word slowly, as if she was stunned by Nijinsky's statement. "Murderer?"

The inspector played with the brim of his hat. "Curious how this whole melodrama played out, Major, but as it turned out, it was most fortunate that I intercepted him at the airport last night."

E-Alexa waited. Nijinsky had a maddening habit of milking the moment.

"As near as we can determine, Comrade Arbat flew to Kiev yesterday for the express purpose of killing an insignificant Party official in Diva. From what we have been able to determine so far, he flew to Kiev and stole

a car from a small restaurant near the airport. The
car was reported stolen earlier in the day, and was
subsequently located in the airport parking lot. The
Kiev police tell us they have matched fingerprints. As
it turns out, Comrade Arbat was not too clever; he even
left the keys in the ignition."

E-Alexa was growing impatient again. She scowled
at the inspector. "Why is it I get the feeling you think
I know more about this man, Arbat, than I am letting
on, Inspector? Am I correct?"

Nijinsky sighed. "Oh, no, Major, I was merely hoping
you could shed some light on this matter. You see,
I thought you might know who some of his friends
were. I'm speaking, for example, of the woman who
purchased his ticket for him. The ticket vendor said a
rather striking woman in a military uniform purchased
the ticket. I thought perhaps you might have some—"

E-Alexa shifted in her chair. "At last count there
were some thirty thousand women in the army alone,
Inspector. I could hardly be expected to identify anyone with such a limited description."

Nijinsky nodded, and continued to worry the brim
of his hat. "Of course you are right, Major—it was a
long shot. I just thought that since you were at the
airport that night, you might have seen someone you
recognized."

E-Alexa crossed her legs. The hem of her skirt
was just above her knees. Nijinsky saw no reason
to pretend he did not notice.

Nijinsky brightened. "Oh, and another thing. I found
this." He reached into his inside suit coat pocket and
produced an envelope. He opened it and handed a
news clipping to E-Alexa. It was the clipping she
had given Arbat. "It's all a little hazy yet, Major, but
I get the feeling Arbat didn't even know the man he
murdered."

"Why do you say that, Inspector?"

"I believe that the reason he was carrying this article

around was that he needed the picture in order to identify his victim. At any rate, I was wondering if you happened to know the man in the picture. His name is Evgeni Koslov. What with him being from the same village where you grew up, I thought there might be a chance. . . ."

E-Alexa studied the picture for a moment. She knew she had to be careful. "It looks like Koslov, all right," she confirmed. "It's hard to say. You know how people change—they never look the way you remember them."

Nijinsky looked relieved. "Well," he said, "sorry to bother you, Major. Sometimes I get lucky when I take these shortcuts. But in this case I suppose I will have to fly to Kiev and check this out. This investigation would have been much easier if Arbat hadn't tried to escape. He'd still be alive and I would not have to bother you."

E-Alexa was relieved when he started for the door.

Before reaching for the knob he paused again. "One more thing. This one you can appreciate. We learned that Comrade Arbat used a 9mm Makarov on his victim. If I remember correctly, you were issued a Makarov when you received your commission. That means you know what a 9mm slug can do to a man. I haven't seen the report, but it is difficult to imagine that there is much left of this man Koslov. Arbat shot him three times."

E-Alexa looked at her watch. "I'm sorry, Inspector, but I really must be getting ready. This is all very intriguing, but knowing how tenacious you are, I'm certain you will get to the bottom of this matter."

Nijinsky apologized and looked at his own watch. "The time always seems to get away from me. I was supposed to meet my wife at the Bolshoi fifteen minutes ago. At any rate, Major, you have a good trip. I will stay in touch. I know you are interested in how this all turns out."

E-Alexa waited for the door to close and the sound of the Belgrade's ancient elevator to be heard before she picked up the telephone. Her message was brief. "I am running late."

LOG:
FIVE: FOUR

Ministry of Trade: Kiev 2130L
4 November

Despite the hour, Achina Budenny was still at her office when the phone rang. She picked it up, half expecting a call from her daughter at Kiev University. A widow for the past 11 years, Achina kept in frequent contact with her daughter, Tarasina, named after the Ukrainian poet Taras Schevchenko. She was surprised, however, when she heard the voice of Pytor Zimrin.

"Pytor, where are you?" It was good to hear his voice.

She was even more surprised when he informed her he was in Kiev. "At the Leningradskaya, a small hotel on the boulevard. Do you know where it is?"

"Of course."

"Can you meet me here in half an hour?" There was an uncommon urgency in his voice.

"Where?"

"There is a small cafe just off the lobby. I will wait for you there."

Achina left the office immediately, summoned a taxi at the kiosk outside the metro station, and arrived at the Leningradskaya less than 25 minutes after receiving Pytor's call. She found him drinking coffee and sitting at a small table in the rear of the cafe. He was alone.

He stood up to greet her, and she could tell that his physical condition had deteriorated even further in the short time since Boris Chinko's funeral.

"This is a happy surprise," she began.

Pytor waved her off. His aging eyes darted around the small room, and he leaned toward her before he spoke. "I must talk to you. You have heard about Yuri?"

The woman nodded. "I received a call," she confirmed. "What about you?"

Again he waved her off. "I am afraid there is not enough time."

Achina frowned. "Time for what, my old friend?"

"We will have to dispense with the amenities." He paused just long enough to regulate his breathing. She could not help but notice he had lost weight. "You know of your brother's true sympathies, do you not?"

Achina braced herself. "If you are asking if I knew that he was a conduit for information to the Americans, yes. Boris told me shortly before he died." She did not tell Pytor that on occasion she had opposed her brother by delivering messages for the militant faction of Reprisal. Boris was too trusting; he was a fool to trust the Americans.

Pytor Zimrin appeared to be relieved—as relieved as a man near death could appear. His expression softened. "Did you also know that your brother was involved in the disappearance of Aleksandr Milatov?"

Achina acted stunned. She did not know how much Pytor knew. "I—I always believed that Milatov had been . . . I guess I believed he was dead," she lied. "That was the way of things in those days."

"It depends on which part of the Reprisal faction you support," Pytor revealed. "He is either in hiding—or he is dead. There are no more than a handful of us in either faction that know."

Achina remained cautious. She did not share Pytor's views.

"Where do your sympathies lie now?" Pytor asked. "I must know."

"I am with the Ministry of Trade."

"That is not an answer," the old man bristled. "You know why I am asking."

Achina lowered her voice. "If you are asking if I support Aprihnen, I tell you I spit on him. He is a cancer. Things are no better now than they were twenty years ago."

She had evaded his question, but Pytor Zimrin appeared to be relieved. "I must warn you," he began, "that what I am about to reveal can cost both of us our lives. For me, what life I have left is of little consequence. For you, the stakes are higher. You are still a young woman."

Achina urged him to continue.

"I was with Boris when he died. He revealed many things. A man close to death does not lie. He told me where Milatov is in hiding. And he told me where his contact book was. It was hidden in the pages of the text he was using to teach Yuri English."

"Where is it now?" Boris had advised her to trust no one.

"That book is the object that Yuri threw into the grave before it was closed. I instructed him to do it."

"Then we need not worry. It will never be found."

Pytor held up his hand. "What I have not revealed is that I also funneled information to the Americans. My code book is a duplicate of the one that is buried with Boris."

Achina breathed deeply. She had decided what her course of action would be the day her brother died. Further contact with Reprisal, regardless of sentiment, would cease. Boris had never revealed that Pytor was involved, nor had he told Pytor about Achina. The landscape was littered with too much deceit and too many lies. "There is no longer a need. . . ."

"On the contrary, I have been contacted."

It did not surprise her. The Americans had no way of knowing that at least one of the many heads that constituted Reprisal was dead, just as they had no way of knowing that Reprisal was actually two factions— or perhaps more; even she couldn't be certain.

She went on. "Boris indicated that contacts have been infrequent since—"

"The Americans are attempting to locate Milatov."

"Why?" she asked.

"That I do not know. So far it is only a preliminary inquiry. They ask only, if adequate assurances were given by the United States government, would those who know where Milatov is hiding arrange a meeting."

"Do the Americans know about the infighting within the ranks of Reprisal?"

Pytor looked at her. "Everyone is on guard," he said.

Again Achina decided to keep her involvement a secret. "The Americans cannot be trusted," she countered.

Now Pytor knew which faction the woman supported. "Are they any less trustworthy than Aprihnen?"

"The KGB and the GRU searched for Milatov for years. They have not been able to establish contact. Why are you so certain the Americans are trustworthy? Are you willing to trust them more than your own people?"

Pytor hesitated. His hands trembled.

Achina lowered her voice. "Why are you telling me all of this?"

The old man's response was lost in a racking cough. "I am afraid the answer is obvious. If Aprihnen's hooligans knew that I knew of Milatov's whereabouts, I do not think it would take them long to get the information out of me."

Achina Budenny reached across the table and captured the old man's hand. It was cold to the touch. "Who here knows besides you?" she asked.

Pytor's answer did not surprise her. "To the best of my knowledge, I am the only one left."

"And you propose to tell me."

"Not unless you are willing to accept the burden." Again he was forced to wait until the cough subsided. "In a few minutes I shall walk out of this cafe. When I arrived I left a package at the registration desk in the lobby. I told them someone had lost the package. If you feel ready to accept the responsibility, simply ask if anyone has found the parcel. It is small, wrapped in plain white paper, with the name Yuri Konyev written on it. If they ask you to identify the contents, tell them it is only an inexpensive and outdated English textbook."

"And if I choose to avoid . . . ?"

"Eventually the two factions must work together. Otherwise there is danger. Is it enough that Milatov is safe? Should the secret die? Even then, one is only able to determine his whereabouts if you decipher the code; the fifth and ninth words at the top of pages five, fifty-five, one hundred and five, and one hundred and fifty-five."

The woman slumped back in her chair. Why her? Why now? Why this test of her convictions? With Boris's death she had believed the days of subterfuge were finally behind her. Milatov should be left alone; no one, particularly the Americans, should have access to him.

Pytor studied her for a moment, stood up, smiled, touched her shoulder as he passed her chair, and left.

Achina Budenny sat motionless for several minutes.

Finally she stirred. She checked her watch, patted her hair, and when she was convinced she would not be connected with Pytor, she left. She did not stop at the desk to pick up the package.

LOG:
FIVE: FIVE

Taganrog: Moscow 2240L
4 November

On a blacktop two-lane road that threaded its way through a winding succession of low-rising hills, E-Alexa drove toward the brooding two-story *dacha* situated by a small lake and guarded by a squad of Aprihnen's handpicked militiamen. Taganrog.

In the eyes of Georgi Kusinien, Taganrog, birthplace of Anton Chekhov, was the taproot of his melancholia. Seldom did he read Chekhov without crying. Kusinien considered sadness to be the burden of all who were born at the northern tip of the Gulf of Taganrog, itself a part of the Sea of Azov.

Rather than deny his birthright and his predisposition, Kusinien had decided to name his *dacha* after the city in which he was born.

Kusinien was considered by most to be the source of Aprihnen's wisdom, the master strategist the President of the Commonwealth relied upon.

The sentry recognized her car, nodded, stabbed the beam of his flashlight into the backseat of her staff Volga, stepped back, saluted, and motioned for her to proceed. There was no dialogue between them; she had not even rolled the Volga's window down.

From the gate to the rear of the house was a little over a kilometer through a heavy thicket that sheltered Kusinien's collection of Siberian dwarf deer. As usual, with darkness the lane was dotted with thick patches of fog, and her visibility was further impeded by the occasional spit of sleet and rain.

She parked at the rear of the house and entered through the rear door. Kusinien himself often used this way of gaining access to the house because it enabled him to avoid the members of his staff and ever-increasing personal entourage.

From the large kitchen, E-Alexa could see into the dining room and through that door into the study, the room where the president's adviser often held his most important meetings. She had learned early on that if Kusinien invited you into his private study, he considered the meeting to be of the utmost importance.

From where she was standing, E-Alexa was unable to determine who was in the room with him, and the conversation had been hushed to a mutually muted whisper. She shrugged, took off her coat, and started up the narrow back stairway to the second floor. At the top of the stairs, she paused just long enough to see if any of the rooms were occupied. With no yellow wash of light peeking out from under any of the doors, she concluded she was alone.

Inside the tastefully appointed room where she knew they would inevitably spend the night, she began to undress. She made certain the black wool skirt and white silk blouse were carefully hung in the closet. She put her bra, panties, and pantyhose in a clothes hamper, and checked to make certain she had fresh ones to wear when she returned to the city in the morning. As she stood in front of the mirror, cupping her breasts in her hands and admiring the lithe yet muscular body reflecting back at her, she wondered what General Vyacheslav Bekrenev would think of his new chief of logistics at Belushya Guba now.

From the bedroom she retired to the bath and began to draw a tub. It was a sunken affair with delicate rose-petal faucets and a recessed area where the drinks Kusinien inevitably brought could be set. Out of the corner of her eye she saw the babushka who tended to upstairs matters in the *dacha*. The old woman emptied the clothes hamper, entered the bathroom just long enough to check the towels, and retired. Like the security man at the main gate, the old woman never spoke. And if E-Alexa was naked, as she was now, the old woman always averted her eyes.

E-Alexa sprinkled a bath scent in the water and slipped into the tub, immersing herself up to her long, slender throat. Then, as if the old woman leaving the compartment had been a signal, Kusinien materialized.

There was an unspoken ritual about his arrival. He handed her the glass of chilled berry juice and situated himself on the unlikely satin loveseat that sat discreetly in the corner of the large room. He was dressed as he always was, in a black suit, white shirt, narrow regimental tie of subdued complementing colors, and black leather rubber-soled shoes. The latter, E-Alexa suspected, were a carryover from his early days in the KGB.

He sat for several moments, studying her through the pinkish blush of the berry juice glass.

"Your drive?" he inquired.

"Harrowing," she admitted. "The roads are slippery."

"I am flattered that you came."

She laughed. "Do I have a choice? If Kusinien commands, I obey."

"You are under no obligation," he said, but she dismissed him with a feminine wave of her hand.

"I am teasing you," she said. She raised herself high enough out of the water that her breasts were exposed.

Kusinien raised his glass to eye level and studied her again. "You have had your conversation with General Bekrenev?"

E-Alexa took a sip of berry juice and nodded. "I acted appropriately surprised. You would have been proud of me."

They sat in silence for several minutes, and she appraised the man who had altered the course of her life as well as that of her country. No one knew for certain, but from what he had told her about himself, E-Alexa had decided that he was at least seventy, if not older. He was tall and painfully thin, a fact that was apparent despite clothes that were tailored to make him appear stronger. His eyes reminded her of tortured amethyst, pale by comparison to hers, but penetrating and haunted. His pencil-thin lips seldom betrayed emotion, and only an occasional and subtle lift of his shaggy eyebrows indicated surprise or anger; E-Alexa was never quite sure which.

For the most part he was bald and his skin had a bluish, almost marbled texture to it. Only his hands betrayed his age. A slight palsy was evident when he was tired.

When she could stand the silence no longer, she spoke. "Why did you select me?"

"Because I can trust you," he said. "And," he added, "you will do what must be done."

"You are referring to the remaining Sino technicians?"

Georgi Kusinien seldom smiled, but he did allow himself an occasional guttural sound that indicated his amusement. "It is one of your charms, Comrade Chinko, your beguiling bluntness. There is a certain appealing economy in your style of communication."

"The Chinese," she reminded him, "is it true what Bekrenev tells me?"

Kusinien leaned his head back and closed his eyes. "We are at a crossroads. Our Sino friends have made their contribution and the matter is reduced to this. We have no further use for them—as they have no further need of us. You realize, of course, that there are always problems in terminating any kind of agreement. If we did not take this measure, what is to stop them from returning home and setting the wheels in motion to duplicate our efforts at Belushya?"

"Is that not already a danger?" E-Alexa asked. "Besides, General Bekrenev indicated that this decision is imminent."

Kusinien still had his eyes closed. "Time is our ally. When we inform them, we must have our plan in place. And, of course, it must appear that the—shall I call it *accident*—is but one of the vagaries of life."

E-Alexa slowly raised herself out of the water and stood in front of him. Kusinien handed her a towel and she made a ritual of the process of drying herself off. Everywhere there were mirrors and no matter where or how she turned, she knew that he was savoring every languid move. She stepped to the basin and unknotted her hair. When she did, the ends were wetted by her still-damp shoulders.

Kusinien stood up beside her, and she knew it was time for the second part of the ritual. She handed him the small vial of body oil and he began to rub it over shoulders, his large, strong fingers gently kneading it into the flesh as if he were caressing a cherished piece of ivory. From time to time E-Alexa permitted a deep-throated moan to escape unchecked, not because she knew the sounds of her gratification pleased him, but because of the exquisite delight she felt over her entire body.

His hands explored, always gentle, over her breasts, against her flat, hard stomach, and in places soft and still moist from the bath.

Then he stopped and she stepped away from him. There was no indication of any emotion on his part.

"Shall we go into the bedroom?" she heard herself asking. At times like this E-Alexa always thought that her voice sounded as though it were disconnected from her being—from the part of her that stood there inviting his assessment.

Kusinien nodded and walked into the bedroom ahead of her. The babushka had turned back the covers of the mahogany canopied bed. The sheets, as always, were rose-colored silk. E-Alexa had selected them herself. In fact, she had insisted that Kusinien redecorate the entire bedroom in colors that pleased her.

"For you," he had said when he showed it to her for the first time after the work had been completed. "For you and you alone."

The babushka had laid out a gown for her, but E-Alexa ignored it. She crept up on the oversized bed and languished across it, stretching and reveling in the luxury of her surroundings. Instead of looking at him, she studied the ballet of flames in the fireplace.

Kusinien had assumed his usual position in a large overstuffed chair close by the bed. His faded purple eyes continued to assess her—not as a lover, but more as a connoisseur appreciating a lovely piece of art.

Again the silence annoyed her. "Will the time come when we make love?"

Kusinien made his sound of amusement, not a laugh, but something that seemed to swell out of his throat. "There was a time when I deluded myself with such visions," he said. "But alas, I am first and foremost a pragmatist. A man of my age and skills is no match for the fire and vigor of youth."

E-Alexa smiled softly, and allowed her hand to creep across the bed with the intent of reaching out to him. She stopped when he continued to speak.

"In addition to being a pragmatist, I am also a student of science and of comparative behavior."

E-Alexa looked at him.

"You, my charming and inviting Major, are a mantis, a member of the family Mantidae. Do you know what happens when the female mantis is done with her male lover?"

E-Alexa shook her head.

"The female devours the male."

"Do you think I would devour you?" E-Alexa smiled.

Kusinien stood up, walked to the nightstand beside the bed, and opened the drawer. He withdrew a small purple velvet receptacle, opened it, and held it out to her. It was a brooch, a delicately crafted gold mantis mounted on a white-ice diamond island.

"Georgi," she heard herself say. She seldom said his name aloud. "It is beautiful."

Kusinien lit a small candle and set it on the nightstand before he turned out the light. He stood beside the bed, and the only sound E-Alexa could hear was the sound of the wind and the sporadic click of ice grains against the window.

"Would you be disappointed in me if I tried to seduce you?" she asked.

He did not answer her, and she could not tell what he was thinking in the darkness.

"Are you going now?"

"I will read for a while before I retire."

"You are aware that General Bekrenev insists that I return to Belushya immediately? I will have to leave very early in the morning. I have an eight-thirty flight."

Kusinien did not speak. Instead, he bent in the darkness and allowed his fingers to trail over her shoulders and touch her hair. Then he left the room.

E-Alexa crawled between the sheets, rolled over on her back, and stared up into the darkness. Her thoughts were no longer of Georgi Kusinien. They had turned to her assignment at Belushya Guba. The Sino technicians and scientists, she repeated to herself, and how to sever the agreement. She began to plan. The candle was still glowing when she closed her eyes. The gold mantis was still clutched in her hand.

TWO

LOG:
SIX: ONE

It was shortly after four P.M. when Bogner walked into the Notre Dame de Montreal, a cathedral more than a century and a half old. Gladys at the Queen Elizabeth had been explicit in her instructions.

"Walk to the front of the sanctuary. Near the communion railing next to the side altar and when you are standing next to the statue of Saint Gabriel, you will see a confessional. Pause to genuflect before the statue and light a vigil candle. You must light the farthest available candle to your right on the top row. Make the sign of the cross and then proceed directly to the confessional. Enter the vestibule on the right."

Even now as he genuflected and studied the icon, Bogner knew he was being watched. He wondered if the priest was one of them, or was it the little man who appeared to be deep in prayer in the first pew, or the . . . Then he decided that would be too easy, too convenient. Reprisal, the organization, the network, the thing, the unknown element that protected and sometimes seemed on the verge of betraying Milatov, was a riddle.

He lit the small vigil candle on the top row, the

farthest to the right, and made the sign of the cross. Then he headed for the darkened confessional. Bogner knew the routine in front of the statue was a way of checking him out. As a passing thought he wondered who had given them the description they were working with: Packer, Jaffe, maybe even Langley.

Inside the darkened cubicle, he knelt and leaned forward with his hands on the prayer rail. In front of him was a small opening covered with a thin, black fabric that allowed him to see the vague profile of the priest.

"Commander Bogner?" the tired voice inquired.

"Is all of this necessary?" Bogner snarled. "You've already checked me out. You know who the hell I am."

There was a muted laugh and then the sound of someone clearing their throat. "It is the way the game is played, Commander. Besides, we're not at all certain that you know who you are dealing with—nor are we convinced that we want to deal with you."

"It's a little late to get picky, Father—or whoever you are. Let's get to the point; you know why I'm here, we need to contact Milatov."

There was another laugh, this one more derisive. "What makes you think Milatov is still alive? How long has it been since anyone has seen Milatov?"

Bogner had rehearsed his lines. He knew what he wanted to say and how much he could reveal. Whoever Reprisal was, he or she wasn't a known commodity. He had to take it one step at a time. This was the gamble part. He had Packer's blessing, but both men knew it was a long shot.

"Our intelligence reports indicate increased activity at Belushya Guba. We are also aware that Viktor Denisov, prior to Zhelannov's assassination, was making arrangements to move the E-1-A Novgorod System to Belushya Guba. . . ." Bogner allowed his voice to trail off to see if the contact would pick up the thread.

"Come, come, Commander, we know you know more than that."

"We're also aware of increased personnel activity and technical exchanges with representatives of the People's Republic of China.

"And we are aware that your government has been shadowing Xo Cho Ping for some time now."

Bogner sucked in his breath. It was like walking on dynamite caps.

There was a prolonged silence on the other side of the thin gauze curtain. When the voice spoke again, it was halting and not quite as confident, an indication to Bogner that whoever was behind that curtain was wavering. "You are aware of course that Aleksandr Milatov disappeared shortly after leaving the Nobel award ceremonies in 1982, and that he has since disavowed his role in the development of the E-1-A after learning the Party's true intentions."

"I know that he intended for the Novgorod to be used as a defense system, not an offensive weapon. We have been led to believe that in the end he was disenchanted with his government, the Party, and with the whole system of Soviet thought."

"Milatov is dead," the voice finally said.

"Dead men don't write books," Bogner reminded him.

There was another pause. "By what authority do you seek this man?"

It was the question Bogner had been waiting for, the code. The answer was one word, "Colchin." Packer had cleared it with Colchin's top adviser, Lattimore Spitz. "If you know Milatov, you know that they are old friends," Bogner answered.

"I know nothing of such matters," the voice said.

Bogner continued to wait for a response. He was beginning to wonder if the man on the other side of the confessional was receiving his instructions from someone else. Finally the voice came through. "Your wishes are known, Commander Bogner. You will be contacted."

"How soon?" Bogner demanded.

There was no answer. A small, sliding panel was suddenly slipped into position, shutting off the dim light that filtered through the gauze curtain and enveloping Bogner in darkness.

Before Bogner could plan his next move, there was the sound of a brief scuffle in the enclosure where the priest was sitting, an even briefer protest, muted and somehow futile, followed by the sound of weight slumping against the wall on the other side of the confessional.

For Bogner there was that old characteristic and familiar sensory sensation—the *odor*, the *feeling*. He had a sixth sense for it. On more than one occasion he had described it as the smell of danger. In this case there was more than an odor—there was the almost imperceptible ticking sound. Before Bogner hit the floor of the tiny cubicle, he had already drawn the Steyr SPP and had disengaged the safety. He threw his weight against the penitent's door, leaped to the safety of the first row of pews, and managed to roll over and bury his head in his arms just as the confessional exploded.

Even before the dust settled, he was on his feet, scanning, listening. Keep running, you son of a bitch, he thought. As long as you're moving I can hear you.

There were two nuns. The one who was no more than 30 feet from the explosion, her black habit covered with dust and debris, was too stunned to react. Her glasses were broken and her mouth was open. She was having trouble breathing. Bogner had the feeling she would have screamed if she could have gotten her mouth shut to get a scream generated.

The other, seemingly unhurt, was already screaming. She sized up the situation, saw Bogner, and pointed toward the back of the sanctuary. The door to the choir loft was swinging shut, and Bogner began to run.

In the vestibule, he threw open the door, raced up two flights of stairs, and shouldered his way through the door into the choir loft. Behind the organ and to the side of the loft was a second set of stairs, obviously leading to the bell tower. The loft was cantilevered out over the sanctuary and he looked down. It was a good 30-foot drop from the prayer railing around the loft to the floor of the sanctuary. Whoever he was chasing was trapped.

A small smile began to play at the corners of his mouth; Bogner figured he had him. There was no place to hide in the choir loft and there were only two ways out; one was up, the other was down. From where Bogner was standing, he knew *down* hadn't been an option.

The chase was over; the game of cat and mouse had commenced. Bogner waited, standing motionless, head cocked to one side to listen.

The area around the shattered confessional was a scene of chaos. Now the two nuns had help. Two parishioners, or at least that's what Bogner assumed they were, had come to the two women's aid. The nuns were hysterical. There was still a blue-gray wispy cloud of smoke, and the acrid smell of things burnt— wood, fabric, and flesh—permeated all the way to the choir loft. They had pulled the priest from the confessional and they were tending to him. From where Bogner stood, it was hard to assess the damage.

He crossed the choir loft, pressed his back against the side of the stairway, and peered up into the darkness. On the other side of the loft the door flew open and a young robed figure stumbled into the room.

Bogner leveled the Steyr SPP at him with both

hands. "Who the hell are you?" he blurted.

"Bro-brother—Brother Regis," the young man stuttered. He had been running. He was having trouble breathing. "I-I-I saw—saw the man that threw the parcel in Father Jerome's confessional—and then—then I saw him run to the back of the church."

Bogner looked up, motioning with the Steyr. "What's up there?"

It took Brother Regis several seconds to get his thoughts collected. "The maintenance area for the pipes—and the bell tower."

"Any other way down?"

Brother Regis was shaking his head, and Bogner could see beads of sweat running down the young man's face. His cassock was unzipped and open to the waist. Under the cassock he was wearing a white T-shirt with the words *Hard Rock Cafe* blazoned across his chest. He was breathing hard. "No," he finally managed.

Bogner's finger tightened on the trigger. He shoved open the door to the bell area. The stairs disappeared into an ominous black hole directly over his head, and he kept the muzzle of the Steyr pointed at it. At the same time, he kept his back close to the wall and tried to regulate his breathing.

"Any place to hide up there?"

Regis shook his head. "I—I don't—don't think so."

"Any lights?"

Again Brother Regis shook his head.

Bogner worked his way up two more of the steps. There were eight to go. He looked down. The young brother was holding his breath, his eyes fixed on Bogner's semiautomatic.

Bogner paused, negotiated two more steps, pressed the muzzle of the Steyr against the underside of the trapdoor, and pushed up. Then he let it drop. There was a loud thud as the door clattered back into place and Bogner ducked back.

The look on the brother's face indicated he didn't completely understand what was happening. "What did you do that for?" he finally blurted out. "Now he knows where you are."

"He knew that long before I manhandled that trap-door. If our bomber had a gun, he would have used it right there and then," Bogner explained. Then he wondered why he felt compelled to answer Regis's question in the first place.

Regis nodded. His mouth was open.

Bogner crawled back up under the trapdoor, put his shoulder against it, and cradled the barrel of the Steyr in his right arm. With his left hand and shoulder he shoved the door up and open, waited while he counted to three, thrust himself up through the opening, and using his legs as springs catapulted his body into the darkened bell tower. He rolled over and lay motionless in the darkness.

What little illumination there was in the room was streaming up through the trapdoor opening. Again he cocked his head to one side, listening. It was the kind of silence a man experiences when he knows someone else is in the same room with him.

Finally he called out. "Regis, you still down there?"

"Still—still here," Regis stammered.

"Then how about a flashlight?"

Brother Regis thought for a moment. "Will a candle work?"

"Anything beats what I've got," Bogner shouted.

It took Brother Regis several minutes to round up candles and work up enough courage to climb up to the darkened bell tower. And by the time he did, Bogner had talked the bomb-thrower into giving himself up. As his captive was climbing down from the choir loft, Bogner heard Regis exclaim, "He's just a boy."

It was after the youth saw Bogner's semiautomatic that the bravado faded and he began to shake. When he quit shaking, he began blurting out his story. In a matter of minutes, the tone of the boy's voice went from cockiness to pure cooperation.

"Honest, I didn't mean to hurt no one. The—the old man in the vestibule—he paid me to do it." The words were gushing out now. "He . . . paid me five dollars . . . I didn't know it was no bomb—honest. He said it was just some stuff that would stink up the church and smell bad—and that all he wanted me to do was throw it in the confessional so that it would get all over the priest and then he would be even with him."

Bogner sagged back against the front of the organ. He looked at the kid who had thrown the bomb and then at Brother Regis. He was shaking his head. "I don't suppose you know this kid, do you?"

Brother Regis nodded. "I've seen him before, hanging around the schoolyard . . . at the academy . . ."

"What did the man look like?" Bogner asked. He was still brandishing the Steyr, and the kid was having difficulty taking his eyes off of it.

"I don't know—old—just old," the boy blurted out. "All old guys look the same to me."

Bogner straightened, stuffed the Steyr back in his coat pocket, and looked at Regis. Outside, in the street, he could hear sirens. He realized that in a matter of minutes, Montreal's finest would be swarming into the church and then the lid would be off. Whoever, whatever Reprisal was, his cover as a naval procurement agent would be completely blown—if it wasn't already.

"It's in your hands now, Brother," Bogner said. "When the authorities get here, tell them what happened." He glared at the boy, smiled at the young brother, slipped back down the stairs, and in the confusion made his way to the church vestibule and out into the street.

Two blocks from the cathedral, he hailed a taxi and went back to the hotel.

LOG:
SIX: TWO

The Apartment of Achina Budenny: Kiev 1842L
5 November

Achina Budenny relived her conversation with Pytor Zimrin over and over through the course of the day. The old man's haunted face and empty eyes burned into her subconscious, and by the end of the day permeated her every thought.

She had been distracted even during a late-afternoon meeting with two trade agents from Georgia and the subsequent briefing session with the Ministry's trade supervisor. After that meeting, and despite the weather, she had driven several kilometers out of her way, only to keep going past the Leningradskaya Hotel after changing her mind.

She was still taking off her coat in her apartment when the telephone rang.

"Where have you been?" Tarasina asked. "I've been trying to reach you all afternoon. I called your apartment and your office."

Achina sat down and kicked off her shoes. "I am sorry, I should have called you. There were meetings."

"You have heard the news?" Tarasina asked. Her voice had an alarming edge to it.

"What news?"

"Oh, God, Mother—I'm sorry. I thought maybe you had already heard. It's Pytor—Pytor Zimrin—he committed suicide."

Achina was stunned. "Suicide?" she repeated. The single word came out fragmented, broken into tiny shards of a near whisper. "Are you certain?"

Tarasina's voice bordered on hysteria. "I heard it on the news, state television. He jumped in front of the metro."

"Are you certain it is the same Pytor Zimrin?" Achina heard herself ask.

"They said he was from Diva," the girl confirmed. "I'm so sorry, Mother. I—I thought . . ."

"It's—it's all right," Achina assured her. She made a conscious effort to steady her voice and reassure the girl. "Just give me a few minutes."

"Do you want me to come over?"

Gradually, Achina was able to regain some degree of composure. She forced the words out. "No—the weather is bad. Do you know where they took the body?"

"Are you certain you don't want me to come over?" Tarasina pressed. "At times like this I think we should be together."

Achina Budenny suddenly felt stronger. "No," she said, her voice growing firmer. "Try to get some sleep. Try not to think about it. I will call you first thing in the morning."

After she hung up, Achina Budenny resigned herself to what she knew had to be done. She put on her coat and went back down to her car. It was 13 kilometers back to the Leningradskaya.

LOG:
SIX: THREE

En Route to Belushya Guba
5 November

For E-Alexa Chinko it was a long and difficult day. She left Kusinien's *dacha* in the early hours of the morning, drove to her section office in the Chesnakov Compound, and made two protocol calls: one to Vyacheslav Bekrenev and the second to Admiral Ilya Dolin, informing him of her approximate arrival time at the Belushya site.

From Chesnakov, she was driven to the airport, took the 8:30 Aeroflot flight from Moscow to Naryan-Mar, and was met by Dolin's personal TU-142 for the four-hour flight to Belushya. During the flight to Belushya there was time to reflect.

Bekrenev's announcement that Aprihnen intended to terminate the joint effort on the E-1-A had come as a surprise to her—and the general had made it clear that he did not expect the scientists from the Yiyang Province to return to their homeland.

Despite the urgency in her new assignment, her thoughts returned repeatedly to Nijinsky. Nijinsky knew; there was no longer any doubt in her mind. The only question was: What would he do with the information? Obviously, he had been involved in GRU matters before. Her prolonged tour of duty in Belushya would certainly allow the situation to cool, but there would be the inevitable return. Nijinsky knew that she was not a common *urka*—he was a realist. Aprihnen's ascension to the presidency had brought with it a return to many of the old ways. The more she thought about it, the more confident she was that in the end, Nijinsky would be instructed to terminate his investigation. Bekrenev had once revealed that both he and the prosecutor general had worked their way together through Moscow University's Law Faculty, and reflected on the fact that both had spent time in the City Collegium of Advocates. She decided to try to forget about Nijinsky.

At other times during the flight she allowed herself to doze off, slipping into fitful spates of half-sleep, anguished periods when her subconscious dealt not with the present but the personal agenda that had become her crusade of revenge. The names of the guilty tumbled over and over in her mind: Ilya Dolin, Kirill Gureko, and of course, Aprihnen himself.

When she awoke, she realized that the interior of the Tu-142 had darkened. Day had become night, the Arctic night. Below her, the last traces of light faded in the west and vast expanses of the Karskiye Vorota Strait were covered with ice—lights from ships were no longer visible. Then it occurred to her that the construction effort would continue throughout the long winter, but there would be no more supply ships.

From time to time the admiral's plane was buffeted by turbulence, and she felt the pilot decrease their altitude in preparation for landing. They were below the cloud deck now, and the blinking red light on the wing gave the occasional glimpses of swirling snow an ethereal appearance.

Overhead another light began blinking, and she tugged at her seat belt to make certain it was secured.

Dolin's plane landed and taxied to the small operations building at the northeast corner of the airfield. She noted that there were lights in both the alert hangar and the larger joint service and repair hangar where Dolin's aircraft along with two modified Sukhoi Su-24 "Fencers" and two gas-turbined Sukhoi R77 all-purpose recovery helicopters were housed. The alert hangar was smaller and contained three MiG-29 Fulcrum A fighters, each of which had been modified for Arctic service and was used only for Belushya security patrols.

Despite her dislike for the man, E-Alexa acknowledged that Dolin was both an administrative and strategic genius. Denisov himself had selected Dolin to spearhead the rejuvenation of Milatov's project, a move, E-Alexa had to admit, that was an indication of Denisov's own brilliance.

E-Alexa gathered her gear and made her way from the plane to operations, past the meteorology detachment, and into the security section. The personnel elevator took her down two levels to the narrow cement underground concourse and the rubber-tired tram that took her to the operations center. The short journey through the network of steel-reinforced passageways always reminded her of the copy of the hopelessly incompetent American G2 report obtained from their Warsaw contact. "Ground operations minimal. Three structure on installation. No discernable activity." The report had made E-Alexa, like most of her fellow officers, laugh.

Of course that was three years ago, and by now even the small-minded Americans surely suspected an operation of more significant dimensions. After all, she reasoned, they had to be aware of the continuous flow of materials into Belushya; a fleet of supply ships was not an easy thing to disguise.

At the entrance to the communications center, a young seaman leaped to his feet and snapped to attention as she passed through the security scanner. After E-Alexa passed, he returned to his focus on the bank of video security monitors.

She passed through COM-CEN and into PuA-49, the project engineering section. Two members of the technical contingent were poring over computer readouts. Both men were wearing the green-red digitized clearance cards. They were so engrossed in their conversation that they failed to notice her.

From the PuA-49 section, she went directly to the project control center, glanced at her watch, and decided there was still time to check in with Dolin, a matter of courtesy. It was a few minutes after ten P.M., and she knew the aging admiral seldom retired before the final security check of the day at 10:45.

She activated the epa-sensor device on the internal CS and tapped out his code. Within seconds, his image appeared on the monitor. He had stripped off his tunic and was clad in a robe. Beyond him she could see the wall-displayed chess board and the blinking images of the chess pieces.

"Ahhh—Major Chinko," he exclaimed.

"Admiral," she said, keeping her voice even. "I arrived a few minutes ago and wanted you to know I am reporting in. I am quite tired, and I think I will go straight to my quarters."

Dolin frowned. E-Alexa knew she had disappointed him. It was obvious Dolin enjoyed the company of women. "Very well. Will you join me for breakfast, Colonel?"

It was the first time anyone had addressed her by her new rank. The promotion was implied; she had anticipated it—but curiously, neither Bekrenev nor Kusinien had discussed it.

"I am curious, Admiral; Colonel Ulitsa has been informed that he is being replaced?" she asked.

"I informed him this evening at dinner. He has been assigned as the liaison officer to the Sino technical contingent."

E-Alexa could not help but ask, "What was his reaction?"

"When orders come directly from General Vyacheslav Bekrenev, one does not have a reaction—one accepts one's fate. As you well know, Colonel, with Vyacheslav, there is no court of appeals."

E-Alexa laughed. She laughed because she was expected to. Dolin perceived their relationship as one in which they could exchange their small annoyances with the vagaries of their fellow officers—even their superiors.

"In Moscow there was," she began cautiously, "talk of the impending termination of the joint effort between us and our Sino colleagues. . . ."

Dolin raised his finger to his mouth and she allowed her voice to trail off.

"Despite Colonel Ulitsa's assurances that this system is now secured, I would prefer to discuss this matter at breakfast."

"Of course, Admiral. Now if you will excuse me, I think I will retire to my quarters."

Dolin allowed several seconds to pass before he spoke. "Tell me, Colonel. I find it curious that you did not activate the image sensor. Is there a reason? In a place like Belushya, it is not often that we are graced with the image of a beautiful woman. You deprive me of one of my rare pleasures."

E-Alexa bit her lip. "It has been a long, difficult day, Admiral. I am afraid you would not be all that pleased with the image you would be receiving."

Dolin laughed.

"Good night, Admiral," E-Alexa said. In her pocket,

her fingers coiled around the diamond-mounted mantis pin. She slipped her security card in the slot, pressed the three-digit code, and waited for the door to open. Then she congratulated herself. She had been able to avoid Dolin after all.

LOG:
SIX: FOUR

Institute of Sciences, Kislovodsk Center for Research: Moscow 2024L
5 November

"So, my old friend, still trying to rid the streets of our fair city of hooligans and nefarious types?"

Nijinsky laughed and slapped his friend on the back. "It is good to see you again, Valari. Or should I call you Doctor Alekseevich now that you have achieved such prominence?"

Valari Alekseevich smiled a bit sheepishly and led his boyhood companion into his office. "It is always Valari to anyone who grew up in the old Lyubimov section. There aren't that many of us who remember what it was like before they tore it down and built that monstrosity called the arsenal."

When both men were seated, they exchanged small talk and reminiscences. Only then did Alekseevich's face sober. "I would like to pretend that it is the past that brings us together, my dear Konstantin, but I remember you too well. You were always deep in thought, and I suspect that it is that overly active mind of yours that brings you here tonight."

Nijinsky's homely face manufactured a smile. He took off his glasses and cleaned them. "It is both flattering and a bit frightening to know that someone you haven't seen for so many years recalls you that well."

Alekseevich leaned forward in his chair with his hands on his knees. "From that do I deduce that you are reluctant to admit that it is business that brings you here?"

The inspector waited. "Actually, it is. Something has come up in one of my current investigations, and I thought that perhaps you might be able to clarify something for me. All I hear are my own signals. Consequently I never seem to come to any conclusions—at least not ones that make any sense."

The doctor folded his arms. "Sounds rather intriguing."

Nijinsky cleared his throat. "For the past several years I have been in contact with a young woman."

"Ahhhh . . . I see. An affair of the heart?"

"On the contrary, this is an affair of the mind. She is from a small village in the Ukraine, well educated, and from all outward appearances devoted to her career. She was a minor security official in the Naval Directorate of the GRU for a number of years, and has since been involved with security activities for a project that she refuses to talk about."

"Sounds to me like the attributes of a good officer," Alekseevich observed.

"Sounds more like a Party loyalist," Nijinsky countered, "but there is something else going on here."

"You'll have to be more explicit."

Nijinsky thought for a minute. "Twice within the past three years she has sought my department's assistance. Each time she has given us information that has led to, in both cases, the deaths of the persons she has reported on. Because of her former GRU affiliation, she always implies that certain high officials believe these people to be enemies of the State."

"Now there's a term I haven't heard for some

time." Alekseevich grinned. "Things haven't completely returned to the ways of the old days. The GRU and the KGB took care of their own problems."

"Exactly," Nijinsky confirmed. "But in each case, these individuals are little more than petty criminals, and in each case they commit a felonious crime after we are informed of their unsavory nature and asked to look into the matter."

"Are you saying you believe your department is being set up?"

"There is more to it than that."

"Perhaps Aprihnen's new RSB is more clever than their predecessors. Perhaps they have decided that if they allow the Moscow police to dispose of their problems they will not draw the same criticism."

Nijinsky tented his fingers and studied his friend through the maze. "These are not the kind of people that the RSB concerns itself with. The more recent one killed a petty Party official after we were alerted that he was involved in black market activities."

Alekseevich frowned. "So what do you conclude from all of this?"

"I don't know. There are too many inconsistencies. It could be that this woman is nothing more than a messenger for Party factions and we are, as you suggest, simply doing their dirty work for them. On the other hand, I have been around long enough to suspect something else."

"Like what?"

"You are a student of human behavior. You understand the profile of the kinds of individuals who peopled the ranks of the KGB and GRU. These people were of a single purpose, correct?"

"Are you telling me that you believe this young woman is using the RSB to accomplish something else? Her own agenda perhaps?"

The nod was hesitant.

"And you are looking to me to tell you that this is possible?"

"Is it?" Nijinsky asked.

Alekseevich sighed. "Entirely. Does this surprise you?"

"I don't know."

Dr. Valari Alekseevich leaned back in his chair. "Perhaps I can shed some light on this matter, my old friend, but we'll have to go back to the beginning. Are you prepared to tell me everything you know about her?"

Nijinsky was ready. He loosened his tie, leaned back, and began.

LOG:
SIX: FIVE

42 Krehchatik: Kiev 2313L
5 November

After picking up the package in the lobby of the Leningradskaya, Achina Budenny drove to the warehouse district in the Vskaya section near the rail depot.

She left her car at the People's Park near the statue of Levitsky, and walked to the service entrance of a building close to the piers on the Dnieper River. The watchman, an elderly man smoking a pipe, huddled close to, and warmed his hands by, an ancient kerosene heater. He made no pretense at stopping her.

The floor of the warehouse was deserted, but there was a light in the small office at the top of the steel stairway leading to the second floor. She could hear voices. She climbed the stairs and waited outside the door until one of the two men looked up. His features were concealed by the shadows.

"Yes?" he said.

"I am looking for Askold."

"What about Askold?"

"I must talk to him. It is important."

The man twisted the cigar out of his mouth and studied it before he looked at her again. "What do you want to talk to him about?"

Achina stepped into the room and removed her hood. "Tell Askold that I spoke to Pytor Zimrin last night."

From the shadows at the far side of the room, a third figure emerged, a ponderous, slow-moving man whose features were obscured by both darkness and shadows. As he walked toward Achina she noticed his pronounced limp. Boris Chinko had once described how Askold had had his left leg blown off by a land mine when he was in the army.

"And you are?" he asked. For a man of his girth, his voice was surprisingly soft and compassionate.

"Achina," she replied, "Achina Budenny."

Askold motioned for the two men to leave them alone. They went into the hall. After they left, he closed the door behind them. He pulled a chair away from the table and motioned for Achina to sit down. Then he took out a package of cigarette papers and a pouch of tobacco and rolled a cigarette. He lit it before he spoke.

"You say you talked to Pytor only yesterday?"

Achina nodded. "I am Boris Chinko's sister," she said.

Askold waved her off. "I know who you are and I know why you are here. Despite your views, Pytor trusted you. He was confident that you would come after you heard the news."

"Then you have heard . . ."

Askold walked around the table, dropped his cigarette on the floor, ground it out with the heel of his boot, and sat down across from her. He rubbed his hand across his brow before he began. "Pytor came here last night—after he talked to you. He told us what he had done—and he told us what he was going to do."

"And you did nothing to stop him?" There was outrage in her voice.

Askold laid his hands on the table. His fingers were gnarled and crooked. He studied them as if they were detached curiosities. "Pytor Zimrin was a man among men. He knew what he had to do."

Achina wished she had not come. They were all the same, these radicals who opposed the Party. A life meant nothing. Their only concern was the cause. How many had to die? She looked into Askold's eyes, trying to get a feel for the soul of the man.

"You have the package Pytor told us about?" Askold asked.

She nodded, and he held out his hand. She would not have given it to him if Boris had not assured her that he believed Askold was above suspicion regardless of his philosophy. In these matters she had to trust her brother's judgment.

"Pytor said there were two. Where is the other one?"

"It was buried with my brother."

Askold smiled. "That is the right answer." He rolled the package over in his hands, examining it. "Have you ever admired the beauty of St. Sophia Cathedral in the early dawn of a winter morning, Comrade Budenny?"

She shook her head.

"Such strength, such power, such . . ." His voice trailed off. "That is the way I felt about your brother. And now that you are here, now the question must be, do I believe you, do I trust you as I trusted him?"

Achina did not know how to answer him. Finally she said, "If you are asking if I am as brave as my brother, the answer is no. I came to give you the book and to tell you what no one knows I know."

Askold leaned forward.

"I know where Aleksandr Milatov is." Her voice was little more than a whisper.

"That secret died with Pytor," Askold thundered. His fist slammed down on the table and Achina shuddered. "How do you know this?" he demanded.

Achina folded her hands. She tried not to look at him. "I overheard them plotting. I heard them make arrangements. It was to look like an abduction, but Comrade Milatov actually engineered it. It was his decision."

Askold leaned back in his chair. "Suppose I told you that we received word several months ago that Milatov was dead."

"I would not believe you."

Askold sighed. He stood up and walked to the window, pulled back the heavy dark curtain, and stared out at the darkness. From where she sat, Achina could see only one distant streetlight. "We have received no such word," he admitted. Then he turned and looked at her. "Such information as you have is a burden in the wrong hands. What do you intend to do with it?"

Achina was surprised at the sudden strength in her voice. "Are you concerned that something will happen to me?"

Askold's hand went to his coat pocket and emerged with a small automatic. In his hand it appeared small and insignificant. "If you were to die, Comrade Budenny, it is true there would be one less to oppose us. It would also be true that we would no longer have to be concerned about what you do with the information you possess."

The woman drew back. Her eyes went from the small handgun to Askold's face and back again. She held her breath.

"You see, Comrade Budenny, we both have the same objective. We just have different philosophies about how we achieve it."

Askold laid the weapon on the table. His full lips were pulled back in a half smile. "I grant you this much; you are a brave woman. It took a great deal of courage for you to come here. And you are very wise to turn this over to us as well. With this"—he held up the package—"others were certain to learn of Milatov's whereabouts. Now the burden is no longer yours."

Achina stared at the man.

"Do you know where Milatov is?" he finally asked.

There was a lump in Achina's throat.

Askold tore open the package and opened the book. He began to thumb through the pages.

Finally Achina answered him. "There is a small village on an inlet north of Saint John's in Newfoundland. I am told it is very much like the place where Milatov spent his youth."

"Go on," Askold said.

Achina continued. "He was given a change of identity. His papers were altered by a contact in Oslo. My brother arranged everything. He is now called Mayevsky, Viktor Mayevsky. He was flown from Oslo to Paris and then to Montreal. A woman by the name of Livina poses as his wife."

Askold continued to stare at her. "You work for the Bureau of Trade. Your brother's daughter is an officer in the GRU. How do we know we can trust you?"

Achina stared back at him. "What would I have to gain by telling you this?"

The man did not answer.

"Even though there are differences, we are all Reprisal," she said softly.

Askold looked at her. Then he laughed. "Reprisal," he said, "must know, Achina Budenny. Do you think it is wise to tell the Americans?"

Achina hesitated. She knew there was no room for vacillation—yet that was exactly what was happening. Originally she had been opposed to telling the Americans of Milatov's whereabouts—but she had wavered when Boris believed otherwise. Now, without him . . .

Askold limped to the door, opened it, and spoke briefly to the two men standing in the hallway. Achina was unable to hear what they were saying. When Askold returned, he was no longer frowning.

"Khrushchev would roll over in his grave if he heard

me say this, Comrade Budenny, but it would appear that the gods have smiled on us this day. You see, earlier today we learned from our contact in Prague that the Americans are making yet another attempt to contact Milatov. Through his emissaries, the American president, Colchin, is seeking the assistance of Reprisal."

"The American president?" Achina repeated. Despite everything Boris had said, the idea was unacceptable to her. The philosophy was too ingrained: Never cooperate with the Americans. She looked at Askold with dismay. "Would you reveal Milatov's whereabouts to the Americans?"

Askold smiled. "Milatov and Colchin are old comrades; did you know that, Comrade Budenny?"

Achina shook her head. "Other presidents have sought audience with Dr. Milatov in the past and his whereabouts have not been revealed. This American president cannot be trusted any more than his predecessors."

"This world is a riddle," Askold said with a sigh. "Is this the right course of action? Should I inform our contact in Prague that we cannot help him? Is there never a time to trust?"

Achina stood up. "In the final analysis, I must be opposed to revealing Milatov's whereabouts to the Americans."

Askold took her arm and escorted her to the door. "Your long-guarded secret is safe with us," he said, "but the question is, is our secret safe with you? What do you do with what you have learned here tonight? Is your opposition so strong that you would reveal our plans to arrange a meeting between Milatov and Colchin's representative?"

Achina looked up at him. She remained silent.

"My comrades will see that you are safe returning to your car. I feel I should warn you, this is a violent neighborhood. I'm afraid there are as many hooligans in Kiev these days as there are in Moscow."

Moments later, when Achina Budenny turned the key in the ignition of her car, there was a violent explosion. The tiny Zaporozhet erupted in a ball of flame.

From where he watched at the darkened window in the warehouse, Askold turned to his colleagues. "Sad," he said. "But you realize, of course, that it was necessary. She revealed Milatov's whereabouts too easily. Neither side could have trusted her."

LOG:
SEVEN: ONE

Queen Elizabeth Hotel: Montreal 0045L
6 November

For Bogner it had been a long evening. He had been on the phone continuously with first Packer, then Langley as he attempted to relay the events of the afternoon. There had been two sessions with Montreal's finest, and only a Lattimore Spitz phone call to a high-level liaison officer for the prime minister had righted the situation.

"I think we got it quieted down," Packer finally said in his third call of the evening. "What's your next move?"

"At this point it's in the hands of the gods, Clancy. It all depends on whether or not my conversation in that confessional was monitored or not. That priest isn't going to relay any information to anyone. On the ten o'clock news they indicated his condition was critical."

On the other end of the line, Packer was silent for a moment. "Langley still thinks they'll contact you. If you haven't heard from them by noon tomorrow, we can pretty well figure they've rejected our request. In that case, pack up your things and come home."

The last conversation with Packer had occurred at

10:30. Bogner fell asleep watching television, then awakened, took a shower, and was preparing to turn in when he heard a knock on the door.

"Room service," the voice said. It was louder than Bogner would have expected.

"Sorry, pal," he shouted, "wrong room, didn't order anything."

"A gift from the concierge," the voice persisted.

Bogner upholstered the Steyr, concealed it in the pocket of his robe, and opened the door. The room service clerk was elderly and slightly stooped, with a neatly trimmed mustache and a white busboy's jacket. He was standing beside a room service cart.

Bogner started to speak, but the man motioned for him to step aside, pushed the cart into the room, pulled the white table linen off of the cart, and began to arrange the dishes on the table.

"Keep your voice down, Commander," the man said one cut above a whisper. "Just listen."

Bogner waited. His finger was curled through the trigger housing of the 9mm.

"At precisely 0100 hours, you are to go down the service elevator, through the laundry room, and out the rear service door. There you will find a taxi. If there is more than one taxi, take number 671. You will be driven to the west end of Montreal International to the Canadian Air Guard Training unit. Arrangements have been made to fly you to the U.S. Air Force Base in Saint John's, Newfoundland. The base commander at PAFB has been instructed to see that you are taken to Brigus Cove on the Avalon Peninsula."

"Contact with Milatov?"

"He has agreed to talk to you—but only because your president intervened. I am told he has great respect for your President Colchin."

"Where will I find him?"

"You will be taken to the Smallwood Chapel. It is a small structure near the wharf at the end of the street.

There you will meet a man by the name of Gehring; he will take you to Milatov."

"Which faction of Reprisal is he?" Bogner sneered.

"One of the few who trust Americans," the old man snapped.

Bogner nodded. "What about security?"

The man smiled. He had a prominent silver tooth. "Don't worry, there will be ample security, Commander Bogner. What happened today was most unfortunate. Be advised that we have been taking good care of Doctor Milatov for quite some time now."

"What about that kid that threw the bomb today?" Bogner probed.

"The police interrogated him for over two hours. He knew he was throwing a bomb, though not why."

"He threw a bomb in a confessional for five bucks?" Bogner asked in amazement.

"Gives a man cause for concern, doesn't it," the man replied.

Bogner thought for a minute, then repeated the instructions, and the man confirmed each phase with a curt nod of the head. Then, as he left the room and stepped into the hall, he elevated his voice. "*Bon appetit*, Commander."

LOG: SEVEN: TWO

Belushya Guba 0802L
6 November

E-Alexa's morning breakfast meeting with Admiral Ilya Dolin was not at all what she had anticipated. Dolin hurried through the meal, ordered the dishes cleared away, and escorted his new logistics officer from the dining room into his adjoining office.

The carpeted room with its large kidney-shaped mahogany desk and leather appointments was opulent even by Kremlin standards. On his desk was a picture of an attractive middle-aged woman. E-Alexa assumed it was Dolin's wife even though he never spoke of family.

To her surprise, Dolin's manner was far less cordial than the previous evening. He sat down behind his desk and lit a panatella. "You will forgive me, Colonel Chinko. These are difficult times, and to compound matters, it has been a long night."

E-Alexa waited for her superior to elaborate.

Dolin exhaled a cloud of blue-gray smoke. "An American Trident SSBN was in the area most of the night. We monitored its activities from the time it entered our waters at North Cape."

"Its intentions?" E-Alexa asked.

Dolin shrugged. "We have no way of knowing, Colonel, perhaps nothing more than simple Arctic maneuvers. Or it could be on a reconnaissance mission. Our surveillance units indicate that it finally took a clearly defined north-northwest course at about 0600 hours this morning."

"If it was south and east of Svalbard," E-Alexa inquired, "is that not the route of most American SSBN Arctic training missions?"

Dolin nodded even though he appeared to be lost in thought. "For the moment, it is no longer a matter of concern," he admitted. "But nevertheless, it gave us a long night. However, our concern with the American Trident is not why I asked you here this morning."

E-Alexa waited.

"Tell me, Colonel, do you recall a conversation with Colonel Ulitsa about one of the Sino engineers assigned to the Lyoto-Straf project during your previous visit?"

E-Alexa thought for a moment. "Yes, Admiral, I do recall. I believe it was a man by the name of Zhou Hu."

Dolin put down his cigar. "Your suspicions were confirmed, Colonel Chinko. Colonel Ulitsa's subsequent investigation uncovered the fact that Zhou was systematically cataloging all of the technical data relevant to the Lyoto-Straf 96 project."

Again E-Alexa waited.

"Zhou suffered a mild coronary," Dolin finally said. "Then, when we informed Comrade Xo, Xo ordered him to return to Lhasa. I am certain you realize this unexpected recall put us in a rather delicate position. Not only the integrity, but the success of the Belushya Guba mission was jeopardized."

E-Alexa nodded.

Dolin continued. "It is a fact: In President Aprihnen's mind as well as that of many others close to the president, our Chinese colleagues cannot be trusted. Zhou's activities were proof of that. But it also put us in a rather delicate position. On one hand, if we detained Zhou, the Chinese would have been aware that we were on to their scheme. If we allowed Zhou to leave with the data, the Dung government would have had sufficient design details and telemetry data to enable them to construct something very similar to the Milatov E-l-A system, and for that matter, an entire structure equivalent to the Lyoto-Straf 96."

"Would that not have been the outcome in either case?" E-Alexa questioned. There were many, like her, who felt the Sino technical agreement had been a mistake from the outset.

Dolin sighed. "You have a way of asking difficult questions, Colonel Chinko. But there was still another consideration—and a very important one; I will come to that in a moment. The answer to your question is probably yes. Ambassador Kusinien was opposed to this joint effort with the Chinese from the outset. But President Aprihnen believed that it could be controlled."

"Was it?"

"In a manner of speaking. We allowed Zhou Hu to leave knowing what the situation was—or at least what we believed it to be. On the afternoon of September 25, Zhou boarded a freighter bound for the mainland, the *Drachev*. It was the last scheduled run before we closed our port for the winter. Prior to his departure, we learned that he retrieved a small aluminum canister from the second of the three flotation pontoons on the first Lyoto-Straf. With that retrieval, we were able to confirm his mission. That, however, presented us with another quandary. If we severed the agreement with the Dung government before we received their contribution, namely a production-perfected method of encapsulating the cruor-toxins in the HORDE warhead, we would have been back to square one."

"Intriguing dilemma," E-Alexa observed, "and your solution, Admiral Dolin, was to . . ."

"The credit goes to General Gureko," Dolin admitted. "He reasoned that we could buy time if Zhou somehow conveniently disappeared. When the *Drachev* left port, it was accompanied by a Moskova-class icebreaker, the *Urhan*. We managed to delay the sailing of the *Drachev* for twenty-four hours under the pretext of correcting some minor but persistent electrical problems in the ship's computers and navigational system. In actuality, we were waiting for a storm over the Greenland Sea to intensify. Captain Zachinsky was not apprised of this. When the *Drachev* sailed the afternoon of September 25, both General Gureko and I were convinced it was sailing into certain disaster. Not only had the *Urhan* been instructed to make it safely to port if there were problems, but General Gureko took one extra precaution. A sweep-assigned Sukhoi Su-24 was ordered to sink the *Drachev* if it was in peril and its fate uncertain. The pilot, of course, was told that certain top-secret instrumentation on board, being sent back to Murmansk for recalibration, was unique to our mission here and dared not fall into the hands of outsiders."

"And?" E-Alexa questioned.

"The *Drachev* was destroyed. It now lies somewhere in the shallows at the bottom of the Stavka Straits."

"You are not concerned that oil slicks will eventually reveal its whereabouts?"

Dolin leaned back in his chair. "Even if Lieutenant Klyuzov had not insured the demise of the *Drachev*, the Arctic would have finished the job for us. A ship without power and navigational aid is helpless in such a situation. By now, several feet of ice obscures her location. And, I might add, the chances of our Sino friends actually ever discovering what happened to Zhou Hu and the *Drachev* are remote indeed."

For the first time, the frown disappeared from

Dolin's face. "Our Sino comrades are probably think-ing that they have cursed luck."

"And the cruor-toxins?"

Dolin sighed again. "Less than a week later, Xo Cho Ping revealed that they have successfully developed a way to encapsulate the toxins that will enable them to survive the blast area. The information is being encoded now—and should be in our hands within a matter of hours. Xo himself will deliver it."

"And you are convinced they suspect nothing about the disappearance of Zhou?"

"Even if they did, how could they say anything? We have admitted that the *Drachev* was lost. How could we be held accountable? What else could we do? Arctic waters are cruel and unforgiving. We lost a ship, an entire crew, and some very valuable equipment. Their losses—a mere one man. In a nation of 1.3 billion people that can hardly be considered a disaster, even if he was a respected scientist. I feel certain they realize they would arouse suspicion if they created too much of a stir over his loss."

"There is still the matter of Zhou's accomplice?" E-Alexa asked.

"That is where you come in," Dolin replied.

E-Alexa realized it was time to put on her logistics officer's face. "Can the Lyoto-Straf project be com-pleted in an air of distrust? You realize, Admiral, that the nature of the work here is rapidly becoming common knowledge—even with the man on the street in Moscow. As for the sinking of the *Drachev*, have I not heard you mention the names of both Gureko and Lieutenant Klyuzov, as well as imply the knowledge of others in your meteorology detachment? And what about Colonel Ulitsa—and now me? Was it not Lenin who said that when more than two people know something, it is no longer a secret?"

Dolin got up from his chair and began to walk about the room. "That is precisely why you are here, Colonel

Chinko. You are here because Kusinien and others say you have a brilliant tactical mind. As soon as we are able to duplicate the Sino experiments with the cruor-toxins and validate the after-blast dispersion models, we will have no further use for our Chinese friends. Their—how shall I say it—'tidy' disposal will be in your hands."

E-Alexa allowed herself a small smile. "Then I see no reason for you to continue to frown, Comrade Admiral."

Dolin put out his cigar. He lowered his voice. "The solution is not quite as simple as you might think, Comrade Chinko. Comrade Zhou is gone—but his legacy is still with us."

"You will have to be more explicit."

"In the six weeks since Comrade Zhou's departure, we have discovered that his activities were even more extensive than we had first imagined. It would now appear that our Sino comrade not only duplicated the original data, but altered the residual data in our computers."

"Meaning what?" E-Alexa asked.

"Zhou was far more clever than we gave him credit for being. Ulitsa considered him to be both an amateur and a fool because of the blatantly obvious way he went about retrieving the information. But Colonel Ulitsa was wrong. Zhou not only managed to alter certain key data in our data bank, he found a way to render our working files useless. We are systematically reviewing our backup files. So far, we have managed to check only ten percent of the data—and all of it is contaminated."

"How is that possible?"

"I wish we knew, Colonel Chinko. I wish we knew."

LOG:
SEVEN: THREE

ISA Offices: Washington 0834L
6 November

While Packer brushed the wet snow off his coat and hung it over the edge of the door, he watched Miller hang up the phone.

"It's a bitch out there, slippery as hell. Damn near got rear-ended on New Hampshire," Packer complained.

Miller ignored him, took a sip of coffee, and picked up the phone again. "Mel Clapoll, please," he said.

Packer could only hear Miller's end of the conversation. His longtime assistant made a couple of notations on his desk pad, barked a curt thank-you, and hung up again.

"What's up?" Packer asked.

Miller rocked back in his chair and sifted through several scraps of paper. "The more I dig, Clancy, the more intriguing this affair gets."

Packer sat down on the edge of the desk. "Like how intriguing?"

"I ran across this in one of the WMO reports," Miller said. He laid a Xerox copy of a page from the WMO monthly satellite analysis in front of Packer. He had highlighted the details of one of the AWS reports.

"I always wondered who read these things," Packer commented.

"Read it."

Packer read aloud. "2142Z—0042 Zone 3—Quad 55E-A; Bl factor. Recorded. Verified. 092594–942509. So what the hell does it mean?"

"Hell, Pack, I didn't know either, so I called Clapoll over at the Weather Bureau. He checked it out. It turns out there was a bright flash in the sky somewhere over the Stavka Straits on the night of 25 September and one of the WMO satellites recorded it."

"What made you check it out in the first place?"

"If you want the truth, I went to the john and picked up the WMO report for something to browse through while I was sitting there. If you look at the entries, there is nothing recorded on any of the passes over that area, or on any of the passes before or after. I wondered why, so I decided to check it out. Call it curiosity."

Packer stood up, started for his office, then stopped. "The Stavka Straits are west of Belushya and northeast of Murmansk; that's why you checked it out, right?"

"Right," Miller said, and picked up another piece of paper. "Let me add a little fuel to our fire. Apparently they had one hell of a storm up in that area; it lasted for several days. Clapoll just informed me that the captain of an Air Canada flight also reported a brilliant flash in the sky. Get this. The PIREP was logged at 2140Z."

Packer came back to his desk. He was frowning. "How long have you been on this?"

Miller shrugged. "Off and on for the past couple of days. I figured if I had an AWS report and a PIREP both reporting the same phenomena . . ."

"Could have been aureole activity," Packer reminded him. "I used to fly the MATS run from Thule to Sondrestrom. The damn instruments started going haywire when we flew above the circle."

"That's what I figured, but Clapoll says no, not when

you've got a low-pressure area kicking up a storm like they had during that period."

Packer picked up the report and studied it again. He looked at Miller.

"Want more?" Miller asked. "How about this? This is a copy of the WBAN entry at 2200Z, actual transmission time 2217Z from Konsoolstva Pagoda Statsiya. Know what the ground observer reported?"

Packer shook his head.

"Well, a loose translation would be, 'Magnetic anomaly phenomenon recorded at approximately 2145Z.' See, it says right here, 'brilliant flash of light.'"

Packer picked up the second report. "So, you've got three sources reporting something that Clapoll is telling you can't be atmospheric phenomena. I still have to ask, so what?"

"Look, Pack, this could be a wild-goose chase, but to all of this let me add one more intriguing little fact." He pulled out the monthly shipping bulletin. "Check this entry here."

Packer scanned it and looked at his colleague. His eyes were squinted and his brow furrowed. "Are there other reports of the *Drachev* making this run?"

"For the past three years the *Drachev* has been pretty much committed to duty in the Barents Sea. Plus, when the Russians report that one of their ships has *apparently* been lost at sea, you can bet your bottom kopek that they've already damn well determined that's exactly what happened."

"What do you make of it?"

Miller hunched his shoulders and tapped his pen on his desk. "Something. Nothing. Hell, who knows? Like I said, maybe it's nothing. But with Bogner talking to Milatov along about now, the whole damn Belushya situation was on my mind."

LOG:
SEVEN: FOUR

*Smallwood Chapel: Brigus Cove, Newfoundland 1447L
6 November*

Gehring was a young man, but his weathered skin
and thick, bushy beard hid most of his facial features.
Bogner was quick to decide that if Gehring was a
member of the Reprisal faction that favored closer
ties with the Americans, he gave no visible sign of
it. He did not smile and he studied Bogner like a man
contemplating a purchase. The depth of the man's
suspicions was evident from the outset.

Bogner crawled out of the USAF blue staff car and
waited.

Gehring continued to glower. "Should I just assume
you are Bogner, or do you have some identification?"

"Any kind you want," Bogner assured him.

"Never mind, that shit's too easy to fake. Besides, if
you aren't Bogner our security sucks, and you'll live
just long enough to regret the day you ever set foot
in this province." He lit a cigarette and continued to
scrutinize him. Finally he said, "Follow me." There was
no ceremony in his voice.

From the vestibule of the chapel, Bogner was led
through a rocky courtyard at the back of the church
and down a steep incline toward a small cabin perched

precariously on an outcropping overlooking the cove. Below him he could see and hear the surge of the waves breaking against the massive boulders that littered the beach some 30 or 40 feet straight down. It occurred to him that it was the perfect place to dispose of unwanted guests.

Gehring opened the door of the cabin and stepped aside to allow Bogner to enter. As he did Gehring's hand emerged from his pocket; his index finger was coiled around the trigger of a Sig 228 automatic. With his other hand he slapped in a magazine and chambered a round.

Bogner tried to size up the situation. In addition to Gehring, there was another man in the room. He was wearing a heavy coat and hefting a Yugoslavian M-85 semiautomatic.

Bogner held out his hands.

At the far side of the cabin there was another door and he saw the knob turn. When the door opened, two men entered. One was young, the other much older. The older one walked with a cane. There was one chair in the room, and he was escorted to it. When he was seated, he removed his hat, gloves, and scarf, then unbuttoned his heavy wool coat. His long white hair hung down to his shoulders. Bogner recognized him even before the old man's raspy voice made his announcement.

"I am Aleksandr Milatov."

Bogner studied the sad face with its faded, tired eyes, flared nose, bushy eyebrows, and expression of perpetual disappointment.

"I must apologize, Commander Bogner," he said. "My hosts take my continued security as a matter of personal pride. I trust Lieutenant Gehring of the Provincial Police treated you well."

Gehring's expression did not change.

"My friend David, he is well?" Milatov asked.

"President Colchin sends his greetings," Bogner said.

"Yes, the president enjoys good health."

Milatov's warm smile revealed a row of worn, smoke-stained teeth. For a moment he appeared to be lost in thought. Then he regained his composure. "I understand you were flown here in the middle of the night for our little meeting, Commander Bogner. If that is the case, I must assume there is some degree of urgency."

Bogner glanced around the room. "We can talk in front of these . . . ?"

Milatov laughed. "Exile is a great deal like being incarcerated, Commander Bogner. These men even know my toilet habits. There are no secrets."

"Belushya Guba," Bogner began.

The old man waved Bogner off. "You must forgive me, Commander. True, I have developed a passion for peace, but I am still Russian. To reveal the secrets of my mother country is a bit like spitting on my mother's grave."

Bogner shifted his weight. The old man had the advantage. The drama would unfold at whatever pace Milatov felt was appropriate.

Milatov looked down at his hands. "When I decided to go into hiding, I knew of General Denisov's plans. Perhaps that may have even spurred my decision. Unfortunately, the turn of events at Chernobyl only facilitated his desires. If your question is whether or not the E-1-A system is being developed in Belushya Guba, the answer is yes. If your question is, is the program active, that is also answered yes."

"More specifically, the E-1-A is what?"

"It was designed along the lines of the SA-X-12B with a range that far exceeds anything that we had hoped to achieve with its predecessors."

"Range?" Bogner asked.

"Seven times that of the SA-X-12B. Initial tests confirmed a tractable range of over seven hundred kilometers."

"Our intelligence reports indicate there is a joint

effort between your government and the Chinese."

The old man hesitated again. He looked around the room and down at his hands again. "Are you familiar with the allegations that my government used cruor-toxins in our war with Afghanistan, Commander?"

"I am," Bogner said.

"Their deployment was not nearly as extensive as indicated in reports," Milatov said, "but your intelligence sources were right; they were used. A very indiscriminate weapon, I fear. You see, we also suffered a great many casualties."

"From what I've heard, they cannot be controlled," Bogner said.

"For every problem, there is a solution," Milatov replied. "A problem our Chinese comrades have solved in theory. I repeat, in theory."

"Explain," Bogner said.

"The cruor-toxins will not survive the initial heat of the blast at the point of impact, Commander, unless, of course, they are properly encapsulated and protected."

"Are you telling me that your government is developing a weapons system that will disperse cruor-toxins as a second deterrent following the initial nuclear explosion?"

Milatov's eyes saddened. "It is a devastating concept, Commander, but that is the goal of the Belushya Guba project. The E-1-A is no longer a tactical weapon, nor is it a defense system; quite clearly, it is a strategic weapon of staggering implications."

"But the range is still a limitation," Bogner countered.

"I see that your intelligence loop has a few holes in it, Commander." For a fleeting moment there was a hint of a smile in the weary face.

Bogner laughed for him. "Then your scientists have overcome those limitations?"

"You have not heard of the Lyoto-Straf 96?"

Bogner repeated the term. "Lyoto-Straf 96?"

"An ingenious system that is both deployable and submersible, Commander; the brainchild of Admiral Ilya Dolin."

Bogner let out a whistle. "Permanent underwater launching platforms?"

"Not only that, Commander. The initial system, I am told, is very near completion. The shakedown mission is scheduled early next year."

"But why? President Aprihnen has repeatedly indicated your government is in total compliance with the parameters of the SALT agreement."

Milatov spit on the floor. "Aprihnen cannot be trusted, Commander. You must tell David that."

"How current is your information?" Bogner asked.

"You Americans are so skeptical," Milatov replied. "You come seeking information and then you distrust it. I assure you, my sources are extremely reliable and equally current."

"You have contacts?"

"I have said enough, Commander. The rest is up to you." There was a subtle nod to Gehring, and Bogner knew that the old man had just informed his protectors that the meeting was over.

"One more question," Bogner bargained.

Milatov hesitated.

"The cruor-toxin encapsulation code?"

"Our sources tell us Xo Cho Ping is on his way to Moscow even as we speak. He is hand-carrying the encapsulation formula."

"Can't happen," Bogner said.

"You are correct, Commander, that must not happen."

LOG:
SEVEN: FIVE

Noginsk Chetvyerta: Moscow 1644L
6 November

Nijinsky's fingers drummed on his desk while he waited for his call to be put through to the inspector with Kiev homicide. When the man finally came on the line, his voice was surprisingly low-key.

"Lieutenant Trusov, this is Lieutenant Nijinsky of Moscow Noginsk. Were you able to obtain the information I requested?"

Trusov had to think for a moment. "Ah, yes, Inspector, you were seeking information on one Aureio Gavrilovich. Yes. As a matter of fact, we had a stroke of luck. First, we checked out the Zaporozhet. MRB records indicate that Gavrilovich sold the car to a salvage company."

"When?" Nijinsky demanded.

"It was picked up at the Kiev airport the day after Koslov was murdered. Gavrilovich reported that the car was not drivable, that he had left it at the airport and that he wanted the salvage company to dispose of it. I am certain that you are familiar with the law that says the owner of the salvage yard must report the identification and road permit numbers to the MRB when an automobile is removed from service."

"Indeed. Were you able to recover it and did you search it?" Nijinsky asked.

Nijinsky could hear Trusov shuffling papers on his end of the line. "Ah, here it is. We have verified everything that you requested, Inspector. We compared prints on the steering wheel with those you wired us of Comrade Arbat and with those of Aureio Gavrilovich. There is no question."

"Good."

Trusov cleared his throat. "But perhaps even more important than the prints is the testimony of the waitress."

Nijinsky waited. "You mentioned a waitress."

"Indeed, the waitress," Trusov replied. "We interrogated her, of course, and showed her a picture of Arbat. She recognized him. She told us he was quite handsome and that is why she noticed him. She indicated that Arbat spoke to Gavrilovich but that her co-worker did not reply. She said he went to the kitchen, returned, and slid something across the countertop to Arbat. She did not know what. When I asked if she thought it could have been the keys to the Zaporozhet, she thought that was a possibility."

Nijinsky slumped back in his chair. He was playing with a small smile, but it was to early to tell if he had anything he could hang his hat on. "Thank you, Lieutenant Trusov," he heard himself saying. "You have been most helpful. I will be back in touch with you as this matter unfolds."

Nijinsky hung up the phone and opened the file folder. Then he made a notation. "6 November, 1655. Trusov confirms prior preliminary reports. Waitress verified Arbat's presence." When he was finished, he rocked back in his chair and looked around the room. Everyone was busy. He had decided he would test his theory on one of his comrades when they had more time.

LOG:
SEVEN: SIX

Staff Room: Belushya Guba 1818L
6 November

E-Alexa was late to the unscheduled staff meeting. When she was notified that Dolin had called the meeting, she was in the pontoon assembly arena, three levels below and at least a quarter mile from where the officers were gathering.

When she entered the room, she looked around the conference table. Dolin and Gureko she recognized. The two junior officers were new to her.

Dolin stood up when she entered the room; Gureko remained seated. The two junior officers followed the example of the admiral.

"Captain Perinchek and Lieutenant Rachmansov," Dolin indicated, "Colonel Chinko."

E-Alexa appraised the two men before she took her seat. Perinchek looked confident. Rachmansov looked anything but confident.

E-Alexa ascertained that her presence and the absence of Ulitsa made her role obvious. She looked at Dolin, who was motioning for them to take seats. "Captain Perinchek, please inform our comrades of your findings."

Perinchek stood up. "At Admiral Dolin's direction, we continued our review of the files on the Lyoto-Straf—"

"Dispense with the formalities, Captain. What did you find?" Gureko demanded.

Perinchek looked at Dolin and then the general. "So far, he admitted, "every file we have accessed is contaminated."

Gureko scowled. "And what percent of the files have you reviewed, Captain?"

Perinchek's air of confidence was gone. "We have accessed all files in sections AA, AB, AC, and we have spot-checked all remaining files."

"How is this possible?" Gureko shouted at Dolin. "Have we not taken every safety precaution?"

"Captain Perinchek assures me that every security procedure and precaution has been taken every step of the way."

"In theory, Admiral," E-Alexa offered, "retained files would not be contaminated. Only those in the unit itself would be subject to—"

Gureko spun in his chair. "We are not talking theory, Colonel Chinko, we are talking reality. Somehow our Sino comrades have discovered a way to render our files useless."

"Where is the Chinese contingent now, Lieutenant Rachmansov?" Dolin asked.

"As you ordered, Comrade Admiral, I have had them confined to their quarters until further notice. I have a guard posted outside each man's door."

"How is all this possible?" Gureko thundered.

Neither Perinchek or Rachmansov volunteered to speculate. E-Alexa shifted in her chair. She had regained her composure. "As I was saying, General"— she stared at Gureko—"data stored in compliance with RGN security procedures is safe—unless of course Mr. Zhou designed a way to walk through our central storage units and contaminate them, which seems unlikely."

Perinchek looked at her. "The files are lined with lead, Colonel Chinko. Each is sealed. Only Lieutenant Rachmansov and I have the access code to the individual file drawers. No file can be removed without the code-key of the individual requesting the file and either the lieutenant's code-key or mine."

"Handprint code-keys?" E-Alexa inquired.

Both Perinchek and Rachmansov nodded. "The only time I have seen data contaminated to this extent," Perinchek volunteered, "was when an exposed magnet on a sensor remained undetected overnight."

"Impossible with lead shields," Gureko sneered.

"The lead shield file liners were a precaution taken in case of just such an event," Perinchek admitted.

Dolin leaned forward with his arms on the table. "Have we checked access logs? Do we know who was in the files and when?"

Rachmansov opened his files. "The first contamination was discovered eighteen days ago. Prior to that there were no reports. It is a little over three weeks since Zhou departed."

"Are you saying that the data was retrievable prior to that?" Dolin asked.

"Let me rephrase that, Admiral. Up until eleven days ago there was no report of contamination."

"Is this not simply a case of bringing duplicate files from Moscow?" E-Alexa inquired.

"Duplicate files were not sent to Moscow," Gureko said, lowering his voice. "Aprihnen's orders, for security reasons."

"Then you are saying there are only two known sets of files," E-Alexa said, "those in the computer and the retained files, both of which are contaminated."

"This could bring the Lyoto-Straf project to a halt," Gureko growled.

Dolin held up his hand. His voice was uncertain. "Conceivably, a third set still exists."

Gureko looked at him. "If there are no duplicates, where? How?"

"At the bottom of the Stavka Straits in the companion room where Mr. Zhou was at the time the *Drachev* went down," Dolin said.

"Nonsense. He could have been anywhere on the ship at the time it went down," Gureko reminded him.

"That is always a possibility," Dolin admitted. "But let me ask you a question, Comrade General. If you were aboard a ship that was taking a pounding like the *Drachev* was during that storm, where would you be?"

Gureko looked at his fellow officer. "What makes you think that Zhou's files survived? Flight Officer Klyuzov reports he recorded a direct hit with his missile."

"Consider the alternative, Comrade General. Either we explore the feasibility of a possible retrieval mission to the unfortunate *Drachev*, or we inform President Aprihnen that the Lyoto-Straf project has come to a halt because of contaminated data."

Gureko sagged in his chair. E-Alexa was stunned.

"If Lieutenant Klyuzov's reports are accurate, the *Drachev* lies in no more than eighty to ninety feet of water," Dolin said. "We have the retrieval technology."

"Under the ice?" E-Alexa asked.

Dolin nodded, "Under the ice, Colonel," he confirmed.

"Then what is our next step, Admiral?" Perinchek asked.

"As I see it, we have two missions. You and Lieutenant Rachmansov will, in addition to checking the remaining files, conduct an intensive interrogation of our Chinese friends. If we can determine how they contaminated our files, there may be a way to rectify the situation." Then Dolin looked at E-Alexa.

"And you, Colonel Chinko, will come with me. We are going to investigate just how long it will take to have the SBK-77-DORO made available."

"SBK-77-DORO, Admiral?" E-Alexa asked.

Dolin nodded. "It is what the Americans call a DSRV, a quite remarkable piece of equipment."

LOG: SEVEN: SEVEN

Prince Edward Island 1616L
6 November

"Where the hell are you?" Packer groused.

Bogner's voice crackled through. " . . . about thirty thousand feet over PWI. At the moment they've got me patched through the ground station at Bangor. . . ."

"We're catching up, Toby. Miller just handed me a copy of your earlier transmission. He says you've already talked to Milatov, that you're on your way back, and that you believe it is essential that we locate Xo."

"Not only locate him, Pack, we've got to stop him. Milatov claims Xo is on his way to Moscow with the final piece of the cruor-toxin puzzle."

"Then Milatov confirmed it?"

"That and more. The old boy has corroborated our worst fears. Aprihnen is tying the E-1-A to a dirty warhead, and Milatov claims they've developed a system that can launch it from anywhere on the face of the globe. Not only that, he claims Xo is in the process of delivering the final component, and when Xo turns over that data, our problems are compounded. In fact, they get a helluva lot worse real quick."

"We're in luck, T.C. It looks like we finally got a

break," Packer revealed. "Our contact in Tibet reports that Xo left Lhasa the day before yesterday. He stopped overnight in Beijing, had several meetings, and caught the BOA flight to London. Less than an hour ago, I got a hold of Jaffe and he put the request through; the Brits let us intercept him. It wasn't as difficult as we thought it would be. M-5 took him into custody and put him aboard a Concorde bound for Washington less than ten minutes ago."

"The State Department is cooperating?"

"The boys over at the State Department don't know anything about it," Packer admitted. "We'll bring them up to speed after we get what we need."

Bogner understood the risk Jaffe and Packer were taking. If the Secretary of State got word of what the ISA was doing with someone as politically influential as Xo, all hell was bound to break loose. "Either way, my ETA at Andrews is 2000 hours," Bogner confirmed. Then his transmission started breaking up again.

Packer placed the phone back in its cradle and took out his pipe. He could smell a break a mile away.

LOG:
EIGHT: ONE

Miller pulled away from the curb and into the flow of Andrews traffic. Then he busied himself changing channels to pick up the restricted relay from Jaffe's car.

Packer looked at Bogner; he had already started his briefing. "So far, no screwups," he grunted. "Xo's flight is on the ground and Jaffe's men should be talking to M-5 along about now."

Bogner looked tired and he needed a shave. "Where are they taking him?"

Packer took out his pipe, tamped it, but did not light it, then reached inside his coat pocket, extracted a small, dog-eared spiral notebook, and flipped through several pages. "After the M-5 boys hand him over, we're slipping him into the Markham."

Bogner looked at his watch. After his conversation with Milatov, he was eager to talk to Xo. "How long?" he questioned.

"Another hour at least. We got the call less than fifteen minutes ago. The guy identified himself as a Lieutenant Frazer of Washington National Security. He said he was relaying information from Bambi.

That's the code name for Jaffe's man, Stag. He helped intercept Xo at Heathrow."

Bogner managed a tired smile. "I know Stag; he plays rough. Let's hope our boy Xo is still in one piece."

Packer nodded. "Jaffe assures me he doesn't rough anyone up when we plan to dump them."

"Where and when?"

Packer shrugged. "When we're through with him, we take him back to Heathrow, dump a quart of bourbon on him, screw up his life a little, dump him in some alley, and deny we know anything about it. I had Frazer make certain Xo's diplomatic papers and personal effects were lost for the time being. Bambi has his briefcase. No papers—no positive ident."

When Clancy looked up, Miller was pointing in the rearview mirror. "We picked up Langley at that last stoplight, Chief. He's right on schedule."

With Langley following, the cars continued south on Bellham until Miller came to an empty field next to an abandoned marina. He pulled off the road, into the shadows. "This is it. Now we wait."

Packer checked his watch.

Langley's dark blue Buick coasted to a stop behind them and he turned off his lights. In a cluster of metal sheds some 200 hundred yards in front of them, a third car blinked its headlights three times.

"That's our man," Packer confirmed. "No one moves until he repeats it."

Miller stared straight ahead. Langley was already out of his car, standing beside Packer's Pontiac. In the blanched illumination from the car's dash lights, Bogner could see Packer's jaw twitching. The ISA chief was getting edgy. The reason was obvious; both Packer and Jaffe had their necks on the chopping block on this one. What they had done was tantamount to abducting Xo, and with the possible exception of Dung, there were few people more prominent and influential in the Chinese Communist Party hierarchy than Xo.

"Hurry it up, dammit," Packer muttered. He lit his pipe. "The last thing that we need is a couple of DC's finest to cruise by and catch us out here with our pants down. It'll be all over the front page of the goddamn *Post* and . . ."

Across the opening the car blinked three times again, and Packer crawled out of the car to accompany Langley. They walked straight ahead until they were standing 50 feet in front of the car, still in the wash of Packer's headlights. At that point, Miller got out of the car and stood beside the open door, left hand concealed in the pocket of his raincoat, his right nervously gripping the steering wheel.

From out of the glare of their own headlights, Bogner saw two men approaching from the other direction. Despite the distance, the difference in the size of the two men was obvious. One was large and wearing an overcoat. His companion was slighter and shorter. The smaller one was handcuffed and carrying a briefcase.

"Look like our boy?" Miller asked.

Bogner nodded. "That's him."

There was a period of animated conversation, and over what appeared to be Xo's protests, Langley took possession of the briefcase. The area was momentarily illuminated by the headlights of two approaching cars. When they passed, the second appeared to slow and Bogner felt his pulse quicken. "Come on," he muttered, "get his skinny ass in the car and let's get out of here."

The conversation continued for several more minutes before Packer and Langley finally headed back toward the car escorting Xo between them. He overheard Packer tell Miller, "We're headed for the Markham; follow us."

A half hour later, with Langley driving drag on the pickup operation to determine that no one was following, Miller pulled the gray sedan under the canopy at the side entrance to the Markham.

Bogner crawled out, and checked his watch; it was 8:30. Out of an old navy pilot's habit, he took a quick check of the weather; the wind had picked up and it was spitting snow again. He wondered what had happened to the M-5 agent. The thought occurred to him that Bambi had a home somewhere. He walked across the Putnam Street lobby and as he approached the elevator, one of Jaffe's men stepped from the shadows. Jaffe's description had obviously been accurate enough that the man recognized Bogner and inclined his head toward the second elevator. "721B, Commander," the man said.

Bogner got off on the seventh floor, glanced down the hall at the conversation alcove, and saw two more of Jaffe's men working hard at not being interested in the latest person to exit the elevator. He ignored them and headed for 721B.

"Bogner," he announced as he knocked.

The door opened and he was face-to-face with the man who had outsmarted him in Stockholm. Now, in the uncompromising overhead light of a hotel room, Xo looked a lot less imposing, like anything, Bogner thought, but a mover and shaker in the Dung government. He was wearing a dark blue but wrinkled three-piece tailored silk suit, a cream-colored silk shirt, black patent leather shoes, and a slightly skewed flowered silk tie. It occurred to Bogner that Xo Cho Ping appeared to be everything that went against Party philosophy. One thing was certain: he was not your prototypical Party heavyweight.

Jaffe's opening was terse. "The gray-haired man's name is Packer. That man over there is Captain Langley. I believe you and Commander Bogner know each other from your recent encounter in Stockholm. My name is Jaffe." Xo's eyes followed the laconic introductions around the room. "Now, Mr. Xo, let me get straight to the point."

Xo was already staring defiantly back at the four men. Bogner had him pegged as the type who found strength in the taciturn role; he showed no expression, and so far he hadn't uttered a word.

Langley seated himself across from Xo; Packer and Jaffe remained standing. Jaffe lit one of his endless chain of cigarettes and offered one to Xo. To Bogner's surprise, Xo accepted it.

"According to your airline tickets," Jaffe began, "you were on your way to Moscow."

"Many people travel to Moscow these days," Xo said.

"Suppose you tell us about your business in Moscow," Jaffe pressed.

"Personal business," Xo replied.

Jaffe looked around the room. "Okay, we'll do it our way. Break the seal on the attaché case, Captain. Let's see what Mr. Xo is carrying."

Langley reached in his pocket, took out a pocket-knife and sprung the lock, then opened the case. It contained three file folders, each in turn containing documents written in Chinese. Langley thumbed through them, stood up, and left the room. He was back within minutes.

Jaffe smiled. "You'll be glad to know, Comrade Xo, that we anticipated as much; we have two colleagues in the next room and both of them read and write several different regional Chinese dialects. We should know shortly whether or not your files contain information we are looking for."

Xo walked across the room and, despite his handcuffs, managed to extract a gold cigarette case from his overcoat. He lit another cigarette. "I am curious; just exactly what is it that I am supposed to be carrying that is of such vital interest to you and your colleagues?" Xo asked.

Packer smiled and looked at Bogner. "Suppose you tell Mr. Xo here all about your conversation with Comrade Milatov, T.C."

Xo's eyes narrowed.

Bogner cleared his throat. "I'm afraid your buddy, Comrade Milatov, didn't hold much back, Xo. Fact of the matter is, when we intercepted you at Heathrow, he had already informed us you were en route from Beijing to Moscow with what he described as the long-awaited formula for encapsulating some heat-sensitive cruor-toxins. In other words, a process that would enable these toxins to survive a nuclear explosion. Or to put it another way," Bogner continued, "a process that would enable these toxins to survive the initial detonation of a nuclear device that is part of the warhead on a Russian E-1-A Novgorod missile."

Xo almost pulled it off. "I'm afraid I don't know what you are talking about, Commander," he said. But the tightening of his jaw and the all but imperceptible twitch of one eye betrayed him. He looked at Packer, then Langley. "You have the wrong man, gentlemen," he said.

"We don't think so, Mr. Xo," Langley said. He was on his feet, moving toward Xo's briefcase again. This time he flipped his knife to Bogner. "Okay, Toby, your turn; start by tearing the briefcase apart."

Xo exhaled. Packer decided that with the smoke curling around his face, Xo was even harder to read.

"Where is it?" Langley demanded.

Xo shook his head. "You were amusing, Captain, until a few minutes ago. I would not have believed your methods were so primitive." Then he paused as though he had violated some inner principle of conduct. He looked at Jaffe and Packer, then back at Langley again. "You appear to be the spokesman for this group, Mr. Jaffe. Is it common practice to treat influential foreigners in this fashion in your country?"

Langley cleared his throat and leaned forward in his seat. There was no point in continuing to beat around the bush. "No, Mr. Xo, as a matter of fact there is nothing common about what we are doing here. Quite obviously, we know who you are and why you were on your way to Moscow. And we are well aware of the international outrage that would develop if officials in your country were to learn that we pirated you right off your flight in London. But they aren't going to find out, Mr. Xo, because if you don't tell us where the data files are for the encapsulation process, you will simply disappear from the face of the earth."

Xo smiled; the smile was small, sardonic, and not quite sincere enough to pull it off. "There will be grave repercussions," Xo threatened, "if I am not allowed to proceed to my destination."

Jaffe stood up. "Your ticket indicates that you intended to fly from London to Moscow tomorrow morning. Then there is a ten-day period before you are scheduled to return to Beijing. Is that because your business in Belushya Guba will occupy you for the entire period?"

"Or is it because it will take a full ten days to teach your Russian friends how to encapsulate the cruor-toxins?" Langley demanded.

Xo looked around the room. He appeared to be less confident. He allowed a small shift in his facial features that Packer interpreted as more than mild irritation with Langley's question. He got up, went to the window, and stared out at the cold Washington night. Bogner sliced open the lining of the briefcase, pulled it out, and examined it. Then he looked at Packer and shook his head.

"Okay, start in on the clothing," Packer said.

Jaffe unlocked the handcuffs. "Take off the coat, Xo," he said.

One by one, Bogner cut off the buttons and examined them. Then he took the suit coat apart, stitch by stitch. "Nothing," he said, looking at Packer.

"All right, Xo," Packer said, "take off the pants."

*   *   *

There was a veiled impudence in the way Xo studied his interrogators. Finally he asked for a drink of water. While Jaffe went into the bathroom, Xo asked for another cigarette. When Jaffe returned with the glass of tap water, Xo took several sips before setting the glass on the nightstand beside the bed. Packer knew it was a stalling tactic, one that he readily admitted he might have tried if he had been in Xo's situation. When Xo finally spoke again, his words were at first measured and then slurred.

"You will understand why I am curious," Xo began, "that your State Department has not been notified. Even in my country, a country your president accuses of excessive human rights violations, one—one is not—not incarcerated without charges."

It was Jaffe's turn. "Make you a deal, Xo. You hand over the data file on the cruor-toxin encapsulation procedures and we let you go."

Xo smiled. "I am beginning to sense that this is a maverick effort, one without official blessing. If that is the case, I will call your bluff. Do as you see fit."

Langley pulled his chair up in front of Xo. "Maverick or not, we know you and your government are involved in the development of the E-1-A Novgorod system now being developed at Belushya Guba. We know that there has been extensive construction activity there the past three years, and we know that Belushya is not the Russian scientific center for Arctic studies that President Aprihnen would have us believe it is."

Xo glared back at Jaffe for several seconds before reaching for the gutted briefcase and retrieving and putting on his glasses. Then he slumped forward and toppled to the floor.

Packer was the first to reach Xo's side. He searched for a pulse, peeled back the little man's eyelid, then looked up.

"Get a goddamn doctor up here now."

LOG:
EIGHT: TWO

Staff Room: Belushya Guba 0808L
7 November

"This meeting will be brief," Gureko announced. He looked at Dolin and E-Alexa. "I have been in contact with Admiral Lyalin at the Moscow Institute of Oceanology."

"He is aware of . . ."

"He knows nothing of the security breach in our computers. Instead I informed him of our interest in the possibility of recovering certain instruments from the downed *Drachev*, explaining, of course, that many of the instruments were unique to our mission and that replacement would be both costly and time-consuming. I indicated that I was merely seeking his advice on the best way to determine the extent of the damage and to determine if a salvage operation was feasible."

Dolin smiled and looked at E-Alexa. "May I point out, Comrade Chinko, that you are watching a master. Our General Gureko has a way in such matters that others only view with envy."

Gureko's ruddy face softened. "Obviously, I inquired as to the availability of the *Akademik Keldysh* and the feasibility of having the Mir 1 or Mir 2 robots explore the condition of the *Drachev*. Admiral Lyalin indicated that because of the ice and our inability to position the *Keldysh* close enough to the recovery site, such a mission would be impossible until the shipping channels open. He suggested instead that we obtain an electronic profile of the wreckage by using the side scan sonar on the *Kuchumov*. If the hull is found to be intact and recovery appears to be feasible, Admiral Lyalin will authorize the deployment of the *Zotov*."

Dolin frowned. "Do you believe that all of this can be done without revealing . . ."

"Need I remind you that it is under the ice, Comrade Admiral. Ask yourself: who will be the wiser about the true purpose of our mission?"

"Do we have a time frame?" E-Alexa inquired.

"Earlier this morning I took the liberty of ordering the *Kuchumov* to be prepared for launching. I am told that the main crane will be ready to lower it into the primary Lyoto-Straf bay within twenty-four hours."

"Then you have a plan, General?"

Gureko nodded. "The crew of the *Kuchumov* will locate and profile the remains of the *Drachev*. Both Captain Beppaev and Captain Stigga, who will pilot the submarine, estimate a mission time of no more than forty-eight to seventy-two hours. In that time, both the site and the status of the wreckage will be assessed, and if it appears that recovery of our Mr. Zhou's files can be accomplished, the *Zotov* will be dispatched."

E-Alexa leaned forward. "As I recall, the *Zotov* is the manned recovery unit that was utilized in the *Komsomoltz* investigation several years ago off the coast of Norway."

"Southwest of Bear Island," Dolin confirmed. "While the Mir 1 and Mir 2 received accolades from a grateful world for their environmental investigation, the robots and crew aboard the *Zotov* recovered certain sensitive information from the wreckage."

"Will mere robots be adequate for our purposes?"

"Ah, Colonel Chinko, that is the beauty of the *Zotov*. The *Zotov* operates with a two-man crew, and in shallow waters such as where the wreckage of the *Drachev* is situated, the crew may actually be deployed outside the vessel. In this case, the robots, if necessary, will merely serve to assist them."

"Divers have adequate protection from the frigid waters?" E-Alexa pressed.

"Indeed, Colonel Chinko, they will have more than adequate protection. In concert with the development of the *Zotov* at our shipyards at Chazhma Bay was the introduction of a protective diving suit with a gel-forming carbohydrate solution between the polyethylene membranes that make up the outer layer of the suit. Our divers can stay in the coldest of waters for up to six hours without impacting their performance."

"Suppose we are fortunate enough to locate Zhou's body and even recover the files," E-Alexa said, "only to discover that those files are also damaged?"

Both Gureko and Dolin frowned.

"In that case, Colonel Chinko, we will have failed," Dolin replied. "If that happens, both our fate and the fate of the entire project will be in the hands of President Aprihnen." He paused for a moment. "And I do not believe I need to tell you that is not a pleasant specter."

Gureko's usual phlegmatic expression was creased into a thin, unattractive smile. "I regret to say that Admiral Dolin is correct. It is not a pleasant specter."

LOG:
EIGHT: THREE

ISA Offices: Washington 1013L
7 November

Bogner finished his briefing and assessed the faces of his colleagues. "I guess the bottom line is, if all of this doesn't scare the hell out of you, what will?"

Miller's face was pale. "It makes you wonder what the hell happened to glasnost."

"I don't think this is what Gorbachev had in mind," Langley said.

Packer drummed his fingers on the table. "Apparently it's what Aprihnen had in mind."

Miller's brow was furrowed. "If I understand what you're telling us, T.C., this damned Lyoto-Straf is nothing more than an underwater launching system for the E-1-A with multiple-kill-potential warheads."

Bogner nodded. "According to Milatov, the first of these launching stations is nearing completion and is capable of being maneuvered into position by two of their nuclear submarines that tow the unit in tandem. Not only that, these launching sleds can be repositioned whenever they damn well get the notion, and in theory at least, we won't have the slightest idea where they have been located. All they have to do is pump the ballast out of the pontoons, refloat the

213

station, and slide the whole affair into a new strategic position."

"But with their missile capability the way it stands now, it seems like overkill. Any one of their bigger SSBNs is capable of launching enough warheads to wipe out—"

"I thought about this all the way back from my session with Milatov," Bogner said. "What this really means is that they can position one of these launching pads in places where we can't get at them. We know we can get *Alvin* down to about four thousand meters and *Jason* to six thousand, but there are a hell of a lot of places out there where they can station one of their launchers that are deeper than that. Four or five of these units situated in the right places and Aprihnen has ninety percent of the world leaders by the nuts."

Langley shook his head. "Think about it. Compound what Toby is telling us with the fact that we are dealing with E-1-As carrying dual warheads. After the initial blast comes the cruor-toxins, and before you know it, everyone in the impact area is bleeding like a stuck pig."

Packer closed his notebook and stared out the window. "Okay, now that we know what we're dealing with, what the hell do we do about it? Second question: How long is it going to take our Chinese friends to realize that Xo never got to the Russians with the formula for encapsulating the cruor-toxins?"

"In some ways, even though he hasn't said anything and we haven't figured out what those files say, I think Xo has pretty much confirmed everything Milatov told Bogner," Miller said. He laid his copy of the report on the table.

"This is where it gets cloudy and Machiavellian, Pack," Bogner interjected. "According to Milatov, one of Chairman Dung's stooges arranged for a member of the Chinese technical contingent to steal the design details of the entire Lyoto-Straf project. The guy's name was Zhou, and he got away with it—for a while. By the time the Russians figured out what happened, they saw to it that when he was called back to China, he never made it."

"So now we've got an open rift?" Packer speculated.

Bogner shook his head. "Not quite. According to Milatov, arrangements were made to allow this guy, Zhou, to leave. He shipped out on the last freighter before the ice closed the harbor at Belushya Guba. But—big surprise, the ship never arrived at its destination, and three days later the Russians announced that one of their freighters was missing."

"Maybe you'd better tie it together for everyone," Packer urged.

Miller arched his eyebrows.

"Milatov figures Chairman Dung only agreed to this joint development project so that he could get his hands on the E-1-A technology. He claims the Chinese already had the problem of encapsulating the cruor-toxins licked some five years ago. He figures Xo was instructed to delay handing over that information as long as possible."

"And we played right into their hands. Now, when we release Xo, he can claim the Americans have the technology; through no fault of the Dung government, I might add."

Langley got up, poured himself another cup of coffee, and stood at the end of the conference table.

"Sounds like the plot of one of those British spy novels," Miller observed.

Bogner laughed. "Hell, Robert, there's more. It seems that Mr. Zhou wasn't content with just stealing the damn files. Milatov claims after he made his copies, he somehow managed to contaminate every damned system-retained computer file in the Belushya complex. He claims that construction on the Lyoto-Straf is at a virtual standstill. He thinks the officers at Belushya Guba are keeping the magnitude of their problem under wraps until they figure out a way of getting their files straightened out."

"You're not saying the E-1-A project is dead?" Miller asked.

"Not dead, but definitely hurting," Langley replied. "They've got to figure out some way of recapturing the data in those files, and that could take a while."

Packer cleared his throat. "If what you're saying is true, T.C., then in theory at least, this guy Zhou has already done the job for us. If Milatov is correct, everything we ever wanted to know about the E-1-A weapons system and the Belushya Guba project has already been spirited out of that damned ice fortress, and it's on a sunken Russian freighter somewhere under the Arctic Ocean."

Packer turned and looked at the map. "We can come a helluva lot closer than that. We can pinpoint it somewhere between the harbor at Belushya Guba and its destination. All we have to do is find out what course they use for supply ships going back and forth between the island and the port."

Miller's fist slammed down on the table. "Of course! Why the hell didn't I see it? Pack, remember me showing you that monthly shipping bulletin about a Russian ship called the *Drachev?*"

"The one that sunk in the Barents Sea?"

"That's it," Bogner said, staring at the map. "Maybe you don't have to sneak into Belushya Guba to find out what's going on after all, Pack. Maybe all you have to do is find out where that Russian freighter went down and go in and take a peek. If Milatov is right, everything we need to know is right there."

"Sounds like a long shot," Packer assessed.

"Not half as long a shot as trying to sneak into Belushya Guba and look around."

Langley leaned back in his chair. "You know something, Pack, T.C. may have hit the nail on the head. The key to all this may be locating the wreck of the

Drachev. If we can, I've got just the toys it takes to go in there and look around."

"Not another *ARCA-DINO?*" Bogner grinned. "Don't forget, we left the last one on the bottom of Negril harbor."

"Even better than the *ARCA-DINO*," Langley said. "All it takes is a couple of phone calls and we can have her piggybacked to the search site in a matter of hours."

"How the hell are we going to find a damned sunken Russian freighter hidden by thirty or forty million tons of ice?" Packer snarled.

"With the most sophisticated underwater tinkertoy you ever laid your eyes on, Clancy. We call her the *Spats* and she comes in two different utilization configurations. Not only that, she just completed her shakedown maneuvers three weeks ago. She's primed and ready. If this mission is doable, she's the gal that can do it."

"So how do we get her to the crash site?" Miller asked.

"We fly her there—aboard a Hercules."

Packer looked around the room. "Hold on. Before we go off half-cocked, we need some verification. How do we know Milatov is leveling with us? We've been making one hell of a lot of suppositions here. I want a chance to go over Bogner's report. We'll meet back here at five o'clock. Then we can make some decisions."

As they started out of the conference room, Packer took Bogner by the arm. "You know what happens if we verify the location of this freighter, Toby. We go looking for it."

"What do you mean 'we'?"

Packer took out his pipe. "Langley will need you."

Packer could feel Bogner stiffen.

LOG: EIGHT: FOUR

Aboard the Kuchumov, *Kilo-class SS 0837L*
8 November

Lieutenant Yuri Zhdanov stood in the cramped control room studying computer-generated quadrant cartograms. Rivulets of sweat etched their way down under his woolen crewneck sweater, annoying him. The drone of the *Kuchumov*'s twin diesel-driven generators annoyed him still further.

For Zhdanov, this mission aboard the tiny Kilo-class was something to be endured. When informed of it by Dolin, he'd commented that the task was unlikely to even afford him a challenge, and in the final analysis would be little more than child's play. Now, despite his discomfort, he had to admit that it was indeed a break from the tedium of the day-in, day-out training sessions for the tandem-sub relocation crews of the Lyoto-Straf launching platform, the device that was now being called Dolin's Sled.

From the beginning, Zhdanov had been trained to operate the RUMR units aboard the giant Oscar-class SSGNs; and now he was being called upon to perform the same duties in the search for the *Drachev*.

Across from him was his comrade, Captain Viktor Stigga, who occupied himself studying the charts.

Stigga, a former Spetsnaz commander, appeared to be as comfortable in the restricted and awkward quarters of the tiny control room as he did the officer's mess back at Belushya.

Now, while Zhdanov watched, Stigga's stylus traced a line from their DP in the undershelf launching facilities of the Belushya complex to the point where the red box recorder on Lieutenant Klyuzov's Sukhoi Su-24 had logged missile impact.

"Here," Stigga determined. "Mark. Sectors 2-b, 2-c, 8-b, and 8-c."

Zhdanov waited for the figures to appear on his monitor before he would confirm. "Verified. I'm getting two vertical, eight horizontal. What's the spread?"

Stigga entered the coordinates into the computer. The screen flashed green and plotted downdrift factors. "Sectors 6-1 and 6-2," Stigga repeated. Then he looked away from the charts for a moment at his radioman. "Ice pack report?"

Mrachkovski keyed the vertical sonar and began reciting a series of readings. "4.7, 4.7, 4.7, 4.9. Mission time 0133."

Stigga looked at his young RUMR officer colleague and smiled. "So, how does it feel, Lieutenant, your first time under so much ice?"

Zhdanov, who was still too young to be completely honest, hedged his answer. "A bit confining, Captain. Of course the Oscar is much larger—there is more room to move around. An additional eighty meters in length provides a few more amenities."

Stigga laughed. "Indeed. On the other hand, there is a cozy feeling about our little girl here, is there not?"

Zhdanov knew better than to engage in a discussion of the merits of size with a former Spetsnaz captain. To a Spetsnaz veteran, small was beautiful. Instead he turned his attention back to his charts. "You have not detailed your mission plan, sir," he reminded his comrade.

Stigga balanced himself by holding on to a polished brass Kingston valve with one hand and the chart table with the other. From time to time he checked the instrument panel directly behind Zhdanov's head. The neutral buoyancy, NEuB, gauge occupied most of his attention. From time to time he gave the controller correction factors.

"The plan is very simple, Lieutenant. I get you to the proper coordinates, you deploy your little seeing-eye friend until we find the *Drachev*, we take pictures of what we find, and then we return to port."

"The RUMR is capable not only of taking laser-embellished photographs, Captain, it is also capable of assessing the damage. Probability of retention factors can be calculated instantaneously. We can advise Admiral Dolin of the probability of . . ."

Stigga laughed again. "One thing you must learn, Lieutenant. We do not *advise* Admiral Dolin, we *report* to him. Admiral Dolin will assess the data. He will determine what action, if any, is taken."

Zhdanov laughed and began to relax. He permitted himself a small smile. "Your point is well taken, Comrade Captain."

"In quarters such as these, Lieutenant, the protocol of units you are familiar with is not possible. Besides, I am looking forward to your RUMR exercise. In the thirty years that I have explored the oceans, I have never had the opportunity to actually see that world. I feel certain that you have noticed we have no windows with which to view what is going on out there."

Zhdanov reflected momentarily on Stigga's statement and looked around the control room. Stigga, Con-Officer Mrachkovski, the radioman, and the young controlman Uritski, along with three seamen, constituted the entire crew of their reconnaissance effort. Dolin had ordered the *Kuchumov* to be stripped of torpedoes, deck guns, and even some of the decking to compensate for the added weight of the hydraulically operated auxiliary sled that launched the RUMR. For that reason alone, Zhdanov figured Stigga would continually monitor the NEuB gages. Then his mind turned to the young seamen in the *Kuchumov*'s galley. It was their first mission under the ice as well. He wondered how they were faring.

"Ice pack report," Stigga ordered.

Again Mrachkovski assessed the four display promoters. The ice thickness had increased. "5.2, 5.7, 5.9, 7.2, mission time 0202."

"Bridge readings?"

Mrachkovski repeated a series of numbers. "027k, 027k."

"Shut down one," Stigga barked.

"Shut down one," Uritski confirmed. "024k, 019k"

"Slow to 03.0."

"Slow to 03.0," Uritski repeated. "Mark."

"There is a condition known as shag ice, Lieutenant," Stigga explained, "tentacles of ice hanging down from the pack." Then, just as he turned to Uritski, the red light began flashing on the sonar display panel. Uritski wheeled his chair around to the full panel display and put on the headset.

"Invader, invader," he repeated.

Stigga leaned on the table in front of the display. "What do we have, Lieutenant?"

"Company," Uritski said with a scowl, "complete with signature cavitation."

Stigga turned. "Go dead. All silent." He waited for several moments. "What do you think?" He was looking at Uritski again.

"Los Angeles-class, no signature. Hard to tell. It's an old one, though."

Stigga folded his arms and looked at Zhdanov. Under the circumstances, his question surprised the young officer. "Do you play cribbage, Lieutenant?"

Zhdanov shook his head. "Are you not concerned, Captain?"

"Yes, of course, but if Comrade Uritski is correct in his assumption, it is one of their older units, and therefore probably a training mission. If that is the case, they are very, very busy."

"Surely they know we are here," Zhdanov protested.

"I am certain they do. They have very likely already identified us as a nonnuclear unit and if they are retro-fitted with profile sonar, there is a good chance they can identify our class by our size."

"And . . ." Zhdanov urged.

Stigga smiled again. "You have much to learn, Comrade Zhdanov. They have a submarine. We have a submarine. They are on a training mission. We are on a training mission. Submarines need water. We are both in the water."

"But these are our waters."

Stigga shook his head. "Look at the charts, Lieutenant. What does it say? Technically, we are both in the Barents Sea. Nowhere do you see the name of our mother country on these charts."

"But they are coming very close to our Belushya site," Zhdanov protested.

Stigga nodded. "They are not close, Lieutenant, until you can see the color of their eyes. Do you see the color of their eyes?"

Zhdanov sighed and shook his head. He wiped his hands on the front of his sweatshirt. He was sweating again.

LOG:
EIGHT: FIVE

The Portland, *Los Angeles-Class SSN-688 0851L*
8 November

Sonarman 2/C Raymond Perkins was finishing his second cup of coffee. What he really wanted was a cigarette, but from where he sat he could see that the CON CEN was too crowded; he could see Lieutenant Mitchell, the ODO; Ensign Smith, the training officer; and even Captain Word. They had been swapping war stories. Everyone, even the new man, a fellow by the name of Goetchel or something close to that who was working the auxiliary radios, and CPO Baker, monitoring the C-con, had been laughing. Screw the chatter, he thought to himself, Ray baby needs a Camel. He fingered the cigarettes in his shirt pocket and wondered when Word would relieve him of duty.

He turned back to his console, glanced at his watch, and drained the last few drops of coffee from his mug. At best it was tepid and he wrinkled his nose. It was his third split shift in the last four nights. This time he was filling in for Mike Cooper, who was still laid up with a bad hand. Coop had gotten careless in a fire drill and someone had slammed the G bulkhead door on his hand. And from the look of that hand, Perkins figured he would be working a lot of split schedules.

All in all, though, that was a concern for another day. In nine more minutes his watch was over. With any luck at all he could clear mess in ten minutes—easy to do because breakfast wasn't his thing—and get some sack time before the 1100 hours inspection. He cleared the C-scope and sequenced the four monitors for the log check. The computer could scan 12 hours of data in six seconds and flag all anomalies in the process. He initiated the final scan and then realized the captain was leaning over his shoulder.

"While you're at it, bring up the review log, Ray." Word yawned. "Did we pick up anything of interest in the last couple of hours?"

Perkins scrolled the ten-minute log with the summary notations. "Nothing out of the ordinary, sir." He pointed at the partial profile on the 0740 sweep. "I pointed this one out to Petty Officer Baker, but he said the image was an old World War II Danish freighter."

Word nodded, and had started to turn away when the CR-SD picked up a minor blip in the DD sector. Perkins magnified the 0100-to-0300 vector and elevated the volume. He could see Word cock his head to one side. At the same time, he changed frequency on the G1-H to coincide with the isolation. Captain Word held up his hand while he studied the 15-second sweep. The banter in the CON-CEN hushed. Word motioned his chief petty officer over to where Perkins was sitting. Now both men stood with their eyes fixed on the scope.

"Can you bring it up a notch, Perky?" Baker asked.

Perkins narrowed the sector. "0130-0230 corrected. How's that, sir?"

Baker held up his hand. In the background Perkins could hear Lieutenant Mitchell tell the radioman to hit the squelch button. Baker continued to study the interval. "Give me a side scan on 3S and 4S."

Smith repeated the order. "Side scan 3S and 4S."

There was a momentary pause before he advised that the starboard sensors had been activated.

"Image sensing 1 and 2," Word barked. "What do you think, Les?"

Baker looked up at the digitized reception being reproduced on the monitor. "Nothing I'm familiar with, Captain. At 20m we get a partial, at 25m it's a little clearer, at 30 we lose it, but the target, if it is in fact a target, is Q and D."

"Then it's not another sub?"

"It could be a sub, Captain, but she's not a nuke. The audio sensors are flat. Whatever we're getting a picture of isn't anything in the computer profile log. The wave sign looks like it could be diesels, but even that could be a residual sound, and it's fading."

"Reference imaging," Word snapped.

"RI up," Smith repeated.

"Length?"

Smith altered the IM. "At this distance it looks to be about seventy or so meters, Captain, about the size of one of their old Kilo-class models."

"I never saw a Kilo with a hump on the back like that. Those first seven digits are probably the con tower, but what the hell are those ten digits near the stern?"

Word straightened up and looked at his communications officer. He was smiling. "Ted, remember that conversation we had the other night when we were talking about how many subs the damn Russians had and you couldn't figure out how they built so many so fast? Well, there's your answer."

Mitchell looked puzzled.

"If you believe that profile, one of their damn subs is giving birth right before our eyes."

Mitchell snickered. "Can you enhance it?"

"Enhanced image, sir," Perkins confirmed.

Baker shook his head. "Who knows what the hell they're up to. Probably some damn training mission."

The soft tone of three bells signaled the watch

change and Perkins waited for orders. Both Baker and Mitchell were still logging the location of the anomaly. The captain ignored it; he was scanning the log.

"See if we can get some coffee up here," Word growled. "Looks like we'll be here for a while."

"Shit," Perkins muttered not quite to himself.

LOG:
NINE: ONE

It had occurred to Bogner that Packer's description of the president's two top personal aids, Lattimere Spitz and Chet Hurley, was right on the money. On this occasion, Spitz was clearly the mouth and Hurley was the mind. He checked his watch; Spitz had been raving nonstop for the last 15 minutes.

"And just what the hell were you guys thinking?" Spitz stormed. "In case you didn't know it when you walked in here, the secretary of state has been on the phone chewing my ass every time he sees a telephone for the past twenty-four hours."

There was little doubt that Oscar Jaffe was the focus of Spitz's wrath, but it was equally apparent that Peter Langley and Clancy Packer were in the same doghouse.

"Dammit, Lattimere, what would you have done?" Jaffe sputtered. He had already puffed his way through half a pack of cigarettes and was reaching for another.

Spitz, standing in front of the fireplace, stared up at the Tade Styka painting of Teddy Roosevelt astride a big bay, and folded his hands behind his back. "Well, I'll tell you one thing, Oscar, I would have used my goddamn head. What makes you think you can intercept someone like Xo in the midst of a busy terminal like Heathrow and not get caught? Do I need to remind you that the goddamn place is crawling with reporters? Did you even stop to think what Xo would say when you were through pounding on him?"

"We haven't laid a hand on him," Jaffe snorted.

"Dammit, Oscar, that's not the point."

Jaffe looked down at the pad of paper in front of him on which he had been doodling. "So Xo is upset, so what?"

Spitz pounded on the table. "I don't give a rat's ass about Xo, Oscar, and you know it. If you walk through that door there, you're not more than thirty feet from the Oval Office—and that's the man I have to worry about."

"It was a calculated gamble, Lattimere," Jaffe sighed. "Xo has information, information we need."

Spitz glared at Jaffe; his thin, hollow-cheeked face and high forehead were flushed with anger. It was several seconds before he managed to bring his voice under control. "The first call I received was from two reporters at the *Post*. You know where they got their information, Oscar? They were standing right there at the exit ramp when Xo got off the plane with a couple of goons from M-5. And what do they see? They see this clown Frazer and the M-5 boys spirit Xo out of the customs area and through a rear door. Hey, both of these guys know there is a procedure, and when the State Department doesn't show and Xo is long gone, they smell something."

Spitz paused just long enough to pour himself a glass of water. He kept glancing at the door leading to Colchin's office as if he expected the president to walk through it at any moment.

"The next thing I know, the secretary of state is on the horn, and he wants to know if Colchin ordered the CIA or the ISA to intercept Xo. So I went straight to the *man*; bottom line, he doesn't know anything about it. In so many words, Oscar, the Maximum Computer is pissed."

Langley shifted in his chair. "When you're through ranting and raving, Lattimere, I'll be happy to share the logic of intercepting Xo before the State Department got in on this."

"Logic," Spitz shrieked, glaring at Langley. "Let me tell you something, Captain, there ain't any fucking logic to this stunt."

At that point Chet Hurley pushed himself away from the ornate conference table and stood up. He took his cigar out of his mouth and looked at Bogner. "Hold it a minute, Lattimere. I'd like to hear what T.C. has to say. He's the one who talked to Milatov."

Bogner shifted in his chair.

Packer loosened his tie. "Take my word for it. There is some logic to all of this nonsense, Lattimere, and if you'll stop shouting and settle down for a couple of minutes, I think Bogner can shed some light on all of this."

Spitz looked at Bogner. Hurley sat down and said, "The floor's yours, Toby. Maybe we should be listening to you instead of Lattimere here."

Bogner cleared his throat. "I think what Oscar means is that Xo is the only man we can get our hands on who actually has firsthand knowledge of the Belushya Guba situation. What we're getting from Milatov is good, but it's secondhand. Xo was there as recently as thirty days ago. Now all we've got to do is make him talk."

"What about your session with Milatov?" Spitz interrupted.

"Milatov explained the system and the hardware, Lattimere, but Xo was the only one who could enlighten us about the current situation. Xo is the key. Until the Russians actually get the encapsulation data from Xo, we've got a chance to bring this down."

"How so?"

Spitz leaned forward. "Look, Toby, I hear you, but now we've got two different situations to deal with. Why the hell couldn't you have interrogated Xo after he was formally granted asylum or charged with espionage?"

"You know damn well why we couldn't, Lattimere. How long did it take Dung to file a protest when word leaked out that we had Xo?" Jaffe snarled. "The damn State Department has more leaks in it than my bathroom."

"There is a procedure," Spitz countered.

"Fuck your procedures, Lattimere," Jaffe spat. "Everyone in this room has a job to do and we are trying to do it. Xo knows what's coming down on that damned ice island and if we can't defuse this situation, our friend Aprihnen is going to have us right where he wants us—and believe me, that ain't a comfortable position."

Hurley cleared his throat and looked at Spitz. "I read Packer's report last night before the president's six P.M. briefing. The president had two questions. One, did NI have any opinion on how effective this Lyoto-Straf concept of a relocatable underwater launching station would be? And two, if it is feasible, is there any indication how soon it will be operational?"

Packer turned to Bogner. "You talked to Milatov. What do you think?"

Bogner shrugged. "Everyone at the Pentagon who knows missiles knows Aleksandr Milatov; most of them will tell you that the former Soviet Union wouldn't have an operational ICBM program if it wasn't for him. Bottom line, the knowledge to put it all together is there. Whether or not they have sufficiently developed the hardware is another matter. In theory at least, the Lyoto-Straf could be one helluva weapon. The way Aprihnen is drifting back to the old Party ways, four or five of these Lyoto-Strafs in strategic locations could give him an unmanned lock on just about any country in the world."

"Unmanned?" Hurley repeated. "Who pushes the button?"

"They can be manned or unmanned. Either way, someone in the Kremlin," Bogner replied, "anytime they want to. With multiple Lyoto-Straf units strategically located, it wouldn't make a bit of difference how they had their missile-toting subs or surface units deployed or who was in charge. In fact, it would probably be the navy's responsibility to go in and mop up the hot spots."

"Did Milatov give you any indication of timing?" Hurley asked.

"He believes the first Lyoto-Straf platform will be ready to tow into position by the time the shipping channels open."

Spitz slammed his fist down on the table again. "And what the hell makes them think that we won't know their every move? The minute they start to move that thing, every damn camera in every damn satellite we've got will be focused on it and recording every move."

"Not when they move it under the surface," Bogner countered. "Our cameras are good, but they're not that good."

Spitz stared back at him. "And how the hell are they going to accomplish that?"

Langley spoke up. "It's simple, Lattimere, two Oscar-class subs. One on each side, especially modified and configured to move the platform. The way Milatov described it to Bogner, the launchers are sitting on massive pontoons nearly three hundred meters long. Purge the pontoons and it moves. Put it where you want it and fill the pontoons, which are actually the system's ballast tanks, when it's in position."

"Not only does the E-1-A have dual warheads, Xo's people have added a nasty little twist. The system has a secondary impact. If Xo gets through, it sprinkles the target area with cruor-toxins," Bogner added.

Hurley let out a whistle.

Bogner looked across the table. Packer had the look of a man who had been allowed to come up for air. Jaffe was still frowning.

Spitz was finally silent.

A smile began to play at the corner of Hurley's mouth. "Okay, so off the record, was it worth pigeon-holing Xo for thirty-six hours before you turned him over to the State Department?"

"The boys at the State Department still wouldn't have him if he hadn't swallowed those damn capsules," Packer allowed.

"There's still the other half of the equation, Chet," Bogner replied. "According to Milatov, Dung and Aprihnen appear to be pulling a double-cross on each other. Apparently, both sides went into this venture with an agreement to exchange technology. But Aprihnen caught one of Dung's technicians with his fingers in the design cookie jar. When he started home, the Russians sank one of their own ships to keep the data from falling into Chinese hands. Then the Russians discovered that this guy, Zhou, had somehow managed to contaminate all of their files. Milatov believes the project is at a standstill until the Russians somehow figure out a way to retrieve the data."

"What the hell are you telling us?" Spitz demanded.

"We're not certain of anything," Packer replied. "But the pieces are starting to make sense."

Langley looked up. "We think there may be a possibility that everything we need to know may be within our reach."

"I'd like to hear about it then," came the voice from the door. There was no mistaking the Texas drawl. It was the voice of David Colchin. He walked in and sat across from his old friend Bogner. "How, Toby? What makes you think we can get our hands on . . . ?"

"It's a long shot, Mr. president. But we've been studying the maps. The problem is ice, not depth. If what we believe is right, and the only working copy of those files is tucked away somewhere on that ship the Russians sank, we think we might be able to slip in there and retrieve it."

Colchin looked around the room. "Mr Jaffe, Mr. Packer, I'd like to hear what you think," he drawled.

"It's a long shot," Jaffe admitted.

"It's reasonable to assume," Packer began, "that this man, Zhou, was taking every precaution to see that the data was well protected. If that's the case, it may have survived. If it survived, the trick will be to find it."

"First we have to find the ship," Langley added.

"Estimate the degree of difficulty, Captain," Colchin said.

"Our Arctic climatologists estimate that we could have anywhere from ten to fifteen feet of ice to work under if the ship is located. That of course would be to our advantage. A three-man crew working out of the *Spats* could probably search her if it looks at all feasible."

Colchin nodded. "What you're describing sounds like more than just a long shot."

"Mr. President, when Milatov informed us that the Lyoto-Straf project appeared to be at a standstill, that made the cheese a little more binding. He thinks it's altogether possible that our Russian friends may be thinking that the quickest way to get back on schedule is to make an effort to recover the data too," Bogner said.

"You've double-checked everything?" Colchin asked. "What about backup files?"

"According to Milatov, duplication of files is one of Aprihnen's phobias," Packer explained.

Colchin's smile began to work the corners of his mouth. He stood up, started for the door, then paused just long enough to motion for Hurley and Bogner to follow.

Then the two men stood in the hall listening while the president voiced his concern. "Look, if push comes to shove, I can handle Secretary Goldberg, but this Xo thing could get blown all out of proportion. As it stands right now, the State Department has egg on its face and Goldberg doesn't like it. And I don't like it because it gives Chairman Dung something to bitch about—and I don't need that either."

Colchin turned to Hurley. "By three o'clock this afternoon I want Xo out of the country."

Hurley nodded.

"T.C., if for some reason you need another round with Xo, contact Hurley. I'll get it approved with the medics. Now, what's the timetable for getting a look at that downed ship?"

"Langley claims he can fly the *Spats* to the staging area as soon as we can determine if it's a go situation," Bogner answered.

Colchin's weathered face continued to work at the making of a small smile. "Keep me advised," he said.

LOG: NINE: TWO

Officers' Quarters: Belushya Guba 2211L
8 November

E-Alexa Chinko finished her shower, put on her robe, returned to her compartment, and removed the three partially filled glass bottles from the Styrofoam container she had taken from the *balneetsa*. It had taken her two days to collect exactly what she needed.

One bottle contained berry juice of the kind Gureko ordered each morning with his breakfast. The second contained the darker wine he often ordered with dinner, and the third was a pale wine, Gureko's standard nightcap.

When she had them carefully arranged on the small built-in surface that served as her makeup table, she reached into her briefcase and removed the tiny vial from the lining. The vial was half empty now. She had emptied more than half of its contents into a smaller vial and hidden it in a plastic ibuprofen container in Colonel Ulitsa's medicine chest. It was wedged in a thin piece of foil and covered with just enough tablets to make it look like an effort had been made to conceal the fact that the vial was hidden. If and when it would be necessary to find the evidence that would convict Ulitsa, she or anyone who conducted a thor-

235

ough search would be certain to find it.

She used a set of tweezers to pinch a small amount of the NAcN from the vial and drop it into the first bottle. She was pleased when after several minutes there was no change in color and the pungent odor of the berry juice concealed the bitter-almond odor of the cyanide crystals. To be certain that the dosage was enough to be lethal, she took another pinch of the cyanide and held it up to the light. Arbat had indicated that such an amount would be more than enough to kill the dog she had been complaining about in her apartment complex in Moscow. Of course there had never been a dog, and even if Arbat had been the wiser, he was no longer a problem.

She waited several minutes, sniffed the container of berry juice a second time, and was satisfied. If anything, E-Alexa decided, it was not the scent of almonds she detected; it was the faint residue of the disinfectant she had used to clean out the bottle.

Another pinch of cyanide was removed and this time mixed with the wine. Like the first bottle, there was no trace of either odor or discoloration. The heavy bouquet of the wine overpowered even the disinfectant. It too would be satisfactory.

Finally, she tried the lighter wine Gureko preferred before retiring. Even after several minutes, the almond aroma lingered. Excellent, she thought to herself, now even a fool could not miss the fact that the general had been poisoned. In all cases, she knew that the dose was lethal. Now it was simply a matter of implementing her scheme.

She checked the calendar. Tomorrow morning, the ninth day of November, the general was expected to accompany Admiral Dolin on the inspection of the fourth and final ballast tank on the Lyoto-Straf's initial superstructure. She, of course, was excused from such formalities while she continued to investigate how the Sino technicians had managed their contamination of the project's central data system.

Her plan was simple. In Gureko's absence, she would simply take the syringe she had stolen from the dispensary and inject the dust with a broken needle that would accommodate the microfine crystals through the cork and into the wine. The berry juice would be even simpler. It would be a case of simply unscrewing the cap and replacing it. If there was any chance at all that the cyanide would be discovered before Gureko consumed it, it would be traced, of course, to Ulitsa.

E-Alexa was pleased with herself. She gathered the bottles, went back to the toilet, and dumped the contents into the bowl. She flushed it, and then she rinsed the bottles with disinfectant a second time, placed the fragile containers in a small hand towel, and smashed them into tiny fragments with the handle of her semiautomatic. Now all that was left was to scatter a tiny portion of the glass fragments on the top shelf of Ultisa's wall locker and put the glass-embedded towel in his laundry. It was a crime that even the unskilled Belushya security force would be able to unravel.

When she returned to her quarters, E-Alexa took out her diary and made a brief notation. It was a quote from a line in a play by Chekhov. "My *lyoobof* endures, outlived only by my *lyoobavatsa*." Then she closed the diary without dating her entry.

E-Alexa Chinko knew that within a matter of hours, the number of names remaining on her list would be reduced by one—and then there would be only two left.

LOG: NINE: THREE

Keplin: Ukraine 2019L
8 November

Tomas Likli's small, spartan apartment was barely adequate even for a man mired in his sixty-sixth year. As he moved about the tight quarters in his tiny kitchen, preparing a cup of tea for his guest, his limp seemed even more pronounced.

He repeated the question. "You ask how well I know E-Alexa Chinko? I would say moderately well, Inspector. She grew up in this village. Her father was one of my dearest friends."

"For the record, you are speaking of Boris Illyavich Chinko, is that correct?" Nijinsky said.

"Yes," Likli confirmed.

"And Boris Chinko is deceased?"

Likli, without the aid of his cane, hobbled the few feet from his kitchen counter and handed Nijinsky a fragile porcelain cup and saucer. The brew was still steaming.

"I would offer you milk and honey for your tea, Inspector, but I have none. A man of my years can do without many things that I once perceived as necessities. But in answer to your question, yes, my friend died recently. It was the sickness. . . ."

Nijinsky dismissed the old man's apology with an understanding wave of his hand.

"I am told that Major Chinko returned home for her father's funeral. I was wondering, Comrade Likli, did you have the opportunity to speak to her at that time?"

Likli shook his graying head. "I attended the funeral and the wake, but E-Alexa and I were not close, Inspector. It was her father and I who were close. Of course I expressed my condolences, but we actually talked very little. She spent most of her time with Achina, her aunt; they have always been very close."

Nijinsky thumbed through the pages of his small notebook until he found the notation he was looking for. "That would be Achina Budenny who was killed by a car bomb in the Vskaya warehouse district."

Tomas Likli nodded. There was a tear in his eye. "A good woman," he confirmed.

Nijinsky closed the book and folded his hands around it. "You were aware of your friend Boris Chinko's disenchantment with the Party in his declining years, Comrade Likli?" he asked.

Tomas paused. "Keplin is a small village, Inspector. It is difficult to keep one's political philosophies a secret. Yes, I knew. Boris was an active Party member for years, but the passage of time brought disenchantment. In the end he was opposed to the mandates of President Aprihnen. He embraced and became a proponent of other views. Eventually, his philosophies and those of his daughter clashed. That is what caused the rift."

"Rift?" Nijinsky repeated.

"Differing political viewpoints often cause chasms, Inspector, even in the closest of families. I am convinced that E-Alexa loved her father and that her father in turn cherished E-Alexa, but that may be nothing more than the traditional perspective of an old man."

"Tell me about E-Alexa Chinko," Nijinsky said. "What kind of woman is she?"

Likli weighed his words. "A brilliant student in her younger days, passionate—and beautiful. Her femininity is and always has been a deceptive mask for her resolve."

Nijinsky took a sip of the tea, set the cup down, and waited. "This next question may seem a little strange, Comrade Likli, and I want you to weigh your thoughts before you answer."

Somehow Tomas knew what Nijinsky was referring to. If the inspector knew about Achina Budenny, he was further into the investigation than Tomas had first supposed. "I will try to help you in any way I can, Inspector."

"Do the names Ammosovich, Koslov, and Mikhail Arbat mean anything to you?"

Tomas did his best to convey the impression the names were cloudy. At the same time he knew Nijinsky would expect him to know the name of Koslov because of his Party position. "Koslov was the local Party director. And Arbat, was he not the man who assassinated him? You must forgive me, Inspector. Because of my infirmities, I can do little else besides read. The newspapers in Kiev covered the story of Comrade Koslov's death, but I do not remember details as well as a younger man."

"What about Ammosovich?"

Tomas realized now just how much Nijinsky knew. He repeated the name. "Was he not the district Party representative; a former member of the politburo? Again, perhaps I should know but . . ."

"Let me refresh your memory, comrade. Serafim Ammosovich was one of several men charged with malfeasance in the Chernobyl incident. But he was murdered before he could be brought to trial."

Tomas nodded. "Yes, I seem to recall that. He was poisoned, is that right?"

Nijinsky nodded. "Comrade Ammosovich, it was charged, was the man who first instructed Comrade Koslov to conceal the magnitude of the situation at the reactor site."

"Many people died as the result of that decision," Tomas confirmed. His voice was weak in its reflection.

Nijinsky took several measured sips of tea and waited to see if Tomas Likli would continue. The old man was shaking.

"I am told that you, a man by the name of Pytor Zimrin, and Achina Budenny, his sister, were very close, that you often discussed politics. Is that true?"

Tomas's voice was barely a whisper, "Yes."

"Did you ever discuss E-Alexa Chinko's plan to seek revenge on certain Party officials because of their delay in warning the people in this area of the magnitude of the disaster?" The manner in which he had articulated the question was as much of a surprise to Nijinsky as it was Tomas Likli. Until that very moment, Nijinsky had not realized that he had arrived at a point in his investigation where he was willing to articulate his suspicions.

Tomas stared back at him. "E-Alexa? Revenge?" he repeated. "I am afraid I do not understand what you are saying, Inspector."

Nijinsky set his cup down. "Forgive me, Comrade Likli, I believe you do. I believe you know exactly what I am talking about."

Tomas was too weary to continue the charade. He began to shake. Finally he managed to speak. "It is true that Boris and his daughter did not share the same political philosophy, but they shared a deep affection for each other. The death of her father and mother was devastating. She spoke to Achina Budenny of her plans. We made every effort to dissuade her. . . ."

Konstantin Nijinsky leaned back in his chair and sighed. "Is it over? Is that all?"

When Tomas Likli did not answer, Nijinsky concluded that there were still more names on E-Alexa Chinko's list.

LOG:
NINE: FOUR

The Kuchumov, *Kilo-Class SS 2323L*
8 November

Captain Viktor Stigga was in the cramped galley of the *Kuchumov*, savoring a bowl of cream ladled over the last of the fresh berries, when he heard the four bells. He sighed, put down the spoon, and picked up the intercom. "This is Stigga."

It was Zhdanov. "We are picking up something, Captain. I thought you might want to have a look at it."

Stigga worked his way through the narrow passage in the engine room, forward to the equally constricting control room, and checked his watch. The RUMR had been deployed shortly after 1800 hours. Stigga had noted the time in the log and marked the sector coordinates 2-b and 2-c. If Chopitski's charts and theories were correct, he did not really expect to uncover anything until they reached the 8-c sector. Chopitski, the senior operations officer on Belushya, had calculated that the *Drachev* would, based on the height of the swell, velocity, and intensity of wind, as well as ice floe factors at the time of Klyuzov's missile launch, be pitched bow first and that the wreckage would settle into the northern two sectors.

Stigga, on the other hand, believed that storm currents would have placed the downed vessel more to the south. Despite that, the decision was made to recon the 2-b and 2-c sectors on the initial pass.

Now Zhdanov had recorded the first significant anomaly, and the crew had watched in amazement as the RUMR circled the remains of a Junker Ju 87. The vertical stabilizer had been shot away and there was some damage to the wings, but otherwise the forest-green fuselage still appeared to be in excellent condition. The aircraft was upside down on its still-closed canopy, and the red circular insignia of a dog was still discernable on the cowling.

"It has probably been here fifty years," Stigga speculated. "They flew those Junkers throughout the Balkans."

"Shall I go in for a closer look, Captain?" Zhdanov asked. He was pleased with the RUMR's performance.

Stigga, aware that the *Kuchumov* had already lost too much time while it waited for the American submarine to lose interest in them, shook his head. "No, we do not have the time."

Zhdanov manipulated the RUMR away from its trophy, and in the process gave Stigga a panoramic view of an underwater world he had survived in while at the controls of a series of Spetsnaz miniature submarines. It was a world that, up until the cameras of the RUMR revealed it, he had never actually seen. Surrounding him was the evidence of man and the debris of time. Still, for the most part, the landscape at the bottom of the Stavka Straits was a pristine moonscape of sand and rock outcroppings. From time to time there was evidence of shifting plankton, but the halogen-bathed waters visible through the synthesized lens of the RUMR indicated a largely lifeless and eternally cold world.

With the skeleton of the Junker behind him, Stigga checked the ice pack report and the NEuB factor before instructing Zhdanov to bring the RUMR around and take pictures of the *Kuchumov*. "That should give me something to show my grandchildren," he joked, "every time they see me in port and wonder what I do for a living."

The two junior officers, Chopitski and Mrachkovski, were laughing. Mrachkovski combed his hair. "If Zhdanov is going to take pictures, I want to be ready," he said, preening.

Even Stigga laughed.

Zhdanov brought the RUMR around, focused the EmlG cameras on the submarine's dull gray hull with the carcass of the Junker barely visible in the background, and began taking pictures. The camera image appeared on one of the two AA4 monitors, and Stigga applauded.

"Entering 8-c sector, Captain," Mrachkovski announced.

Suddenly the atmosphere in the cramped control room was more businesslike.

"What are we picking up?" Stigga inquired.

Zhdanov pointed to the monitor. The RUMR was gliding no more than 20 feet from the broad flank of a plate-steel hull. The images were bright and clear.

"Determination?" Stigga ordered.

Zhdanov adjusted the lens and scanned. His fingers danced over the nine-button primary controls of the unmanned RUMR and the camera lens retreated, giving them a wider view of the target area.

Stigga turned to control. "Verify and record."

The control officer confirmed the command.

Stigga squinted at the somber images on the screen. "Let's take your little friend topside, Lieutenant Zhdanov. Back off a bit more and let's see what we have."

The RUMR began to drift away from the hull and Zhdanov elevated the bow camera. As the remote was ascending, Stigga ordered the Con-P&S video activated and the shields removed from the HMI lights on the upper conning tower.

Chopitski confirmed both commands. "Shields removed and video systems activated."

Light flooded the twisted metal deck of the *Drachev* and the icy image of the freighter's wreckage materialized on the small video screen.

"Log detail, Lieutenant Mrachkovski, we have confirmation." Stigga smiled. The Con-Pts camera was slowly scanning the fading CCP 4147 still inscribed on the quarter bow.

The control officer continued to study the detail. "It would appear, Captain," he assessed, "that the bow broke away following impact." The RUMR continued to scan the exterior from the ship's deck; the stern from midships aft was missing. "That would make the quarters fore of the rupture."

Stigga loaded and tamped his pipe. "How about it, Lieutenant Zhdanov, can you bring your nosy little friend around to the rear of the bow and put some light into the cavity?"

Zhdanov's fingers danced over the hand-held control panel again and the RUMR responded. It began to glide up and over the ruptured hull plates and protruding beams to reveal the agony of the Drachev's last minutes. Mrachkovski grumbled at the lack of detail as the lights probed up into a charred world of tarry blackness.

"I can make nothing out of it," Chopitski complained.

Stigga glanced down at the schematic of the *Drachev* spread over the chart table and studied the details. Then he pointed to the drawing and back at the monitor. "The galley should be about there. If that is the case, the crew quarters should be one deck up."

Zhdanov rotated the lights on the retractable landing boom until they were pointed into the twisted metal maze that constituted the crew quarters.

"Get me in tighter," Stigga ordered.

Zhdanov extended the manipulator arm with the remote video camera. The light was swallowed up in a spectrum of gray to black nothingness. "Definition, sir?"

Stigga shook his head. "No," he muttered.

Zhdanov maneuvered the extender out and back in again.

"No," Stigga repeated. He leaned back against the bulkhead, tapped out his pipe, and studied the images being transmitted by both the conning tower cameras and the RUMR. "What do you make of it, Comrade Mrachkovski?"

Mrachkovski adjusted his glasses, glancing from the camera images to the chart and back. "I think"—he hesitated—"that we have very little time before we begin to get some shifting in the ice pack. You will notice, sir, the hull of the *Drachev* is actually on the bottom. But as the depth of the trailing ice increases, there will be less and less room to maneuver and undertake any form of recovery operation. From the size of the ice bases, it is even possible that the hull could be moved."

"In this direction?" Stigga asked, pointing to the Sverdna Trench.

"It would depend on the actual shift of the floe, Captain. If it moves west and south with the prevailing winds, the pack will push the heavier ice in that direction and that could result in a sweeping motion of the bottom."

"How long before that happens?" Stigga repeated.

"We will have to consult our weather specialists, Captain. But I am certain they will tell you the same thing—that it all depends."

"What you are saying is that the shallow depth here is both our ally and enemy," Stigga muttered. "Is an icebreaker out of the question?"

"Several years ago the *Leonid Brezhnev* was able to journey some twenty-five hundred kilometers beyond the Northern Sea Route. I have heard she encountered and conquered ice four meters thick—and some of it was 'multiyear' ice."

"Ice pack report," Stigga barked.

Chopitski activated the absorption sonar and repeated the last five readings. "ASA activated and confirmed. Prior 4.1, 4.1, 4.0, 3.9, 3.7. Current 3.7, 3.6, 3.7, 3.2, 3.0."

"Thin ice any sector?" Stigga questioned.

"Sector 8-b and 8-c," Chopitski informed him.

"Range?"

"Three hundred meters."

Stigga turned to Zhdanov. "I ask this qustion out of ignorance, Lieutenant Zhdanov. You will forgive me, I am but a mere Spetsnez captain. But—how close would the mother ship have to get to the site of the *Drachev* in order to deploy the *Zotov* unit?"

"It is only an estimate, Captain," Zhdanov said, "but with three men, one pilot and two divers, perhaps within ten kilometers; because of the ice I would recommend that it be tethered."

"And if it were not tethered?" Stigga questioned.

"It would be very risky," Zhdanov replied.

"And if it were swept into the trench, Lieutenant, what then?"

"According to our charts, Captain, manned recovery would be impossible. The trench is fourteen hundred meters. Even the giant whales do not go that deep."

Stigga sighed. "A riddle within a riddle. A gamble within a gamble. What we are concluding, comrades, is that if we are to attempt a recovery, it must be attempted immediately. The ice grows thicker by the day."

"What will you report to Admiral Dolin?" Zhdanov asked.

Stigga thought for a moment. "I will tell him what we know to be a certainty. The *Drachev* is accessible. I will also advise him that I believe launching the

Zotov from one of our larger icebreakers appears to be the operational approach with the highest probability of success." Then he turned to Mrachkovski and Chopitski. "Secure all. We are returning to Belushya."

LOG: TEN: ONE

*The Barton Plaza Dining Room: Washington 0735L
9 November*

Langley was smiling as he crossed the dining room.

"Colchin made the call, I assume?" Packer also grinned.

"The system works," Langley quipped. "A C-130 Hercules left Norfolk at 0600 hours this morning. She is scheduled to pick up the *Spats* at Queens Point at 1100 hours and deposit her at Berisvag, Norway, where the Norwegian icebreaker *Hiltava* is already being rigged with piggyback grids. I got a call from Lattimere Spitz at five-thirty this morning confirming every last detail."

"What about the crew?" Bogner asked.

"They gave us the best," Langley confirmed. "Cody Filchak of the Queens Point oceanographic Institute is your pilot. He's the one that put the *Spats* through her shakedown cruise. He knows this little gem of ours stem to stern and inside and out."

"How did we get him?"

"Standby reserve officer. I asked for him. He didn't have any choice. Besides, we need him to do some tweaking while she's en route to Berisvag. The other diver will be an old academy buddy of mine, Mitch

Cameron. Everyone calls him Geronimo. Simply the best retrieval man we've got. Six hundred meters in the Jim suit, twice."

"You said 'other diver.' "

Langley chuckled. "You're riding shotgun." He reached inside his coat pocket, produced an envelope, and laid it on the table. He was smiling. "Signed, sealed, and delivered. Don't bother to read 'em, Toby; Spitz faxed me a copy. They're signed by Admiral Hampton."

Bogner looked at the envelope. "Any last-minute instructions?"

Langley shook his head.

"When do we leave?"

"A staff car is waiting. We leave as soon as we can get out to Bolling. With any luck at all, we'll arrive in Berisvag before the *Spats*."

Bogner leaned back in his chair. It was his turn to smile. "I don't suppose you thought to bring along any of the familarization and performance manuals on your new toy, did you?"

Langley was ready. He opened his briefcase and shoved it toward Bogner. There were three manuals, all at least two inches thick. Each was marked *confidential*.

"Next thing you'll tell me you already know these," Bogner quipped.

"I better, T.C. I wrote the damn things."

LOG: TEN: TWO

Officers' Quarters: Belushya Guba 1641L
9 November

Lieutenant General Kirill Gureko waited in the corridor while the corporal struggled to position the bulky package in the corner of his quarters. The dark-haired young man straightened up with an air of expectation, an expectation of being summarily and curtly dismissed. Instead, Gureko inquired about his place of birth.

"Leningrad, General," the corporal answered.

Gureko's face softened. "Leningrad," he repeated. "My father is buried in Piskaryovskoye Cemetery."

The young man was not quite certain how he was expected to respond. He had only seen the general from a distance, and the general had a reputation for being abrupt.

"He was a Hero of the People," Gureko reflected. "Lenin himself decorated him."

There was another round of uncomfortable silence before Gureko dismissed the corporal with a casual wave of his hand. The soldier came to attention, saluted, crossed the room, and left, closing the door behind him.

Alone, Gureko stared at the package for a moment,

then seated himself at the small writing table in the corner of his spartan quarters. After the 36-hour stint in the communications center waiting for Stigga's transmission from the overdue *Kuchumov*, he was weary. He glanced in the mirror at the heavily lined face and the abiotic, colorless eyes. Finally, he permitted himself a deep sigh. At 65 years of age, an age long past the official age for retirement of officers, he wondered if his comrades knew how little energy was left to invest in the mission.

He poked at the pockets of sagging skin that had collected under his eyes, and undid the top button on his tunic collar.

As he sat there, he reflected on his personal interrogation of the two remaining members of the Sino technical delegation. He had been with the one called Cho Pin for nearly two hours and learned nothing. Cho was an iceberg. He had infuriated Gureko with his bland, empty, noncomprehending manner. And, as Gureko had anticipated he would, he had denied any involvement with Zhou and his former colleague's efforts to steal and sabotage the Lyoto-Straf plans.

The interrogation of Po Lia had been slightly more enlightening; through Po Lia he'd learned that Zhou was a last-minute replacement for one of Po Lia's fellow professors who had originally been assigned to the project. It proved nothing, of course, but Po Lia made no effort to cloud the issue, and readily admitted that no reason was given for the sudden switch in colleagues. That was an aspect of the investigation that Gureko intended to pursue.

With little forethought he picked up the intercom phone and directed a call to Colonel Chinko. When she did not answer, he tried her junior officer, Lieutenant Siddrov.

Siddrov picked up the phone on the first ring. He recognized Gureko's voice. "Yes, General," he snapped.

"I want an update on Colonel Chinko's investigation," he snarled.

Siddrov hesitated. "I must apologize, General. Colonel Chinko is not available and to the best of my knowledge, she has not yet documented her progress."

"I have been unable to reach her. My question is, has there been *any* progress?"

Lieutenant Ivan Siddrov, a product of a field promotion in Afghanistan and not a graduate of one of the numerous Soviet military academies as were most of the other officers at the site, disliked the idea of operating outside of the chain of command. Now he was being pressed for information by another officer; even if Gureko was a general, Siddrov was uncomfortable with the breach of protocol. Colonel Chinko was his immediate superior, and if she had not relayed the information Gureko was seeking, there was probably a reason. "We continue to investigate, General," he finally said. He realized even when he said it that it sounded feeble.

Gureko grunted. "Could it be, Lieutenant, that Colonel Chinko does not know how to proceed with an investigation of this nature? Because if that is the case, I can bring in an investigator from the Institute."

Siddrov knew better than to respond. He suspected that Gureko was baiting him. He had seen the old Bolshevik in action when he replaced Colonel Ulitsa. "I believe we are making progress, Comrade General," he finally said.

"Good," Gureko replied. "Inform Colonel Chinko that I inquired about her progress." He did not wait for Siddrov's response.

After Gureko hung up, he began to undress. He took off the thick leather waist belt, unbuttoned his tunic, and threw it over the back of the chair. Then he went to the cabinet, removed several audio tapes from his collection of music, and reached for the bottle of red wine on the top shelf. Selecting a cassette that included Rimsky-Korsakov's "Russian Easter Overture," he lit a cigarette and took off his boots. From a small compartmentalized area over the writing surface of his desk, he removed an ornate leather journal and picked up a pen. He entered the date at the top of the page.

9 November

Then he took a sip of the wine and began to write.

A moment later, he coughed—and thinking he could alleviate the small spasm in his throat, he consumed the rest of the wine in three or four gulps.

Within a matter of seconds the cyanide had etched acid furrows into his throat. Gureko tried to scream out; he rocked forward, trying to gulp in air. Finally he fell from the chair to his knees and began to cough. At first only traces of pinkish mucus appeared—but finally a torrent of thick, black blood erupted and spewed from his mouth onto the worn, faded expanse of carpet in front of him.

Gureko's stomach and lungs felt like they were on fire and his heart was pounding. He could feel the trip-hammer-like throbbing in his chest and he could no longer breathe. Clawing at his throat, he made repeated futile attempts at screaming for help.

Finally a shudder raced through his body, and a violent chainlike series of spasms resulted in a paroxysm of involuntary but vain efforts to hold on to life.

And then his heart stopped.

For the few microseconds that he lay suspended between life and death, Kirill Gureko knew not why it had happened—but he knew what was happening. All of the efforts to hold on to life ceased, and he felt himself being sucked down hard against the floor.

There was the sensation of departure and the cessation of pain. His vision became blurry and there was both hopelessness and futility.

After 65 years of life, 41 of them in the service of the military, Lieutenant General Kirill Gureko was dying. The battlefield of his final struggle was the sanctity of his own quarters.

LOG:
TEN: THREE

Belushya Guba 0309L
10 November

Even though E-Alexa had planned the entire episode down to the most minute detail, even to anticipating the moment when she would receive word that something had happened, she was not prepared for what she saw when she entered Gureko's room.

Dolin stood sullen and silent in the corner of the room, apparently too stunned to acknowledge her entrance. Both Lieutenant Siddrov and Doctor Konyev, the Belushya medical officer, were kneeling beside Gureko's body. A large pool of congealed blood covered most of the area under the general's head, and his white undershirt and uniform pants were stained an ugly brown color. The full, fleshy face was twisted sideways and had turned an ugly purple where the blood had settled in the soft tissue.

E-Alexa sucked in her breath and held it for several seconds until the unexpected wave of nausea subsided. She had seen men die before, even relished the site of Serafim Ammosovich gasping for his final breath, but somehow this was different. Perhaps it was because she had actually known Gureko.

E-Alexa turned to Dolin. "When did this happen?" she finally managed.

Dolin was too numb to speak coherently. He tried several times before the words came out in an understandable fashion. "He—he was with me—waiting for radio contact to be established with the *Kuchumov*. We had instructed Captain Stigga to make no efforts at radio contact until he surfaced from under the ice pack. We did not want our transmissions to be monitored. . . ."

Dolin continued to mutter, and E-Alexa turned to Siddrov. "What happened, Lieutenant? Who found him?"

Siddrov's hands were shaking. His voice was strangled. "One—one of the security guards, a-a Corporal Vestna, awakened me at 0230. He was making the 0200 security check and tried General Gureko's door; it was not locked and the lights were still on. He attempted to alert the general and when he received no response, he entered. What you see is what he saw. To the best of my knowledge, no one has touched anything except Doctor Konyev. He rolled the general's body over. . . ."

E-Alexa looked around the room. "But I don't understand what . . ."

"Doctor Konyev believes he was poisoned," Siddrov said. "He said that the moment he walked into the room and saw the general's body . . ."

"Is he certain?"

"No, he will have to do an autopsy, but he indicated he had seen this type of violent internal reaction before."

E-Alexa turned back to Dolin. She knew that the admiral would expect her to oversee the investigation. He was still unnerved. "Has Doctor Konyev estimated the time of death yet?" She had already rehearsed what she would say. Other than her reaction to the scene when she first entered the room, the scenario was now beginning to unfold exactly the way she had envisioned it.

Dolin again tried to marshal his senses. "I—I must return to the dock area," he muttered. He checked his watch. "I—I must be there when Captain Stigga files his report."

"Very well, Admiral," E-Alexa said, steeling her voice. "I will take over here. I will report back to you the minute I have something."

Dolin delayed for several moments before deciding to leave. When he left the room he was still looking back at Gureko's body in disbelief.

E-Alexa knelt down beside the doctor. "Lieutenant Siddrov indicates you believe General Gureko was poisoned," she said.

Konyev, a small stocky man with an unlikely crop of reddish brown hair and shaggy eyebrows, looked at the new logistics officer. Even though they had not been introduced, he knew who she was. "It looks like poison," he assured her. "I was the medical officer at the Muravev Naval Academy when a young ensign poisoned his roommate. When I entered the room earlier, I encountered that same pungent odor. Death has many odors; often it is an indication how the individual died."

"Poison has an odor?" E-Alexa repeated. Even in the early planning stages she had decided to pretend that she knew nothing of poisons.

"Strychnine, cyanide, arsenic, each has a characteristic odor. Often you can tell by breathing close to the area around the victim's mouth, but in General Gureko's case I cannot tell for certain. He has been dead for several hours and there was excessive bleeding."

"An autopsy will reveal what kind of poison was used?" E-Alexa asked.

"Yes, but unfortunately, knowing the type of poison will not do us much good, Colonel. All of them are stored in our chemical laboratory and many people have access to them."

"Could it have been suicide?" she asked.

Konyev studied the scene for a moment. "In my estimation, it was not suicide, Colonel. A man who commits suicide prepares for his death. I see no preparations here. I see only the body of a man whose last few moments of life were filled with excruciating pain. No, I do not believe General Gureko took his own life."

E-Alexa turned to Siddrov, and as she did, she looked around the room again. "Well, Lieutenant, we know one thing."

Siddrov waited.

E-Alexa bent over and picked up the wineglass. "If General Gureko was indeed poisoned, then we can start our investigation right here—with this glass. Take it to the chemical section and see if anyone there can run some tests to determine what kind of poison we are dealing with."

"I can run those tests for you, Colonel," Konyev volunteered. "I will correlate the results of the tests with my findings after I conduct the autopsy. Between the two, we should have a fairly good idea of what to look for when you begin your investigation."

Konyev was playing right into her hands. E-Alexa was careful not to smile.

"How soon can I expect word, Doctor?"

"Within a matter of hours," Konyev said. "Where will you be?"

"We will both be in our respective quarters waiting for Captain Stigga's briefing. Lieutenant Siddrov and I will not begin our investigation until we know what to look for. Will you make arrangements to have General Gureko's body moved?"

"Of course," Konyev said.

LOG:
TEN: FOUR

Briefing Room: Belushya Guba 0739L
9 November

Captain Viktor Stigga stood in the middle of the darkened briefing room with a pointer in his hand waiting
for the discussion to end. Behind him, the site of the
downed *Drachev* glared from the lighted image on the
projection screen.

Mrachkovski, Chopitski, and Zhdanov from the
Kuchumov were seated on one side of the table, while
Dolin and his staff sat on the other. Altogether there
were 11 people in the room including E-Alexa.

"Proceed, Captain," Dolin ordered. The admiral's
voice was still subdued, but he had regained his
composure.

Stigga cleared his throat and turned back to the
display. "The *Drachev* is located here. The position is a
sector eight fix, two hundred meters south and southwest as indicated here in 8-c-aa and c-ab. Average
depth in this part of the strait is eighty-seven feet."

He turned off the overhead projector and activated
the video.

"As you can see here from tapes made through the
rotating con camera, there are periodic indications of
illumination through the thin ice. You will also note

that it darkens as the ice thickness increases to more than three to four meters. And as the floe thickens, we begin to encounter vertical buildup here and here." He pointed to protuberences of the underside of ice formations. "At this point there was also evidence of significant compacting."

Mrachkovski, working the controls, fast-forwarded the video to the site of the wreckage and Stigga continued.

"It would appear that the beam of the *Drachev* was snapped at the point of missile impact. The bow forward is here, situated on this small underwater plateau. The remainder of the hull is approximately two hundred meters south of the bow section. When we discovered this, I instructed Lieutenant Zhdanov to maneuver the RUMR into such a position that you will be able to see into the bow section from the perspective of the rupture in the hull."

Mrachkovski fast-forwarded the tape a second time until they were looking into the cavernous opening at the location of the explosion.

"From this camera angle you will be able to observe certain finite details. That object to your right is the remains of the crew ladder leading down to the galley. There is evidence of excessive fire damage in this area, probably as the result of brief but extremely intense fires ignited by the impact of the missile. Lieutenant Mrachkovski believes that because of the location of the boilers aft, none of the damage you are viewing is the result of residual fire. In other words, this is all impact damage. In this dark section here, you can see the corridor leading to the officers' quarters. We have compared this to a schematic of the ship and we believe this is the passageway that leads to the cabin where Mr. Zhou was assigned prior to departure."

"Is it accessible, Captain?" Dolin demanded.

"If our only problem was getting to Mr. Zhou's room, perhaps it would be feasible to use underwater torches to cut away the debris," Stigga speculated. "The problem, however, as Lieutenant Zhdanov, who has twice been on missions aboard the *Zotov*, informs me, is that we cannot get the craft close enough to use the two extensible manipulators—which of course would operate the acetylene torches that would enable us to cut through the debris."

Dolin stood up, walked to the monitor, and studied the image. "So what is your recommendation, Captain?"

Stigga turned off the video and turned back to the projector display. "There is considerable compacting of ice in this sector, Admiral. If we go in with the *Zotov*, we may not have enough room to perform this operation. Most assuredly, we cannot depend on piggybacking the unit in on one of our submarines. There is too much danger of losing—"

"I will determine what we are willing and unwilling to risk, Captain Stigga," Dolin reminded him.

"But of course, Admiral," Stigga said. "I was only going to say that if it is imperative that we do attempt to recover something from the *Drachev*, there is another approach that may be more feasible."

"Continue, Captain."

"One of our larger icebreakers could perhaps be moved to this position here, in sector 8-a, near the cove west of Kickana Island. Then the *Zotov* could be lowered from the mother ship, through the thin ice, and personnel could be dispatched from the *Zotov*, recover the objective, and return to the *Zotov* in the allotted exposure time."

"Which is how long, Captain?"

Stigga looked at Zhdanov, and the young lieutenant pursed his lips. "No more than sixty minutes at a time, Admiral; at the very most, seventy-five minutes maximum exposure per egress."

"Can it be done?" Dolin asked, looking around the room.

Stigga hesitated before he nodded. "If the mission is simply to go in and recover some object, the answer is yes. If the divers have to torch their way through any of this debris you see clogging this area where we believe Zhou was at the time *Drachev* went down, it could require two, perhaps more dives."

"I am curious, Captain Stigga, what makes you think Zhou was in his quarters at the time the *Drachev* went down." The statement was made by a direct, almost gravelly voice coming from the far end of the table.

E-Alexa tried to identify the voice in the darkness. But it was only after Dolin acknowledged Captain Brerkutev, the site salvage officer, that she knew. She had never met the man, but Dolin had already indicated that if a recovery effort was attempted, Brerkutev would be the man.

For a moment, Stigga faltered. "My assumption is only based on what I know about human nature, Captain Brerkutev. It has been my experience that men who are not at their stations during a crisis aboard ship often return to their bunks to pray or whatever. Mr. Zhou, in all probability, was sufficiently unnerved by the storm to seek the only shelter he had. And that would have been his quarters."

There was a silence, and Dolin looked around the table again. In the muted light he found it difficult to determine what his staff was thinking. "Captain Stigga," Dolin said, "I must repeat my question: based on what you and your men saw, do you believe it is possible to retrieve the electronic data files from the *Drachev*?"

Stigga knew that it would be inappropriate to vacillate. "Yes, sir," he said.

"And the best way of doing that?" Dolin pushed.

"To go in with an icebreaker, position the *Zotov* in the recovery area, and make a series of short-interval dives until we recover the data."

Dolin looked across the table at Fleet Admiral

Nikolayev. "Your opinion, Comrade Admiral?"

Nikolayev got up from the table and walked to the situation display. He looked at Stigga and then the map. Dolin could tell he was apprehensive. "If we had a ship the size of the *Brezhnev*, I could give you an unqualified yes, Admiral. If at all possible, I would recommend that we have the *Brezhnev* deployed here from her permanent station in Uroska."

"No," Dolin thundered. "We do not have the luxury of time. My question, Admiral Nikolayev, is can one of your ships make it to the sector on the chart that Captain Stigga has indicated?"

E-Alexa could read the uncertainty in Nikolayev's expression. "Yes," he finally agreed. His response lacked conviction.

Dolin glanced at Stigga and Perinchek. "How much preparation time do you need?"

Perinchek was busy calculating the installation time of the deployment crane on the stern of the mother ship. The two officers conferred briefly and Stigga nodded. "Thirty-six hours, Comrade Admiral."

Dolin stood up. "Very well, we are working to an estimated departure time of 2000 hours on 10 November. Admiral Nikolayev, you will assure me that the crew of the *Pitki* will be readied, and Captain Brerkutev, you will likewise give me your assurance that the *Zotov* and your divers will be prepared."

"We will be ready, Admiral," Brerkutev replied.

LOG:
TEN: FIVE

.

Fredrikstad Pier: Bersivag 1451L
10 November

From the temporary steel-grid catwalk that had been erected around the *Spats,* Peter Langley launched into the second session of the premission briefing. From where they were standing, Bogner was able to get an overall perspective of the DSSV.

"Not counting the manipulators, which can be extended eighty-eight inches, she's thirty-one feet, seven inches from the fore viewports to the horizontal stabilizer on the elevated aft wing. Notice that the gimbaled main thruster is actually aft of those horizontal controls. Prevents turbulence," Langley added.

Bogner studied the configuration and pointed to the larger of the two topside plates midships.

"Explosion hatch cover; one to the dive chamber, the other to the control pod," Langley answered. "Both are sealed from the outside after the crew enters the personnel sphere. Tight and right, T.C., but it can be dispatched from the crew capsule in the event of an emergency. There's a small D ring rigged to an explosion capsule under the guard. Pressure has to be equalized before the release mechanism will trigger, though."

"The UW access hatch is underneath?"

Langley nodded. "Exactly. The pilot hovers the *Spats* over the salvage site, and accesses the diver right on the target. We had both Arctic and Antarctic missions in mind when we designed her. It cuts down on exposure time for the divers. The insulation factor in those suits drops off rapidly after sixty minutes. In most cases, the pressure-compensating factor is the greater of the two considerations. In this case, however, we aren't operating at depths that deep."

"How long before the diver turns into a popsicle?"

"If you're outside of this little gem longer than sixty minutes, we've got problems."

Bogner grinned. "I like that 'we' attitude."

Langley turned back to the *Spats*. "There are four ballast spheres in all, two fore, one aft, and another under the control pod. Each ballast tank has its own pump. She has swiveling side thrusters port and starboard—the same with the sonar arrangement, except we've augmented them with units on the top and the bottom as well as the sides."

The two men descended the personnel ladder to study the bow configuration, and Langley began to point out bow detail. "Two, count 'em, Toby, two bow manipulators, eighty-eight inches and sixty-six inches extended. The E2T picked up a forty-seven-pound weight in the tests, and the E1T disassembled a small black box that required the removal of four screws in the rear panel. Nifty, huh?"

Bogner looked up at the lights.

"Two HMI lights on each boom, seven hundred power. Both booms are retractable. Each boom extends seven feet from the central fuselage so you can direct a twenty-two-foot light bank. We can flood an area the size of a ranch house with these babies. With four cameras, IMAX in the personnel pod, a three-D video on the bow undercarriage, a top three-sixty video rotator scanner, and an aux infrared, we've got it all covered."

"Depth?"

"Are you ready for this—five hundred meters. We can go deeper but the exterior personnel can't and we're not ready to commit to a total robot mission. That comes somewhere down the pike."

Langley stepped off of the catwalk and lowered himself through the personnel hatch. Bogner followed. They descended into the personnel sphere and Bogner let out a whistle.

"It's all here. A totally integrated control system. Either pilot can take command. There are four panels, A panel upper left, 1 and 2, all lighting, interior and exterior, actuators and depressors; plus your cameras. The B panel is your support systems: oxygen, mix, ESS systems gauges, that sort of thing. The C panel is the nerve center, all controls and safety: flap control, aileron control, trim tabs fore and aft. The D panel is the toys: your manipulators, the Roby 2 unit and external systems other than power. Seat A handles panels A and C. Seat B monitors B and D. All crossover and duplicated—and the computer can handle everything if you've got your hands full with something else. During the shakedown, Geronimo handled the whole ship from the A seat and recovered that forty-seven-pound package I was talking about—in a three-knot current."

Bogner crawled through the access door from the personnel sphere into the dive chamber and began to look around. In all, there were six capsule control valves on the bulkhead near the hatch, all diver controlled: flood, or ballast, evacuate, pressure up and pressure down, and two "pause and hold" switches. Langley informed him that they were merely emergency backups because all operations were handled from the control pod's D panel.

"If, for some reason, the diver is incapacitated, the pilot is still in control."

The dive gear, at least the part of it that Bogner

could see, was stored in a series of compartments behind clear-view acrylic panels in the walls of the flood pod next to the intercom speakers. There were four compartments in all. Each was sealed.

"What about the communications and LS systems outside of the pod?"

"Don't sweat it; computerized and in the helmet, T.C., no valves or gauges to check, all cabin-regulated, all miniaturized. The pilot monitors everything. We've done everything we can to make the personnel outside of the pod free as a damn fish. But just in case you do have some difficulty and the system isn't responding, there are four auxiliary LSS ports on the exterior. All you have to do is plug in. The LSS analyzer on the computer takes over and corrects the mixture. If that doesn't solve the problem, Cody turns control over to the APU and comes out after you. DPs can work with or without a tether."

"Vision aid?" Bogner asked.

"Night vision—right in the helmet, along with the IFO display in the visor. The only time you'll need the halogens is for up close, less than six feet."

Bogner continued to study the controls and configuration of the dive chamber until they heard footsteps coming down the access ladder.

"Heard you guys were down here," the voice was saying even before Bogner could get a look at him.

"T.C. Bogner, meet the only man on the face of this earth who knows more about the *Spats* than I do, Commander Cody Filchak."

Bogner's first impression was that Cody Filchak looked as though he could have played any kind of role except that of the man who piloted the navy's newest and most sophisticated DSSV. He was average height, average weight, and average build. He smiled at Bogner with a bland face that was partially hidden by a pair of wire-rimmed glasses and a neatly trimmed mustache and goatee. Only the eyes, blue-black and surprisingly large, gave any indication of intensity.

"Heard a lot about you, Commander," Filchak said. "Happy to have you aboard."

"Peter here has been singing your praises too," Bogner admitted.

"Enough of the mutual-admiration bullshit." Langley grinned. "I was just giving Toby here an overview of the *Spats*."

Filchak leaned against the bulkhead, crossed his arms, and looked at Langley. "Some interesting news topside, Peter; from the sound of things, we won't be operating in total darkness. Apparently they've got a lead for us."

"How so?" Langley asked.

Filchak looked at his watch and hunched his shoulders. "Don't know, but it looks as though we're going to find out at 1530."

LOG:
ELEVEN: ONE

Officers' Quarters: Belushya Guba 1743L
10 November

E-Alexa Chinko planned her moves cautiously. She had instructed the security officer to initiate a systematic search of quarters starting with the highest-ranking officers and proceeding down until it encompassed even the site's enlisted personnel. Like everything else in her plan, she made certain that someone was always with her; any discovery would thus be verified.

Now, in Colonel Boris Ulitsa's quarters, she made certain she was assisted in her search by Lieutenant Siddrov. Siddrov had posted a gawky young corporal at each door while they conducted their investigation. The corporal had repeatedly expressed his awe at what he termed "the splendid quarters enjoyed by the Belushya officers."

Now, while Siddrov systematically went through the drawers in Ulitsa's desk, E-Alexa searched the medicine cabinet in the colonel's toilet area.

"Nothing," Siddrov grunted, still kneeling in front of the desk. He continued to run his hands along the underside of the center drawer.

E-Alexa stepped from the toilet area and looked at

the closet. "Be certain to check the clothing area. Look in the pockets and hems of all of the uniforms. I will go through the linen."

Siddrov was still kneeling on one knee. "Colonel Ulitsa hardly seems like the type of man who would . . ."

"Nor was Admiral Dolin," E-Alexa reminded him. "But we searched his quarters. At this point, we must assume that no one is above suspicion. I intend to search every corner of this facility, Lieutenant Siddrov, including your quarters as well."

"Of course, Colonel. I was merely observing that Ulitsa does not seem like the kind of man who . . ." As Siddrov spoke, he ran his hand along the storage shelf of Ulitsa's built-in wall locker. Suddenly his hand recoiled. "Shit," he exclaimed.

E-Alexa paused. "What is it?"

Siddrov was looking at his hand. There were several small fragments of glass embedded in the palm of his hand and fingers. E-Alexa could see a trickle of blood.

"Nothing," he said. "Colonel Ulitsa must have broken something on this shelf and didn't get it cleaned up."

E-Alexa frowned. As far as she was concerned, this was simply the first in a series of critical discoveries that would implicate Ulitsa in Gureko's death—and she had staged it well. So far, it was working perfectly.

"Let me have a look at it," she said. She took Siddrov's hand and moved him over to the desk under the lamp. "Tiny splinters of glass," she said. "Where did you find it?"

Siddrov tilted his head toward the wall closet. "On the shelf."

E-Alexa went to the unit, picked up one of Ulitsa's handkerchiefs, wrapped it around her hand, and wiped it along the shelf. Like Siddrov's hand, it was embedded with splinters of glass. Then she carefully folded the piece of fabric and laid it on the desk.

Siddrov was shaking his hand. "There is a burning sensation," he complained.

E-Alexa paused. "Perhaps you should go to the clinic and have Doctor Konyev clean out the cuts."

Siddrov looked at his hand, then at his superior officer. "But the search . . ." he protested.

E-Alexa insisted. "Have the matter tended to," she ordered. "It will only take a few minutes."

When Siddrov left, E-Alexa picked up the handkerchief containing the fragments of glass from the shelf, put it in her uniform coat pocket, and waited several minutes. Then she followed. The timing was critical; with any luck at all, she would arrive just as Konyev was making his diagnosis.

She entered the clinic on cue. Konyev looked up. "Your culprit is cyanide, Colonel. The lieutenant has several pieces of glass embedded in his hand that are coated with cyanide."

"Cyanide," E-Alexa repeated.

"The same thing that killed General Gureko," Konyev announced. "Fortunately, however, Lieutenant Siddrov has only a few superficial ruptures of the skin; discomfort, but no long-term damage."

"Are you certain it is cyanide, Doctor?"

Konyev nodded his head. "The odor is unmistakable." He reached over, picked up a small vial similar to the ones E-Alexa had taken from the medical requisition area, uncorked it, and held it out for E-Alexa's inspection. "Cyanide's signature is the aroma of almonds. Quite evident, wouldn't you say?"

"The lieutenant will be all right?" E-Alexa inquired.

"As I indicated, he will experience some discomfort. It is not unlike a second-degree burn," Konyev explained.

Slowly, E-Alexa extracted the handkerchief containing the fragments of glass from Ulitsa's shelf. "I—

I wiped off the shelf where the lieutenant found the splinters. Is it possible to determine if this is where . . ."

Konyev carefully took the piece of fabric, placed it under the microscope, and examined it. When he looked up, his face was expressionless. "One and the same, Colonel; even the particles of glass are the same. This is cyanide—and cyanide killed General Gureko. Where did you find it?"

"It wasn't me that found it," E-Alexa stressed. "Lieutenant Siddrov was inspecting Colonel Ulitsa's clothing locker as part of our investigation." She made certain that Konyev knew it was Siddrov who'd found the broken pieces of glass.

"And where is Colonel Ulitsa now?"

"He was assigned to the records administration when it was discovered that the computer records had been contaminated," E-Alexa said. "The file checks are being conducted in E-Section. He is working with Perinchek and Rachmansov."

"Is he aware of your investigation?" Konyev asked.

"Of course," E-Alexa said. "He is not aware, however, that we are searching all personnel quarters."

Konyev looked at the microscope and shook his head. "I would not want to be in Colonel Ulitsa's shoes," he said with a sigh.

LOG: ELEVEN: TWO

Ministry of Security: Moscow 1818L
10 November

Inspector Konstantin Nijinsky had been waiting for over an hour. While he waited, he gazed at an elaborately framed photograph of a young ballerina over the minister's secretary's desk. Unfortunately, the secretary herself looked nothing like the woman with the lithe young body in the picture.

Nijinsky lit a cigarette, took two drags, and put it out. The woman was glaring at him.

Efforts at even casual conversation with the woman had been fruitless. She contented herself with thumbing idly through the pages of one of the current news magazines. There was a picture of an American basketball player on the cover. The man was soaring through the air, high above the rim and the other players.

While he waited, Nijinsky considered how he would weigh his words. Major General Vyacheslav Bekrenev's reputation made the encounter all the more difficult. Not only was he, along with Georgi Kusinien, reputed to be among the architects of Aprihnen's rise to power; it was also said that he was the man who shaped both the president's internal and external security policies.

Finally the door opened and Nijinsky looked up.

Bekrenev was scowling, but his manner was affable. "Sorry to keep you waiting, Inspector. I have been on the telephone."

Bekrenev was a broad, squat man who wore all of the medals of a former Soviet hero. He had a round-shaped head and a ruddy complexion, and walked with a limp. After studying Nijinsky for a moment, he motioned the inspector inside to a chair, took out a cigarette, and sat down behind his desk.

"So, Inspector, I should tell you, it is not often that I am graced with a visit by our local constabulary. Is there something I can do to help you?"

Nijinsky knew the footing was treacherous. He hesitated, even though his lines were rehearsed. "I," he began, "have been investigating a series of events."

"Events, Inspector? What do you mean by events?" It wasn't at all what Nijinsky had expected; Bekrenev's manner was smooth—smooth enough that it caught him off guard. Most of the old-guard Bolsheviks who had moved back into power with Aprihnen were less polished.

"If you prefer—murders," Nijinsky said. He was surprised at how easily the word had slipped out.

"Murders?" Bekrenev repeated. "Murder is a serious charge, Inspector. Whose murder? And why should I be interested? Am I correct to say that murder is something that is handled by your department?"

Nijinsky hesitated. "Quite so, comrade; murder investigations are indeed under the purview of my department. But I fear this one leads my department into areas where the lines of authority are somewhat blurred."

Bekrenev leaned back in his chair and exhaled a cloud of smoke in Nijinsky's direction. "You will, of course, explain?"

Nijinsky reached into his pocket, took out a piece of paper, and unfolded it. "Do the names Serafim Ammosovich, Evgeni Koslov, and Mikhail Arbat mean anything to you, General Bekrenev?"

The man though for a moment, then shook his head. "No," he replied. "Why?"

"Those are the names of the victims," Nijinsky replied. "I was hoping you might know one or more of them."

"Did I not read somewhere that there are upwards of eight or nine murders a day in Moscow, Inspector? I know none of them. So I am curious as to why you should ask me about these three."

Konstantin Nijinsky braced himself. He looked straight at Bekrenev to maintain eye contact. "These men," Nijinsky said evenly, "were all somehow involved with the decision to delay notifying the people of the magnitude and ramifications of the reactor failure at Chernobyl."

"Let me understand what you are saying, Inspector," Bekrenev insisted. "Are you saying that one man is killing officials because he believes that they needlessly delayed evacuation orders?"

"Not exactly, General. Let me clarify: first, I did not say it was a man. And second, I wish to further clarify that this individual did not necessarily pull the trigger in each case. However, I have a feeling that the individual in question engineered all three deaths, and in one case may have actually committed the crime."

Bekrenev's face softened. "Did anyone ever tell you, Inspector, that you are a master of the art of vague accusation?"

"Let me be more specific, General. Our investigation shows that Mr. Arbat killed Comrade Koslov; and I myself killed Mr. Arbat in a shootout at the airport. Comrade Ammosovich's murder investigation, because of its apparent tie-in to the aforementioned, has only recently been reopened."

Bekrenev put out his cigarette and lit another. "My first question, Inspector, is, why are you telling me all of this? The second, and perhaps more obvious one, is, why is any of this a concern to me? From what you indicate, your investigation appears to be proceeding."

"Suppose I told you that I believe the person responsible for these crimes is one of your people, Comrade General."

"I would doubt your veracity, Inspector," Bekrenev said. He appeared to be slightly amused at the thought.

"Are you familiar with an officer by the name of Colonel E-Alexa Chinko, General?"

Bekrenev nodded, "Yes, I am." He was no longer amused. His face sobered.

Nijinsky broke eye contact. He looked down at the hat cradled in his lap. It was still damp from the snow.

Bekrenev cleared his throat. "I feel certain you realize these are serious allegations, Inspector Nijinsky. Are you aware that Colonel Chinko is not even in Moscow? She is stationed at a remote joint military-research installation located . . ."

"In Belushya Guba," Nijinsky finished.

Bekrenev continued to study the disheveled little man who had made the accusation against one of his officers. Then he stood up, walked to the door, dismissed his secretary for the evening, and returned to his desk. He reached into his desk drawer and withdrew a small voice recorder. "Do you mind, Inspector? I do not want to confuse any of the details of your report."

Nijinsky braced himself. "Perhaps we should start with the case of Serafim Ammosovich. . . ."

LOG: ELEVEN: THREE

Admiral Dolin's Office: Belushya Guba 2022L
10 November

"Colonel Ulitsa?" Dolin repeated. "Are you certain?"

E-Alexa crossed her legs and straightened the hem of her skirt. "Ulitsa," she repeated. "Lieutenant Siddrov discovered the remnants of the broken cyanide vial, Admiral." Again, she had worded her response with the utmost care. Without saying it, she had implied that she was not even with Siddrov at the time of the discovery.

Dolin shifted in his chair. "And Doctor Konyev has verified that it was poison that killed General Gureko?"

"Actually, it was cyanide," she confirmed. "Our investigation found traces of the broken vial in a soiled washcloth taken from Colonel Ulitsa's laundry hamper. Doctor Konyev also examined that. He informed me that those fragments indicated that at least some effort had been made to destroy the fact that the fragments were from a cyanide vial."

Dolin sighed. "This is difficult to accept, Colonel. I have known Colonel Ulitsa for a long time."

E-Alexa waited.

Finally Dolin asked the question she had been waiting for. "Your conclusion, Colonel?"

It was all E-Alexa could do to keep from smiling. "It would appear that Colonel Ulitsa put the cyanide in General Gureko's drink as some sort of retaliation. It would also appear that Colonel Ulitsa used a syringe with a broken needle to inject the cyanide through the cork." She held the syringe out for Dolin's inspection. "In addition, I took the bottle of berry juice that I found in the general's quarters to Doctor Konyev. He was able to determine that it was also contaminated with the same poison. Here is a copy of his report for your files."

Dolin turned around in his chair and looked at his telephone. His shoulders sagged and his voice was halting. He sat there for several minutes repeating the names of Gureko and Ulitsa. "Now comes the difficult part," he said. "Now I must inform General Bekrenev."

E-Alexa walked around the desk and put her hand over the telephone. It was a bold gesture. "What about the contaminated data, Admiral? Are you prepared to answer Bekrenev's inquiries?"

Dolin hesitated. "The survey is nearly complete," he admitted. "Perinchek informs me that he is virtually certain that all of the classified data has been contaminated. It may well be that our efforts to complete the project on schedule now rely totally on the success of Comrade Brerkutev's retrieval mission."

E-Alexa decided that the time had come. "I have been thinking, Comrade Admiral. Is there not wisdom in delaying your call until Lieutenant Siddrov and I have had an opportunity to interrogate Colonel Ulitsa?"

Dolin waited for her to elaborate.

"Does it not seem curious to you that the Sino technician was able to complete his mission without Colonel Ulitsa's detection? This is followed of course by the question, how did the Sino contingent gain access to restricted areas without the knowledge of Colonel Ulitsa? And one final question. Is it possible that Colonel Ulitsa knew of all of this and was, in fact, part of it?"

When E-Alexa finished, she knew she had selected the right moment. Dolin was obviously unnerved by the series of questions. He looked at her in a way he had not looked at her before.

His voice faltered. "You must understand, Colonel, I am the one who selected Colonel Ulitsa for this assignment. He was chosen from a number of candidates. He was chief of security at Mandaska."

"Did it occur to you that it is curious that a man would apply for a post at Belushya when he was stationed at a base situated near the Black Sea?" E-Alexa's question was designed to seal Ulitsa's fate.

Dolin was wavering. What had first seemed impossible to him now seemed not only plausible, but perhaps even likely.

"If the retrieval mission is not successful, Admiral, Ulitsa's involvement will make the entire situation . . ."

"More palatable?" Dolin finished the sentence for her and began to smile.

"Perhaps not more palatable, Admiral, but in view of the fact that it was an act of internal espionage, our superiors may view the situation in a slightly different manner. If we report the fact that our former chief security officer is guilty of treason and that the contaminated data was part of his scheme, it may not appear that we have been remiss in our vigilance."

Dolin's smile intensified. He knew exactly what his new logistics officer was recommending. He turned away from the phone. "Do you believe that Colonel Ulitsa knew of the Sino activity, Colonel Chinko?" His conversion was almost complete.

"What does it matter what I think, Admiral? If the colonel confesses to such activity, who am I to refute it?"

Dolin sat back in his chair. He was pleased. "When Ambassador Kusinien advised me he was sending you to Belushya to fill the vacant chief of logistics position, I was opposed. But now, I see why the ambassador was so enchanted. You are very good, Colonel."

E-Alexa smiled. "Then I have your permission to focus my investigation on Colonel Ulitsa, review his files, take him into custody, and interrogate him about both his role in the untimely death of General Gureko as well as the Sino contamination of our computer files?"

"There must be no holes in your case," Dolin cautioned.

"I understand, Admiral."

"By all means, Colonel Chinko. Proceed."

E-Alexa was exhilarated. She turned and started toward the door, only to be stopped by Dolin.

"How long do you think it will take you to *determine* the degree of Colonel Ulitsa's involvement, Colonel Chinko?"

"In order to answer that, Admiral Dolin, I must first ask you a question. How long will it take us to determine if the retrieval mission is a success?"

Dolin thought for a moment. "I see what you mean," he said with a laugh. "But in answer to your question, not less than seventy-two, no more than ninety-six hours . . . but of course those are estimates."

"Then that is how long I have to obtain what you need. Is that not correct, Admiral?"

Dolin nodded. As he did, he said, "I have noticed that you wear a pin on the underside of your uniform lapel, Colonel Chinko. May I inquire what it represents?"

E-Alexa turned up the lapel to display the figure of the gold mantis mounted on the white-ice diamond island. "It is from an admirer," she informed him.

"I am certain you have many of those, Colonel," Dolin said.

LOG:
ELEVEN: FOUR

Briefing Room, Fredrikstad Pier: Bersivag 1530L
10 November

It was precisely 30 minutes after the hour when Colonel Gustav Berggen, the Bersivag IO, stepped to the front of the room and began the briefing. "I will dispense with the formalities; any necessary introductions can be handled later. The purpose of this meeting is to make you aware of recent information obtained from two different NATO sources."

Bogner looked around the table. He recognized Langley and Filchak, and from the name emblazoned on the pocket patch of the dark-haired, hawk-faced officer who had arrived late, he could identify the third member of the *Spats* crew, Mitchell Cameron. He was a choleric-looking man who took a seat at the end of the table by himself.

Berggen dimmed the lights, turned on the overhead projector, and pointed to a map of the Stavka Straits. "Please note this coordinate at the tip of Morkarov. This is NATO sector DD. Our Russian friends designate this sector as 8-a and 8-b and 8-c on their charts. The transparent red overlay will indicate the precise area. At the request of the Bersivag-based United States NI officer, we conducted a search of all data and

transmissions from all ships in the DD sector from
the period 0000MST 9/25 thru 0000MST 9/27. During
that period there was an intense low-pressure area
over the sector and, I'm told, for those of you who
weren't here, quite a blow. The storm held traffic
to a minimum. Nevertheless, we were able to verify
four separate Russian vessels in addition to our
own traffic. Also, we were able to verify that our
Russian friends did report the loss of an apparently
Murmansk-bound freighter, the *Drachev*. Based on ice
pack reports and normal Russian shipping practices,
it is safe to say the *Drachev* more than likely sailed
from Belushya Guba the evening of September 23.
Our assumption is that she would not have sailed
any later than that because the intensity of the
developing storm would have been apparent and
they would have held her in port. Our information
also indicates that one of their icebreakers, a Moskova-
class designated the *Urhan*, was accompanying the
Drachev. They became separated during the storm.
The *Urhan* arrived at port—the *Drachev* did not. Any
questions?"

"Were we able to determine what the ship was carrying?" Langley asked.

Berggen glanced down at his sheaf of papers.
"According to the report they were carrying instruments for recalibration."

"Seems we've heard that one before," someone said
from the other side of the table.

"What else?" another asked.

"If that storm was that intense, she was bobbing
around like a cork out there," a voice observed.

Berggen tapped the table with his pointer. "Because
of the storm and the ice pack, the *Drachev* may have
altered course. However, I have indicated the normal
Russian course from Belushya to Murmansk with this
line. I believe it is reasonably safe to assume she did
not deviate far from this course."

"No radio transmissions or distress calls?" Langley asked.

"None," Berggen confirmed, "but that is not unusual for our Russian friends."

"That's a helluva lot of water to cover," Filchak whispered to Bogner. "This could take us a while."

Berggen overheard the comment. "Perhaps not. For whatever reason, Belushya has dispatched at least one search party that we know of."

Bogner sat up. "Search party? When?"

Berggen checked his notes again. "On the morning of November 6, the *Portland*, SSN-688, encountered a Kilo-class Russian submarine in the designated sector, 8-a, 8-b, 8-c, or DD as we know it. Captain Word reported that at first he thought the Kilo was on a routine training mission, but the more he observed her, the more he was convinced she was up to something. The *Portland* also reported that the configuration of the Kilo was non-standard-profile. Which he later indicated his computers identified as some sort of deployable DSSV or DSRV."

"Bingo," Langley blurted out. "Milatov was giving us the straight skinny after all."

"Question: Did that Kilo know we were monitoring her?" Bogner asked.

Berggen looked at Langley. "I would only be speculating," he admitted. "The *Portland* did incorporate her gas envelope to confuse the Kilo's sonar and detection devices."

Langley leaned back in his chair. "If I was the captain of that Kilo, I'd be working along one of two lines of logic. Either I was under such time pressure to get something accomplished that I had to take the risk—or I was really on a deployed submersible training mission and really didn't give a damn whether the Americans watched or not."

Berggen listened, waited for comment, then continued his briefing. "According to Captain Word of the *Portland*, the Kilo deployed the submersible on three separate occasions. All of these deployments were remote, two were short-interlude missions, which to me indicate they did not find what they were looking for. The third deployment was protracted, lasting a little over five hours. To me, a mission of that duration indicates they either found what they were looking for or were close enough to be encouraged."

"The question is," Bogner said, "did they *get* what they were looking for? Or did they just locate it and then head for home to get the right equipment?"

Filchak studied the chart. "Okay, if I understand everything you've shown us, Captain Berggen, that X marks the spot of the bogie. But X is out there a piece and it looks like we've got both open water and ice pack to contend with. How do we get there?"

Berggen laid down his pointer, walked to the head of the table, bent over, placed his hands on the surface, and lowered his voice. "Subterfuge, Captain, subterfuge. We are playing in their waters this time. They are the ones who have the sensors salted along the main shipping routes. They will know our every move— as we will know theirs. If we piggyback the *Spats* in on one of our NATO nuclear submarines, the Russians will monitor our every move. This does not even take into consideration the fact that our climatologists estimate that we cannot get you within the operational range of the *Spats* because of the west-to-east compaction of the ice floe."

"We're going in with an icebreaker?" Filchak asked.

"Nor are we going in with an icebreaker, Commander. We have quite an ace up our clever Norwegian sleeve. For the last fifteen years we have deployed the WMO weather ship *Akershus* at the edge of the ice floe, always for Arctic observation purposes. While we speak, the *Akershus* is receiving a few minor deck alterations that will enable us to transport the *Spats* to within a few miles of the operation site as well.

Obviously, to maintain some element of secrecy, your DSSV will be concealed by a series of false crates and other supply containers. To our Russian friends' satellites, I feel quite certain everything will look perfectly normal. Then, while you and your crew are going about your business, the crew and complement of weather specialists aboard the *Akershus* will go about their jobs. Our Russian friends will be receiving hourly observation reports from the *Akershus* just as they have in the past."

Langley smiled and looked at Bogner and Filchak. "What do you think?"

Bogner smiled. "I like it," he admitted.

"When do we sail?" Filchak inquired.

"We will be ready when you are," Berggen announced.

LOG:
ELEVEN: FIVE

Taganrog: Moscow 2241L
10 November

General Vyacheslav Bekrenev's Volga rocketed through the low hills outside Taganrog and through the security gates at Kusinien's *dacha* with only a token slowing at the security gate. When the patrol guard saw the two stars on the front of the general's staff car he was waved through with minimum ceremony.

The car came to a halt in the main drive at the front entrance. Bekrenev instructed his driver to wait, and was intercepted at the door by another guard. The militiaman waved him through, and Bekrenev headed for Kusinien's study.

As the ambassador stood up to greet him, Bekrenev took off his hat and coat, laid them over an ornate antique table, and went to the fireplace to warm his hands.

"I have seldom seen you display such urgency," Kusinien observed.

"There is a problem," Bekrenev said. "The matter dictates urgency."

Georgi Kusinien took the time to pour a glass of brandy for his longtime comrade. "Here," he said, "this will take the chill out of the night air."

Bekrenev sipped twice, then bolted the remainder. He handed back it to Kusinien for a refill.

Kusinien filled it, set it on the mantel of the fireplace, took a seat, and looked at the clock on the other side of the room. "It must be urgent. Are you not normally at the officers' club informing your fellow officers of your heroic deeds in one battle or another at this time of night?"

Bekrenev did not laugh. "How well do you know Colonel E-Alexa Chinko?"

"Why?" Kusinien asked. Georgi Kusinien could be as diplomatic or as abrupt as the occasion required. The art of subtlety was lost on someone like Bekrenev when he was agitated.

Bekrenev took another sip of brandy and studied the reflection of the flames in his glass. He repeated the question. "Just exactly how well do you know this Colonel Chinko?"

Kusinien smiled. "Are you implying . . ."

"I am implying nothing, Georgi," Bekrenev snarled. "I am simply trying to determine how well you know this officer that you recommended we send to Belushya to take over the vacant position of logistics officer."

"Are you saying Gureko is complaining because we sent him a beautiful woman to fill a vacancy on his staff?"

"Gureko is not complaining, comrade. In fact, your longtime political nemesis, General Kirill Gureko, is not doing anything. He is dead."

Kusinien sat upright. He sounded as though the breath had been sucked out of him. "Gureko? Dead?"

"More precisely—he was murdered."

"Admiral Dolin informed you of this?"

"Of course not, I was informed by my contact. Dolin has said nothing."

Kusinien's faded eyes blinked behind the shaggy mask of his eyebrows. His palsied hand reached for his pipe. "Exactly what does Colonel Chinko have to do with this?"

Bekrenev turned so that his back was to the fire. "Late this afternoon, an inspector from the Moscow homicide department came to see me. He chose his words very carefully, but he finally admitted that he believes Colonel Chinko is directly or indirectly involved in the murder of three men."

If Kusinien was surprised, he was able to conceal it. "Did he tell you who these three men are?"

"Two of them were minor Party officials, one was a known hooligan. I checked the files on all three of them."

Kusinien lit his pipe. "Did this inspector tell you what he believed Colonel Chinko's motive was for her involvement?"

Bekrenev was in no mood for Kusinien's measured line of questioning. "He did," he snapped.

"And?"

"It seems that all three men were somehow involved in the decision to delay information on the magnitude of the reactor failure at Chernobyl."

"Were you aware that Colonel Chinko lost both of her parents to the radiation poisoning that we still insist on telling the world never existed? The day she came to see you to receive her appointment to Belushya, she was returning from Keplin where she'd buried her father."

"Gorbachev's blunder, not ours," Bekrenev reminded his comrade.

"Or a Party blunder?" Kusinien asked. "What did you tell the inspector?"

"I thanked him for his information and told him I would look into the matter."

"And now you have word of Gureko's death—and you are wondering."

"I am told he was poisoned. The police inspector indicated one of the three men in the case he has been investigating was poisoned." He paused. Finally he said, "You were the one who recommended Colonel Chinko. Gureko is your longtime political adversary . . . do you understand why I have questions?"

Kusinien put down his pipe. "Come, come, General, she was but one of several candidates. You reviewed all of the dossiers; you concurred with my recommendation. Colonel Chinko has an excellent record. She is well qualified—and she is a former GRU illegal. That fact alone more than qualifies her for consideration, does it not?"

Bekrenev blinked. "There is a good chance that I would have done nothing with the information had it not been for this subsequent news about General Gureko."

"Gureko is not a loss," Kusinien scoffed. "At times he was a blundering, posturing fool. The time is long since past when there is a place for the prototypical Bolshevik in the higher echelons of the Party."

"It is not the Party I am concerned about," Bekrenev said. "It is the Lyoto-Straf program that concerns me. Gureko was vital to its success."

"The development of the Lyoto-Straf will continue with or without Comrade Gureko."

"This woman, this E-Alexa Chinko, she is more to you than an officer for whom you have great respect?" Bekrenev probed.

Kusinien got up from his chair and walked to the fireplace. He stood for several moments watching the flames. "If I were a younger man, old comrade, I would be angry at your insinuation. However, at my age, I am flattered." He inhaled the smoke drifting up from the fireplace until it filled his lungs, and for a fleeting second, Bekrenev thought he saw his old comrade draw strength from the gesture.

"This woman," Bekrenev pushed, "she is capable of committing the crimes the inspector accuses her of?"

"Most assuredly."

"Then we must do something about her, comrade. It is possible that President Aprihnen would view this matter as jeopardizing the entire Belushya project. We cannot stand by and do nothing."

"What would you have me do, General?"

"Order her back to Moscow?"

Bekrenev heard his aging comrade utter the strange guttural sound that for Kusinien indicated amusement. "You forget, Comrade General, that it was you who promoted Colonel Chinko to her post. I have no authority in this matter. If you wish her removed from her post, you must be the one who orders her back to Moscow."

"And then what?" the general demanded.

"Then we will know if Colonel Chinko has more names on her list."

"Does she know of your role in advising Chairman Gorbachev at that time?"

Kusinien sighed. "At the time I was a mere under-secretary in the ministry of information reporting to Gureko. How could I have influenced anyone?"

Bekrenev walked slowly over to the table where the bottle of brandy was located and filled his glass again. Then he held it up and examined the contents of the glass through the flames.

"Just for the sake of discussion, comrade," he said, "let us suppose we wanted to and were able to convince Colonel Chinko that Moshe Aprihnen was ultimately the one who made the decision to withhold the Chernobyl information. What then? Do you think she would attempt to murder the President of the Commonwealth as well?"

Kusinien smiled. "All of this, of course, is just for the sake of discussion," he said.

"By the same token, if we were to ultimately attempt to arrange such a twist of fate, would it not be wise to remove her from the Belushya situation before she becomes too closely associated with it?"

"There is wisdom in such a move," Kusinien admitted.

"Then it is settled. Tomorrow I will issue orders to have Colonel Chinko returned to Moscow."

Georgi Kusinien sighed. "As you see fit," he acknowledged. He saw no reason to tell his longtime comrade that the move suited his purpose for more reasons than one.

LOG:
ELEVEN: SIX

Officers' Quarters: Belushya Guba 2307L
10 November

When Boris Ulitsa returned to his quarters at a few minutes past eleven that evening, he was exhausted. Working with a team that consisted of Lieutenant Perinchek and two computer technicians, he had reviewed over 17 hours of retained files. If nothing else, he was now convinced that all of the files were contaminated. He opened the door and turned on the lights. Colonel Chinko was sitting on the edge of his bunk.

"Colonel Chinko," he exclaimed.

"It has been a very long day, has it not, Colonel Ulitsa?" Her voice was uncharacteristically cold and stripped of emotion.

Ulitsa took off his tie and unbuttoned his uniform top. He threw both of them on the bunk next to E-Alexa. "I suppose there is some logical reason why I find myself returning from my shift to find you sitting in my room, Colonel."

"There is," E-Alexa confirmed.

Ulitsa opened his wall locker and removed a bottle of vodka. He splashed two or perhaps more ounces into a tumbler and gave his fellow officer a mock

294

toast. "Here's to ice," he said. "Now, since we will both readily admit that there is no love lost between us, Colonel Chinko, I am certain you will understand why I don't offer you a drink." He bolted the drink, refilled his glass, turned the chair around, straddled it, and sat down. "So—to what do I attribute finding Belushya's chief logistics officer in my room at this time of night?"

E-Alexa continued to smile. "You are aware, of course, that I am conducting an investigation into the murder of General Gureko."

Ulitsa threw his head back and laughed. "Murder, is it? I thought it was suicide. Which is it going to be, Colonel? Whatever you want it to be?"

E-Alexa did not laugh.

"This place is rampant with rumors. Some say he killed himself, others say he was murdered. Which is it? Or aren't you allowed to discuss these matters with an officer who has fallen out of favor?"

"I will tell you anything you want to know," E-Alexa said. "Ask me."

"Okay then, who killed him?" Ulitsa laughed. "Anyone I know? I'd like to send them something for their trouble."

"General Gureko was poisoned."

Ulitsa thought for a minute. "Poisoned? Really? Poison sounds rather melodramatic. That's the kind of thing they used to do back in the days of the czars." He looked around the room and laughed. "Rather ironic, isn't it. Here we are, surrounded by some of the most sophisticated high-tech killing machines in the world, and the killer resorts to something as outdated as poison. Do you mind telling me what kind of poison?"

"Cyanide. Someone put it in his beverage. General Gureko consumed it—and it was all over. Death was instantaneous."

Ulitsa let out a whistle, drained his glass, and filled it again. "Just think, Colonel, if it hadn't been for our thieving little Chinese friend slipping out of here with those documents, I would still be the logistics officer and it would be me conducting this investigation instead of you."

E-Alexa waited.

"So," he said, "do you have a prime suspect?"

"I do indeed, Colonel. You see, *you* are my prime suspect."

Ulitsa stared back at her and set his glass on the desk. He looked at E-Alexa as though he was unable to comprehend what she said. Finally he unleashed a nervous laugh. It was much too strained to be effective. "Did I hear you correctly, Colonel?"

E-Alexa still hadn't moved. She was staring at him, and finally he looked away. "Admiral Dolin ordered me to conduct a search of all personnel quarters earlier today. Do you know what we found in your room, Colonel?"

Ulitsa continued to stare at her in disbelief. He had been caught off guard.

"We found the remains of a broken vial that formerly contained cyanide," she informed him. "Then we found broken pieces of glass in a small cloth that you obviously used when you tried to destroy the evidence. Doctor Konyev was most cooperative. He confirmed that the glass came from small cyanide vials that were stolen from the supply area in the clinic."

By now the smile had completely faded from Ulitsa's handsome face. He sat motionless for several minutes, and then he shook his head. "Preposterous," he said emphatically. "I had nothing to do with General Gureko's death."

"It would appear that you had the motive," E-Alexa said. Her voice was cold.

"Why, because he relieved me of my duty station? On the contrary, he did me a favor. All it means is that I can rotate back to the mainland in a few weeks. Just in case you hadn't noticed, my dear Colonel Chinko,

Belushya Guba is not exactly a choice duty station."

"Is that why you killed him?" E-Alexa said.

Ulitsa ran his fingers through his hair. For the first time, E-Alexa thought she was beginning to see a crack in the veneer of self-assurance. "I repeat, Colonel, I did not kill him."

"How do you explain the cyanide?"

"I don't know anything about the damn cyanide."

Suddenly E-Alexa's hand emerged from the folds of her uniform holding a 9mm semiautomatic. Ulitsa's eyes narrowed and he stared back at her.

"What the hell is going on here?" he stammered.

E-Alexa said nothing.

"Look—I told you, Colonel Chinko, I had nothing to do with killing General Gureko." By now his voice had lost all semblance of composure. It even cracked when he tried to say the general's name.

E-Alexa allowed her pleasure to surface. The thought of Ulitsa cowering, pleading for her understanding, amused her. Through it all she remained seated, shoulders squared. It was proving to be even easier than she had anticipated.

Ulitsa's eyes narrowed; the vodka was taking effect. He reached for the bottle again, but his hand faltered.

"What—what the hell is—is happening," he slurred.

"You have been sufficiently drugged to destroy your coordination, Colonel."

Ulitsa tried to stand up, discovered that he was too unsteady, and staggered toward the bed. As he did, E-Alexa stood up. He pitched forward on the bunk and fell facedown, sprawled across it. "Why? Dru— drugged?" he muttered.

E-Alexa rolled the former Belushya security officer over on his back. Then she reached into her pocket, removed the gas-chambered silencer, and attached it to the barrel of the semiautomatic. Methodically she wiped away the fingerprints with a small damp cloth, took Ulitsa's right hand, curled his index finger through the trigger guard, and bent his arm up and in until the nose of the barrel was pressed against his right temple. Then she gripped his hand and laid her finger over his—until she could squeeze the trigger.

There was a muffled thudding sound followed by instant carnage. Ulitsa's head jerked violently to the left, and the side of his head exploded, splattering the pale green cinder-block wall of his room with bone and tissue.

There was a ringing sound in her ear . . . and then there was a terrible and empty silence.

Finally E-Alexa straightened up and looked around the room.

It had all been so very, very simple. She walked over, picked up the half-empty bottle of vodka, and dumped the remains in the toilet. Then she filled it with a small amount of water, tipped it over, and allowed the water to trickle under Ulitsa's bunk. She placed the glass on its side beside it. She placed the unsigned requisition slip for the semiautomatic on the desk with his key to the stores room and other personal effects.

It was done. She surveyed the room one last time, left, tripped the safety lock from the inside, and closed the door. From there, she went back to her own room, three doors down the corridor.

As she undressed and prepared for her shower, she complimented herself. The alternate periods of remorse and elation kept her awake well into the small hours of the morning.

LOG:
ELEVEN: SEVEN

Ministry of Records: Moscow 2331L
10 November

Konstantin Nijinsky removed his hat and coat, laid them over the back of an adjacent chair, and slumped down at the records table with the file folder in front of him. The files clerk, a pale little man wearing a coat sweater to ward off the chill of the night chamber, stood anxiously by.

"Will you need anything else, Inspector?"

Nijinsky looked up from the file and shook his head. "This should be adequate," he said, looking at the stack of files.

"We seldom have anyone in here this time of night," the man went on. "About the only people who use the record files at night are police officials and researchers."

Nijinsky nodded, and the clerk waited as though he expected Nijinsky to say something. When there was no response, the little man cleared his throat.

"I have some files to put away, Inspector. I will be in the next room. If you need anything, just ring the bell on my desk."

Nijinsky nodded again and opened the file. The first document was a summary of the file. All routine

military orders were arranged by successive dates.
He rummaged through the papers in the back of
the folder until he found the one marked *lyekarstva
zapeesnaya*, opened the medical file, and sifted through
the papers.

There was the usual assortment of documents: shot
records, physicals, base clearances signed by the installation medical officer, and a sealed envelope. It was
dated 24 March 1987. Nijinsky opened it and began
to read:

> I have advised Major Potemkin Lieutenant
> Chinko's tests are now complete.
>
> While Lieutenant Chinko, during my observa-
> tions, exhibited infrequent periods of depression,
> she likewise demonstrated the ability to, even
> during periods of high stress, make clear and
> rational decisions. At no time during the tests did
> the subject exhibit evidence of hallucination and
> improper emotional response such as charged by
> her commander. To date, neither I nor Doctor
> Gokol, who assisted me in these tests, has viewed
> evidence of the more overt manifestations indi-
> cated by Major Potemkin. We have, however,
> cataloged occasional inappropriate responses
> to authority and external influences. Lieutenant
> Chinko's perception of moral right and wrong,
> according to our tests, is clear and logical.
>
> It is our recommendation that she be returned
> to active duty and Major Potemkin's charges dis-
> missed, further disregarded, and files purged.
>
>   Dr. Anatoly Fomin
>   24 March 1987

Nijinsky completed his notes and turned to the front
of the file and the access record. He recognized none of
the names until he came to the fourth one on the list. He

scribbled the name and date in his notebook: Natalia Taksis, secretary, Ambassador Georgi Kusinien, 11 February 1989. Then he closed the file.

Then he pushed himself away from the table, stood up, and walked to the desk of the files clerk. He rang the small bell and waited for the little man to emerge from the records vault.

"I note that the last access date was almost six years ago. Is there any other way of telling how long it has been since anyone reviewed this file?" Nijinsky inquired.

The clerk brightened, nodded, and went to the computer. He called up the access file and frowned as he evaluated it. "The date is valid, 11 February 1989," he confirmed. "Actually, Inspector, by comparison, the file you are reviewing has been quite active. We have many files here that have never been opened."

THREE

LOG:
TWELVE: ONE

The Akershus: *Barents Sea 0707L*
12 November

Bogner finally managed to get some sleep.

Langley had finally run out of training drills.

The 4,000-ton, 366-foot-long *Akershus* "weather station" had departed Berisvag at 2200 hours the evening of November 11. For the first 12 hours following their departure, Commanders Bogner and Cody Filchak and Lieutenant Mitch Cameron were continuously hammered with Langley's mission detail.

There had been three dry launchings of the *Spats* and three "wet" runs, during which Cameron and Bogner tested the re-engineered AUS gear for Arctic operations.

The *Spats,* because of its size, had been positioned on the aft deck adjacent to the starboard 20-ton crane that would hoist the craft into the water and recover her when the mission was complete. The hybrid DSRV was concealed by a series of cartons and tarpaulins designed to look like equipment and supplies to be used by the *Akershus* during her winter deployment.

To assuage Langley's fears and to show that the *Akershus* was mobile enough even in floe ice, the ship's captain had demonstrated the starboard and port side thrusters that enabled the ship to maneuver in a tight 360-degree circle, thereby assuring a quick recovery. Berggen had likewise demonstrated the Wartsila bubbling system, a continuous curtain of compressed air bubbles released from beneath the waterline of the *Akershus*'s hull which impeded the compacting of the adjacent ice.

"We learned that little trick from the Russians," Berggen quipped.

It was against that backdrop of fitful sleep that Bogner first heard the knock at his cabin door. He squinted at the clock, realized the time, and sat up.

"Door's open," he muttered.

It was Filchak and Cameron. "Geronimo and I figured we'd better see that you were out of the sack," Filchak said with a grin. "Langley's got us scheduled for an 0730 briefing."

Bogner grunted, threw his legs over the edge of the bed, and pulled on a pair of trousers, a sweatshirt with the words *U.S. Naval Academy* emblazoned across the chest, and the pair of battered black Reeboks his daughter, Kim, had given him several Christmases earlier.

"Where is this briefing?"

"C level, by the crew infirmary in the superstructure," Cameron said.

Minutes later, Filchak led the *Spats* crew through the maze of interior corridors to the C level, one level below the aft wheelhouse, and into the cabin area. Langley was waiting.

Before the three men could be seated, Langley laid a series of photographs on the table. "There you are, gentlemen, compliments of NATSCOM," he muttered. "Look familiar?"

Bogner studied the series of photographs and looked up. "We're not alone."

Langley passed the photographs around the table. "T.C. is right. That first photo was taken yesterday afternoon at 1500 Zulu. The second was taken on the 2100 orbit at 2141Z last night."

"Did we get a reading on her?" Filchak asked.

"Photo 3, Cody, it's as clear as anything you get from Olan Mills. According to NI, you're looking at pictures of the *Pitki*. It's a pre-Yermak-class icebreaker. Just in case you're not impressed, we're being told that it's still one of the most powerful icebreakers they've got—and it's been making steady progress through the ice pack."

"Progress to where?" Cameron asked.

"According to our computer models, the *Pitki* is headed right where Berggen put the big red X on the bogie site."

Bogner leaned forward. "Did NI give us any kind of ETA on the *Pitki?*"

"Best guess, by 0500 hours tomorrow morning."

"What's the ETA at our launch site?" Bogner asked.

"A couple of hours later. The weather boys estimate she can make better time because of the east-to-west drift of the ice pack causing more compacting in our waters. They're estimating that we will be encountering ice pack one to one and one half meters thick by early tomorrow morning."

"Can we handle it, Peter?"

Langley smiled. It was rare for Cameron to say anything at a briefing session, and he had already asked two questions. Langley considered it a good sign. "Berggen thinks we can," he began. "But there is some question in his mind about how close he can get us to the bogie site before we have to launch the *Spats*."

Filchak gingerly rubbed his hand across his three-day growth of beard and studied the photos. "Well, it's safe to assume they are not going in there without some way of getting down to that ship. What do you think? Do you suppose they're bringing in one of their Mir submersibles?"

"NI claims they have a hybrid version of the Mir I

and II called the *Zotov*. Our pictures indicate there is some kind of anomaly on the stern of the *Pitki*, but we can't identify it. So our assumption at this point is that they're going diving too."

"That's good news and bad news," Bogner muttered. "If they're coming back with a submersible, that means they haven't recovered the files yet. That's the good news. The bad news is that we're going to have company while we're trying to poke around down there."

"That's the way I read it, T.C. Between the Russians and the ice, it may actually get a little dicey down there." Langley looked at each of the three men before he continued. "This may help," he said. He laid what appeared to be a chart on the table and unrolled it.

"Gentlemen, what you are looking at is an engineering drawing of the *Kinta*. The *Kinta* is the sister ship of the *Drachev*. The two hulls are identical and were laid simultaneously at the Yevtushenko Shipyards in 1964. It is also true that both ships underwent extensive modifications in 1981, so there is some dissimilarity. But focus on the similarities; notice the fore superstructure with the radar mast, the INMARSAT antenna, and the radio gear—the same on both ships. During the retrofit the *Kinta* was given a satellite navigation system. To the best of our knowledge, the *Drachev* wasn't. Everything else is pretty much the same; the primary layout hasn't been changed; the engine room, the engine control room, boilers, generators are all aft."

Bogner and Filchak studied the drawing from one side of the table, Cameron from the other.

"We were able to get these drawings from the British Admiralty archives. As it turns out, the *Kinta* went down in the North Sea in '85 and the Brits assisted in the salvage operation.

"Note particularly the location of the crew and guest quarters. Under interrogation, Xo admitted he was on the *Drachev* twice. He called it a 'dreary experience.'

But the thing that registered with me was his comment about there being nothing for a passenger to do once he went beyond the amenities of the superstructure."

"He was on a damn freighter," Cameron sniffed. "What the hell did he expect?"

Langley smiled. "My point is this. If the *Drachev* was actually battling heavy seas and ice, it couldn't have been much of a night for passengers and crew to be out and about. Best thinking is, this guy Zhou was probably in his cabin when the *Drachev* went down."

"And that's where you figure the files are?" Bogner asked.

Langley shook his head. "Not necessarily. They could be anywhere, T.C. He could be carrying them. They could be in his luggage—or he may have hidden them somewhere on the ship. The latter option seems like the least likely of the three to me. When you get down there and actually see the layout of the ship, it's conceivable that you could develop a whole new set of theories."

"Interesting question," Cameron drawled. "How do we learn to think like a Chinese technician in the next twenty-four hours?"

"Yeah," Filchak muttered. "If we knew how they think we might have some clue as to where he hid the damn thing."

Langley rolled up the drawing and checked his watch. Beyond the porthole was darkness, the Arctic darkness, a total absence of light. He was aware that the *Akershus* had slowed. The grinding sounds of the ship's encounters with ice were becoming more frequent. No one had to tell them that they had begun to move into the ice pack.

Finally, he looked at Bogner. "I hope to hell they don't find that damn set of computer files on their first dive—because the way I calculate it, they'll have already been down there a couple of hours before we even get the *Spats* launched."

LOG:
TWELVE: TWO

The Russian Icebreaker Pitki *1856L*
12 November

Ilya Dolin had designated Sergi Brerkutev as the man who would lead the recovery efforts at the site of the *Drachev*. Now Brerkutev, who had served as the mission specialist and commander on the *Zotov* during two previous recovery assignments, was reviewing launch details.

The 44-year-old ex-GRU assistant in the Naval Directorate had been constantly assessing the stream of site data since their departure from Belushya.

On the surface, Brerkutev did not appear to be the type who would be leading such a mission. He was taciturn and, for the most part, uncommunicative. Yet he double-checked every calculation, and even when he was satisfied, he insisted that both Zhdanov and Stigga verify his findings. He was an angry man with demanding ways and the uncommon habit for a commander of brooding instead of ventilating.

For a diver he was deceptively tall man. He had a thick brow, broad shoulders, and a barrel chest. His crop of black, close-cropped hair and tightly bunched muscles further confused the picture. In the bulky, dark wool, turtleneck sweater he wore to protect him-

self from the biting cold, Brerkutev looked top-heavy
and uncoordinated.

As the time of their launch approached, Brerkutev
began to communicate with abrupt, only half-articu-
lated commands that both Stigga and Zhdanov were
forced to interpret while disregarding his frequent
habit of thinking aloud.

"The transponder is where, Captain?" Brerkutev
wanted to know.

Stigga pointed to the photograph taken by the
RUMR. "It is here, on this section of the hull. We
attempted to place it as close to the location of the
crew quarters as possible. We were able to maneuver
the extensible manipulator past this stanchion and into
this area of the bulkhead."

"Range?"

"No more than ten kilometers," Stigga estimated.
"Perhaps less."

"Is it activated?"

"No. But it can be triggered—whenever we are ready
to begin our initial search," Stigga advised. He studied
Brerkutev over his reading glasses for several moments.
"I am curious, Comrade Brerkutev, why you selected
me for this mission. As you well know, I have no
experience with . . ."

"You are a former Spetsnaz commander, Captain.
There is little to recommend a man other than his
profession and the way he performs his duties, and
you, like Lieutenant Zhdanov, have gone repeatedly
to places where too many of our comrades are too
full of fear to venture. That is all the recommendation
I need."

Stigga nodded.

Brerkutev continued. "You will be in command of
the *Zotov* during the actual recovery effort. Lieutenant
Zhdanov will be at the control of the support equipment. In the event more than one diver is required,
Lieutenant Zhdanov will assist me. At all other times,

the *Zotov* will be under my command."

With that, Brerkutev turned his attention to the
weather charts and the ice reports. After appraising
them for several moments, he began to draw a series
of red lines parallel to a small island close to the site
of the downed *Drachev*.

"You will note, gentlemen, this small outcropping
known as Kickana Island. It is uninhabited, of course,
except for occasional military or meteorological bil-
lets. It is not quite five kilometers long and no more
than one-third kilometer in width. I point this out,
comrades, because this wretched little rock greatly
influences the flow of the ice pack in the area. West
of Kickana there is often a thin ice estuary that extends
out from the outcropping two and sometimes three
kilometers. Because of this, I have instructed Captain
Koshkin to position the *Pitki* in the shelter of Kickana.
We will launch the *Zotov* from there."

Both men nodded. "The red lines?" Zhdanov questioned.

Brerkutev frowned. "Because of the east-to-west
movement of the ice, Lieutenant, there are often
buildups which form pressure ridges. Those ridges
can extend out from the island for quite some distance.
If I have calculated density and flow correctly, our
target has more than likely changed position since
your reconnaissance. What's more, the shape of the
ice under the surface is constantly being changed by
the fluctuations in pressure. I rather imagine that what
was at that time mere lace ice and tentacles may now
present us with more formidable obstacles."

Stigga continued to scrutinize the chart. "If we
launch from the thin ice here"—he pointed to the
lee side of the island—"then we will be much closer
to the site of the wreckage."

Brerkutev, engrossed in the chart, reached in his
pocket and removed a small leather pouch containing
his cigars. He lit one and continued to dissect the

possibilities. "It may well be, Captain, that we have reduced the distance from launch to the wreckage by half. At the same time, we must recognize that we may have even less room to maneuver then when you took these photographs. In either case, I applaud you for your foresight. We will be able to get much closer with the *Pitki* than we would have with one of our submarines."

Zhdanov leaned over with his hands on the chart table. "Do I detect concern?" he said.

Brerkutev straightened and studied his cigar as though he had never seen it before. "My primary concern, Lieutenant, comes from the fact that we are attempting this mission early in the season. That means that the ice is still young. Young ice is unpredictable ice; it shifts, often quickly and unexpectedly, sometimes for no apparent reason. It crushes, often without warning. It menaces, always. The ice can crush a ship's hull and wad it up like a discarded piece of useless paper."

Zhdanov sobered. "Do you think we will be able to recover the files?"

The mission commander shrugged his bull shoulders. "That depends on where the files are, Lieutenant."

"Our assumption all along has been that they are either on Zhou or in his parcels."

"And if they aren't, Lieutenant, then what?"

Zhdanov knew there was no answer. If Zhou had hidden the files in some obvious place, their mission would be a success. But if the little man had hidden them in a less-than-obvious place, there was the distinct possibility that they would never find them.

"We will soon know the answer," Brerkutev muttered, answering his own question. "Captain Koshkin advises me that we will be at the salvage site at 0600 hours tomorrow morning—and then our adventure begins."

LOG: TWELVE: THREE

Admiral Dolin's Office: Belushya Guba 1900L
12 November

"Is there any word from the *Pitki?*" E-Alexa inquired as she took her seat at the conference table.

"Indeed, Admiral," Konyev reminded him. "We have heard nothing about the mission?"

"Captain Koshkin has been ordered to maintain radio silence," Dolin admitted. "We have taken this precaution because suddenly there is a great deal of activity in our area. We have been informed that no less than two of the American nuclear submarines are conducting maneuvers in an area off the coast of Bear Island; and the Norwegians are deploying their weather ship much too close to our objective."

"Do you believe they suspect something, Admiral?" Perinchek asked.

"Have you ever met an American who was not suspicious?" Dolin laughed. "But in answer to your question, Lieutenant, I do not want to give them cause to be suspicious. If there are inquiries, I can simply inform our curious friends that the *Pitki* has been dispatched to Kickana Island to accomodate some experiments which I will not be at liberty to discuss."

Dolin's droll comment triggered a round of laughter, but their faces sobered again when the admiral reached for E-Alexa's report.

"I must congratulate you, Colonel Chinko. Your investigation into General Gureko's murder and the timely manner in which you brought the matter to resolution is indeed commendable," Dolin offered.

"Thank you, Comrade Dolin," E-Alexa acknowledged. "However, I must give Lieutenant Siddrov most of the credit. It was he who found the evidence that implicated Colonel Ulitsa, and it was he again who conducted the investigation of the colonel's suicide."

Siddrov, the youngest officer at the table, acknowledged E-Alexa's recognition and began passing out copies of his report. "Shall I proceed, Admiral?"

Dolin nodded.

"With the admiral's permission, I will dispense with Doctor Konyev's autopsy report on General Gureko and begin with my investigation of the death of Colonel Ulitsa."

Again Dolin nodded. "Please continue, Lieutenant."

"Colonel Ulitsa's body was discovered at 0630 on the morning of November 11 by Corporal Vessey of the Administration Detachment. Corporal Vessey informed me that Colonel Ulitsa had ordered him to make certain that he arrived at the zone A complex before both Lieutenant Perinchek and Lieutenant Yakovelev arrived to begin reviewing computer files."

Dolin looked at both Perinchek and Yakovelev for confirmation. Both officers confirmed the time that they had intended to start. "We had agreed to get started early that morning," Yakovelev said. "At that point we believed that it would take no more than another eight hours to complete our review."

"I am curious," Konyev interrupted, "to know if either Colonel Chinko or Lieutenant Siddrov had advised Colonel Ulitsa that he was under suspicion at that time."

E-Alexa shook her head. "On the contrary, I had spoken to Admiral Dolin only a few hours earlier. Doctor Konyev has established the time of death for Colonel Ulitsa at somewhere between midnight and 0200 hours the following morning. In fact, even Lieutenant Siddrov was not aware that Admiral Dolin had advised me to proceed with charges against Colonel Ulitsa. You will perhaps recall that Lieutenant Siddrov was involved with the final security checks aboard the *Pitki* at the time."

"Continue, Lieutenant," Dolin ordered.

"When I arrived at Colonel Ulitsa's quarters, it was almost 0700. Colonel Ulitsa was dead by his own hand. He'd used a 9mm semiautomatic which he had checked out of armament stores. The requisition slip, unsigned and unauthorized, was lying on his desk.

"He fired a single shot into his right temple. According to Doctor Konyev, the bullet passed through and shattered the sphenoid bone, traumatizing the brain interior known as the lateral ventricle and the corpus callosum. The bullet exited the left side of the skull eroding the temporal, zygomatic tissue. Death was instantaneous." As an afterthought, Siddrov added, "The bullet ricocheted off of the cement wall after impact and we found it under Colonel Ulitsa's bunk."

Perinchek, who had audited the report, confirmed it. "Under Colonel Ulitsa's bunk we discovered both a bottle and a glass. Apparently Colonel Ulitsa had been drinking."

"Excessively?" Dolin asked.

"I did not check blood alcohol," Konyev admitted. "The cause of death was apparent. It is quite obvious what happened, Admiral. The behavior pattern of Colonel Ulitsa in this case is almost textbook. General Gureko removed him from his position as chief of logistics and replaced him with Colonel Chinko. He brooded, sought revenge, and poisoned the general. But the brooding only intensified—and there is little doubt that he worried that Gureko's death would be traced to him. Finally, he despaired, drank sufficiently to find the courage to put the gun to his head, and pulled the trigger. As they say in those old American movies, 'an open-and-shut case.'"

"You conducted the investigation, Lieutenant Siddrov; do you agree with Doctor Konyev's conclusions?" Dolin asked.

"I do, sir."

"I do wish to interject the following," Perinchek observed, "for the record. It seems curious that neither Lieutenant Yakovelev nor I observed anything in Colonel Ulitsa's behavior the past few days that would have indicated . . ."

"May I remind Lieutenant Perinchek that his speciality is computers," Konyev said. "We do not expect him to be an astute observer of the vagaries of human behavior. Colonel Ulitsa was a professional soldier by training, but we do not always know what goes on in the brain of a man who has committed so heinous an act as the murder of a fellow officer."

Dolin pursed his lips and closed the file. "There is still the matter of informing General Bekrenev."

E-Alexa leaned forward. "How much does General Bekrenev know? Is he aware of the death of General Gureko?"

Dolin did not conceal his apprehension well. "I have avoided informing General Bekrenev until our investigation into the matter was complete. At the same time, I have been reluctant to establish any kind of direct contact other than the usual operations report in the hope that we could recover the files from the *Drachev* before our dilemma had to be reported."

Dolin's admission surprised his staff. He was playing a dangerous game. As he stood up, he advised E-Alexa to remain. When the other officers cleared the room, he handed her an envelope.

"What is this?"

Dolin hesitated. "You have been recalled to Moscow," he said, "by order of General Vyacheslav Bekrenev. Your orders arrived earlier today, in the packet from the Special Purposes Detachment."

"Were you aware this was happening?" E-Alexa demanded.

"No," Dolin said, but he looked puzzled. "You are not pleased with orders that recall you to Moscow? Do you not think that there is a possibility that your reassignment is the result of a need for your capabilities in a more important capacity?"

As far as E-Alexa was concerned, Dolin's response was out of character. She stared at him. "Tell me, Admiral, what is more important to President Aprihnen's agenda than the success of our mission here at Belushya Guba?" Her face was flushed with anger. "I do not like this. I have been led to believe that the successful development of the Lyoto-Straf project was absolutely critical to the reemergence of the Party and the reunification of the Soviet people."

"That is true," Dolin admitted.

"Then request a delay," E-Alexa demanded.

Dolin stiffened. "Under the circumstances, Colonel Chinko, I am in no position to request anything. Your return to Moscow was ordered by General Bekrenev."

E-Alexa stared back at the man. "Are you not concerned that I might say something about the situation concerning the file contamination?"

"Is that a threat, Colonel Chinko?"

"It is not a threat, Admiral," she said, her voice suddenly softening. The frown faded and she summoned a quick, and to Dolin almost sinister, smile. "You can count on my discretion."

"Good," Dolin said.

"When am I to report back?"

"Immediately," he replied. Then he extended his hand.

LOG:
TWELVE: FOUR

The Russian Icebreaker Pitki *0542L*
13 November

In the empty, cold darkness punctuated only by illumination from a bank of lights from the *Pitki's* squat superstructure and two sets of auxiliary lights set up by the rigging crew, Yuri Zhdanov and Viktor Stigga watched the launch crew scurry about on the ice below.

The ground crew, dressed in hooded parkas, their faces shielded by heavy felt masks and tinted goggles, struggled to keep the ice from reforming over the 30-by-30-meter hole in the ice.

The detonating C-cord had finally completed the job after holes had been augered at two-foot intervals around the circumference of the launch area. The initial tests indicated that the ice, even in the shelter of the lee side of the Kickana inlet, was almost two meters thick.

Now, while the launch crew went about their final preparations, Stigga could hear the *Zotov*, suspended by two steel cables some 20 feet in the air over the hole in the ice, creaking and groaning as its titanium hull adapted to the minus-37-degree air temperature and 30-knot winds.

Brerkutev was already down on the ice, directing the touchdown. The shielded heating coils on the underside of the saucer-shaped craft were glowing and the umbilical cord carrying the power from the mother ship's generators to the *Zotov* would not be disconnected until the crew had powered up all systems aboard the hybrid DSRV.

Overhead, Stigga scanned an Arctic sky that was a panorama of blackness imprisoning tiny specks of icy light. The immenseness seemed to mock them. Stigga shivered. The undersea world that he knew had never seemed as hostile or terrifying.

The *Zotov* was lowered until it settled into the temporary slurry of ice and seawater. Meanwhile the launch crew encircled the craft, submerging a series of barrels through which the *Pitki* would pump compressed air that would keep the water agitated and allow the *Zotov* to resurface. All Brerkutev and Stigga had to do now was hope the ice floe allowed them to surface somewhere near the launch point.

On touchdown, Brerkutev gave the signal and Stigga and Zhdanov were hoisted over the side and down on the ice. They worked their way to the craft, mounted the detachable access ladder, and lowered themselves into the personnel chamber. By the time the launch crew closed the hatch, Brerkutev was already at the controls. When Stigga began peeling off his gloves he heard the hiss of the seals engaging on the hatch cover. He looked at Zhdanov. Zhdanov was smiling. He was in his element. He moved into the third chair, where he could operate the exterior systems and monitor the primary.

Stigga in turn slipped into his seat just before the umbilical was disconnected, the lights flickered, and the conversion to battery power was completed. From where he sat he could see the darkness out of the starboard viewport only.

"Ballast spheres open," Brerkutev barked.

"Ballast spheres open," Zhdanov confirmed. "Pump off."

Stigga heard the rush of water into the spheres. There were two chambers directly over the personnel bubble, one fore, directly under them, and one in the stern, near the rear thruster. They began to descend as Brerkutev played touch-and-go with the control panel, and his monotone voice began issuing a series of commands to Zhdanov. Each was verified almost as soon as Brerkutev recited them.

Beyond the acrylic viewports there was pitch darkness, and the only illumination in the cramped cabin was a series of tiny red, green, and blue miniature lights shining up from the array of panels. For the moment there was a ghostly blue-green cast to his comrades' faces, and even though he had lost track of the number of missions he had been on in the cramped confines of miniature submarines in the service of the Spetsnaz, this time Stigga felt more confined than he could recall.

"Report, Lieutenant," Brerkutev snapped.

"ROD, six meters per minute, ballast ninety, ninety-one, equivalent buoyancy reading 0.04." Each time Zhdanov made a reading, Brerkutev confirmed it.

"Now, Captain Stigga, let's see where we are," Brerkutev said. He depressed the switch on the boom that operated the retractable lighting rack and fixed the lights in the first position, slightly fore of the viewing ports. The two outboard HMI lights flickered to life and bathed the viewing area in a surreal greenish-white color. Stigga blinked.

The seascape looked altogether different than it had on the monochrome monitors of the *Kuchumov*. What had appeared to Stigga to be little more than amorphous curtains of icy lace reaching down from the ice pack above were now bleached white, ghostly columns of ice, gigantic, oddly shaped, and contoured pillars that supported the massive monoliths of ice above them.

"Very impressive, is it not, Captain Stigga?" Brerkutev whispered.

Stigga's hands inched toward the number-2 controls as the *Zotov* moved closer to a tusk-shaped column of ice that reached to what he imagined to be a few feet from the bottom and disappeared in a mushroom-shaped canopy over his head.

"Range?" Brerkutev demanded.

A series of computer sector images rolled on the monitor above Stigga's panel, and behind him he could hear Zhdanov's readings.

"Sector 8-a, 21.2 kilometers, sector 8-b, 22.2 to 22.4., speed, three knots."

"Main thruster on, Lieutenant Zhdanov, please confirm."

Stigga felt the craft accelerate, and he could hear Zhdanov. "Four knots, five knots, one quarter."

"And now, Captain Stigga," Brerkutev breathed, "activate your so carefully placed transponder. Let's see where our beloved *Drachev* is hiding."

Stigga pressed the switch that had been taped to the console and activated the low-frequency C1 unit. A tiny red light began to blink.

"We are receiving a signal," Zhdanov announced.

"Compute coordinates," Brerkutev directed, "and fix."

"333.4 and 333.6. Plot. Auxiliary activated, Captain Brerkutev."

"I take it that you are impressed, Captain Stigga?"

Stigga's throat was dry and he felt the pressure. He nodded rather than betray his discomfort. By the time he found his voice, Brerkutev was engaged in a new series of commands.

"Forward 3020," he said, and turned to Stigga again. "The computer processor will determine the range based on multiple arrival paths of the transponder signal. The signal, of course, will vary depending on what it encounters. Without the processor, we could conceivably lose our signal behind the stanchions of one of these many ice bases."

"Multipath ranging," Stigga acknowledged, "I am familiar with it." Brerkutev nodded and reduced the speed on the main thruster. The *Zotov* was approaching the ice barrier.

"Side scan sonar, Lieutenant, port and starboard."

"Activated," Zhdanov confirmed. Both Brerkutev and Stigga watched as the resultant pings were reduced to a series of digitized readings on the central monitor.

"Shut down the HMI lights, Captain Stigga, save our batteries. Retrieve the boom. There will be nothing to see for several moments now—and I should warn you, even if you did continue to watch, the view through the central port would be quite alarming. Even my own reaction time and decision-making does not equal that of the computer."

Brerkutev released his hold on the twin pistol-grip controls and leaned back. Stigga watched him depress the switch on the auto pilot and the *Zotov* slowed.

"2 knots, Captain," Zhdanov informed. "Auto engaged."

"Mission time?"

Stigga studied the two-phase chronometer. "Elapsed, twenty-two minutes, forty-seven seconds, margin 147.13, minus 2.1 to 2.7."

"We are losing too much time," Brerkutev complained. "Range, Lieutenant?"

"17.2 to 17.4, DR computation."

"We are not DR, Lieutenant," Brerkutev snapped. "Factor."

Zhdanov recited the range to speed factor. "17.2 to three, 15.1 to four, 14.2 to five knots."

"Maintain current, Lieutenant."

"We have a continuation on port, Captain," Zhdanov said. "It reads like a wall of ice."

"Lights, port and scan."

Stigga sucked in his breath. Out of the port viewport he could see what amounted to a whiteout. He felt the computer adjust the *Zotov* to a 345-degree plane. Brerkutev's jaw tightened.

"Compaction," he announced. "Those are pressure ridges of ice extending out from the base of Kickana."

"We're losing the signal, Captain," Zhdanov said.

"I'm afraid our computer is having a difficult time threading its way through this maze, Lieutenant. We are losing precious time."

"347.1 to 347.7 course alteration," Stigga said, repeating the latest readings.

Brerkutev's hands reached involuntarily toward the controls. "Mission time, Lieutenant?"

"Elapsed 27.2."

Stigga could see Brerkutev juggling the math in his head. His hands were still poised over the controls.

Zhdanov continued his recitation, and finally the readings began to come around. "We're back to 344.2, 344.0, adjusting to 339 . . . 338 . . . 337."

Brerkutev activated the port illumination again. Stigga saw the captain's hands flex, and he leaned back in his chair again.

"We have clearance," Zhdanov said, "and I'm receiving the signal again, sir."

Brerkutev let out a sigh. "Have you ever been tempted, Captain Stigga, to trust your own instincts over the capability of the computer?"

Stigga did not answer.

"In case you have, Captain, don't," Brerkutev said.

LOG:
TWELVE: FIVE

Sector 8-a, 8-b: Stavka Straits 0648L
13 November

"Slow to three, correct to 323.4, Lieutenant Zhdanov," Brerkutev ordered. "Target?"

Zhdanov corrected. "Sixty meters and closing."

Brerkutev employed the reverse thruster. He was peering intently through the forward viewing port. "Lace ice, Captain Stigga—one minute it is a thing of beauty, the next minute it becomes a hazard."

Stigga nodded and watched the transponder signal grow steadily stronger. The tiny red indicator light now blinked incessantly.

"Speed three knots, range .5 kilometer." Zhdanov indicated.

"Activate the light boom, Captain Stigga. Any moment now we should be getting our first look at the reason we have undertaken our little adventure."

Stigga leaned forward and peered into the viewport.

"Slow to two, range one hundred meters."

Suddenly Stigga could see it, a dark, nearly shapeless mass, a sheen of thin, semiopaque ice coating its otherwise dull gray hull. Ice curtains, like trailing tentacles of some great surface monster searching for victims, undulated around it. Without waiting for

Brerkutev's orders, he reached for the acoustic intercept receiver and listened to the sound waves of the *Zotov* bounce off the heavy steel plating. He looked at Brerkutev. "Closing fast," he advised.

With the retractable lighting boom extended and the hull bathed in the flood of light from the HMI units, Brerkutev used the base thrusters to bring the *Zotov* up to the top deck of the *Drachev*'s ruptured bow. In the half-light, backdropped by the ice, the three men studied the skeleton of the superstructure, a montage of twisted steel, coated with the streaked oil-blackened remnants of the fire.

"Take the controls, Captain Stigga," Brerkutev barked. He reached for the controls of the IMAX. "Bring me as close as you can to the wheelhouse. Let's see what we have."

Stigga rotated the side thrusters until the *Zotov* began to rise, then increased the drag on the horizontal stabilizer until the stern of the whale-shaped craft was elevated higher than the bow and the viewing ports were pointed directly at the wheelhouse. The windows had been blown out and the interior consumed by fire. The sonar array on the aft bulkhead, the radios, and a bank of no-longer-recognizable supporting gear had been reduced to charred metal and a tangle of wiring. A single light bulb, unbroken, along with charts and code books, cluttered the floor. Now and then, something billowed in the minor turbulence created by the *Zotov*'s thrusters.

The *Zotov* slowly and methodically circled the wheelhouse, its high-intensity lamps constantly being rotated to probe into every corner of the structure. The blast had peeled away most of the interior paneling, and the door leading to the captain's quarters immediately adjacent to the control area had been blown off, exposing the man's personal effects and leaving them to the vagaries of the sea.

"It is like looking into a tomb," Stigga muttered.

Brerkutev was silent. He kept the camera running. Finally he leaned back in his observation chair and rubbed his eyes. He pressed the video-replay button and watched the tape that Zhdanov had filmed from the RUMR.

"All right, Captain Stigga," he said with a sigh, "let's take her over the edge and down so that we can view this section of the bow from the opening in the hull."

Stigga brought the *Zotov* around 180 degrees by using the horizon indicator to level the craft and decreasing the port thrust. He could hear Zhdanov counting in the background: "60.1, 60.5, 60.9, 70.3 . . ."

"There's your target."

Brerkutev used the remote to reposition the lights. "Hold steady." He scrolled through the video to the sequence of RUMR images. "Is that the place?"

Stigga nodded. "We were using the galley as reference. The schematic indicates that it is directly under the passageway leading to . . ."

Brerkutev frowned. He turned in the pilot's seat and watched as Zhdanov scrolled the data a second time. "There," he said. "Freeze it, Lieutenant."

Stigga, now viewing the opening in the *Drachev*'s hull illuminated by the intense light of the *Zotov*'s bank of HMIs, could see more detail than he had in the original images captured by the *Kuchumov*'s cameras. "That's it," he confirmed.

"Lieutenant Zhdanov, assume the second seat," Brerkutev snapped. "Captain Stigga, primary control." He studied the two images, comparing the one on the video monitor with the one through the viewport. Stigga, meanwhile, hovered the DSRV directly in front of the cavernous opening in the bow.

"Swing the light booms forward, Lieutenant, and direct the lights down that passageway."

Stigga watched the booms pivot forward and the darkness at the end of the passageway give way to a pale wash of limpid light. The *Zotov* continued to drift, and Stigga was forced into a series of corrective maneuvers. Once again, Brerkutev accessed the situation. "We won't know until we go in and have a look around," he finally said. He opened the door to the egress chamber and sealed it behind him.

Zhdanov scurried about the personnel pod to make certain that the Ac line and the ABA systems had been activated. "All support systems on and functioning," he advised. Then he repositioned himself in front of the second console. He scanned the AMS and LSS gauges and opened the InCom to the egress tank. "Pressure valve is now open," he informed Brerkutev.

There was a momentary lull until the diver's voice crackled over the InCom. Both Stigga and Zhdanov could hear Brerkutev's muffled voice through the ARB mask and the repetitive whooshing sound of the air regulator.

"Open the F1 valve, Lieutenant, and give me a pressure reading."

"87.2, 89.7, 94.9," Zhdanov recited.

"Hold it steady, Captain Stigga," Brerkutev ordered.

"Chamber sixty-nine percent capacity," Zhdanov advised.

"Open egress."

Zhdanov leaned forward and depressed the switch. Stigga felt the *Zotov* lurch and drift into a slight lift. He quickly rotated both side thrusters and corrected to the 0.0 reading on the vertical and horizontal indicator screens. He looked at Zhdanov and nodded. "Holding steady."

Zhdanov stared through the viewport. He appeared to be holding his breath. Finally he stabbed his index finger against the four-inch-thick acrylic lens. His voice was excited. "There he is."

When Stigga was finally able to make out the lace-ice-shrouded image of Brerkutev, he was adjusting the series of tiny butterfly valves on his wrist monitor. As Stigga and Zhdanov watched, he pulled the neoprene seal back up over his LSS monitor, massaged his wrist where it had been exposed to the icy water, and tugged the insulated neoprene wrist band down till it snapped onto his glove. Then, from his tack belt, he unsnapped his halogen lamp and directed the beam into the bow cavity.

"Correct egress E time, Lieutenant?" Brerkutev's voice crackled.

"Seven minutes and thirty-one seconds—mark."

Brerkutev tapped his chest twice, circled his index finger and thumb, and extended his arm.

"Everything seems to be working," Zhdanov sighed.

Stigga depressed the "on" button on the mission recorder and tapped in the time code. "Converting to analyzer."

Zhdanov squinted into the viewport. "From here on out, Captain Stigga, it is in the hands of Comrade Brerkutev and the *Zotov* computers."

"And now we wait," Stigga said.

"Yes—we wait," Zhdanov confirmed.

Brerkutev's first obstacle was the twisted personnel ladder to the deck above the galley. He wedged his foot into a twisted vertical support beam and clawed his way through a series of shredded panels into the B deck passageway. A thin glaze of ice had begun to form on the inside of the lens on his facemask, and he held his breath until he was certain that it was warm enough. Then he released his mouthpiece, exhaled through his nose, and watched the lens cloud and then clear. On the LSS system in the personnel pod, both Stigga and Zhdanov noted the irregularity in the recorded breathing pattern.

The passageway had been heat-warped by the blast. The corridor was littered with ice-encased debris and a puzzle of twisted metal. There was no easy access to the passage to the crew quarters beyond the damage area. From where he stood, he could see two distinct ruptures in the hull. He traced the beam of his flashlight down the length of each of them. The bow had actually split open, engulfing the crew, and subjecting them to a lingering death in the 34-degree water.

Brerkutev paused a second time to regulate the mixture on his LSS. He paused and attached his L line to a small metal D ring at the fire extinguisher station. The glass was broken, but the red cylinder was still locked in place and the hose was still coiled in its cradle. From that point on, he could see that the blast had twisted the companionway at a sharp angle down and toward the port side of the bow. He nudged the beam of his light deeper into the aphotic recesses, crawled over a mangled I beam, and squeezed into a small section where he could stand erect. A network of steam and water pipes had been ripped loose from the ceiling and blocked the entrance to the first cabin. He danced the beam of light around the room. The bunk was made, the door to the wall locker open and empty. The amenities were such that he reasoned he was in the area where the infrequent *Drachev* passengers were quartered. He stepped back and redirected the wash of light further down the passageway.

"E time?" he questioned.

Stigga's voice came through. "Seventeen minutes, twenty-three seconds."

Brerkutev checked his monitor. The device was off one second. "I'm in the area," he informed them.

In the undulating silence, disrupted only by the sound of his own breathing, he turned back into the passageway and turned on his recorder.

"2-E is clear. I'm entering 2-D."

There was no confirmation from the control pod, but the periodic muted beep in the InCom indicated his crew had activated the mission recorder. 2-D had not even been made up for the *Drachev*'s final journey. The mattress was still rolled up and the bedsprings were coated with rust. He opened the wall locker, and the mirror on the backside of the locker door momentarily caught his reflection. It startled him. Brerkutev sucked in his breath. As he was working his way out of the cabin, he heard and felt the ice shift.

LOG:
THIRTEEN: ONE

Operations Control: The Akershus *0813L*
13 November

Two latecomers, both officers, entered the control center, and Bogner seized the opportunity to look around the operations control facility at the crew Berggen and Langley had summoned for the final prelaunch briefing session.

In addition to the captain of the *Akershus* and the chief of NI, the cast included Dr. Simon Penser, the British representative of WMO and the *Akershus*'s chief climatologist; Lieutenant Timothy Bagley, the communications officer; Bryan Coltrain, the weather ship's operations officer; and Dr. Anita Howard of Lockerbie University, the ship's Arctic meteorological specialist. During the past 36 hours, Bogner had been briefed by each of them.

"Check your watches, please," Langley advised. "We have a lot to cover here before the 0900 launch time. The sole purpose of this gathering is to give Toby, Mitch, and Cody any last-minute information we've picked up. We'll start with Tim."

Bagley stood up and methodically leafed through his log. He was a phlegmatic young man with a scraggly red beard and his hair tied in a haphazard ponytail. Like Penser, he had a heavy British accent. Unlike Penser, he had a sense of humor.

"All right, boys and girls," he began. "Let's clear up the matter of the NATSCOM reports first. By now I believe everyone here is aware that we have been tracking the progress of a Russian icebreaker, the *Pitki*, for the past several hours. In the past, when our Russian friends have sent one of their breakers out this time of year in these waters, their normal course is straight to Murmansk. Not so this time. As recently as two hours ago, the *Pitki* was located just off the leeward coast of Kickana, a rather dubious chunk of uninhabited rock and ice about thirty kilometers due east of us. The two NATSCOM reports we have received confirm that she has not moved since approximately 0500 hours this date. I will leave the significance of this piece of information up to Captain Langley's speculation.

"The second item you need to be aware of is that at approximately 0555 hours, we began to pick up a signal. At first rather anemic, but after we changed frequency, strong enough to lock on to." Bagley walked to a map and pointed to a location west of Kickana. "That signal emanates from here," he emphasized. "Curiously enough, this is 8-c on your international OMO sector chart, or NATO Sector DD. Again, I will leave the interpretation to Captain Langley."

When Bagley sat down, Langley turned to Anita Howard. "It's your turn, Doctor."

Anita Howard was a tall, rawboned woman with volumes of gray hair pulled back in an unappealing bun. She was wearing a black turtleneck sweater, a vest, and no makeup.

"As you know," she began, "we are still being subjected to a rather significant west-to-east surface flow. By comparison to other years, we are getting significantly more ice activity both on and under the surface than we normally do at this time of year. Normally I would say you gentlemen would not encounter much in the way of pillaring and cathedral formations under the surface at this time of year. But I have taken two standard 4LM scans since our arrival, and there appears to be significant ice formation of the type mentioned even at this time."

"Meaning what, Doctor?" Bogner asked.

"Two things, Commander," Howard warned. "First, you may encounter some difficulty maneuvering your DSRV in the areas around 8-b and 8-c. Pillars and cathedrals can and will provide significant navigational impediments if you encounter them. On the other hand, Captain Langley assures me that Commander Filchak, who will be piloting the *Spats*, is familiar with both of these obstacles."

Filchak studied the chart and looked at Dr. Howard. "How about it, Anita? Do you think those pillars extend all the way to the floor of the strait?"

Howard chewed on the end of her pencil. "It depends on the depth, Commander. At depths of more than eighty-five to ninety meters, probably not. The thing that I'm really more concerned about is the compaction factor. In the area of the operation we have both new and old ice. The new ice is aggressive—hence compacting is not only possible, but likely."

"What you're saying," Bogner observed, "is that even if we can get in there, we could have a little trouble getting out if the ice shifts or if we have excessive delays."

"Exactly," Anita Howard confirmed. "It's something you'll have to watch every minute."

Langley turned his attention to Bryan Coltrain. "What do you think, Bryan, can they make it?"

Coltrain thought for a moment. Then he shrugged. "I don't see why not, Peter. It looks like you've got a capable crew and one hell of a little piece of equipment. Looks to me like all we need now is a little bit of luck. We've got the technology; the question is, do we have Lady Luck on our side?"

It was Langley's turn. He cleared his throat. "This is the way I read it, Toby. It's risky—but these missions always are. It goes with the territory. Captain Berggen, Commander Coltrain, and I put our heads together before this meeting started. Based on what we know, and combined with what Bagley reported at the start of the briefing, it appears that we may even have some company down there."

Bogner could feel the muscles in his shoulders tighten. Rapid-fire flashbacks of his encounter in the *Arca Dino* at the bottom of Negril harbor strobed through his mind. And for a moment, Langley's voice seemed to come and go, to fade and intensify.

"Putting what Bagley picked up this morning with everything else we've learned, it's a pretty good guess that the *Pitki* is on the same mission we are."

"If they are down there, they're running silent," Bagley added.

Langley went back to the chart. "The signal we're picking up is here." He pointed to the 8-b sector. "The *Pitki* is here, just off the coast of Kickana, a distance of less than eight kilometers."

"Is there any possibility we're too late?" Filchak asked.

Langley frowned. "There sure as hell is, Cody."

"Seems to me it's a hell of a lot like looking for a needle in a haystack," Cameron grumbled. "We're talking one hell of a big ship. A man could hide a damn computer tape almost anywhere."

"We've gone over all of this before, Mitch. We think it's likely this guy Zhou knew his ship was in trouble. That makes it even more likely that he would have had the tape with him just in case he could find his way out of there. We also think it's equally unlikely that the Russians are using an unmanned recovery device because they wouldn't have any way of going into the actual wreckage and conducting a search. Add to that our intelligence reports which indicate they have only one known DSRV capable of this kind of mission in these waters. That would be the *Zotov*. The *Zotov*, according to our information, has an elapsed mission time of twelve hours. That means they have only twelve hours to get from the mother ship to the *Drachev*, find what they're looking for, and get back to the *Pitki*. Our guess is that if they don't find it the first time, they are going to keep going back again and again until they do."

Bogner looked at Langley. "If they find it the first time, then we're out of luck."

"Exactly," Langley confirmed, "and we go back to the Maximum Computer and tell him we were a day late and a dollar short. Believe me, that's something I have no intention of doing."

"Remember, there are other options," Cameron reminded them. "A little less desirable maybe, but clearly other options."

"So how do we play it?" Bogner pressed.

Langley shoved his hands in his pockets and continued to glare at the chart. His voice was hesitant. "I think we go in now. But we hang back and we wait—and we keep an eye on them. If the *Zotov* hightails it out of there early, it's a good bet that they found what they were looking for. Allowing for something like an hour each way to and from the mother ship, another thirty to sixty minutes for recovery operations, and a hedge safety factor, it's my guess that they are thinking they have eight hours to work with on their recovery operations. Using Bagley's information, we have to figure that they planted the transponder and activated it only when they started their search. That was at 0555. Eight hours would be 1355. If the *Zotov* is still there at that time—they haven't found it—if they leave, go back, recharge their batteries, and come back again for a second look, then that means we're still in the hunt. Make sense?"

"If they leave, we go in and look around, right?" Filchak asked.

"Exactly," Langley confirmed.

Coltrain leaned forward with his arms on the table. "Cody tells me the *Spats* can stay down there for thirty hours if need be. That gives us a decided advantage. If we launch at 0900, you should be in sector 8-b and 8-c by 1030 even if Dr. Howard's forecast on subsurface conditions is correct. That should give you an opportunity to find a hiding place and observe the *Zotov*. Theoretically, you can get close enough to monitor any transmissions between the craft and any deployed divers. Your digital decoder can handle most of it. But like Peter says, if the craft cuts out early, we're probably too late. If she's still there, it's a safe bet she hasn't found what she's looking for."

Langley looked around the table. "Very well; any questions?"

The room was silent.

"All right then," Langley said. "Let's hit it."

As Bogner stood up, he realized he had that old familiar knot in his stomach. The only difference was, this one was a little bigger than the last one.

LOG:
THIRTEEN: TWO

In the Wreck of the Drachev *0921L*
13 November

"E time?" Brerkutev demanded. Despite his proximity, his voice sounded distant.

"One hour, thirty-one minutes, and seven seconds," Zhdanov informed him. The RUMR controller's voice sounded mechanical. "Any progress, Captain?"

Brerkutev realized that it had been too long since he had relayed a progress report, and he stopped his search long enough to activate the recorder.

"I am in Cell four, still in the auxiliary crew and passengers' quarters. It appears that none of these quarters were occupied," he recorded. At the same time his observations were being transmitted to and recorded in the personnel pod of the *Zotov*. "So far, no sign of our Mr. Zhou."

In the tangled passageway, following his transmission, Brerkutev was again confronted with a maze of support beams and partitions that blocked his access to the last two cabins at the end of the hall. He tried to move one of the beams, noted the increasing sensation of numbness in his extremities, and checked the body temperature gauge on his environmental panel. His fingers felt stiff and bulky, and he had begun to notice a degree of fatigue.

A check of the gauge indicated his body temperature had creeped down to 97.7 and there was the growing sensation of isolation. He tried to loosen the beam, and gave up when it refused to budge.

At that point, he had already decided that if he could not squeeze through to the last two cabins, he could loosen his LS pod, crawl through, and pull the pod through after him. It was a bit tricky and more than a bit risky, but he had done it before—although never in such cramped quarters.

He studied the barrier for several seconds, and finally decided that loosening the life-support system, slipping out of the harness, and swimming backward through the opening was his only alternative. He informed Stigga of his intentions, unbuckled the LS and DS apparatus harness at both points—the chest and between the legs—switched to the auxiliary LS system inside the ARB mask, kicked off the fins, and began backing through the opening feet first. It had occurred to him that if he did not find Zhou's cabin, and what they were looking for, he could work his way on through to the crew quarters and up to the bridge.

He was halfway through the narrow opening when he heard the ship shudder and begin to groan under the pressure of the compacting ice. The *Drachev* shifted, and Brerkutev's world twisted violently to port.

He felt the beam begin to slip. There was a grating sound and a protracted guttural moan from the hollows of the severed bow. Involuntarily, he held his breath, waiting for the beam to slip further. Then he realized it was holding.

Brerkutev swallowed, continued backing through until he knew he was clear of the debris, and pulled the LS pod through the narrowed opening after him. Now, in a more confined area, it took him several more minutes to slip back into the harness and reattach and readjust the LS system controls.

For the moment he concentrated on regulating his breathing, and switched from the auxiliary ARB supply to the LS supply. With that done, he checked the ARB and realized that he had used 78% of the available air supply. The needle gauge was fluttering on the 20% indicator. He did a quick calculation of the time required to get back to the *Zotov*, decided he had time, and slumped back against the bulkhead to get oriented. He was all too aware that if the beam had slipped another inch or two, he would not have made it, either in—or out. To be on the safe side, he knew he needed to find another escape route.

Brerkutev checked the reserve on his halogen lamp, flexed his fingers to enhance his circulation, and directed the beam into the first cabin on the starboard side. His heart quickened and he felt an involuntary shudder race across his shoulders. When he had least expected it—there he was. Zhou's bloated, milky white body undulated in a comical burlesque in the unseen currents over his bunk. He appeared to be suspended, mouth and eyes open, frozen in a pantomime mask of horror as if he realized what was happening.

Brerkutev caught his breath, hesitated, and reached out. Zhou's body floated away from him, slowly rotating in the macabre ritual over his bunk. There was a thin sheen of ice encasing the cadaver, and it made him look varnished, yet jagged; minute crystals of ice had gouged away small parcels of flesh to reveal the tortured remains of the man's muscle structure.

The ship shuddered again and Brerkutev, momentarily off balance, felt himself teeter and fall against the bulkhead. There was a roaring sound, and Zhou's body, like an inflated water toy, banged against the bulkhead and settled again, this time closer to the bunk.

Brerkutev could not help but wonder how the man had died. Was it as the direct result of the explosion?

Had he drowned—or suffocated—or what? He looked at the body; there was nothing to indicate that the body had been severely traumatized. Had he frozen to death? There was always the possibility he had suffocated in the thick oily smoke of the dying freighter. He reached for the body to move it out of the way, and a slime eel the size of his arm erupted from Zhou's open mouth, its eyeless head the size of Brerkutev's fist, its misshapen sucking mouth seeking more.

Brerkutev jumped aside, and the revolting creature slithered to the floor like a serpent in search of still another hiding place. He thought about trying to stomp on it, but the resistance of the water and the slowness of his reaction rendered it a fruitless gesture. The eel, spewing a gray-green trail of slime, disappeared into the darkened corridor.

Brerkutev steadied himself, trying again to regulate his breathing. He waited, counted to ten, eyed the contents of Zhou's cabin, and tried to determine the most likely hiding place for the data.

He worked his way to Zhou's wall locker and began rummaging through the small pile of clothing and personal effects. Then he went through the pockets of the two or three hanging garments. Again, nothing. Now there were only two obvious places left, the medicine cabinet and Zhou's luggage. He decided to go through the latter last—a suitcase was too obvious. He rummaged around in the wall cabinet, cut open Zhou's tube of frozen shaving cream and toothpaste, dumped the ice-crystal contents of a small leather choke case. Nothing. As a last resort, he broke open the man's deodorant stick and crumbled it in tiny pieces.

Nothing.

Finally he turned to the luggage. If Zhou had not put the data capsule in his luggage, all bets were off—and Brerkutev knew there was no way of telling how long it would take to find it. He opened the single suitcase, threw aside two silk shirts and a framed photograph of two children. Then he saw it, a bulge in the lining of the case. He took the knife from his pack belt, cut the lining open, and found the small aluminum canister. It was no more than ten centimeters in diameter, less than a centimeter thick, and it was carefully sealed. Even as Brerkutev checked his watch and studied the small package, he had to fight off the sensation of elation.

I give you credit, Comrade Zhou, he thought to himself, credit for being clever enough to devise your little bit of chicanery and espionage—but not very clever in where you hid the spoils of your efforts. To Brerkutev, it meant only one thing. Zhou was not a professional; he was a zealot. For Zhou, no doubt his departure from Belushya Guba meant that he was safe and he could relax. A professional would have known he was never safe. Brerkutev was mildly amused. If Ulitsa hadn't been able to find it in such an obvious hiding place, Ulitsa was either a fool, or Zhou had moved it from its original hiding place.

Brerkutev depressed the small orange button on his transmitter. "We are in luck, comrades, I have located it," he said. "I'm coming in."

In the personnel pod of the *Zotov*, Zhdanov and Stigga smiled at each other.

LOG: THIRTEEN: THREE

Aboard the Spats *1039L*
13 November

While Filchak and Cameron readied the OS search gear, Bogner assumed the controls of the *Spats* and continued to monitor the telemetry display above the central control panel. The imaging video in the pressure capsule gave him a picture of both men as they went about their preparations.

Filchak was calling the shots; on the initial foray, Cameron would lead the dive with Bogner patrolling the drag.

The less-than-two-hour voyage from the *Akershus* to the site of the downed *Drachev* had gone easier than the crew anticipated. Filchak had locked on to the signal of the transponder and turned the controls over to the *Spats* central computer. Bogner figured that they had gained at least an hour because a major portion of what was expected to be a tedious search effort had been all but eliminated by the incessant signal of an indiscriminate Russian transponder.

"How we doin', Toby?" Filchak inquired from the dive area.

"Nothing to it; just following the yellow brick road. The signal is getting stronger."

The signal was strong enough now that Bogner could look away from the data display to the camera monitoring the activity in the pressure pod. Filchak was putting the RSB masks through their final check and he was smiling. If he could have requested a favorable dive scenario for the *Spats*, it would not have read any different from the one they were encountering. They were ahead of schedule, they were less than one half kilometer from the site—and from all indications, the *Zotov* was giving no indication it was aware they were even in the area.

"Just like they do it in the training manuals," Filchak quipped coming back into the control pod. "Our Russian friends out there are about to get the surprise of their lives."

Bogner turned back to the telemetry display and pressed the "record" button to log the mission track. Thus far the *Spats* was proving to be even more remarkable than Langley's claims. From the forward thruster ducts and viewports, both eight inches in diameter, and the nose sonar cone, all the way back to the main propulsion motor with both the gimbaled and tilting shrouds aft, the *Spats* was a monument to American ingenuity.

"How we doin', Toby?" This time it was Cameron. His voice was edgy.

"I'm starting to pick up fragments of conversation between the Russian DSRV and her deployed personnel. Can't make much out of it, though."

"They're talking to each other?" Filchak asked.

"Affirmative. They don't know we're here."

"What's their situation?"

Bogner shook his head. "Garbled."

"Have you tried any of the lower frequencies?"

"Negative—but I get the impression they're getting ready to take their diver aboard."

"Pan forward," Filchak advised.

Bogner started to smile. "Got a lock. Getting feedback. Two targets confirmed—both passive."

Filchak was grinning. "Lock and load; the big one is obviously the *Drachev*. It looks like the smaller one is coming from the submersible."

Cameron was hovering over them. "Ready to start taking pictures? Advise when you make visual."

Bogner shook his head, "Not yet, but I can see a faint illumination at 075 degrees. The way I read it, whoever is out there is working their way back to the submersible. I'm logging more chatter than we were getting initially."

Filchak put on his headset and listened. His face was creased in a scowl. He looked at Bogner and mouthed the words, "They're making a hell of a lot of noise for being on a clandestine mission."

Bogner lowered his voice to a barely audible whisper. "Why the hell do you suppose they are running with their ears down? So far I haven't heard anything that even indicates they're in touch with their mother ship."

"Trying to extend battery life?" Cameron guessed.

"Beats me," Filchak admitted. "Maybe they bought that weather ship bit." Like Bogner, his voice was barely audible.

He leaned forward, adjusted the volume on the squencer-receiver, and opened the key that activated the red warning light in the pressure capsule.

"Image up," Filchak instructed. "Full infrared."

"Camera on," Cameron confirmed. "Tell me when you start to get a picture."

Filchak and Bogner watched the capsule monitor while Cameron stood motionless waiting for further instructions.

Bogner continued to scowl, interpreting each series of sounds. Finally he looked at Filchak. "No image, but there's no mistaking that sound, Cody, that's the pressure plate. Whoever was out there thumping around in the popsicles has just gone back on board."

Filchak took off his glasses, wiped them off, put them on again, squinted at the hazy images on the monitor, and leaned forward. "Shit, I can't make anything out."

"Maybe we don't need pictures," Bogner said. "We'll have a pretty good indication of what's up if they hightail it out of there. That means they got what they came after."

LOG:
THIRTEEN: FOUR

Aboard The Zotov *1131L*
13 November

For Stigga and Zhdanov, the wait until Brerkutev had equalized the pressure in the chamber seemed like an eternity. But when he emerged, he held the canister up in triumph, and the perpetual guarded scowl was gone. It was the first time the two men could actually recall Brerkutev smiling.

He dropped into the second control seat and began turning the canister over and over in his hand. Zhou had played it safe; the container had been wrapped in plastic, and sealed in a second watertight heavy polyethylene bag as an added precaution.

"The proverbial needle in the haystack," Brerkutev exclaimed, "and we found it."

Zhdanov peered over his shoulder. As he did, the ice pack shuddered again and the cabin of the *Zotov* was filled with the alarming sounds of the compacting and shifting wall of ice. Brerkutev and Zhdanov appeared to ignore it; only Stigga seemed to be concerned. His question betrayed him. "We are finished, comrade?"

"Yes, Captain, we are finished," Brerkutev said, "just as soon as we run this through our computer." He began to cut away the thick plastic coating on the

347

container. When it was open, he discovered a small tray with two reels of tape. Each reel was encased in a small plastic envelope. There were no apparent markings on them. Without knowing why, Stigga watched Brerkutev's smile begin to dissipate.

"There is a problem, comrade?" Zhdanov asked.

Brerkutev continued to frown. He selected one of the two reels, opened it, and examined it. Then he slipped it into the adaptor on the Zotov's auxiliary computer. The screen was momentarily blank and then the monitor began displaying and repeating a series of meaningless digits.

Stigga, watching the monitor, scowled. "I do not understand," he said.

Brerkutev ripped open the second packet, dropped the cartridge into place, and received more of the same. When he looked at Stigga, his face was flushed with anger.

"It is contaminated," he spat. "It too is useless. We have been duped. This is the cartridge Zhou intended for us to find."

Stigga stared at the unit in silence.

"But—how could that be?" Zhdanov said.

"Did you not say you found the tapes in Zhou's effects?" Stigga asked.

"It was too easy," Brerkutev spat, "too easy. Only a fool would have hidden them in such an obvious place. He knew we would discover them if we searched him prior to his departure. If we believed we had the tapes, we would have discontinued our search, and Comrade Zhou, even though he was in disgrace, would have escaped with the real tapes."

"But where are the real tapes then?" Stigga demanded.

Brerkutev studied the two worthless cartridges. Then he held them up again. "What impresses you about these tapes, Captain Stigga? Does anything strike you as unusual about them?"

Stigga selected one of the tapes, weighed it in his hand, and examined it. On the surface at least, there was nothing unusual about it. Both of the cartridges were of the size and type used to make backup tapes of retained files. They even had the Red Army seal on the plastic jackets. "They are the type used on all military computers I am familiar with," Stigga said. "They are even compatible with the ones used on the *Kuchumov*." He handed the cartridge back to Brerkutev.

"Look at the size of the container," Brerkutev said. "Does it not strike you as quite large considering the size of the reels?"

Stigga nodded. "Larger than necessary," he confirmed. "Because if we did"—he began to reason his way through the riddle—"conduct a search prior to Zhou's departure, they would be quite obvious, hidden as they were in a large container, and the real tapes would, of course, go undetected."

"Then the real tapes still must be somewhere on board the *Drachev*," Zhdanov concluded, "and in a much smaller container."

Stigga nodded. "But the question is where?"

"Indeed," Brerkutev said, "where? This time, Comrade Zhdanov, you and I will both search."

LOG: THIRTEEN: FIVE

Aboard The Spats *1242L*
13 November

"What the hell do you suppose is going on over there, Cody?" Cameron complained.

Cameron, like Filchak and Bogner, continued to watch the distant image of the *Zotov* on the survey monitor. "Mitch is right. They've been sitting there for damn near an hour now."

"Exactly one hour and twenty-three minutes," Bogner corrected. He adjusted his headset and leaned forward in the obs seat, straining to pick up the infrequent fragments of conversation aboard the hybrid Russian DSRV.

"You picking up anything at all, T.C.?" Filchak asked.

"They're not doing much talking, Cody. But they're sure moving around in there."

Cameron, with his feet propped against the console, focused his attention on the pod speaker over his head and nodded. "Hell, I can't make heads or tails of it. What do you think, T.C.? Do they have problems?"

Bogner shrugged. "Can't tell. What I'm hearing doesn't make a whole lot of sense. All I'm getting

350

is an occasional fragment. They seem to be talking about their equipment."

"Maybe that's it," Cameron said. "Maybe they brought their diver in because of equipment problems."

"Possible," Bogner admitted.

"According to Langley, they've made some real technological breakthroughs since they developed the Mir series," Filchak interjected. "One report said that with this new ARB headgear, their external personnel are supposed to be able to work outside the unit for up to six hours at a crack. Based on the information we have, we know their diver wasn't deployed near that long."

"Or . . . maybe they simply haven't found it yet," Bogner speculated.

"Then why did their diver come in?" Filchak asked. "The way I see it, they're losing a hell of a lot of time in that pressure changer . . . and those batteries won't last forever."

"Has to be equipment malfunction," Cameron decided.

Bogner shook his head. "I don't think so, Mitch. At first I thought maybe they were waiting for some kind of verification from their mother ship—but they haven't transmitted anything back except that one short burst, and they haven't received any transmissions since that time. The way I have it figured, their mother ship doesn't know much more than we do."

"They can't possibly know we're here, so why the silence?" Filchak said.

In the surreal red light of the *Spats*'s control pod, the three men waited. With their viewports shielded and all systems powered down to absolute control minimums, Bogner was beginning to experience a gnawing and growing uncertainty. The frequent, and now not so distant, rumble of compacting ice only exacerbated the situation.

Cameron slumped back in his chair with his arms

folded across his chest. "They're no damn different than we are; hurry up and wait."

Suddenly Bogner held up his hand. "Hold it," he whispered. "I think I'm getting something."

Cameron leaned forward and Filchak looked at the monitor.

"Unless I miss my guess, gentlemen, that was the old familiar egress hatch hiss." Then he began to smile. "That's it—they're taking on water."

"Shit," Cameron hissed, "I'm beginning to feel like a blind man trying to thread a needle. Crack the shield on the bow viewport, Cody. Let's see if we can pick up a visual."

"You sure it's their egress hatch?" Filchak questioned.

"Go red, kill the monitors; what do you see?"

Filchak opened the fore viewport to a narrow one-inch slit and put on the night vision gear. "We've got egress, all right. There he is," he confirmed. "What are you getting, T.C.?"

"Chatter, a lot of it, inter and inner. Confirmed deployment—only this time, there are two of them."

"Two divers?" Cameron questioned.

Filchak chewed on his lower lip. "Well, there's the answer to one of our questions, gentlemen. They still don't have what they came after. They're sure as hell not crawling back into that old tub to have a picnic."

Filchak stood up. Even in the pale red light of the control pod, Bogner could see the tenseness in the man's face. "What now, Cody?"

"We're out of options. We can't sit here any longer. If they find it on this pass through that old tub, it'll be too late. Once they get it on board that damn submersible of theirs, our only option will be to ram them and take it away from them."

"Are we going in?" Cameron pushed.

Filchak peered through the slit in the viewport. "Give me a reading, T.C. How far from them are we?"

Bogner scanned the USD. "Less than five hundred meters, closer to four hundred and fifty."

"I think you'd better get dressed, gentlemen. It looks like we're going in. If Langley is right, the crew complement of that damn thing is limited to three men. If two of them are headed for the *Drachev*, that means they've only got one man at the controls. With two divers deployed he's got his hands full. That means he won't be watching his sonar—and he damn sure won't be looking for company. We're about to give our Russian friend the biggest damn surprise of his life. When he looks up, we're going to be sitting right on top of him."

Cameron was grinning. "Scrap plan A and go to D, right?"

Filchak could feel the rush. "You got it. First we make damn sure that toy of theirs doesn't go anywhere—then we get what we came after."

"We're coming in directly on the target's stern," Filchak confirmed, "and we're in luck. It looks like we've got him boxed in. Don't have a visual, but sonar indicates he's got a wall of ice on two sides and the *Drachev* sitting right in front of him. It looks like the only way he can get out now is to try to squeeze through us and the ice pack."

While Bogner listened to Filchak describe the conditions outside the *Spats*, he watched the gauges in the pressure capsule creep up. The LOSC suit felt bulky and restricted his movements. A small magnification lens had been inserted over the LS system gauges, and even with the slight distortion caused by the thickness of the viewing lens in his RM helmet, he could confirm readings to the nearest one-hundredth. He would wait until the last minute when the *Spats* began to settle to activate the SM-A computer; then he would initiate the systems check.

Compact and weighing only four pounds, ringed by a

buoyancy compensator, the computer itself was sealed in a small compartment near the support pack, but the telemetry appeared on the view-through of his mask as an ancillary to the night vision. Finally the *Spats* began to settle. He checked the readings, and signaled to Cameron. He mouthed the word "ready."

Cameron opened the hatch, each of them aware that when they dropped through the transfer skirt, they would be completely dependent on the LOC. From that point on, it would monitor their breathing, air supply, blood pressure, heart rate, body temperature, and fatigue factor. It was at times like this that Bogner was always reminded of astronaut Gus Grissom's comment about the concern of knowing your fate was in the hands of the *low bidder*.

"How about it, T.C., am I coming through?" Cameron's voice sounded clear in the recessed speakers built into the RM helmet. "Any distortion?"

"None," Bogner advised, and checked with Filchak in the control module. Filchak confirmed the reception and cleared.

"E-time 1333," Bogner recited. "We're running on blinkers from here on out . . . no chatter unless absolutely critical."

Cameron confirmed with a hand signal, and opened the hatch to the transfer skirt.

"Valves open," Filchak advised.

Suddenly the B pod of the pressure capsule began flooding with icy black water, and Bogner could feel the pressure against his legs as it swirled around him. Within seconds he felt the same pressure against his chest, and microseconds later it eddied around his viewing lens. Then the pressure began to subside and he depressed the illuminator switch on the LS system to activate the LED display. All systems were functioning. He took a deep breath, felt the immediate reassurance of the measured oxygen mixture, closed his eyes, and stepped onto the transfer platform. When he opened them, he was standing on the floor of the Stavka Straits.

Cameron was ten to 12 feet in front of him, already working his way in the direction of the *Drachev*. They were approaching the *Zotov* from the blind side, the stern. Cameron was giving hand signals. Their plan had two stages: First they had to make certain the Russian craft was unable to get away, and when that was accomplished, they had to make certain it was unable to communicate with its divers. Only then could they risk going into the *Drachev* after the files.

By the time Stigga was able to separate the confusion of sounds caused by the shifting ice pack and the bombardment of the hull of the *Zotov*, it was too late; Cameron had snapped off the antenna platform and cut the cables to the HMI lights on the retractable lighting boom. The damage could be repaired, but the *Zotov* would have to deploy a diver to do it. Through the craft's port lens, Bogner could see the distorted image of the *Zotov*'s one-man crew frantically trying to correct the situation and reestablish contact with his divers. Bogner moved to the port side of the Russian DSRV, where he loosened the casing on the side scanning sonar, jammed it, and plugged the vents leading to the CO scrubber. From there he worked his way over the roof of the craft and jammed the rotating side thruster. He had just started for the belly pan when he saw Cameron emerge from the starboard side of the craft waving the wire cutters. The man signaled by scissoring his gloved fingers. He pointed to the hull of the *Drachev*, and motioned for Bogner to wait the customary five-count before following.

When Cameron moved away, Bogner began his count. Disabling the *Zotov* had been the easy part. Now was when things could get complicated, and Bogner knew it. It was the questions he didn't have answers for that troubled him now. Had they severed the *Zotov*'s communications before the crew of the Russian submersible had gotten through to the divers to warn them? Was there a COM alternative they hadn't anticipated?

With Cameron already on his way to the wreckage, Bogner turned around, his eyes searching the icy black waters to see if he could still determine the location of the *Spats*. There was a shadow, all but indiscernible, immediately behind the *Zotov*—but it was there. If he could see the craft, was the commander of the *Zotov* or its divers able to see the same thing? And . . . did the Russian captain realize that his craft was now hemmed in between the edge of the ice shelf and the larger *Spats?* The question haunted Bogner; how disabled was the Russian DSRV?

He turned back toward the hull of the *Drachev*, searching for Cameron. Finally he spotted him. He was following the tether line of the Russians.

Bogner shoved the beam of his halogen back to where the tether was attached to the transfer skirt, and caught the quick reflection of light bouncing off of a metal object dangling from the *Zotov*. It was the hook on the haul-down winch. Suddenly everything began to fall into place. At least it explained why the Russian diver had returned to the *Zotov*. He scanned the area with his lamp and saw the depressions on the ocean floor—twin depressions, a sled—the Russians had gone back with a sea sled. Why? Did they need it to transport something back to the *Zotov?* Or did they need tools, a torch maybe, to get through to the place where they believed the files were? He remembered a previous dive: the twisted mass of metal, the tortured plates, convoluted passages, the remains of a sunken and tortured ship. Most of all, he remembered the uncertainty. That ship had been a maze that went nowhere, a puzzle without a solution.

That had to be it. That had to explain the long delay. It wasn't battery life or equipment limitations;

they came back because they were stymied—they needed tools.

Bogner traced the depressions for a few yards, saw where the craft had lifted off, grabbed the tether line, and started for the *Drachev*.

LOG: FOURTEEN: ONE

The Drachev *1334L*
13 November

Cameron located the battery-powered sea sled at the point where the *Drachev*'s broken bow nestled closest to the ice wall. The sled's crew had positioned it on an ice shelf projecting out some eight to ten feet from where the gas and charge hoses led from two insulated steel tanks up to the second-level passageway.

Cameron circled around Bogner with an elaborate set of hand signals, and finally resorted to his diver's slate. "Let Cody know this?" he scribbled.

Bogner moved around the sled, weaving the beam of his lamp over the contents. He shook his head, wrote out the word "torch" on the slate, and pointed into the hull. For Bogner it was obvious; if the Russians had gone to all this trouble, they had to believe they knew where to find what they were looking for.

Cameron turned off the broad-beamed halogen lamp and unholstered the bullet-shaped high-intensity light from his crew pack. From where they were standing they could see where the hoses disappeared into the bowels of the *Drachev*. He held up two fingers before scratching the words "wait" and "go in" on the slate.

Bogner nodded.

Cameron started for the yawning hole in the *Drachev*'s hull, for the second time tracing the thin beam of his knife light up the length of cable to the point where it disappeared into the mass of twisted metal.

Cameron's gestures were easy to interpret; one of them would follow the cables, the other would work his way topside and circle back, both working their way down to the cabin area from the bridge.

Bogner nodded. He was recalling the detail and configuration of the bridge from the schematic— more specifically, the location of the gangway leading down from the bridge. The mental images began to crystallize: the captain's quarters adjacent to the bridge, first officer's quarters on the port side, stairway leading down to the second deck and cabin area. Second level and the radio room and the . . . He sketched the layout in his mind as he worked his way through the mental maze.

Even in the blackness that surrounded them, Bogner was beginning to see detail in the *Drachev*'s hull. The LED display on his support pack reflected like a firefly in Cameron's facemask.

"Ready?" Cameron signaled.

Bogner nodded.

Cameron reached down and intensified the halo illuminator on his LS display. He pointed to the red "13:51."

Bogner circled his gloved forefinger and thumb. When he did, Cameron again turned toward the cavity in the *Drachev*'s hull, activating his LD-Night Vision system and turning off his lamp. Suddenly they were in total darkness until Bogner was able to activate the scanner. When he did, Cameron was little more than a distant and surreal red image. Next, Bogner locked the darkened sweep halogen in the insert holder of his LS harness to free his hands and start his ascent. Illumination was virtually nonexistent and what little there was, was quickly sucked up in the inky blackness no more than eight to ten feet in front of him. They were at a point where every step had to be planned in advance. Langley had emphasized it repeatedly; there was no such thing as being too careful.

Bogner took his readings, did a final systems check, and started up. Langley had calculated that Cameron had the more difficult of the two routes into the area where they expected to find Zhou's quarters. Consequently, it would take him longer. Cameron had to work his way through the wreckage with only the knife light and the operational constraints of the infrared . . . and at the same time avoid alerting the Russians that they were there.

Bogner methodically worked his way up through a thin layer of crystallized plankton, wedged through a narrow opening where the encroaching ice pack had moved to within a few feet of the hull, and crawled over the gunwale onto the heat-buckled short deck in front of the wheelhouse. Most of it was encased in a silvery-green sheen of ice, and the steel plates that constituted the top of the bridge had been peeled back by the force of the explosion. Only then did he realize that the reference charts from the British Admiralty would be next to useless; the force of the explosion had twisted, destroyed, or dislodged most of his reference points.

It was too risky to use any form of light, and he was totally reliant on the ANV unit. He moved the reference venue from right to left and tried to orient himself. There was a hole the size of a city transit bus in the short deck where the metal had been ripped up and peeled out, reminding him of the holes in the beer cans when he had plinked them off of the fence with his father's .22 back in Texas.

He leaned over and peered down into the hole. His field of vision dissipated in blackness after only a few

feet. Still, he could see that the wheelhouse had been
ravaged by the blast; the walls were charred, the console torn away, and the instrumentation destroyed.
What the blast hadn't demolished, the flash fire that
followed had finished off. The area had been annihi-
lated. It was a charred world of oily black on more
of the same. Charts, debris, pieces of brass, broken
glass, and what appeared to be a pair of pants littered
the tiny area. Bogner swam around to the door, open
but twisted to one side, though still on its hinges, and
wedged his way through. Now in a blackness where the
ANV was proving even less adequate, he was forced to
use his knife light. It was risky. He bounced the thin
beam of light along the back wall of the wheelhouse
tracing the thin trickle of oil coming from one of the
gauges. Then he played it over the frayed, burnt wiring
that undulated in unseen currents. His light scoured
the walls of the wheelhouse and he saw a second door.
If he remembered the schematic correctly, it would be
the one leading to the passageway and the captain's
quarters. Off that passageway was a stairwell that led
down to the B level and transient accommodations.
Bogner opened the door and leaped back. His breath
went out of him and he felt an instantaneous constric-
tion in his throat.

There was a body. It was only half there—the top
half. The rest of it had been blown away. Entrails, some
a corrupted blue and others bleached white by the icy
salt water, trailed from the remains of the torso. While
Bogner watched, it pirouetted back and forth in some
kind of morbid dance.

For some reason, Bogner could not take his eyes off
it. It was what was left of what had once been a man.
The head was bloated and burned, the face perverted;
a capricious mask, life's final fatal cruel joke. There
was no tongue, no eyes; the fish had already come and
gone, and the arms were extended as though the torso
was contemplating flight. It floated toward him, and

Bogner reached out to push it away.

For the next several moments he had trouble regulating his breathing. Twice he changed the breathing air mixture on his LS gauge. He stepped into the passageway, and the torso suspended itself in the disturbed currents behind him, floating like some kind of grotesque balloon doll.

In the captain's quarters he poked the beam of the knife light along the wall in the hope of finding the ship's safe. Bogner laughed to himself. There was always the possibility that Zhou had practiced the ultimate irony and placed the data packet in the ship's safe for keeping.

But there was no safe, at least not in the captain's quarters, and he turned back to the passageway again, pushing the thin stream of light ahead of him until he saw a place where the steel plates had been twisted away. The metal stairway down was actually twisted off to the port side and then up again. Two steel support beams had been dislodged from the skeleton of the superstructure and had fallen across the corridor leading to the quarters. For all intents and purposes, the passageway was blocked. There was a hole in the decking where he could get to the second level, but it was a good six to seven feet on the other side of the tangled support beams.

He backed out of the passage, worked his way back through the maze of destruction that had once been the *Drachev*'s wheelhouse, and slipped aft on the narrow decking until he came around on the other side. Again there was a door, this one leading from aft into the wheelhouse. He managed to force it open, and discovered he was on the other side of the obstruction. All he had to do now was inch his way from where he had entered, across the buckled steel plate decking, to where the hole was through to the B deck. A wall had been blown out of the compartment on the starboard side of the passageway and had been crumpled up into a 45-degree angled steel obstacle. There was just enough room for Bogner to get through, and he managed it by scaling over the top. That was when he saw the first brief indication of light. He turned off his knife light and waited in the darkness. Finally he saw the light a second time: a momentary, muted flash.

He squinted, still uncertain—twice before the bioluminescence had fooled him—but now the white-yellow distant glow occurred a third time and he froze.

He was looking down through the hole in the A deck when the light seemed to intensify. It moved along the passageway beneath him, through the water, intensifying as it approached. It moved rhythmically, from right to left and back again, in a sweeping motion, until it began to light up the entire area beneath him.

Bogner waited until the diver was directly beneath him. He had to be certain it wasn't Cameron. He felt his heart begin to pound and his pulse quicken. He kicked off his fins and dropped through the hole just as the diver turned, looked up, and brought the barrel of his 5.66mm APS underwater assault rifle up to a firing position.

The Russian managed to squeeze off one round before Bogner hit him. Bogner heard the errant six-inch serrated-steel rod plow through the water, but it missed its mark. He had timed it perfectly—his feet caught the Russian in the chest and the force of the blow spiraled the man backward with his lamp clutched in one hand and the empty APS in the other.

Bogner's advantage was brief. The Russian was quick. The man righted himself, and stabbed the beam of halogen back in his face. Bogner blinked, ducked, and catapulted himself forward. He was surprised at how slowly he seemed to be moving. It was as if he were looking at the man one frame at a time. The advantage was gone. Bogner lunged again, unsheathed his shark knife, slashed at the Russian's LS tubes, and missed. For Bogner, his adversary seemed cat-quick, but his own movements seemed clumsy and slow. The Russian finally dropped his underwater assault rifle, unsheathed his own shark knife, feinted right, then left, and lunged at Bogner, a killer marionette in half-light, going for the air lines.

The force of the blow sent Bogner reeling back into the bulkhead. He bit down hard on his mouthpiece and recoiled. He brought his right knee up to protect himself, and slashed back across the diver's body. This time the knife caught, dug in, dragged, and gouged its way through the Russian's belly before freeing itself.

Suddenly Bogner was enveloped in a ruptured, belching, billowing cloud of red black. His now-frantic opponent tried to spin away from him, but Bogner lunged again. The eight-inch blade caught the man in the side, under the rib cage, and Bogner jerked the blade up and out. For Bogner, time was suspended; it was either an eternity or one fleeting, terrifying, numbing moment; he could not tell which.

His thrashing adversary was suddenly no different than a wounded shark—a vengeful, dangerous, dying shark—with a knife.

Bogner knew now that ultimately he would win. Behind the Russian's mask, he could see the unstrung eyes and the frantic mouth desperately working an LS mouthpiece that was no longer connected to anything.

As Bogner watched, a thin pinkish substance began to ooze into and fill the interior of the man's mask. Then he began to convulse. Bogner knew what the Russian was trying to do; he was trying to scream, trying to express his outrage, his anger, his pain— but there was no sound. He was trying to retaliate, but there was no control. All Bogner had to do now was wait. He took a step backward and the Russian's body, awash in the surreal light of his own halogen, began floating away. His LS system was pumping the

precious air mixture into the black emptiness of the
Drachev's passageway.

It took Bogner several seconds to regain his equilibrium. He was still shaking. He struggled to regulate his
breathing and tried to focus his attention on the display
panel on his LS system. One of the man's blows had
caught his mask, causing a malfunction in the telemetry display in the lens of his facemask, and now there
was an endless stream of meaningless, mocking digits.
He tried to ignore them, counting instead in unison
with his still-accelerated heartbeat. For the moment,
everything was devoted to what seemed like a futile
effort to shake off the image of the dying Russian's
face. He swallowed and closed his eyes.

He shook his head, opened his eyes, swallowed hard
again, counted to ten, reached down to deactivate the
digital exhibit on his LS monitor, and made note of the
fact that his hands were still shaking. Shaking, hell, he
mumbled to himself, they were almost useless.

He counted to ten a second time, and sagged back
against the bulkhead in the darkness, still waiting, still
gathering his senses, still trying to sift through the
mental chaos. He told himself he had to reconstruct
his plan, reorient his thinking, get his act together—
whatever the words were.

All right now—what was the Russian doing—searching—searching for what? Put the pieces together, Toby.
If he had the APS poised and ready, it was obvious it
was not for the data capsule, but for another diver.
In other words, Bogner reasoned, the Russians knew
they were there. But how? He had disabled the communications on the *Zotov*—or had he? Where was
Cameron? What about Cameron? Had he stumbled
into an ambush or what?

Gradually Bogner began to get his thoughts organized and his breathing regulated. He checked the LS
display for confirmation, and turned it off again. He
had begun to think again—in logical, connected, and

organized patterns, the way he had been trained to think. If the dead man's partner was prowling the *Drachev*'s passageways like his comrade, Bogner did not want the illumination of the tiny panel to give him away.

He began inching his way back down the passageway, using the knife light to check for obstacles. He had worked his way into an area where there were cabins on both sides of the passageway, and surprisingly little damage. At the first opportunity, the first open door, he slipped in, pushed his back to the wall, and turned on his halogen. When his eyes finally adjusted, he realized there was nothing in the cabin. Even then, he took the time to study the layout of the empty compartment. If Zhou was quartered in a cabin in this section, the cabin layout was likely to be the same. And there was a good chance that he was. Bogner tried to think; where would he have hidden the container, assuming of course that he had actually hidden it in his cabin?

When he finished, Bogner turned off his light, groped his way back out into the corridor, and in and out of three more cabins before he saw the giveaway sign of another light. It was moving in a somewhat erratic pattern not more than 30 feet further down the passageway. Bogner stopped, and adjusted his low-frequency RF scanner. For the first time he was picking up sounds other than the shifting and groaning of the ship and the compacting the ice against the *Drachev*'s hull. It had to be the Russian—Cameron wouldn't be transmitting. Bogner reached down and loosened the flap on his holster.

Filchak had insisted that each of them carry a four-barrel 4.5mm underwater pistol in their U belt. At the depth they were operating, it had an effective range of no more than 15 to 18 feet, but in the tight quarters of the *Drachev*, Filchak had calculated that in most cases 15 feet would be more than enough. Filchak was right; Bogner slipped the compact stainless-steel dart gun out of his aux-holster, released the safety, checked the six-round magazine, and shoved his gloved finger through the oversized trigger guard.

When he looked up, the light seemed dimmer, farther away even than when he had reentered the passageway. He decided to hang back, to conceal himself as long as possible, and shield the knife light. He kept close to the bulkhead with his back pressed against the wall, and continued to inch his way forward. In what was now a clear passageway, he felt his foot brush against something, and aimed the thin beam of light toward the floor. It was Cameron's halogen. For the second time in the short space of the last ten minutes, Bogner's stomach rebelled on him and he was forced to choke back the rush of bile.

Less than six feet from him, Cameron's body undulated just a few inches above the plate steel flooring. There was a messy hole in the front of his dive suit where his stomach should have been, and a wispy, disturbingly pink cloud of mucus, blood, and flesh fragments swirled around the body. The AB system had been disconnected and his facemask smashed. Cameron's face was distorted, pushed to one side by the force of the blow that broke the lens and crushed his skull.

Again Bogner was forced to regain his equilibrium. But this time the pieces came together quicker. Cameron had stumbled upon the Russians. They had disposed of him and now they were out, trying to determine if Cameron was alone.

Now the question was, how much did the Russian recovery team know? Were there transmissions going back and forth between the DSRV and the deployed divers? Did they somehow know about the *Spats* now? Did they know that the *Spats* had them hemmed in? Maybe he and Cameron hadn't disrupted communications between the Russian DSRV and the divers after all.

He looked at Cameron's body and began counting until he had control again. For one fleeting moment he considered breaking silence and trying to contact Filchak in the *Spats*, but there was always the chance the Russians had found a way to monitor his transmission. Would he simply be enabling them to confirm what they now only suspected? And if that was the case, would they learn more than they already knew? Doubts were beginning to creep in; did Filchak really have them trapped? Maybe Filchak had left. He opened his own receiver on the helmet radio again and selected the widest low-frequency band. He figured that if the Russians were talking to each other, he might be able to pick up fragmented portions of the transmission and locate them on a narrower band.

Bogner leaned over, got hold of Cameron's arms, and dragged his body out of the passageway into one of the empty cabins. As he did, their was another long, loud grinding sound, the loudest one thus far. As the bow portion of the ship shuddered, it rolled a few more degrees to starboard. Bogner momentarily lost his balance, ricocheted gently off the bulkhead, and held on until the bow settled again. In the icy darkness he could hear his heart pounding.

Now he realized he was fighting a strong temptation to get out of there and head back to the *Spats*. He counted to 100, settled himself, and using his knife light, worked his way back into the passageway. There he encountered the first of the cut-through support beams the Russians had been forced to torch their way through. Either Cameron had interrupted them— or they were in a big hurry; the special underwater acetylene torches had been discarded right where they had used them.

Bogner crawled over the beams and shoved the narrow beam of light along ahead of him. At the end of the passageway was the hole where the explosion had occurred. He was in luck; at least now he knew how to get out of the maze of buckled steel without threading his way all the way back through the wheelhouse. All he had to do now was follow the gas cables back to the tanks on the sled.

The faint light that he had seen earlier was gone now and the transmissions had ceased. Either the Russian was one deck below him—or he had worked his way topside, maybe even returned to his own DSRV. Bogner activated the chest harness halogen. The cabin door to his right had been twisted off by the force of the blast. The one on his left was open. He squared with the door so the light of the halogen bathed the room. It took him several seconds to recognize what he was looking at. Zhou's bloated body rippled in unseen currents, and what was obvious now was the fact that the Russians had already been there. The man's personal effects poppled in a world of unseen eddies and currents. There was nothing but debris.

Bogner reached out, pulled Zhou's body to him, and ran the light over it. In life Zhou had been an exceedingly small and frail man; his hands, like his feet, if Bogner hadn't known better, could have been those of a child. Bogner looked at him and decided that the montage mask of death was indescribable.

Then he turned away and surveyed the contents of the tiny enclosure; under tons of Arctic ice, in frigid Arctic waters, he was searching for the logical illogical. Where would a man hide his most cherished possession? The cabin was spartan; there were few accoutrements and even fewer amenities. He could tell by the debris that the Russians had been thorough. The only question was, had they found what they were looking for? Was that it? Had they finally found it? Was that why the other Russian was gone? Was he on his way back to the DSRV? Bogner paused long enough to check his E-time. The cold had numbed his senses in a way that he could not remember. E-time was

now 90:47. Had Langley advised them to curtail each
mission at the 120:00 mark, or was it . . . Suddenly
he was having difficulty remembering. Cold fatigue—
Langley had talked about "cold fatigue." What about
it? What the hell was it? He couldn't remember. He
turned back to Zhou again and shook his head, still
trying to clear his thoughts. There was still no evidence
of any transmissions between the Russian DSRV and
the deployed divers—no make that singular—he knew
that at least one of the divers would not be making any
more transmissions—he knew that much for certain.

Everything seemed cloudy, and he checked the readings on his LS system. The numbers were hazy. The
7-H gauge indicated his heartbeat had slowed and that
his breathing was both shallow and irregular. None
of it was making any sense until he checked his
body temperature; it had plunged to 94.2 and he felt
himself slipping into some kind of vague and stylized
dream world. He increased the oxygen content of the
BA mixture and began inhaling, counting backward
from 100 until he reached 91 and felt the surge in his
lungs. He was still unsteady, but he could tell that his
equilibrium was starting to come around. His fingers,
hands, and arms were less numb and his vision began
to clear. He checked the monitor, and the readings on
the dythermic scale were beginning to inch up again.
He took a deep breath, and then another, carefully
timing the intervals between each.

All the while he continued to stare at Zhou's bloated
body. He was trying to remember the session with Xo.
Had Xo actually let something slip that might serve
as a clue? What about books, or logs, or ledgers?
Too obvious. Personal effects? No, the Russians had
already been through those. Damn it, what had Xo or
Milatov said?

Bogner shook his head. Was there anything there?
Any clue? Any . . . any what? Zhou had been released
from the infirmary on Belushya Guba, cleared to

return to his duties—and then abruptly ordered to
return to China.

Curious how even the Chinese were becoming
Westernized. Now they were manifesting the ultimate
symbol of the Western lifestyle, the heart attack. It
occurred to Bogner that it was a helluva place to
get philosophical—and he laughed to himself. Next
thing they knew, they would be fighting the air-quality
problems associated with exhaust emissions. Then
he repeated the words—heart attack—heart attack—
pacemaker. Bogner wheeled in the murky water and
looked at the body. It was a long shot, but it could
well be the answer. He peeled open Zhou's shirt
and saw the blanched but still telltale incision. He
took out his shark knife, pushed the distended body
down on the ice-covered bunk, and sliced through
the dilated chest. Then he pried up with the blade of
the knife and lifted the pacemaker out of the cavity. The
smile didn't have to be invited—it came automatically.
There were no prods, no wires, no batteries; nothing
more than a small superficial chest wound, a neatly
crafted pocket under Zhou's chest flesh. It was a small,
one-by-two stainless-steel receptacle no more than a
half-inch thick.

Bogner could feel his heart hammer as he examined
the container in the eerie light of his halogen. Zhou,
you conniving little bastard, he thought; there wasn't a
damn thing wrong with your heart. He studied it for a
moment before he slipped the tiny case into the pocket
on his U belt and turned around. For a moment the
light blinded him.

He saw just enough to record the fact that the
diver standing inside the door of the cabin had an
APS underwater assault rifle like the one he had
encountered earlier. The piercing light from the man's
halogen lamp blinded him, and twice he heard a sound
like that of an air rifle. There was pain and confusion. It
was a searing pain, glancing and momentary in his left

shoulder. And even though it was momentary, he felt himself rocketing backward, tumbling across Zhou's bunk and up against the bulkhead.

The Russian was moving toward him, but Bogner felt paralyzed. It was all freeze frame, one image at a time: First the fingers uncoiled, then they reached out, and then they twirled around the tiny stainless-steel packet. For one fleeting moment, Bogner feared that his assailant was going to squeeze off another round; at this range he couldn't miss. Instead, the man straightened up, examined his prize, and began to back away. He kept the APS trained on Bogner.

Bogner's world was hazy, images were unclear, the pain in his shoulder came and went. He reached down and felt the butt end of the second dart. It had plowed into his U belt by the APS unit and had barely penetrated his dive suit.

The Russian studied him for a moment, probably figuring that the second dart, the one aimed at the stomach, had done more damage than it actually had. Then he backed away, turned, and disappeared back into the passageway.

The orderly universe of T.C. Bogner began spinning. He could feel himself being sucked down into chaos, a morass of disembodied movements. His heart was pounding and nothing made any sense. He tried to get up, succumbed to a kind of vertigo, and dropped back again. It occurred to him that if he rested for a moment he would be all right. Just a little rest, he repeated to himself . . . just a minute or two so I can get everything together . . .

Awareness for Bogner came on slowly. Images began to materialize and then faded before crystallizing. Reality took shape, then quickly dissolved into fragments. There were periods when living seemed important—and equally unimportant. Reality skated on the edge of palpability. Bogner opened his eyes and closed them. Up was down. In was out. Consciousness was painful.

Awareness came in leaps. There were realizations of elapsed time, perceptions of cold and pain, wariness, cautiousness. When Bogner opened his eyes, it was to more darkness. Sight revealed nothing.

He tried to move his arm and felt pain. He tried to reorient himself and experienced confusion. Then, somehow he managed to connect brain and muscle, and groped for the switch to his halogen. With the light came another level of comprehension.

He lay there for a moment, on his back, staring up at the sheen of ice on the ceiling of the cabin. A char darted up, in, and was gone, its silver body an uncertain blur. He managed to move one leg and then the other, slowly pushing himself with his good arm into an upright position. As his chest moved, so moved the lamp and the illumination.

Then the questions began. How long? How much was left? He fumbled for the illuminator switch on the LS panel; blood pressure—elevated, heartbeat—above normal, E-time—113.2, body temp—96.4. He closed his eyes again. Screw it. Go back to sleep, Toby, he thought to himself. Just let your eyes drift shut, old buddy. Lay back down. To hell with it. Who the hell cares?

The next awareness was that of collapsing metal. Shrieks of protest from a not-yet-dead ship—either that or someone was violating the corpse. Bogner was rolled out of the bunk and onto the deck, sliding across the cabin and coming to a halt near a stanchion. A support beam began to bend under the pressure, and the heavy steel plates of the hull screamed as they separated. The world tipped to a 45-degree angle, and he found himself lying against the wall of the cabin. He tried to clear his head, and reached again for the LS monitor. This time there was no illumination—and no display. He managed to extricate the knife light and get it pointed at the lens. It was cracked and the LED icons had drowned in a bath of salt water. He pulled one leg up under him and then the other. The LS system was still functioning, but if the water seal on the computer had been compromised, there was no telling how long it would operate. Suddenly there was a whole new sense of urgency. He managed to push himself into a standing position, but he was standing on the wall; the ice pack had tipped the bow portion over on its side and he was in a wedge between the deck and the vertical.

Bogner pulled himself through the access and back into the passageway. He activated the halogen again and began probing for the acetylene cables. He found them, tangled under twisted beams and ruptured plates from the hull. The passage was blocked, and the only way out was back up through the wheelhouse. E-time was becoming a factor; a critical factor. He turned and scaled his way over the debris back to where he had encountered the first Russian diver. He found the body in much the same position he had left it. From the looks of things, his comrade hadn't even bothered to check on him. The only difference was that now the man's body lay under a tangle of bent piping, wedged between a hull plate and the ice where the massive column had fractured the seams. Despite the pain, Bogner swam up, clawing his way back through the same maze he had conquered earlier. He struggled back to the wheelhouse, through one of the damaged panels, and out on the short deck. By the time he was able to get down to the rupture in the hull where the sled had been located, he realized he was too late. The Russians had left it behind. It was wedged under tons of ice and there was no sign of the other diver. It was now or never. He searched out the COM switch on his LS panel and pressed it. There was static and more static, but the green indicator light began to flash.

"*Spats*, this is D2, do you read me?"

The green indicator light began to blink and Bogner held his breath. Finally he heard Filchak's voice. "Toby, is that you?"

"Damn right. I'm coming in."

"Have you got it?"

"Long story. I'll tell you when I get there. They may be monitoring us. My guess is that one of their divers made it back to their submersible with the canister."

"What about Mitch?"

"I'm coming in alone."

There was silence on the other end.

"What's my E-time?"

"151.33," Filchak confirmed.

"Damn," Bogner muttered. "Let's hope it lasts another ten minutes."

LOG: FOURTEEN: TWO

The Russian DSRV Zotov *1647L*
14 November

At 47 minutes after the hour, Brerkutev fed the first of the two miniature tapes into the *Zotov*'s computers. By the time the two men had reviewed all four tapes, they knew they had what they were after.

"It is accomplished, Comrade Brerkutev," Stigga said, "and you are to be congratulated. Admiral Dolin will be pleased."

Brerkutev held one of the microminiature cassettes up to the light and admired it. "It is like a fine jewel, yes?"

Stigga looked at him for a moment. He had not asked the question.

Brerkutev understood. "Zhdanov," he said slowly, "is gone. But the Americans have paid an even higher price. There were two of them. I killed both of them."

Stigga remained silent. In his earlier days, as a Spetsnaz captain, he would have rejoiced in Brerkutev's achievement; now it seemed hollow and pointless. The loss of life, even if they were Americans, saddened him. He stood up and walked two steps to the console. For all intents and purposes, the *Zotov* was shut

376

down, conserving what little battery life was left. "You assessed the situation before you entered the pressure chamber, comrade?"

Brerkutev nodded. "The retractable lighting booms have been sabotaged as well as the rudders. As it now stands, we have no external lighting. Which means, of course, that we will be entirely dependent upon our side scan and forward sonar for navigational purposes. Range and depth detectors have likewise been damaged but appear to be marginally operable."

"They have vandalized the forward cameras and the LR antennas," Stigga added, "but in their haste they overlooked the stern camera. I have rewired the controls and can now rotate it a full three hundred sixty degrees."

Stigga activated the bank of standby batteries and demonstrated the capability of the stern video. The position of the American DSRV could be pinpointed by the external lighting. "There is the American craft, directly off our stern," he said.

"The question is," Brerkutev muttered, "why have they made their proximity apparent? It would seem to be to our advantage to know they are so close, yes?"

Stigga studied the echo from the sonar. "There is ice pack to our bow and starboard. They have maneuvered their vessel into a position that they believe stymies us."

"We are like two blind gladiators," Stigga mused.

"On the contrary, now is when we show our American intruders true Russian ingenuity," Brerkutev countered. "The ice columns on our port side appear to be too compacted, but if we elevate to just under the surface ice, it would appear that there is sufficient room to go out over them."

Stigga looked at the ice profile on the scope. To him, there did not appear to be room, but he knew that Brerkutev understood the *Zotov*'s capabilities as well as, and perhaps better than, anyone. "Without visual contact?" he asked.

The mission specialist scanned the console again. "Do you play chess, Captain Stigga?"

Under the circumstances, Stigga was surprised at Brerkutev's question. "I have played it," he admitted. His voice was subdued.

Brerkutev slumped into the pilot's chair in front of the console. He tented his fingers and stared at the shielded viewport. He lowered his voice to a whisper. "If you were an American, Captain Stigga, and you had put your quarry in jeopardy, such as they believe they have us, what would you expect your quarry to do?"

Stigga thought for a moment. "I do not know, comrade," he admitted.

"Exactly," Brerkutev smiled. "We are an enigma to the Americans. They do not understand us and therefore they do not know how we think. For now it does not matter how they knew we were here. We will deal with that at the appropriate time. Consider their situation. They dispatched two divers and their divers have not returned to their vessel. On the other hand, we know that the Americans have very sophisticated equipment, and we can assume that they know one of our divers has returned. This presents a quandary for them, does it not? If we were to attempt to leave, by whatever course, do you think they would pursue us?"

Again Stigga did not answer. Brerkutev had made his point and he waited for the senior officer to continue.

"I do not think they would, Captain Stigga; they would not leave their divers in peril."

"But they are dead," Stigga said. "You yourself confirmed as much."

"The pilot of the American DSRV does not know that." Brerkutev frowned. "In fact, they know nothing for certain. The only thing they are convinced of is that they have us trapped. I feel certain that at this very moment, their biggest concern is the safety of their divers. Americans are such fools; they place too much value on life. It is a predictable trait."

"You have a plan?" Stigga asked.

A smile creased the Russian's face. He leaned down toward the console again and studied the telemetry. "Have you been monitoring the ice pack, Captain?"

Stigga shook his head.

Brerkutev pointed to the 8-c sector on the grid. "This profile would indicate thin ice, would it not?"

Stigga studied the sector grid. "Perhaps," he admitted. "There is no way of knowing for certain until we test it with an absorption beam."

Brerkutev continued to smile. "And there is no way of our American friends knowing either, is there?"

"There must be an absorption beam to determine thickness—and an absorption beam can be detected," Stigga confirmed, "So far I have detected none."

Brerkutev smiled. "Then I have a plan, Captain, but as in a chess match, we must wait until our opponent is sufficiently distressed and distracted. At this moment, the captain of the American vessel is concerned that we will attempt to escape before he is able to bring his divers in. He is also, I am confident, reasonably certain that when we do try to escape, we will attempt to go out over his vessel. If he did not believe this, he would not have attempted to jam our vertical thrusters."

Stigga waited for the mission specialist to elaborate.

Brerkutev activated the absorption sonar on the vertical and set it for random readings. "Yes, Captain, we will respond exactly as our American friends think we will. Except we will add our own little wrinkle. We will make it appear that we are attempting to do exactly what they expect, elevate and attempt to escape by going out over them. Instead, we will elevate, but instead of attempting a horizontal maneuver, we will go right on up—through the thin ice to the surface."

Stigga reserved judgment. Brerkutev's plan was both risky and brilliant.

The senior officer leaned forward and placed the acetate overlay on the display monitor. "Now, Captain, let us make some assumptions. Getting through to the surface is one thing, but we must recognize that the eight or nine kilometers back to the *Pitki* will be just as difficult."

LOG:
FOURTEEN: THREE

The American DSRV Spats 1737L
14 November

Bogner bolted down his second cup of coffee. And even though it was laced with a double shot of bourbon, the chill persisted. The four-inch steel dart buried in his ANA pack had penetrated deep enough to render the unit useless.

"The other dart creased your shoulder, Toby. It broke the skin and I salted it down with sulfur and quinine. It's clean. If it starts to hurt, I'll load you up with some novocaine. You're lucky. An inch to the left and we could have had some major problems."

Bogner looked past Filchak at the systems monitor while Filchak bandaged the shoulder wound with gauze and two strips of adhesive.

"What happened to Mitch?" Filchak asked.

Bogner's voice was still edgy. "I couldn't tell. He was dead when I found him. . . ." His voice trailed off and he shook his head. "I don't know what the hell was wrong with me, Cody. For some reason I fell asleep at the switch. I had that damn container right in my hand and that son of a bitch snatched it away from me."

Filchak finished his task and began putting away the medical supplies. "The cold has a way of . . ." His voice trailed off. "Don't be too hard on yourself, Toby; this whole operation was a long shot from the outset."

"Helluva price to pay for a long shot."

Filchak peered through the bow viewport. "At any rate, he's still sitting there. Are you sure their diver made it back to the ship?"

"He didn't have a lot of options."

"Well, if he's got the data tapes, why the hell doesn't he try to bail out?"

"I figure they must have some way of determining whether they've got what they came after. They're probably running it through their computers to verify what they've got."

"The question is, now that they have it, can they get out with it?"

Bogner was still scowling. "The way I see it, if their diver got back to the craft, it would be a simple enough task to correct the situation on the vertical thrusters. If they assess the situation the way we think they will, they'll figure the only way out is to go up and out over the top of us. And we can stymie that maneuver."

"Then what?"

Bogner stared at the video display. "We start by establishing contact—and then we negotiate. We tell them they have two options. One, they can hand over the data file and we'll let 'em out, or two, they can hold on to their precious little package and we keep them hemmed in until the damn ice shelf wads up and crushes that little underwater jewel of theirs. Of course, somewhere along the way we point out that if that happens, we leave without the data file, but at least we're leaving with our skins."

"Think they'll buy it?" Filchak asked.

Bogner shrugged his shoulder. "We know one thing. If nothing else, we can outwait 'em."

Filchak looked at Bogner and then the console. "So what do we do in the meantime?"

Bogner got up and went over to where the coffee-pot had been plugged into the timer on the side sonar auxiliary unit. "We wait, Cody, we wait. The minute we hear them fire up, that's when we go into action."

LOG:
FIFTEEN: ONE

Sheremetyevo Airport: Moscow 1803L
14 November

Aeroflot flight 171-G from Leningrad to Moscow was an hour behind schedule when the Tu-204 broke through the overcast over the northwestern lights of the city. The leaden clouds, heavy with sleet, had concealed any indication of the city until the flight was within 17 minutes of the announced landing time.

In the seat behind E-Alexa, two American businessmen, one of them obviously visiting Russia for the first time, discussed the obstacles they expected to encounter in the passport/visa control area.

"Whatever you do," the older of the two men advised, "don't lose your customs certificate. If you do, you won't be able to exchange your damn rubles when we get ready to leave."

E-Alexa, when not occupied with her own thoughts, listened to the Americans and wondered what the area they talked about was really like; she repeated the name to herself, Memphis. For the second time in the hour-long flight, E-Alexa asked for a drink of water. The stewardess, a young woman in whom E-Alexa had detected a distinct Estonian accent, brought it to her and quickly turned her attention to the two Americans,

384

in the process confirming for E-Alexa that the young woman was angling for a night on the town with the two men.

For E-Alexa, weary of travel, and bundled in her gray-green dress uniform with the cluster on the epaulets and the red star stitched both on her C hat and tunic collar, it had been a long and uncomfortable day. When she heard the pilot announce that surface temperature at Sheremetyevo airport was only 22 degrees Fahrenheit with winds up to 15 kilometers, she wished she had not decided at the last minute to check her greatcoat through with her luggage. It would be a long, cold wait at the domestic carousel.

During the flight from Murmansk to Leningrad, she had speculated about the reason or reasons she had been so unexpectedly recalled from Belushya Guba. If Dolin knew, and she suspected that he did not, he had concealed it well—and Dolin did not conceal things well. The name of General Bekrenev carried a great deal of weight, and with Dolin's seemingly unending series of misfortunes, or was it more appropriate to call them blunders, it was more than obvious that the admiral could ill afford to plead her case. She chastised herself for even mentioning the fact that she might inadvertently reveal that the Belushya files had been compromised. That had been a major blunder on her part.

From time to time during the Leningrad-to-Moscow portion of her flight, she had also allowed her thoughts to turn to the recovery effort that she knew was under way near the tiny ice island of Kickana. She had dined with both Captain Stigga and the younger Lieutenant Zhdanov before they embarked upon their mission; she knew both men and had wished them well. Stigga, she had decided, was a simple man who had long since quenched the fire in the belly so often associated with a former Spetsnaz commander. Zhdanov, on the other hand, was at the age when he considered himself invincible. He radiated that aura of overconfidence that men often exhibit who have mastered new and dangerous technology.

Thinking of them for the moment made her forget her own difficulties.

Now, just minutes from landing, the Tupolev Tu-204 began to encounter turbulence and the no-smoking light started to blink. E-Alexa checked her seat belt and closed her eyes. She recalled that her father had advised her that it was always best to both fly and land with one's eyes closed when the weather was inclement.

For the next several minutes the huge aircraft seemed to float amidst a cacophony of disturbing hydraulic and mechanical sounds. The landing gear was deployed and the aircraft yawed as the crew fought the unpredictable crosscurrents just before landing. The fuselage creaked and groaned, the nose of the craft came up, and then there were the reassuring sounds of the tires making contact with the snow-packed runway. When that happened, E-Alexa opened her eyes and watched the blur of lights pass by her window. As the huge plane slowed for the turn on to the taxiway, she realized that there was even more snow than she had anticipated. It would be difficult to get a taxi—taxis were always hard to get when the weather was bad.

By the time the plane had taxied to its ramp, E-Alexa had gathered her personal effects and was ready to deplane. The two Americans juggled luggage and briefcases, again revealing their uncertainty with the upcoming customs encounter by making a series of tasteless jokes about Russian culture. The fools, E-Alexa thought to herself, probably did not realize that more than half of the people on the plane spoke English, if not fluently, then certainly well enough to understand what the men were saying.

The Tu-204 was capable of carrying well over 200 passengers, but this particular flight from Leningrad was not crowded. As she looked around the craft, she estimated that there were fewer than 100 passengers aboard. She slipped into the aisle, and was the fifth person off the aircraft. By the time she had reached the end of the portable causeway into the terminal, she had formulated her plans for the evening. She would get something to eat, sign out a vehicle at the militia motorpool, and drive to the *dacha*; Kusinien would be pleased. E-Alexa was just reaching for one of the red military telephones when she saw him approaching.

"Colonel Chinko," Nijinsky said in greeting. His voice could not have been more pleasant.

"Inspector," she replied. E-Alexa wondered if she had successfully concealed her annoyance. She was in no mood for small talk, particularly with Nijinsky.

The inspector stuffed his newspaper in his coat pocket and smiled. He had the look of expectation.

"Do you make it a habit of sitting around airports, Inspector?" she tried teasing.

"No—actually, well, yes, in this case, yes." It was the first time E-Alexa had ever seen the homicide inspector appear lost for words. "I have to admit," he whispered, leaning toward her, "that I knew you were arriving on this flight."

His admission caught E-Alexa off guard. "But only a few people knew," she said.

Nijinsky held up his hand. "I called your office, just by chance this morning, and wouldn't you know it, just my luck, this young officer informed me that you were returning to Moscow some time today. Well, you know how it is, after twenty years with the Noginsk, a few phone calls and I was able to determine that you were on flight 171-G out of Leningrad. The manifest listed a Colonel Chinko, so I figured that you must have received your long-overdue promotion and took a chance on meeting this flight." The lie was his way of acknowledging her promotion and, at the same time, avoiding revealing his meeting with Bekrenev.

"I'm flattered," E-Alexa said. She made the response sound as icy as possible without revealing her agitation. "But it was not necessary."

Nijinsky was clever enough to know that he had caught her off balance. "We are old friends," he reminded her, "and I was able to recover something that belongs to you. I have been keeping it for you."

"Recover?" E-Alexa said.

Nijinsky reached into the inside pocket of his raincoat and took out a parcel. It was large and bulky. "Forgive the poor wrapping job, Colonel. I fear that in such matters I am not so adept. But I thought I should conceal it so that people wouldn't be alarmed when they saw me handing it to you. A place like this— well, you know, people become alarmed when they see someone brandishing a semiautomatic."

E-Alexa took the parcel from him and peeled back the wrapping. It was the 9mm Makarov she had given Arbat and the one she reported as having been stolen from her hotel room.

"Every now and then we accomplish our objective, Colonel," he said. "Now you are saved the embarrassment of reporting it to your military superiors."

"I had given up hope that it would be found," E-Alexa lied. "I must admit, I confessed—and I have requisitioned a new one."

Nijinsky smiled. "I rather imagined that would be the case," he said.

LOG:
FIFTEEN: TWO

Norwegian Maritime Weather Ship Akershus *1818L*
14 November

Berggen, the captain of the *Akershus*, Langley, and Commander Coltrain had gathered in the COM CEN when Bagley had first reported picking up the sporadic transmissions. For the past hour they had been standing by while Simon Penser, the British WMO representative, monitored the exchanges.

"Are you certain?" Langley asked for the second time.

"Quite," Penser said, holding up his hand. "Rest assured, the combination of short range and low frequency is S.O.P. for them."

"There's no way we can be one hundred percent certain, Peter," Coltrain observed. "The signal is weak and intermittent. We're now looking at an elapsed mission time of close to thirteen hours if we were anywhere close on their estimated launch time. Based on everything we know, the *Zotov* is pushing the limits on its EMT. Unless, of course, they've upgraded those fancy nickel-iron batteries of theirs, she simply can't stay down there much longer."

"You're convinced those transmissions are between the *Zotov* and the *Pitki?*" Langley asked.

Bagley laughed. "Put it this way, who the hell else would the *Pitki* be talking to? There isn't another damn Russian vessel within three hundred kilometers."

"It's curious that they would risk a transmission when they know we're in the area," Coltrain speculated.

"Maybe they don't have any alternative," Penser said.

"What about the *Spats*?" Berggen inquired.

"They're under strict orders," Langley said. "If I know Bogner, we won't hear a damn thing until it's either over or too damn late."

Berggen turned away from the console and walked across the room. He took out his pipe and began to pack it. Then he looked at Langley. "It is a curious world you live in, Captain. It is a world with which I am entirely unfamiliar. Hearing all of this, how do you assess the situation?"

Langley chewed on his lip. He sat down, studied the charts in front of him, and sighed. "Frankly, Captain, I guess a lot—and I pray a lot."

"Pray?" Berggen repeated.

"Yeah—I pray that I'm guessing right. Right now I'm guessing that if Penser and Bagley are correct, then the *Zotov* is still down there. If the *Zotov* is still down there, it can mean one of two things; either our Russian friends haven't found what they're looking for—or the *Spats* has them cut off. Taking that logic one step further, if the *Zotov* hasn't located what they went in there after, given the fact that we are told they have a twelve-hour EMT, they would have returned to the mother ship by now to recharge their batteries."

Berggen lit his pipe. "Then you believe there is a confrontation?"

"It's a distinct possibility," Langley admitted. "Either that or something has gone drastically haywire."

"Elaborate," Berggen insisted.

Langley shrugged. "Follow the logic. We know that

the *Spats* has a thirty-hour EMT. That's in our favor. If it becomes a waiting game, we're holding the high cards."

Penser looked up from the notepad where he had been jotting the fragments of radio conversation. "I don't know how significant this is, Commander, but if I interpret it correctly, the *Pitki* has just confirmed that she is under way."

"Leaving Kickana?" Berggen asked. "Curious."

Langley looked up. "Which direction is she headed?"

Penser shook his head. "Can't tell yet. There was a brief exchange between the *Pitki* and the detachment commander on Kickana."

"Kickana is manned?" Langley demanded.

"We never know," Berggen admitted. "From time to time the Russians deploy a small group of scientists there. Most of the time, however, they rely on remote instrumentation to take their readings."

"Is it possible that the transmissions between Kickana and the *Pitki* are what Penser has been monitoring for the last hour?" Langley asked.

Penser shook his head. "It is altogether possible that the transmission from the *Pitki* was simply relayed through the unmanned transmitter on Kickana," Penser said.

Langley leaned forward and smiled. "All that prayer helps, Captain. One of our guesses was just confirmed; the *Zotov* is still down there." He turned to Coltrain. "How soon can we confirm which way that icebreaker is heading?"

"The cat's out of the bag with the next transmission. The minute she lets a peep out of her radio, we can fix her position within fifty yards."

Langley stood up and looked at the surface charts. "Ask Dr. Howard to come down here."

"I am already here, Captain," he heard her say. "I just came up from the forecasting center. I thought you would find this interesting." She laid the latest surface chart on the light table in front of him. In the corner under the WMO legend she had scribbled the latest compaction report.

Langley bent over the charts.

"This is our computer model based on the 1800 readings. It is interesting from two aspects. One, the pressure ridges of the forward ice north and west as well as south and west of Kickana have increased significantly within the last twelve hours. Two, there is some breakup in the surface floe west of the island. The latter is to be expected with the amount of pressure-ridge compaction going on under the surface."

"All right, Doctor, interpret it for me," Langley said.

Anita Howard began chewing on her pencil again. Then she pointed to the charts. "Here," she said, "the ice base is moving rather rapidly, Commander, particularly in sections 8-b and 8-c, where the *Spats* is deployed."

"Meaning?"

"Meaning that your primary concern should be getting your crew out of there. Under conditions such as these, lace ice forms rapidly, the tentacles quickly postulate into columns, and the columns rapidly evolve into rather formidable underwater cathedrals. The crew of your DSRV is no doubt being treated to a rather disturbing timpani of sounds not unlike that of an earthquake."

"Can it happen quick enough to trap them?"

"Two-hundred-and-fifty-ton ice boulders are not uncommon," she said matter-of-factly. "I fear, Commander, that all of the conditions for setting such underwater mountains of ice in motion are there."

Langley frowned. "You said something about a breakup in the ice floe west of Kickana."

"Try to picture a great wave, Commander, pushing millions of tons of water ahead of it. There is considerable agitation. Pressure ridges give way to this agitation and the floe moves rapidly, thinning and thickening."

"The *Pitki* just transmitted her position," Penser exclaimed. "She's moving west southwest, two hundred forty degrees. I'd estimate the speed at something close to one and a half knots."

Langley traced his finger from the tiny inlet at Kickana to the red X on the map in sector 8-c. He glanced at Berggen and Dr. Howard, then took a pencil and began to sketch. He drew a rough cube and quickly scratched two disc-shaped figures near the bottom of the cube. "Tell me, Captain, if you were trapped between a rock and a hard place, with ice here and here, and were blocked here, what alternatives would you have for escape?"

Berggen studied the drawing and puffed on his pipe.

"Isn't straight up an alternative?" Langley finally asked.

"Are you forgetting about the ice?" Berggen asked.

"Didn't Dr. Howard say that there is an area of agitation just ahead of these pressure ridges? And didn't she say that this can result in alternating thin and thick pack ice?"

Berggen frowned. "You are suggesting perhaps that our Russian friends will try to go up and out instead of up and over?"

"Why not? Bogner and Filchak were under instruction that, if they got there late, they were to make it impossible for the Russians to get out of there; in other words, a blockade—the oldest navy trick in the book. Now Penser is telling us that the *Pitki* is moving in that direction—toward the 8-c sector. At the same time, Dr. Howard is assuring us that we have surface agitation in the same area—and she is predicting both thin and thick ice. Add to that the fact that there is every reason to believe the *Zotov*'s batteries are weak."

Anita Howard scrutinized the surface map again. "I do not know much about your world of DSRVs and DSSVs, Captain Langley, but if the *Pitki* were to move into this area and further break up the surface ice, what you are suggesting appears to be a distinct possibility."

Langley began to frown and looked at Bagley. "Best guess at how long it will take the *Pitki* to get to sector 8-c, Byron?"

The *Akershus*'s operation officer hedged. "Given what Dr. Howard is telling us the ice compaction factors are, and given the distance between the two points, two hours at the most, maybe sooner."

Langley looked around the room. "Now comes the big question. If the *Zotov* makes it through to the surface, how do we stop them from handing over the data to someone on that damn icebreaker?"

"We can't," Berggen said. "It's up to your crew on the *Spats*, Commander. Are they sufficiently armed?"

"They sure as hell don't have anything that'll stop an icebreaker," Langley admitted.

LOG:
FIFTEEN: THREE

The American DSRV Spats *1831L*
14 November

Bogner tried to rest propped in a cramped corner of the *Spats*'s control pod. Filchak, meanwhile, tried to monitor the intermittent transmissions from the *Zotov*.

"No doubt about it now, Toby. They've got a handle on their situation. I'm only able to get about a third of what they're saying—but I do know they're talking to the mother ship. The *Pitki* knows we've got them hemmed in."

Bogner moved to the B console. "What are they saying to each other?"

"As near as I can make out, they're telling the *Pitki* that they've got two concerns. Their batteries are damn near gone, and they are concerned about the shift in the shelf ice."

Bogner grunted, adjusted his headphones, and studied the situation display. "What's our mission time?"

"We're zeroing in on the ten-hour mark," Filchak confirmed.

"If Langley is operating on good information, then that explains their battery situation. If they launched two to three hours before we did, that means they're probably operating on reserve by now."

Filchak, for the third time in the past 30 minutes, activated the 2072-A signal processor on the flank array passive sonar and opened the view shields. He plunged the *Spats* into a red condition, and the eerie red light concealed the open viewports in the control pod. Both men looked out at the world of darkness beyond the bow viewport.

"They sure as hell can't wait much longer, T.C. They're damn near surrounded by the ice pack already."

Bogner peered out. The columnar formations were becoming an underwater jungle. "Can you get an extension factor?"

"They go all the way to the bottom, Toby. Just east of the *Zotov* I'm picking up a couple of formations about the size of a housing project."

Bogner slammed his fist down on the chart table. "Damn it, Cody, what are they waiting for? They've got what they came after; why the hell don't they bail out?"

Filchak held up his hand. "Hold it, they're talking to the *Pitki* again. I wish to hell my Russian was better. I'm only getting every third word or so."

Bogner picked up the auxiliary headset again and listened until the transmission stopped. "That's another thing. They know we're out here, they know we're monitoring their transmissions, yet they're making no effort to scramble."

Filchak nodded. "They could be thinking that they've got a pretty good profile on us and they probably figure that because of our size, they can outmaneuver us."

"Then why the hell are they waiting?" Bogner said.

Filchak shook his head. "Beats me—unless they've got some damn angle we haven't figured on."

LOG: FIFTEEN: FOUR

The Russian DSRV Zotov *1844L*
14 November

Sergi Brerkutev rubbed his hands together to ward off the growing chill in the *Zotov*. Meanwhile, Stigga's hands moved quickly over the console, checking, rechecking, shutting down the last of the DSRV's control systems. Only the arrangement of makeup air valves continued to operate. "What was our last reserve reading?" Brerkutev demanded.

Stigga's voice betrayed him. "Eleven, perhaps twelve percent."

Brerkutev shivered. He was trying to calculate the power required to activate the vertical thrusters and break through the ice to the surface. He knew it would take every bit of what they had left to break through—even if the *Pitki* did sufficiently agitate the surface ice. Not one to calculate the odds of success or failure in such an undertaking, he nevertheless found himself wondering what factors he had overlooked in his calculations. When he was convinced that he had overlooked nothing, he went over the figures in his mind again.

Brerkutev realized it would be foolhardy to think that even the thin ice would be less than one and a half to two meters thick. But if the *Pitki* could somehow foment the ice enough, and incite a sufficient number of small fissures, and if the crash plates surrounding the personnel hatch withstood the collision, the two of them could escape onto the surface of the ice—and once they were aboard the *Pitki*, the data capsule would be safe.

His plan was both desperate and daring—but Brerkutev was convinced that the Americans would not figure out what was happening until it was too late. By then the *Zotov* would be on the surface.

Using his penlight, Brerkutev scanned the console to make certain he had not overlooked anything, and then checked his watch. Koshkin had estimated he would have the *Pitki* over the 8-c rendezvous site at approximately 1915 hours. The two men had synchronized their watches, and Brerkutev had been instructed to open his receiver at 1910 to confirm the ETA. Now there were less than 20 minutes to go.

He turned to Stigga in the darkness. "There is a spare dive suit in the pressure chamber, comrade. I think it would be wise if you were to put it on."

Stigga hesitated. "I see no—"

"When we get through to the surface," Brerkutev continued, "it will afford you additional protection from the cold. If my calculations are correct, the *Pitki* could be positioned as much as a kilometer away from where we surface. Unfortunately, breaking through the ice to the surface is only our first obstacle. Getting to the *Pitki* will be another test of our resolve."

Stigga opened the air valve in the second pod and moved into the pressure chamber. Brerkutev could see the thin beam of his personnel lamp as the Spetsnaz captain searched for the equipment locker.

Again Brerkutev checked his watch and went over the ascent procedure in his mind. As soon as Koshkin indicated that he was in position and had completed his first pass, Brerkutev would activate the flank and

vertical sonar to determine the position of the thinnest
ice. If the HMI lights worked, and there was no way
of knowing whether the Americans had completely
disabled them or not, he would activate the topside
camera to confirm the location of the thinnest ice.
If not, he would be relying totally on data from the
absorption sonar. In either case, the moment he had
some indication of the ice configuration over them
and knew which way to maneuver the craft, he would
funnel all available power to the vertical thrusters and
head for the surface. If he failed to break through on
the first thrust, at a ten-percent reserve factor, he estimated he had enough power to try three times. If three
did not do it, there was always the even longer shot of
escaping through the diving skirt and swimming until
they found breaks in the ice, a possibility he had not
discussed with Stigga.

Brerkutev shuddered at the thought of the alternative; if the *Zotov* did not break through, the latter was
unlikely.

When Stigga returned, he was wearing the standard
black and red neoprene diving suit. He carried his
helmet under his arm, and slipped into the copilot's
chair at the console. He said nothing.

"Your thoughts, Captain Stigga?" Brerkutev asked.

"I was thinking of young Lieutenant Zhdanov,"
Stigga admitted. "How did he die?"

Brerkutev did not answer him. Instead he asked,
"How long have you been in the Spetsnaz, Captain?"

"Twenty-seven years."

"Surely you have lost men before." Brerkutev's voice
was detached; dry and brittle.

"How old do you think Yuri was?" Stigga asked.

"Perhaps as old as my own son was when he died. He
was only twenty-seven when he was killed by a Muslim
terrorist at a border crossing in Chaman."

"It must be a terrible thing to lose a son," Stigga
offered. The admission had given him new insight into

the man Dolin referred to as the ultimate warrior.

"It is," Brerkutev confirmed. His voice had softened.

Before Stigga could say anything else, he saw the mission specialist check his watch. When he did, Stigga stiffened, leaned toward the console, and opened the gate on his own receiver.

"For the record, Captain Stigga, in a very few minutes we will know if our fate is to be any different than that of young Zhdanov."

Stigga was holding his breath.

Brerkutev glared at the console, waiting. Outside the *Zotov* the ice continued to shift and moan. The hull of the DSRV continued to protest.

At 1917 the red *alert* light on the receiver finally began blinking. Brerkutev adjusted the volume and put on the headset. The five-digit ident code came through in pristine fashion. Stigga recognized the voice of the *Pitki*'s young communication officer, Sergi Yakovelev. He was reciting the vector coordinates in the 8-c sector. Brerkutev turned on the panel light and activated the computer.

"Plotting," he confirmed. "Vector A-B, CD heading 14. Vector A-B, CD corrected. Repeat. Vector A-B, CD heading 14. Vector A-B, CD corrected."

"Confirmed," Stigga acknowledged.

Stigga waited with his hand on the controls of the port and starboard vertical thrusters until Brerkutev activated and checked the systems monitor. The lights in the control pod seemed harsh after the period of prolonged darkness, and Stigga blinked involuntarily. Brerkutev nodded and Stigga pressed the controls to the coil heaters on the VT units. He counted to ten, watched the needle climb into the G zone, and initiated vertical thrust. The *Zotov* began to vibrate and lift.

There was the momentary grinding sound of the titanium hull against the ice as the DSRV brushed against the encroaching ice pack. Then there was a brief downward drift before, slowly, it began to lift.

Brerkutev had used the security system to seal the doors to the egress chamber as a precaution against leaks resulting from the collision with the surface ice. Stigga braced himself against the bulkhead and watched the depthometer. Brerkutev recited the readings. "Seventy-two, seventy, sixty-eight."

LOG:
FIFTEEN: FIVE

The American DSRV Spats *1921L*
14 November

"I'm starting to get some chatter," Filchak reported.

"What kind?"

"Can't tell for certain, but it sounds like they're repeating a series of coordinates. So far there's been no confirmation."

"Nothing from the *Zotov*?"

Filchak shook his head. "They're stirring around over there. I'm picking up some operational chatter."

"Open the front viewport and hit the lights," Bogner barked. The lens shield opened and all Bogner could see was a wall of ice. "Damn it, Cody, we're sealed off. I can't even see them."

"They're lifting," Filchak confirmed.

"Throw this baby in gear," Bogner ordered. "Make sure we've got vertical thrust."

Filchak powered up on all systems. "Stand by." There was a momentary pause. "Power on. Video scan on."

Bogner waited for the *Zotov*'s image to appear on the monitor.

"Hit the reverse thrust," Filchak ordered. "That damned ice is peeling back over us. I'll have to back her out."

Bogner felt the *Spats* lurch backward as he watched the *Zotov* start its ascent. There was a brief scraping sound and then silence. "We're clear," he shouted. "Now—where the hell are they?"

Filchak looked down at the sonar scope. "067 degrees at 0200, they're starting to come around."

"Full vertical thrust," Bogner shouted.

"She's coming straight at us," Filchak warned.

"There's no way I'm letting that son of a bitch get past us," Bogner snarled.

"Hey—she's elevating."

"She can't be—there's nowhere to go."

"Still elevating . . ."

Bogner looked down at the sonar display. "What the hell is going on? She looks like she's trying to go straight on up through the ice."

"She just rammed it," Filchak confirmed.

Bogner switched to the ice pack monitor. "She'll never make it. That ice is at least two feet thick at the thinnest point."

Filchak watched as the *Zotov* descended and applied vertical thrust a second time. "In addition to everything else, I'm picking up some disturbance on the surface."

Bogner wheeled and looked at the monitor. "Damn it, Cody, that's what that was all about; they got help. That's diesel noise. They've got that damn icebreaker of theirs churning up the ice on the surface."

"So far it isn't working," Filchak confirmed. "She's settling again."

"Thin ice in sector 8-c quads 4 and 5," Bogner reported. "She's off target. She'll never get through where she's at."

"She's going up again—but she's too close to that ice cathedral," Filchak said.

The two men watched as the *Zotov* slammed into the ice pack, ricocheted slightly, and came to a halt, listing slightly to her port side, on an ice shelf, wedged between the shelf and the surface ice. Then the image disappeared from the screen.

"Where the hell is she?" Filchak muttered. "Did she make it?"

Bogner studied the monitor while Filchak brought the *Spats* around and focused the HMI lights at the ice shelf. "There she is," Filchak exclaimed, "just like a damn fish caught in a net." He looked at Bogner. "What now?"

"Kill the lights and go silent. It'll take them a couple of minutes to figure out what kind of trouble they're in and I want you to get us in as close as possible."

"Don't tell me you're thinking what I think you're thinking," Filchak whispered.

Bogner's plan was already half formulated. He brought the bow video around until he had a clear image of the trapped *Zotov*. "That was probably their last hurrah. Now it's all starting to make sense, Cody. They figured they couldn't get past us by going over us and decided the best way out was to call in the mother ship to break up the ice. And it might have worked if they had hit the thin ice . . . but from the looks of things, they missed their coordinates."

"Meaning?"

"Assuming they're still alive, it's my guess they'll contact that icebreaker and tell them they need to dig them out. The icebreaker can find them if they send out a homing signal. It won't take the surface crew long to dig them out after they locate them. With a couple of G lines and some augers it shouldn't take more than thirty or forty minutes."

"What's to stop them from using their thrusters to back out of there and try again?"

"My guess is that they don't have any power left. They've probably got a couple of small auxiliary units for standby—enough to keep them from suffocating and to transmit a homing signal, but not enough to power up."

Filchak craned his neck around so that he could see the ops console. Then he looked at Bogner. "You're not going to try to board that damn thing, are you?"

Bogner continued to frown. "You got a better plan? We've come this far, we might as well give it one final shot."

"It's suicide," Filchak protested.

Bogner shook his head. "It's a helluva lot less risky than crawling around in that damn freighter. Besides, this time I know where the Russians are."

"Think you can get aboard?" Filchak questioned.

"I think so. I got a good look at the egress bell when Cameron and I tried to disable it. There is a manual hatch wheel inside the transfer skirt where they lower the haul-down winch. If they don't stop me before I get in that pressure capsule, they're mine. The door to the hatch and the one leading from the pressure chamber to the control capsule can be sealed—but they can't be locked; that's international convention."

"I still think it's suicide," Filchak repeated.

"We'll know how good our chances are as soon as they reveal what their condition is to the mother ship. The minute we're sure they're hung up on that ice shelf, I'm going in."

Filchak shook his head and turned back to the situation display panel. "They're chattering," he said and began to smile. "You called it, Commander. That was our boy on the *Zotov*. In so many words he's telling the surface that they are in a heap of shit. They're trapped and out of power." Filchak paused and continued to listen. "Now the mother ship is responding—she claims she needs a fifteen-minute delay before the *Zotov* starts broadcasting her homing signal. The icebreaker needs more time to get additional equipment deployed on the ice."

Bogner started for the pressure compartment. "That means I've got twenty minutes, more or less, to get on board that damn thing and get that data capsule before that DSRV starts crawling with a bunch of their comrades."

LOG:
SIXTEEN: ONE

Norwegian Maritime Weather Ship Akershus *1941L*
14 November

Berggen and Langley, waiting in the galley of the *Akershus*, had just sat down with their coffee when Coltrain's voice crackled over the intercom. "Captain, thought you'd better know, we're picking up those transmissions again."

The two men raced to the COM CEN, where Penser was still at the console wearing the headset and scribbling down the words he could identify. Coltrain was listening on a second set of headphones.

Langley leaned over his shoulder and began reading Penser's notes; *bataryeya, oopatrye, paisilat, pamaget.* Then he looked at Penser. "Okay, what the hell does that mean?"

Penser removed his pipe and shook his head. "Out of context, nothing I'm afraid. The only thing we do know is that the transmission has been repeated several times. There was a certain urgency about it."

Langley scowled. "Yeah, but you wrote these words down; what the hell do they mean?"

Penser was not the type to be intimidated. "If you're looking for a rather literal translation, the sender is indicating that the ice is thick, their power source is

407

depleted, and they are asking for assistance."

"Is the source of this transmission that same as you were logging earlier?" Langley demanded.

Penser nodded. "Indeed. However, it was much clearer and much stronger then."

Langley turned to Berggen. "What do you make of it?"

Berggen paused before he answered. "If your earlier assumptions were correct, then I imagine we are thinking along the same lines; the Russian craft has indeed attempted to surface through the ice pack. From the sound of things, it did not make it, and is asking for additional assistance. Am I correct?"

Langley nodded. "Exactly what I was thinking."

Berggen cleared his throat. "But your primary concern is what has happened to your own crew—and are they capable of handling the situation?"

Langley nodded. "There's been no Russian distress signal? Do you think we're reading the situation right?"

"There never is with the Russians."

"What happens if we take a look?"

"It wouldn't be the first time." Berggen smiled. "Three years ago, you Americans insisted on, shall I call it, 'assisting' us when we had to fly in to Kickana on a medical emergency. Two of their men were burned in a chemical fire. While we tended to medical manners, you blokes had a look around."

Langley stared out the obs window at the *Akershus's* stern. "What about the chopper sitting on the fantail?"

"An ancient, but serviceable Agusta-Bell, Captain, a 1955 AB-204B, I believe. It was purchased by the WMO from one of your surplus auctions. We use it to facilitate our ship-to-shore emergencies. Its use has been infrequent, of course, but the second officer, Mr. Ewing, is a quite capable pilot."

Langley turned around and looked at the surface

chart. "How long would it take to get it ready?"

Berggen raised his eyebrows and picked up the phone on the intercom. "Bridge, this is Captain Berggen. See if you can locate Mr. Ewing. I wish to speak to him." When he was finished, Berggen placed the phone back in the cradle. "We will know in a minute, Captain," he said.

LOG: SIXTEEN: TWO

The American DSRV Spats *1957L*
14 November

Bogner struggled into the dive suit, pulled the mask into position, checked the LS monitor, cleared his DP, and slipped through the egress hatch as Filchak brought the *Spats* around directly under the ice shelf supporting the *Zotov*.

The DSRV pilot's voice sounding off the readings was the last thing Bogner heard as he cleared the chamber and dropped down into the icy black water. He was using the spare RM helmet, which meant that he again had the benefit of the infrared AVS and the SM-A systems monitor. Now, when he needed it least because his target was in sight, a steady stream of telemetric data flashed through the helmet lens, and he decided not to attach the L line to the D ring on the transfer skirt. He needed to play it by ear—nothing restricting—the *Zotov* looked anything but stable.

Bogner swam up, out, over the ice shelf, and dropped down to within 20 feet of the *Zotov*. He kept low, doing what he could to avoid a chance detection in the *Zotov*'s system of exotic external mirrors. Finally he was able to slip into position under the transfer skirt.

"So far so good, S-1, I'm home," he informed Filchak.

Bogner was no longer concerned whether or not the *Zotov* was picking up their transmissions. "I'm down to the short hairs. Read?"

Filchak acknowledged. "Read you."

Bogner checked his E-time and studied the detail of the external hatch access wheel; two turns to the left would do it. "What's your mark, S-1?"

"Working nine down," Filchak recited. "They're crawling all over the ice with air hammers and ice augers."

Bogner acknowledged; now he had less than nine minutes to pull it off. From here on out, every second was critical. He would have to act fast and he would have to be careful to coincide his actions with the cacophony of noise emanating from the surface. He was banking on the rescue crew using the augers and placing a series of small charges in the ice rather than using the more powerful G lines.

Even now, the disturbing sounds of the compacting ice alarmed and distracted him. He watched the shelf ice heave and buckle before settling again. A disturbing six-inch-wide fissure had appeared in the floor of the shelf, just aft of the craft's bow ski. It trailed back along a fault line that traced its way directly under him. It had already occurred to him that if the shelf took another blow like the one he had just experienced, the ice, the *Zotov,* and one Tobias Carrington Bogner would take a long, nasty drop 70 to 80 feet straight down. He pulled his legs up under him, gripped the hatch wheel, and checked his LS system. The readings were slightly elevated but still within the NO range. "NO," he repeated, "normal operations." He laughed to himself. What the hell was normal when you had your back pinned to an ice shelf 25 to 30 feet under the Arctic ice pack in the middle of the Stavka Straits?

He had taken up position inside the shield. Now all he had to do was wait until the right minute to force his entry.

"Mark—eight and down," Filchak recited. The *Spats's* pilot's voice sounded even closer than it had on the first transmission.

Bogner acknowledged and continued to wait. Where the hell were the Russians on the surface? He didn't want silence, he wanted noise—lots of noise—any kind of noise—noise that would indicate there was activity and maybe even a little confusion on the surface. It was exactly what he needed to distract the Russian crew while he worked his way into the *Zotov's* dive chamber.

"Mark—seven and down," Filchak's voice counted. "How about it, Toby, any progress?"

"Where the hell are they?" Bogner hissed.

"They're ready to start cutting their way through."

"What's taking them so damn long?" Bogner complained.

Still there was no sound of the augers. He moved his arms, and flexed his hands and fingers. More silence. Where the hell were they? He decided maybe the word wasn't silence; maybe the word was stillness. Then he thought about the word stillness, and decided that stillness wasn't quite right either. Maybe the word he was searching for was aloneness. He checked the time. Where the hell were they?

By now he figured the ice would be crawling with every damned crew member the *Pitki* could muster—trying to spare their comrades in the *Zotov* from one damned unpleasant fate. He shimmied back toward the bow to examine the crack in the ice again. It was wider, by several inches. As far as Bogner was concerned, a little too wide to risk waiting in the hatch skirt.

Then he heard it—the chewing, growling, sound-muffling snarl of an auger. At first there was only one—and then two. It was exactly what he had been waiting for. When the third auger kicked in, he reached up and began to turn the hatch wheel.

Suddenly he had the distraction, and he had the

noise. Now all he needed was a little bit of luck.

Logically the crew of the *Zotov* would remain in the personnel pod during the rescue effort—that was where the topside hatch was located. The dive chamber would require makeup air; makeup air required batteries—the door to the dive chamber was likely to be closed.

Bogner turned the wheel and realized he was muttering a prayer. Mickie often accused him of praying only when he was in a tight spot. Maybe she was right. She was right about a lot of things. He gave the hatch wheel another twist, tugged, and felt the seal break. Then he paused to make certain the augers were still chewing their way through the ice. They were getting serious now; a fourth auger had been cranked into action.

He pushed up on the hatch and felt the rush of water swirl past his helmet as it flooded the air lock. Now he had to pull himself into a sitting position with his head inside the skirt cavity. He had to overcome the numbness and the cold. His legs were stiff, his body even stiffer. He checked his breathing on the LS monitor.

There was a brief moment when all the augers were silent and he had to wait. When they cranked up again, he knew it was now or never. He pulled himself up and into the dive chamber of the *Zotov*. The water quit climbing when it reached midthigh. He looked at the buoyancy gauge. The air pocket was holding. But now he had a new problem. When he opened the door into the control pod, would the sudden rush of water disturb the delicate balance that was keeping the craft on the ice shelf? He didn't want to think about it.

Then he caught himself—he was playing mind games with himself again. If he continued to conjure up ghosts he would never go through with it. He hesitated just long enough to remove his glove, lift the flap on his E pack, and slip the 4.5mm out of its sling lock. Once was enough. This time he would be the one who was ready. He gripped the wheel, pulled down, turned it clockwise, and shoved it open. The water tumbled in from the dive chamber and flooded the darkened control pod with a torrent of water.

One body was slumped forward over the control console. The other, on the floor of the pod, twisted and turned in the eddies created by the swirling water. The mouth and eyes were open and a thin trickle of blood had coagulated around the man's nostrils and the corners of his mouth. Bogner lifted the man's head up out of the water and pulled the body up on the chart table. He was an older man, almost bald; but the gray, vacant, and still-open eyes were not the eyes of the man who had attacked him and left him for dead in the bowels of the *Drachev*. He let go of the man and the body slipped back beneath the surface of the churning water.

The other, head down, was slumped against the console. He was a broader, thicker man with a pronounced brow and deep-set eyes. He was wearing an insulated, neoprene dive suit, and there was a two-inch-long gash in the side of his head. It extended from the right ear toward the bridge of the nose. Bogner groped for a pulse. The man struggled, his eyes opened, and he gasped for air.

Bogner buried the barrel of his 4.5 in Brerkutev's throat and pulled the man's face up close to his. Just as he did, he heard the sounds of the Russian rescue team on the roof plates near the access hatch. They had made their way through the ice pack. Brerkutev's eyes were glazed but still defiant. He made a futile effort at twisting away, and Bogner slammed him back against the console.

"The cartridge, dammit," Bogner demanded. "The one you took away from me down in the hold of that ship."

Brerkutev looked back at him with vacant eyes, and Bogner pressed down on the barrel. The Russian's protest was weak, yet laced with epithets half English and half Russian. "Is Russian," he finally managed.

"At this point, Ivan, or Boris, or whatever the hell your name is, I couldn't care less who that cartridge belongs to. I want it. Now quit stalling."

Brerkutev snarled his defiance and Bogner pressed harder.

"There's a guy named Cameron down there in the carcass of that freighter of yours, Ruski, so I owe you one. Don't push your luck."

Brerkutev continued to glare back at him, and Bogner could hear the *Pitki*'s rescue crew pounding on the access hatch.

"Have it your way," Bogner said. "What you don't seem to realize is if I put one of these stainless-steel darts through your brain, you've got a piss-poor chance of getting out of here."

Brerkutev stiffened, his eyes desperately trying to search out the face behind the thick acrylic lens of Bogner's faceplate.

Overhead Bogner heard the seal on the personnel hatch hiss and disengage, and he felt the *Zotov* shift and the bow of the craft dip as it started to slide forward on the ice ledge. Water was gushing through the open access door to the pressure chamber. It cascaded down and swirled around the Russian's chest.

"Another two or three seconds and I won't have to pull the trigger. You'll be sucking ice water."

Brerkutev glared back at him.

Bogner's voice sounded metallic filtering out of the speakers on each side of the RM mask. Brerkutev's hand began to inch up toward the sealed pocket on his dive suit. Finally he pointed to it. "There," he choked.

Time was running out. Bogner leaned into the man, buried his elbow in the Russian's throat, ripped up the seal, and tore open the pocket. He found the container, pulled it out, glanced at it, decided that he had to gamble that it was the same one he had recovered from Zhou, stuffed it inside the sleeve guard of his dive suit, and let go of Brerkutev.

As it turned out, he was releasing the pressure on the Russian's throat just as the water was beginning to swirl around the man's chin.

Brerkutev struggled away from him gasping for breath. Bogner spun and ripped open the access panels of the data storage unit on the *Zotov*'s computers. Then he smashed the circuit boards with the butt of his APR. "Just in case you and your friend were clever enough to duplicate this little gem when you were reviewing it."

Brerkutev's eyes shot up toward the personnel hatch, and Bogner slipped beneath the swirling water. He clawed his way through the debris back to the access door to the pressure chamber and started to crawl through it—but it was too late.

At first it sounded like a slow ominous roll of approaching thunder. Then he felt the *Zotov* lurch, shift, and begin to slide. He knew there could only be one reason; the ice shelf was giving away.

There was the sound of tearing metal and another, not unlike that of snapping bones. He saw the outraged face of the Russian struggling toward him with the APS clenched in his hand.

Brerkutev never made it.

The *Zotov* toppled off of its icy precipice and spiraled down, pinballing through the jungle of ice monoliths until it crashed to the floor of the Stavka Straits.

The man was peering into the wraithlike infrared world of half-formed, half-tone, meaningless images. It was all, he decided, very annoying and amorphous; flitting, disconnected, confusing, and perplexing. But instead of wanting to solve the puzzle, the man wanted to close his eyes and say to hell with it, to hell with everything and everyone.

The man's head hurt. No. "Hurt" was inadequate,

he decided; his head "pounded." "Pounded" was accurate.

When the man moved his head he felt the pain. When he tried to move the rest of his body, he felt more pain.

Finally, when he opened his eyes, he realized he had no idea where he was nor how long he had been wherever he was. His chest ached and there was pressure. He coughed—more than once—often?—the sensation was cold and dry—then there was the awareness of the mouthpiece and the difficulty he was having breathing. He tried to think—and decided that the pain meant one thing. He was alive—but maybe, just maybe that wasn't a good thing. Maybe it meant he still had to die.

One by one he began to sort through the tangle of thoughts. At best, his thinking was muddled and his heart was pounding. The systems were functioning, but not in any kind of efficient fashion. On the other hand, his fingers and hands, like his feet and legs, were thick and bulky, and there was a burning, stubby sensation in each of them.

Words flashed in his brain, but they were empty icons, symbols with no meaning. Then, slowly, and with no definite pattern, he began to realize where he was. Things fell into place. When he began to realize where he was and why he was so cold, he involuntarily elevated himself to a higher level of awareness, something he was not so sure he wanted to experience. After all, if he was going to die, he was not particularly interested in being alert enough to record every last detail of the incident.

He realized there was a comfort in his unnerving numbness.

Gradually his eyes began to focus. But what good did it do? There was nothing but darkness.

Then, out of nowhere, it occurred to him to activate the LED display on his monitor. The phrase "system malfunction" began flashing on the mask's lens, and he closed his eyes. Screw it. Who needs it? The hell with it. Things have hurt worse—I'll just lie here. Maybe the transition will be easy.

But for Bogner, all the years of training were too ingrained, too much a part of him. It was the fireman's involuntary flinch when the alarm goes off. It was the fighter's response to the bell. He began counting to himself again.

One thousand one, one thousand two, one thousand three.

He forced himself to breathe on the count; each breath was a little deeper.

The air slammed into his lungs and he repeated the process.

One thousand one, one thousand two, one thousand three.

Again—one more time—this time a deeper breath—and he inhaled again. This time he was giddy as he began to count; the damn thing was still working.

Finally he opened his eyes again. The telemetry was parading system vitals across the display lens. The figures were meaningless, but the LS system continued to pump its stream of data. The AVS had a crack in one of the lenses and he unplugged it. Then he reached down and activated the chest halogen. Finally there was light in his world.

The beam pierced the icy black water and he saw the ill-defined image of the Russian undulating in the water near the transfer hatch. The lifeless body was still clutching the ominous-looking APS.

Another piece of the puzzle locked in.

Bogner closed his eyes, unsure of reality. But it was real—it, whatever *it* was, was still there. He stared at the morbid scene until he could marshal his senses and bring his breathing under control. The sensation of final reality was intensifying.

He groped out with his right hand, searching for

something to hold on to. He had the unnerving sensation that he was floating free in space and at the same time being confined. Underneath him was a smooth cocoon of metal and glass. He fumbled in the unfamiliar darkness, gradually coming to another realization; he was still in the Russian DSRV and for some reason, it was upside down. The vehicle's egress hatch and the transfer skirt were directly above him.

He framed a mental picture of his surroundings, and decided that the next test was to see if he could move the rest of his body. The hands worked, not well, but enough; now he had to try the legs—and maybe even standing up. He sent out the commands and to his astonishment, the parts responded. They hurt—but they worked. He pulled his knees up, cocked one leg up under him, and managed to get to his feet. A wave of nausea swept over him, and he momentarily sagged back to his knees. He realized he was off balance, and now there was a question in his mind. Could he make it?

He stood up again and began the count. The slightest movement brought on the sensation of total exhaustion. One thousand one, one thousand two, one . . . and then he saw it, beyond the transfer skirt, a light, at first dim and distant, but now getting brighter.

He reached up and began to hoist himself into the mouth of the transfer skirt. By the time he managed to pull himself through the egress hatch, he could see it. The *Spats* was hovering directly above him. He closed his eyes and began to count again—or was he praying—in numbers?

LOG:
SIXTEEN: THREE

Taganrog: Moscow 2121L
14 November

When E-Alexa entered through the back entrance and
started up the stairs, the ancient babushka stopped her.
Even then she did not speak. She simply inclined her
graying head toward Kusinien's study.

The gesture perplexed E-Alexa. "He is alone?" she
asked.

The old woman nodded.

E-Alexa turned, went back down the stairs, and down
the hall to the study. The old man did not look up when
she entered the room. He chose instead to continue to
stare at the flames in the massive fireplace.

She paused near the doorway, standing with her
hands on her hips. She was still wearing the drab
gray-green winter uniform. "Is there some reason why
I was recalled from Belushya?" she demanded.

Kusinien looked at her, then returned his attention
to the flames. "How was your trip?" he asked.

To E-Alexa his voice sounded even more weary than
usual. There was a husky quality to it, not of passion,
but as if he did not care whether or not she understood
him. Finally she settled on the words lethargic and
indifferent.

"Tiring," she admitted. Now she knew that Kusinien was aware of her recall. Up until now, she had hoped that he did not know and that she could make her appeal to him.

Without looking at her, he said, "Please make yourself comfortable. Abuta will be here shortly—with some tea."

E-Alexa chose instead to sit across from him, with her back to the fireplace. She wanted him to have to look at her. Her face was in the shadows, but his face, long and gaunt, reflected the orange-yellow cast of the flames. Advantage: E-Alexa.

The once passionately purple eyes now appeared empty and faded, like the dried flowers that were sold in the Yunoski open-air market. "You did not answer my question," she reminded him.

"I am disappointed in you," he said.

"Disappointed?" she repeated. "Why?"

Still he did not look at her. He folded his hands and looked over them at the flames. "Tell me about General Gureko's death," he said.

She was no longer certain how to respond. Dolin had told her that he was keeping the general's death under wraps until the investigation was completed. Had he changed his mind? She hesitated just long enough for Kusinien to express his displeasure.

"One of your charms, Colonel Chinko, has always been your candor. This sudden reticence does not become you."

"I do not understand," she said, stalling.

"My question was simple enough. Gureko is dead. I am told he was murdered. How did he die?"

"He was poisoned," she said.

"And were you able to discover the identity of the man who killed him?"

"And why are you so certain it was a man?"

Kusinien made his usual guttural sound of amusement. She had heard it before, many times. But this time it was different; somehow he had also managed to convey his annoyance with her evasiveness.

While E-Alexa waited for Kusinien's interrogation to continue, the old woman arrived with the tea. There were two cups, already poured, along with a container of cream. The old woman placed the service on a small, ornately carved marble-topped table next to the old man's chair, then left. When Kusinien turned to pick up his cup, his hand was shaking.

"Colonel Ulitsa was charged with the crime," she finally said.

"You conducted the investigation?"

"Of course. As senior logistics officer, the investigation was my responsibility."

"And you, of course, discovered the incriminating evidence?"

E-Alexa smiled. "On the contrary, it was Lieutenant Siddrov, a member of the security staff at Belushya, who made the discovery."

"And what was Colonel Ulitsa's motive for this outrageous act?"

"We may never know. Lieutenant Siddrov discovered Colonel Ulitsa's body in his room. He committed suicide. The board of inquiry felt that Colonel Ulitsa's motive was that General Gureko demoted him from his position as chief of Belushya logistics to the position of a mere administrative officer."

Kusinien leaned back in his chair, closed his eyes, and allowed E-Alexa to see the full extent of both the mental and physical prostration that had overtaken him. His never-quite-idle fingers searched out the Chekhov play he had been reading and idly thumbed through it.

She waited for several moments before she repeated her question. "Why was I called back to Moscow?"

With his eyes still closed, he said, "You were brought back at the insistence of Marshal Vyacheslav Bekrenev."

"Do I need to remind the ambassador that it was General Bekrenev himself who promoted me to the position of chief of logistics at Belushya?"

"That was before Inspector Konstantin Nijinsky appeared on the scene," Kusinien said flatly.

"Nijinsky? What does Nijinsky have to do with this?"

Kusinien opened his eyes and leaned his near-skeletal head forward again. He reached into the inside pocket of his suit coat and removed a piece of paper. He unfolded it and handed it to E-Alexa.

It was a list of names and nothing more: Serafim Ammosovich, Evgeni Koslov, Kirill Gureko, and Moshe Aprihnen. "I do not understand," she lied. "What is this supposed to mean?"

Kusinien inclined his head to one side. "With the exception of President Aprihnen, they are all deceased. Or perhaps I should say, with the exception of our beloved president they have all died rather unexpectedly—all in the last twelve months. And that does not include the names of Mikhail Arbat and Colonel Ulitsa."

E-Alexa's voice was cold. "You surprise me, Comrade Kusinien." She dwelled on the word *comrade*. She had never addressed him in that fashion before. "But you overlooked the more obvious connection. Each of them, in their own fashion, contributed to the death of my mother and father. Our beloved president was minister of information at the time. It was he who decided to withhold information on the magnitude of the disaster at Chernobyl from Secretary Gorbachev. When he did, he signed the death warrant for the people of my village."

"And Ammosovich?" Kusinien asked.

"A puppet information lackey; he knew the truth but he did not speak up."

"Spoken like a true Party member," he said. A rare smile began to play at the corners of Kusinien's thin mouth. "Yet now we know that it was your father who was instrumental in helping Comrade Milatov escape into exile."

"A falsehood," E-Alexa bristled. "He was a true Party loyalist."

For the first time, Kusinien looked at her. "Such a waste. My lovely mantis, she not only devours her lovers, she devours the truth as well."

E-Alexa sagged. "What will happen now?" she asked.

Kusinien shrugged his withered shoulders. "I can only surmise that General Bekrenev will arrange for you to be turned over to the Moscow police sometime tomorrow."

"And you will do nothing to protect me?"

Kusinien sighed. "I am afraid, Colonel Chinko, despite your loveliness, you have become a diversion that I can no longer afford."

E-Alexa stood up. When she did, the fragile china teacup fell to the floor and shattered. The word *diversion* was like a knife in the heart. "You will not try to stop me from leaving?"

"I will not try to stop you," he confirmed.

Moments later, as E-Alexa climbed back into her car, she looked around the icebound, darkened *dacha* for what she realized would be the last time. In the window she saw the face of the old babushka. The old woman was smiling.

LOG: SIXTEEN: FOUR

Norwegian Maritime Weather Ship Akershus *2355L*
14 November

In the cramped quarters of the *Akershus* sick bay, Peter Langley and Cody Filchak maintained their vigil outside Bogner's room. While Berggen was in the COM CEN making arrangements for Bogner to be flown to the medical facilities at Tromso, Filchak used the opportunity to fill in the details for the NI officer.

"Then, I figure, when the rescue crew tried to gain access to the *Zotov*, over she went. Scared the hell out of me. I had visual contact and I knew T.C. was on board. The thing I didn't know was whether the rescue crew from the icebreaker had gotten everyone out before she took the plunge."

Langley urged him to continue.

"To tell the truth, I was half afraid to go down there and poke around. He took a helluva ride. If you ask me, it's a miracle he's alive."

Langley shook his head. "He appears to be all in one piece, but Berggen thinks we ought to get him to the medical center at Tromso and have them go over him." He paused for a moment then asked, "Anything left of the *Zotov*?"

"Depends on the scrap value of titanium," Filchak said.

Langley stood up and began to pace back and forth in the cramped stateroom. "Between Mitch, Toby, and the *Zotov*, we paid a helluva price for that damn data."

Filchak shook his head. "Mitch led the first excursion into the *Drachev*. I don't know exactly what happened, but T.C. found his body."

"Any chance of recovering the body?"

Filchak thought for a moment. "Possible, Peter, but it would be a long shot—and I don't think it's technically feasible until the ice shelf recedes. After I was finally able to get T.C. back on board the *Spats*, it took me almost two hours to thread my way back to the *Akershus*. Doc Howard knew what she was talking about. That compaction is scary stuff. The fact of the matter is, I think there is a damn good chance we might not even be able to find it."

Langley smiled. "That means if we can't, they won't be able to either."

He was still pacing when Berggen and the ship's doctor came back down the passageway. Berggen looked relieved. "We're in luck, Captain. The base commander at Bersivag is sending a helicopter to pick up your Commander Bogner."

"How is he?" Langley inquired.

Berggen looked at his pipe. "Well, I think it's safe to say he doesn't have much of a sense of humor at the moment."

"How long will it take that chopper to get here?" Langley asked.

Berggen checked his watch. "Three hours, perhaps sooner. They are sending a modified Huey UH-60B to pick him up. I am told that there will be sufficient room for you and Commander Filchak to accompany him if you so wish."

Langley smiled. "Only if you'll agree to take care of the *Spats* for us."

"Most indubitably, Commander Langley. In fact I might even take it out for a little spin myself."

LOG:
SEVENTEEN: ONE

The Kremlin: Moscow 1013L
16 November

Ilya Dolin's driver, a young corporal with a penchant for driving too fast, guided the black Pobedas through the midmorning Moscow traffic. At times he traveled at speeds that prevented Dolin from focusing his attention on the upcoming meeting with Vyacheslav Bekrenev.

Dolin, who had spent the entire night on flights that carried him from his Belushya outpost to the Russian capital, had not slept. He had hoped to arrive in sufficient time to take a shower, shave, and don a fresh uniform before the meeting with his superior, but delays en route had made that impossible.

Now he was reduced to rubbing his hand across his chin, feeling the stubble of his whiskers, and wondering what the outcome of the meeting would be. There were any number of questions. Who, if anyone besides Bekrenev, would be there? How severe would the reprimand be? And what of the entire Lyoto-Straf project? Now that Brerkutev's mission had failed, it would take many months, perhaps two years, to reconstruct the project's data files. He shuddered. At the moment Dolin considered this to be even more of a crisis than the botched *Zhukov* affair.

The Pobedas zipped past the Kolomenskaya Metro Station on Proletarsky Prospekt and the Church of the Ascension of Christ, then turned on Fadeyeva toward the Kremlin.

It was raining, a dreary, cold, steady rain that formed a thin crust of ice on the pockmarked surface of the dirty snow piled along the six-lane boulevard. When the Pobedas turned again and came to a halt in a parking stall close to the Alexandrovski Gardens, Dolin stepped out and breathed a sigh of relief.

"The shortest route to General Bekrenev's office is through the west entrance nearest the tower," the driver informed him.

Suddenly the chill, sodden air of the Moscow morning depressed Dolin as he climbed the stairs to the elevation and bridge leading from the tower to the structure itself. At the west entrance, a militiaman wearing a slicker that concealed his insignia saluted Dolin and opened the door.

Inside, on the worn red carpet of the corridor leading to the elevator to the second floor, the dryness in his mouth became more pronounced.

To Dolin, it seemed that the elevator took an interminable amount of time to reach its destination. He stepped off and went down the corridor, along the way passing a young woman in a militia uniform. She neither spoke nor looked his way. It occurred to him that it was a shame that such an attractive young woman would go to such extremes to conceal her femininity.

He hesitated outside the door to Bekrenev's office, straightened his tie, and smoothed his hair. Then he knocked.

"Come in," the voice instructed.

Dolin entered. Bekrenev was standing behind his desk. Through the window beyond him, Dolin could see the gray somber wash of the Moscow day. Bekrenev motioned for Dolin to sit down without so much as a greeting.

It was then that Dolin noticed the thin, pale presence of the other man in the room. It was Georgi Kusinien. The frail little man was seated in an oversized wingback leather chair to the right of Bekrenev's massive desk. Kusinien acknowledged him with a condescending nod and a slight hooding of his curiously purple eyes. Dolin had not expected Kusinien. It was obvious now that the Party considered the situation to be graver than even Dolin had imagined.

Bekrenev sat down behind his desk and leaned forward with his elbows on the surface. He was rotating an ornate pewter letter opener in his hands. "I suppose you know why we have sent for you, Admiral," Bekrenev began.

"Yes," Dolin admitted.

Bekrenev laid the instrument down with the tip of the blade pointing toward Dolin. Then he picked up a bulky file nearly two and one half centimeters thick. When he opened it, his face was flushed. "It is curious to me, Admiral, how a man of your apparent military stature and with your heretofore impeccable performance record could allow this to happen."

Dolin was already aware that none of his responses would be satisfactory, yet he was determined to explain what had happened.

"One does not expect to find an incompetent, especially one who has served so meritoriously in other endeavors, on one's own staff," Dolin replied.

"You are referring to Colonel Ulitsa?" Bekrenev asked.

Dolin nodded. "If you will check the promotion record, you will see that it was General Gureko himself who selected Colonel Ulitsa as the logistics officer at Belushya." After he said it, he realized that he'd sounded defensive.

"I am well aware of that, Admiral, but you were the

senior operations officer at Belushya; you should have been aware of his activities."

Kusinien's eyes were closed and his head inclined back against the chair. His raspy, always brittle voice commanded attention whenever he spoke, even when he spoke, as he did now, in a near-whisper. "Tell me, Admiral, when did you become aware of Doctor Konyev's involvement?"

Dolin looked at the sparse man in his ill-fitting black suit. "Only after Captain Koshkin aboard the *Pitki* radioed back the information from the site of the recovery effort. Brerkutev informed Koshkin that he had discovered the data capsule in Zhou's chest cavity where Koshkin supposedly had implanted the pacemaker."

"Very clever of Mission Specialist Brerkutev," Kusinien acknowledged. "And prior to that you had no reason to suspect Doctor Konyev of treasonous activities?"

Dolin indicated that he had not.

"Did it ever occur to you, Admiral, that the poisons used to kill General Gureko had to have come from the clinic—and that Doctor Konyev would be the one to both inventory and monitor such materials?"

"In retrospect, I see that, Comrade Ambassador, but at the time we were reaching a critical phase in the Lyoto-Straf program. You will recall that it was at this time I received word from General Bekrenev that the Sino contingent was to be phased out of the effort." Again Dolin immediately regretted his choice of words; he did not want it to sound as though he was trying to blame Bekrenev.

The general shifted in his chair. He continued to glare at Dolin's file. "There is a mountain of evidence to support our claim that the Sino scientists intended to steal our data from the outset," Bekrenev huffed.

"And I have heard," Dolin ventured, "that it was

President Aprihnen's intention to sever our agreement as soon as the Chinese perfected the process of encapsulating the cruor-toxins."

"Your concern is not strategic policy, Admiral," Bekrenev snarled. "Your concern is, or should have been, the successful launching of the Lyoto-Straf program."

"Admiral," Kusinien interrupted, "exactly what did Mission Specialist Brerkutev say when he notified the *Pitki* that they were coming in?"

Dolin breathed a sigh of relief. Kusinien wanted fact, not conjecture. He opened his briefcase and extracted a large gray envelope. "This is Captain Koshkin's statement." He began to read aloud:

At 1850L, 14 November, the *Zotov* broke silence. Mission Specialist Brerkutev indicated that the crew had retrieved the capsule and that they desired to return to the *Pitki*. It was then that MS Brerkutev informed us that because the mission had been extended beyond power capacity, there was not sufficient power to return. He asked me to investigate the feasibility of maneuvering the *Pitki* to and over the 8-c sector site, at the same time breaking up the ice pack, a maneuver MS Brerkutev believed would enable the *Zotov* to make a vertical surface maneuver.

At 1930, we advised MS Brerkutev that we were in position. I deployed crews with G-lines and ice augers. The *Zotov* made at least three attempts to penetrate the ice. Only on the last attempt were we able to determine its precise location. My crew bored through the ice, located the access hatch, and opened it. One of my men attempted to enter. As he did, he claimed one of the crew began firing at him.

"Began firing at him?" Bekrenev exclaimed. "One of the *Zotov's* crew opened fire on him?"

Dolin nodded. "Captain Koshkin claims he too heard what sounded to him like some form of gunfire."

"Most curious," Kusinien said, waving his hand. "Please continue, Admiral."

Dolin returned to the statement. He continued reading it aloud.

> At that point, the *Zotov,* which had apparently been wedged onto a small ice shelf, began to slip, and eventually plunged to the bottom."

Kusinien shook his head.

"At that point," Dolin continued, "Captain Koshkin reported that a helicopter from the nearby Norwegian maritime weather ship *Akershus* appeared on the scene and hovered over the area for several minutes. The pilot of the helicopter established contact and inquired if Captain Koshkin needed assistance. The pilot indicated that he had been dispatched by the *Akershus* because they had been receiving garbled transmissions for the previous two hours and felt that the crew of the *Pitki* might need assistance.

"The DSRV that MS Brerkutev described as having them trapped, Admiral Dolin, did you ever stop to think where that DSRV came from?" Kusinien asked.

Dolin looked at him. He did not want to admit that he had assumed the DSRV had been launched from a nuclear submarine if that was not the case. He thought it best not to admit his assumption.

Bekrenev cleared his throat. "Two facts remain, Admiral: the *Zotov* is lost . . . and we did not recover the data capsule. Is that correct?"

"I must assume," Dolin admitted, "that the data capsule still lies at the bottom of the Stavka Straits. Another effort can be made to recapture the capsule when a suitable retrieval vehicle is available."

"The *Zotov* was a suitable vehicle for such a mission," Bekrenev reminded him.

"Quite a record, Admiral," Kusinien said with a sigh. "Frankly, it is hard to conceive of a more butchered operation. Gureko and Ulitsa both dead, the entire Lyoto-Straf program brought to a halt because of the contamination of the design files, the loss of the *Zotov*—not to mention your lack of awareness of the presence of a Sino spy ring operating in your very midst."

Dolin had no defense, at least not in the sense of the military tradition, and he knew that. He hesitated, looked down, and put Koshkin's report back in his briefcase.

The old man stood up, walked to the window, and looked out at the lifeless courtyard dotted with patches of dirty snow. The window was streaked with rivulets of ice. With his back still turned to Dolin and Bekrenev, he began to speak.

"Is there any chance that any of the data contained in the Belushya data files is usable, Admiral?"

"It would appear that it is all contaminated," Dolin admitted.

"And your estimate to reconstruct the data is?"

"Months—perhaps years. Comrade Milatov spent six years developing the concept of the E-1-A system prior to the design phase. That information is available. And of course, the Belushya facilities are still intact."

"A decision that, in retrospect, I regret approving," Kusinien said.

"I can return to Belushya and begin now," Dolin offered.

Kusinien turned away from the window; the haunted, hollow face of the ambassador conveyed only weariness. "On the contrary, Admiral. You will not be returning to Belushya. At 0900 hours tomorrow morning, you will present yourself to the Ministry of Justice and the marshal provost. At such time you will be bound over and charged with crimes of sedition and malfeasance in your assigned duties for the Russian Commonwealth."

Dolin was stunned. He had expected a reprimand, at the very worst, a reduction in rank—but this was outrageous. He was being made a scapegoat. "I protest," he objected.

Kusinien closed his eyes. "You are dismissed, Admiral Dolin," he said.

Dolin stood up, hesitated, and finally left the room. When the door closed behind him, Bekrenev turned in his chair and looked at the man Aprihnen had entrusted with the staggering responsibility of launching the Lyoto-Straf program. "Who will you appoint to take over the project?" he finally asked.

"I do not know," Kusinien admitted. "More precisely, the question may well be, will there be a program? We must ask ourselves, how much are we willing to pay?"

Kusinien sighed, walked across the room, picked up his coat and hat, and paused after he opened the door. His voice was barely audible. "Some dreams are better left to die, General," he said.

Bekrenev stared back at him, regarding him with the uncompromising appraisal of a man who had been trained to think and act like a general. To Bekrenev's way of thinking, there was no other way to say it; Kusinien was speaking treason.

"There is still the matter of Colonel Chinko," Bekrenev reminded him.

"I have taken care of that matter as well," Kusinien said with a sigh. He nodded to the senior officer, stepped out, and closed the door behind him. Bekrenev sat motionless, waiting until he heard the elevator doors open and close at the end of the hall. Then he went to the window and watched until

Kusinien's spiritless figure appeared in the courtyard below him.

Perhaps, he thought to himself, President Aprihnen would be interested in Kusinien's comments.

LOG:
SEVENTEEN: TWO

Diva: Ukraine 1721L
17 November

E-Alexa pulled the collar of her coat up around her throat and trudged through the ankle-deep snow. The snow had been falling for the last several hours and, despite the gray chill of the late day, she moved toward the gate. Tomas had given her the key.

"The guards will be gone after five o'clock," he had warned her. "They figure the curiosity seekers will not come after darkness."

She inserted the heavy brass key into the bulky lock and twisted. It clicked—and the gate creaked open. She put the key in her pocket and her hand momentarily brushed against the diamond mantis pin Kusinien had given her. Then she entered.

The guards were gone, but the haunting sounds of the music continued. She recognized a composition by Mussorgsky and, for a moment, hummed along with it. The haunting emptiness of her once-bustling birthplace now seemed sadder than ever. She walked across the deserted, debris-littered highway that ringed the town and into what had once been a park where she had played. What she remembered most about the

437

park was her father pushing the swing and her mother laughing.

The swings were gone now.

Across the park was the statue of Tchaikovsky, and behind it the old music theater where she had first watched the touring troop from the Bolshoi; how lovely they had been. Even now she could remember telling her father how someday she would be just like them.

There was the museum and the small conservatory and the band shell where the concerts were held. She remembered the night her father took her to hear the army chorus, and how she had walked home with her tiny hand tucked in the safety of Pytor Zimrin's hand. Pytor had been her father's most trusted friend. Pytor, who loved the music almost as much as she did, had sung folk songs to her all the way home.

"You could be one of them," he had teased her.

She'd giggled. "How could I? I am not a man. Men go into the army. Women have their babies."

Pytor had laughed, and she had asked him why.

"It is more complicated than that," he had answered.

At the time she did not understand—but now she did. It was more complicated than that—much more complicated. She turned and began walking up Obraztsov, past the Party hall toward the high-rise complexes where the workers had been housed when the tractor factory opened. The doors were boarded up and most of the windows were broken out. She counted the floors: six in one, eight in another, seven in still another. She remembered the white one, the one where the women would hang their laundry on the balconies and shout at the children playing in the courtyard.

She turned at Gertsena and trudged through the snow up to the door of the Technical Academy. Visions flooded her mind, recollections vaulted back through time. She'd met her father there on the coldest winter nights when he went to the academy to study electronics so that he could get a better job at the tractor factory. Often the snow was so deep that he would carry her on his shoulders on their way home.

She turned again, into the wind, and the bitter cold made her forehead ache and her lips crack. Still, there were tears. They traced their way down her cheeks until they turned to ice. And finally, when she could bear it no longer, she dropped to her knees in the snow and gave vent to the deep racking sobs that had been imprisoned for so many years.

When the hurt and fear played out, she struggled to her feet. She listened to the haunting sound of emptiness and music and the years—and began to work her way back to the gate where she had entered.

In the gathering darkness she saw the white-yellow of the headlights splayed out on the snow. A car was waiting.

As she approached the gate, the car door opened and Konstantin Nijinsky stepped from the vehicle. He walked to the gate and opened it for her. As he took her arm, she paused and looked at him.

"I'm sorry, Inspector," she said. "I'm afraid that this time I have no tickets for you. But perhaps this will do." She handed him the diamond-studded mantis.

LOG:
SEVENTEEN: THREE

Chambers Avenue & 13th Street: Washington 1847L
20 November

"Are you certain you don't want me to wait?" Mickie asked. "He might be late and it's cold out there." She had a young voice that went well with her youthful appearance. Even Bogner had difficulty believing she would soon celebrate her 40th birthday.

Despite the fact that she was bundled up against the chilled winter night, to Bogner she looked small and vulnerable sitting behind the steering wheel of her convertible.

"Unless I call you, plan to pick me up right here in one hour," Bogner said. He glanced at his watch, conducted one of his frequent weather appraisals, and got out of the car. When he saw how much the weather had deteriorated in the last hour, he regretted the fact that he had agreed to meet Packer.

On the other hand, when Packer insisted on meeting him, Bogner knew the ISA chief had a good reason. He pulled the collar of his coat up around his throat, turned his back to the wind, and gave Mickie a wave as she pulled away from the curb. The taillights of the red Chrysler convertible looked luminescent under the thin sheen of ice. It was a chilling reminder of the deadly sheen of ice in the sunken *Drachev*.

Thus far they had not had the opportunity to really sit down and talk. Since arriving back in Washington, Bogner had been the key figure in a series of briefing sessions regarding the Lyoto-Straf project. The most recent one had been earlier that day before a closed-door Senate foreign affairs subcommittee chaired by a former Navy preflight classmate, Jeb Hawkins. Now Hawkins was the senior senator from Oklahoma.

Hawkins had put him on the stand and questioned him for well over two hours. The questions were endless . . . and when Hawkins ran out of new questions, he rephrased and reframed old ones. Was Milatov on the level? How effective was the E-1-A? What was the effective range? How did the Russians plan to relocate the submerged launching pads—and more.

Did Bogner know where Xo was being kept? Did Bogner think the Chinese had made more than one set of provisions to get the methodology for dispersion of cruor-toxins to the Russians? Or did Bogner believe what Milatov had told him about the impending curtailment of the Sino technical agreement? Finally, did Bogner believe that any further attempts to recover the data from the destroyed *Zotov* were feasible?

At 1600 hours, Hawkins had dismissed his committee and gone with Bogner to the Fairfax bar, where the two former Navy pilots sipped Cutty and water and exchanged war stories.

Finally Hawkins had gotten around to asking the inevitable. "Off the record, Toby, where are they hiding Xo?"

Bogner had laughed. "Even if I knew, Jeb, do you honestly think I'd tell you? No way. The boys over at the State Department will probably come unglued on this one before it's over. I don't want any part of that action."

Later, with Mickie, at dinner, Packer had hunted him down. The waiter had brought the phone to the table, and Bogner had seen Mickie's smile cloud.

Now, standing in the biting cold, he didn't have to wait long. Packer's Pontiac splashed through the slush to the curb and the door opened. Bogner crawled in, and the ISA commander eased his way back into traffic. "Sorry to cut in on your evening," he said.

"What's up?"

"Tying up some loose ends," Packer replied. "Tell me again about the data cartridge."

"You've got my report. You know as much about it as I do. Our Russian friends had to make two trips to find it. Which means they either came up with something they couldn't use, or were empty-handed the first trip. When they went in the second time, Mitch and I went after them. The rest is history."

"How did you know they didn't have what they were looking for after their first excursion?"

"Why else would they have gone back?"

Packer nodded in agreement. "Same conclusion. Second question. What made you think the data capsule might actually be Zhou's pacemaker?"

"Just a hunch. Zhou was a little guy—not the kind I think of as a candidate for a heart attack. Guess I can be accused of stereotypical thinking—but the hunch paid off. Besides, I wasn't having any luck anywhere else, so I took a stab at it, no pun intended. When I dug it out—there were no wires, no leads, nothing but a sealed cartridge. The rest was easy. All of a sudden all the bits and pieces started to make a whole lot of sense. At that point I figured his accomplice had to be the doctor. Milatov indicated Zhou had been diagnosed as having a minor heart attack, which meant the doctor made the bogus diagnosis and planted the bogus pacemaker. Logical?"

Packer nodded. "Somewhere in your report you describe listening to the crew of the Russian DSRV trying to transmit data back to the *Pitki*. Best guess: Do you think they were able to put together anything from the data they recovered?"

Bogner shrugged. "There's no way of knowing for certain, Clancy. Their batteries were weak and their transmissions were sporadic. Maybe they got through and maybe they didn't. We recorded everything they transmitted on the *Spats* mission recorders. If our guys can reconstruct the data from the tape of the transmissions, I suppose the Russians probably were probably able to capture enough to work with as well."

Clancy was frowning.

Bogner looked at him. His friend's face was hidden in shadows with only the occasional illumination of oncoming headlights. "Why the questions, Pack? We've got the capsule. Once we're able to determine what the Russians were able to recapture in the way of data, we'll figure out how to handle it. Besides, there's one thing for certain. We blew the lid off of their Belushya project."

Packer's voice was strained. "There's something you need to know. The *Spats*'s recordings are worthless, and the data capsule you recovered from the *Zotov* contains nothing of value. To coin a phrase, that cartridge is a piece of shit."

"What?"

"Worthless. No good."

"How?"

Packer shrugged. "We've run that damned tape past every damned computer expert in this town. They all say the same thing; it's not some exotic code that we don't know how to break and it isn't some sophisticated icon cluster code, it's a"—he searched for the phrase—"piece of nothing."

"But . . ."

"Like it or not, Toby, so far all we've got is a bunch of educated guesses. Things like the power available when they attempted transmission from their DSRV to the *Pitki*, exposure to prolonged temperature extremes, maybe even faulty recording technique. According to the so-called experts, any or all of the above could impact the data integrity. Like I say, plenty of theory, but nothing concrete."

Bogner sagged down in the seat. "So that's what we got for all our effort—a bad data cartridge?"

"Looks like it. The bottom line seems to be, we don't know what our friends in Belushya were able to recapture and we don't know whether or not our Sino friends made more than one attempt to put the cruor-toxin encapsulation formula in the hands of the Russians."

"In view of the impending breakup of their joint technical agreement, the question may be, did they even try?" Bogner speculated. "Maybe we should try beating it out of Xo."

Packer shrugged and, as he did, turned the car into a narrow alleyway. It was lined with aging brick buildings on both sides. He pulled to a stop and a steel service door opened. A big man in a white medical coat stood illuminated in the wash of light from a single incandescent bulb hanging over his head. He closed and bolted the door behind them.

Packer led the way down a narrow passageway to a service elevator. On the third level they stepped off and into an antiseptic world void of color and comfort.

"Looks like a morgue," Bogner quipped.

"It is a morgue," Packer acknowledged.

They passed through two more sets of doors and into a refrigerated room where a wiry-looking black man checked their credentials. Satisfied, he pressed a buzzer and the doors opened to a world where the walls were lined with headers for stainless-steel vaults. Packer walked to 121-B, opened it, and pulled the sheet back.

Bogner was stunned. "Milatov," he muttered.

"So we're told. That's why I needed you, to make a positive ident."

"When?"

"Reprisal delivered him last night. They wanted us to know. According to them, Milatov had decided to return to Russia. Reprisal was determined that wouldn't happen."

"How did he die? Or shouldn't I ask?"

"Reprisal didn't say and I didn't ask. We do know, however, that the medical examiner found a .22 bullet hole in his mouth and an exit wound at the base of the skull."

"I don't get it," Bogner said. "When I flew to Saint John's those people would have defended him with their lives."

"That was the one thing Reprisal could agree on. As long as he was willing to turn his back on the E-1-A, they were willing to protect him."

"The focus is a little clearer now," Bogner admitted. "If the Russians were unable to recapture the design data from the *Zotov* and Milatov is dead, then it's reasonable to assume they've run into a brick wall." Then he looked at Packer. "Which leaves Xo."

Packer shook his head. "If the Dung government actually had an alternative plan to get the information to Belushya, we won't have any way of knowing whether or not it was successful until it's too late. On the other hand, we're reasonably certain Xo won't give it to them."

Bogner looked at him.

"Xo never did crack," Packer reflected. "Jaffe figures we didn't find it because Xo was carrying the encapsulation formula around in his head."

"Which means the moment we release him, he either hightails it to Moscow to complete his mission—or he heads back to Beijing."

"We got a confirmation; he went to Moscow," Packer said. "Less than two hours ago we received a phone call. It seems that Russian airport authorities reported that the Aeroflot flight that departed Montreal for

Moscow carried a little bonus with it. When the Russians began unloading luggage, they got a nasty surprise. They found a frozen body stuffed in one of the airliner's wheel wells."

"Xo?" Bogner asked. "How? Who?"

Packer shook his head. "Who knows? The State Department insisted that we release him. We tried to warn them it was dangerous. Guess somebody must have tipped off Reprisal."

Bogner thought for a minute. He repeated the name, Reprisal, and looked at the vault containing the remains of Milatov. "Looks like there's not much more we can do about this tonight."

Packer agreed.

RED SKIES

KARL LARGENT

"A writer to watch!" —*Publishers Weekly*

The cutting-edge Russian SU-39-Covert stealth bomber, with fighter capabilities years beyond anything the U.S. can produce, has vanished while on a test run over the Gobi Desert. But it is no accident—the super weapon was plucked from the skies by Russian military leaders with their own private agenda—global power.

Half a world away, a dissident faction of the Chinese Red Army engineers the brutal abduction of a top scientist visiting Washington from under the noses of his U.S. guardians. And with him goes the secrets of his most recent triumph—the development of the SU-39.

Commander T.C. Bogner has his orders: Retrieve the fighter and its designer within seventy-two hours, or the die will be cast for a high-tech war, the likes of which the world has never known.

_4117-0 $6.99 US/$7.99 CAN

THE SEA

SEA

R. KARL LARGENT

At the bottom of the Sargasso Sea lies a sunken German U-Boat filled with Nazi gold. For more than half a century the treasure, worth untold millions of dollars, has been waiting—always out of reach. Now Elliott Wages has been hired to join a salvage mission to retrieve the gold, but it isn't long before he realizes that there's quite a bit he hasn't been told—and not everyone wants the mission to succeed. The impenetrable darkness of the Sargasso hides secret agendas and unbelievable dangers—some natural, other man-made. But before this mission is over, Elliott Wages will learn firsthand all the deadly secrets cloaked in the inky blackness.

___4495-1 $5.99 US/$6.99 CAN